"I need a wife," Reuben murmured. "My son needs a mother."

Ellie tensed. She picked Ethan up and gave him to his father. "You want to fall in love and marry again?"

"*Nay*, I'll marry, but I won't fall in love."

"You'd wed without love?"

"I'd wed for Ethan." He combed his fingers through Ethan's baby-fine hair. "But love? *Nay*. I don't want or need it."

What woman would agree to such an arrangement? "I see." She reached for her satchel on the other end of the counter. "I should get home."

She felt Reuben watching her as she picked up her bag. She was conscious of him as he followed her out of the house.

With a last look in his direction as she pulled away, Ellie wondered how a man who obviously loved his son could dismiss love in marriage so easily. What woman would be happy to be married to such a man and not fall in love with him? And with his son?

Rebecca Kertz was first introduced to the Amish when her husband took a job with an Amish construction crew. She enjoyed watching the Amish foreman's children at play and swapping recipes with his wife. Rebecca resides in Delaware with her husband and dog. She has a strong faith in God and feels blessed to have family nearby. Besides writing, she enjoys reading, doing crafts and visiting Lancaster County.

By sixth grade, **Meghan Carver** knew she wanted to write. After a degree in English from Millikin University, she detoured to law school, completing a Juris Doctor from Indiana University. She then worked in immigration law and taught college-level composition. Now she homeschools her six children with her husband. When she isn't writing, homeschooling or planning another travel adventure, she is active in her church, sews and reads.

REBECCA KERTZ

His Suitable Amish Wife

&

MEGHAN CARVER

Amish Covert Operation

LOVE INSPIRED
INSPIRATIONAL ROMANCE

LOVE INSPIRED®
INSPIRATIONAL ROMANCE

Recycling programs
for this product may
not exist in your area.

ISBN-13: 978-1-335-22988-5

His Suitable Amish Wife and Amish Covert Operation

Copyright © 2020 by Harlequin Books S.A.

His Suitable Amish Wife
First published in 2019. This edition published in 2020.
Copyright © 2019 by Rebecca Kertz

Amish Covert Operation
First published in 2019. This edition published in 2020.
Copyright © 2019 by Meghan Carver

This edition published by arrangement with Harlequin Books S.A.

For questions and comments about the quality of this book,
please contact us at CustomerService@Harlequin.com.

Harlequin Enterprises ULC
22 Adelaide St. West, 40th Floor
Toronto, Ontario M5H 4E3, Canada
www.Harlequin.com

Printed in U.S.A.

CONTENTS

HIS SUITABLE AMISH WIFE

Rebecca Kertz

With love for my niece Sarah, my brother's daughter, who has grown up to be a sweet, loving and hardworking young woman. I'm so proud of you.

Be strong and of a good courage,
fear not, nor be afraid of them:
for the Lord thy God, he it is that doth go with
thee; he will not fail thee, nor forsake thee.
—*Deuteronomy* 31:6

Chapter One

Elizabeth Stoltzfus stared at the small residence surrounded by a yard filled with junk—wood scraps, rusted cars and other debris she couldn't identify. She'd been cleaning houses for years now, but she'd never seen a place like this. The family who'd recently moved to their church district lived here? This was the place the bishop wanted her to clean?

She frowned. The house wasn't large enough for a typical Amish family, and it certainly wasn't big enough to warrant a cleaning lady. But she'd do it because Bishop John had asked her, although she was afraid of what she might find inside.

She steered her buggy to the end of the driveway, where she secured her horse to the hitching post, which looked brand-new. Ellie reached into the back of her vehicle for her cleaning supplies, including her broom. When she cleaned houses for the English, she used her clients' vacuum cleaners. Her corn broom or a damp mop was the best way to clean Amish floors, most of which were made of wood or linoleum.

She approached the side door with her plastic supply tote in one hand and broom in the other. She leaned the broom handle against the building and rapped hard on the door. A child's high-pitched cry rent the silence before the door opened. A young woman with a baby on her hip studied her, then saw the supplies and smiled with relief.

"Sarah Miller?" Ellie realized the woman was actually a teenage girl.

"*Ja*, I'm Sarah. Come in," she said as she moved aside to allow Ellie entry. "You're here to clean for us, *ja*? Thanks be to *Gott*. The house needs it badly."

With a smile, Ellie quietly took in her appearance. Sarah wore no head covering, and tendrils of hair were pulled out as if she or her baby had tugged on the blond locks. Her light blue tab dress was stained with what looked like baby food and who knew what else. She had dark circles of exhaustion under her eyes.

"The bishop sent you."

Ellie nodded. "You're the one who spoke with him, then? He's a *gut* man." She meandered around the room, taking stock of what needed to be done, which looked to be a great deal. "Is there any particular place you want me to start?"

She hid her horror at the condition of the kitchen as she tied on her apron. The floors were stained and warped, and the walls needed several coats of white paint. The countertops didn't look much better. She wondered why this young family had moved here and about the state of their finances.

"You can start here, in the kitchen," the girl said, gesturing about the room. The baby cried louder, and Sarah tried to soothe him.

Ellie felt bad for the young mother, who looked

ready to keel over. The girl clearly needed her rest. She'd offer to hold the little boy, but she had a job to do and the work had to be completed first. She grabbed her broom and started on the floor, which was covered with dust and dirt. With even sweeps of the corn broom bristles across warped wood, she swept the filth into a pile, then onto a metal dustpan, which she dumped outside.

The floor done, she began to wipe down the countertop with a wet, soapy sponge. After checking inside the cabinets, she removed the meager contents and ran a damp sponge over the shelves. Sarah had left the room. She could hear the baby crying from upstairs. Trying to ignore the sound, Ellie did what she could to clean the kitchen. The stove looked new and required little but a damp cloth. She spent a good amount of time on the small gas-powered refrigerator at the end of the counter, removing the food that was inside—a carton of eggs, milk, a pack of sausage and a few other items—and scrubbing it inside and out. It was a heavy task, for it looked as if the appliance hadn't been used in a long time and the last person who'd owned it hadn't taken the time to clean it thoroughly. Satisfied with the results, she went into a back room where she found a gas-powered freezer along with washer and dryer. She checked over each appliance, pleased to find them in better condition.

The baby continued to wail as Sarah descended the stairs, the sound growing louder as she approached. Ellie came out of the back room.

"I'm sorry," the girl apologized. "I can't get him to stop."

"May I hold him?" Ellie asked gently, softening her gaze.

"Ja, danki." Sarah handed her the child.

The baby instantly quieted in her arms. "What's your *soohn*'s name?"

The girl shook her head. "He's not my son. He's my nephew. I've been watching him for my *bruder* while he works." She eyed the baby helplessly. "Ethan," she murmured sadly. "His name is Ethan."

"I see." Gazing into the baby's bright blue eyes, Ellie smiled. "Do you have a clean diaper?"

"Ja, but I don't think it will help. I just changed him."

"Has he eaten?"

Sarah glanced at her wristwatch. "'Tis not time."

"Babies know when they are hungry. Do you have milk for him?" The girl nodded. "Will you make up a bottle?" Sarah proceeded to fix it. "Where's his mother? She busy, too?" Ellie asked, curious.

"She's dead. She died right after she gave Ethan life."

"I'm sorry," Ellie said with genuine sympathy, although she believed that the woman was in a better place. God would have taken her into His house and made her happy that she'd sacrificed her life for her son's.

Sarah approached with the bottle and reached for the boy.

"May I feed him?" Ellie watched her closely. "Why don't you wash up," she suggested softly after Sarah nodded. "Do you have fresh garments?"

"Ja."

"Go, then, and take a few moments for yourself.

You deserve it. I'll watch Ethan for a while until you feel better."

"Danki," Sarah murmured shyly before she headed upstairs.

Ellie heard the slam of a door. "Sarah?" a man's voice boomed. "How's Ethan?"

He entered the room and froze when he saw her. She released a startled breath as she recognized him. The baby's father was Reuben Miller, her sister Meg's former sweetheart, the one who'd lost control of his buggy one rainy night and sent Meg into the cold, dark depths of a creek.

"Ellie?" he said unhappily. "Ellie Stoltzfus?"

"Reuben," she greeted, acknowledging that she knew him.

"What are you doing here?"

"I'm cleaning house."

He scowled. "Why?"

She raised her chin. "Because the place needs it, and—"

"And?" he prompted.

She stared at him. He was sweaty and disheveled but still an attractive man. He had removed his straw hat and his blond hair was matted. Golden hair a shade darker than the hair on his head ran along his jaw, the beard proclaiming him as having married. But it was his eyes that drew her attention the most. They were a beautiful shade of blue, like the light blue of a bright sunny summer sky. His features were strong and symmetrical. She suffered a fluttering like butterflies in her belly. Reuben Miller was an extremely handsome man.

"Ellie?"

"Bishop John told me to come."

"I didn't ask for someone to clean for me."

He clearly didn't want her here. She saw his face change as he realized that she was holding his child. Reuben approached and extended his arms.

Clutching the baby closer, she resisted his unspoken request and stepped back. "I won't hurt him."

He sighed. "I know you won't." The man closed his eyes, looking tired beyond measure, and Ellie felt a deep welling of sympathy for him.

With a soft murmur for Ethan, she gave Reuben his son, then turned for her cleaning supplies with the intent to continue on to the next room. To her surprise and relief, the baby snuggled against his father's chest without a whimper.

"Ellie?" Reuben said when she headed toward the gathering room beyond the kitchen.

"Ja?" She faced him.

"I don't need you here."

She flushed with anger. "I'm not here for you, Reuben. I'm here for Sarah and Ethan." After a brief pause, she added, "If you have a problem with me, talk with the bishop." Ignoring him, she began sweeping the floors in the other room, hoping he would stay away and not give her grief.

The ensuing silence in the house unsettled her. Reuben hadn't followed to harass her, and his absence after their mild altercation worried her. She returned to the kitchen for a peek, and what she saw made her heart pause before it started to pump harder. Reuben leaned against the counter cradling his son as he fed the baby his bottle. She experienced an odd sensation in her chest as she watched man and child together.

Suddenly, Reuben looked up as if sensing her presence. They locked gazes, and she lurched back a few steps, eager to escape the odd intimacy of witnessing a tender moment between a father and his son.

"Ellie!" Sarah bounced down the stairs and stopped abruptly when she saw her brother. "Reuben, you're home! How was work? Did your crew get the job done? Will you have time to work on the *haus* tomorrow?"

Expecting him to scold his sister, Ellie was shocked to see his face soften with indulgence as he smiled at Sarah. Reuben chuckled, and the sound rippled along her back from her nape to her lower spine. "In answer to your questions—*ja*, I'm home. *Gut*, work was *gut*. *Ja*, we got the job done. And as to your last question, most definitely *ja*." He'd held up a finger with each yes, the last of which caused Sarah to squeal with pleasure.

"You've met Ellie," Sarah said with a smile.

"We're acquainted," Ellie confessed, meeting the girl's light blue eyes. She transferred her attention to Sarah's brother. "I didn't know you'd married. It must have been soon after…" She bit her lip, her voice trailing off before she could mention his breakup with Meg.

"I met Susanna not long after," he began. "We married six months later." He studied his son. "We were happy until…"

"'Tis *oll recht*, Reuben," his sister said softly. "I know how hard this is for you, but I'm here to help for as long as I'm able."

His smile for Sarah was soft and filled with affection. "I know you wish to be with our family in Ohio. I appreciate that you're here for now. I'll find someone to take care of Ethan so you can go home."

"I don't mind being here, *bruder*."

"I know you don't." Sorrow settled on the man's features, touching something deep inside Ellie. "But you're too young for this worry."

Overwhelmed by conflicting emotions, Ellie turned away. "I'll finish the gathering room and return tomorrow to do the bedrooms and baths."

"Ellie—"

"Don't say you don't need me to clean for you, Reuben, because from the look of this place, you most certainly do."

She caught a quick glimpse of anguish on his features as he turned away. Her gaze once again moved about the room. Was he concerned with money? She didn't know what to say to make him feel better that wouldn't offend him. She had no intention of being paid for the work. Reuben and his family needed her, and she was always happy to help someone in need. If she told him that, however, she knew he'd glare and order her to leave. Now that she understood the situation, leaving was the last thing she wanted to do.

She returned to the gathering room to dust the furniture. After a brief visit to the kitchen sink to fill up her bucket, she worked to scrub the walls. As the grime fell away, leaving the room brighter, Ellie smiled. It always felt good when she could see the fruits of her labor, and the new look of the room was a vast improvement.

"Ellie." Reuben's quiet voice startled her. She gasped and spun to face him. She looked behind him, but there was no sign of Sarah.

"Is something wrong?" she asked. Ellie saw that he'd noted the bright cleanliness of the room. "Do you need something?"

His lips firmed. "I don't think you should come back tomorrow."

She lifted her chin. "Then don't think, because I will return, Reuben. You have a baby to consider. He should have a clean place to crawl." She narrowed her gaze as she took his measure. "Is it because it's me? You're angry because I'm Meg's sister?"

He looked shocked. "*Nay!* The fact that you and Meg are related has nothing to do with this."

She went soft. "This isn't paid work for me. I'm here as a favor to Bishop John."

"I can pay," he said sharply.

"Reuben—" She started to object, but he'd left the room.

Ellie closed her eyes as she sighed. The man needed help, but clearly accepting it didn't sit well with him. She thought of young, tired Sarah and felt rising sympathy for the teen. She firmed her resolve. She'd be back whether or not Reuben Miller liked it. She'd do all she could to help Sarah and the baby. Short of his throwing her bodily out, she'd return tomorrow and the next day for as long as she could help in any way.

A glance at her wristwatch confirmed that it was late afternoon. She'd started the work at one, after having finished housecleaning for the Smith family, English clients. Tomorrow she'd come after she worked at the Broderick house. She made a mental list of what this house—Reuben—needed as she searched through every room on the first floor. She gathered her cleaning tools, then left after calling out to Sarah that she was leaving.

Ellie was conscious of Reuben's stare on her through the kitchen window as she climbed into her buggy and left.

* * *

Reuben held his sleeping son close as he watched Ellie Stoltzfus leave. He'd never expected her to come here, and it bothered him that she had. The house was a disaster, and he was ashamed with how little he'd been able to get done.

He'd known the house and land needed work. His uncle had purchased the property from a poverty-stricken English family who'd needed the money desperately. It had always been Uncle Zeke's intention to clear the land and fix up the house for him and Aunt Mary to live out their remaining years, but then Aunt Mary had passed on, and he'd gone into his own decline. When Zeke died, the house went to his only remaining relative, his brother, who was Reuben's father, who gave it to Reuben after his wife Susanna's death.

When he'd first married Susanna, he'd made plans to build a house for them on a section of his father's farm. They had lived with his parents for the first months while Reuben had saved nearly every dollar he'd earned from his construction job. They'd been excited when he learned Susanna was pregnant. They decided to remain in his parents' house during Susanna's pregnancy and wait until after the baby was born to start construction on their home. But then everything in his life had changed after his wife died within minutes of delivering Ethan. He'd gained himself a son but had lost his life partner, and he'd been devastated. He'd barely been able to think. It had hurt too much to feel, to breathe, yet he was responsible for the tiny newborn he and Susanna had made together.

Susanna's medical bills and funeral had taken all of his savings, and he was left with no choice but to stay with his parents until he could finish paying off his late wife's hospital bill while trying to save whatever money he could to have a place of his own. During those awful first grief-filled months, his mother and sister had stepped in to care for Ethan while he took every opportunity to bury his grief with work. Then Mam and Dat had decided to move to Ohio to be closer to Mam's parents. Dat had suggested that he and Ethan move with them, but Reuben hadn't been able to bear the thought of another change in his life. When his father gave him Uncle Zeke's property, it had been like an answer to Reuben's prayers. After his parents had sold their property, Reuben had moved into Uncle Zeke's place. It was a disaster, but he could fix it up and make it a home. His sister Sarah had offered to stay and help with Ethan until Reuben could make other arrangements for his son's care while he was at work.

Life was tough. He worked hard to feed and clothe Ethan, and although he'd finally paid the balance owed to the hospital, there never seemed to be enough money or time to fix up the house and clear the garbage from the yard. He briefly closed his eyes. *So much to worry about.*

Reuben knew the best solution would be for him to marry again, something he didn't want to do. Still, he had to think of his son first, so he would find a wife, if only for Ethan to have a mother. He would need to find a woman who would watch and protect his son and be content to simply be a quiet, calming companion for him. He wouldn't promise love, although he would honor her. He didn't want to marry for love. Love hurt too much.

He would be practical in his choice of bride. He'd

already lost a wife. While Susanna and he had started their relationship as friends, deep affection and love for each other had come with time. When she died, a part of him had died with her. He never again wanted to feel that depth of pain.

"Reuben, are you hungry?" Sarah entered the room with a smile. "I can make us eggs, toast and sausage."

"That sounds *gut*, Sarah." He smiled his thanks while he noted something different about her. She looked rested, pretty. She'd redone her hair, and the dress she wore looked freshly laundered. It was only at that moment that he realized how hard it must be for her to care for his young son. His sister was only fifteen, and she received no help or relief from Ethan's care, except for when Ethan was napping. It wasn't fair for Sarah to be saddled with a child. He would have to start looking for a wife, and soon.

Reuben shifted his son in his arms and softened as he studied Ethan's perfect, smooth baby facial features. His son lay content against him. It had taken him a while to bond with Ethan. His grief had been too stark, at first, that it had been painful to look at his son, who reminded him of Susanna. But his parents' decision to move had spurred him to change and take full responsibility and care of his child. He'd held his baby frequently, staying up with him at nights when he cried. He'd bathed, fed, and changed his diaper. His time spent with Ethan had created a deep parental bond. He'd discovered a love for his son that was overpowering and joyful. Every time he saw the way his baby lay trustingly within his arms, his love overflowed, overtaking his grief and cementing an even stronger link. There wasn't anything he wouldn't do for his child—and that included taking another wife so Ethan could have a mother.

After supper, he left Ethan in Sarah's care and built a cradle large enough for a toddler to use on the first floor for when he and Ethan were downstairs together. Tomorrow, he would work to replace old and damaged shingles on the roof of his house. The job shouldn't take long. The area of roof was small, but the house had two floors, with the bedrooms and bathroom upstairs and a second smaller bath downstairs. Plenty of room for three or four, even possibly five people. *Although there will be only three of us living here.* He had no intention of having more children. He'd learned the hard way that the health risk to a woman was too great.

The next morning, he got up and checked on Ethan, who continued to sleep. He began to assemble what he'd need to fix the roof. He briefly considered bringing Ethan outside while he worked, but was afraid that his son would get hurt as he stripped off shingles and tossed them to the ground. Ethan would have to remain inside with Sarah. Today, he'd get a lot done with the building supplies that he'd already purchased and stored in the small barn. Money was tight, but he would get paid by the construction company in the next couple of days.

Reuben felt a measure of peace at his plans for the day, until he remembered that Ellie Stoltzfus had said she'd be back. His good humor and sense of well-being abruptly left him.

He sighed as he recalled the first time he saw her years ago…sweet, lovely, with golden blond hair and bright blue eyes. He'd been attracted to her.

He forced the memory away. He had to stick to his plan and find a wife who would accept that they would be companions but nothing more. The last thing he needed was for Ellie to interfere with his life. He had enough to worry about without the attraction he still felt complicating things.

Chapter Two

Ellie had no idea why she felt as if she shouldn't tell her family about Reuben. Yet she decided not to tell anyone about her experience at the house or that Reuben had moved into their church district. They'd find out soon enough when Bishop John introduced him to the community, or in the event that someone such as their neighboring busybody, Alta Hershberger, learned about the new family in Happiness and nattered about them.

She told him she'd be back today. And she'd made the decision to return tomorrow and the day after that until he no longer needed her. But once she'd arrived home last evening, she'd worried about the cleaning jobs she already had scheduled. Ellie couldn't abandon her housecleaning business yet, even if she wanted to help someone in need. She'd worked too hard to get it going, and she wasn't about to let any of her clients down now that they'd come to rely on her. Thankfully, the Broderick family, her job for this morning, had changed the day and time that they wanted her to clean. Which left Ellie free to head to the Reuben

Miller residence first thing to continue the work she'd started yesterday afternoon.

The early summer day heralded warm temperatures and sunny skies. Ellie enjoyed the trip to Reuben's as she viewed the green lawns that looked lusher after an overnight rain. She was happy with her life and pleased with how well her cleaning business was doing. She figured she would clean houses until she had children after marrying.

She wasn't in any hurry to wed. Her sisters Nell, Leah and Meg were happy with their husbands, and her youngest sister, Charlie, would be marrying Nate Peachy, the man she loved, come autumn after harvest time in November. Once Charlie moved out of the house, Ellie knew that she would be the only one there to help Mam and Dat with chores. Her parents were getting older, and she noticed that they were starting to show their age. She caught her father walking with a stiff gait as if in pain, especially before it rained. Her mother often needed help lifting baking pans out of the oven, and she seemed to have slowed down some. Though she was away from the house with her work each day, Ellie always made it a point to help them in any way she could when she was home.

The house would be too large for her parents if she wed and left the nest like her sisters. If her mother and father were settled in a smaller home, Ellie would feel better about moving on. But as things stood, with five daughters and no sons to take over the property, there would be no one to help her *mam* and *dat* if she left. And there was no *dawdi haus* on the property, since neither Mam nor Dat had parents who lived in the area. Her *dat*'s *eldre* were deceased, and her *mam*'s non-Amish parents lived in Ohio. For now, she'd keep a close eye on them. If they needed her, she could adjust her cleaning schedule to spend more time at home.

Ellie saw Reuben immediately as she steered her horse onto the short driveway next to his house. He knelt on the roof, working on removing shingles. He wore his black-banded straw hat to protect his face and neck from the sun and a short-sleeved light green shirt with black suspenders and navy tri-blend work pants. As she climbed down from her vehicle and tied up her horse, she heard the *thud*, *squeak*, *thud*, *squeak* of his hammer claw as he pried nails out of old roof shingles before he ripped them up and tossed them to the ground.

She stood a moment, her hand shadowing her eyes against the sun so she could see him better. She couldn't help but notice the way his forearms flexed as he worked. Reuben moved to another area to tear off a section of the roof, then suddenly stopped as if he'd sensed her presence. He stared down at her, his expression unreadable. He rose to his feet as if planning to come down, and she feared that the wood might not be sturdy enough to hold his full weight. Sorry to have disturbed him, she turned away without a word, hoping that he wouldn't follow. She didn't want to get into a discussion with him when he was that high off the ground, and she didn't want him to send her away before she could finish cleaning his house.

Heart thudding, she retrieved her cleaning tools and approached the side door of the house. To her surprise, the door opened, and Sarah waited with a smile and warmth in her expression. There was no sign of Ethan.

"You came back!"

"I said I would."

Sarah nodded. "I know you clean houses for a living and that you have other work that needs to get done. I don't expect you to ignore it to help us."

"Not to worry. The family I was going to clean for this morning rescheduled. Even if I have to work, Sarah, I'll clean for you. I may have to come later in the day, but I will come," Ellie said softly. "I always keep my word, and I want to help."

Sarah blinked back tears. *"Danki,"* she whispered. She followed as Ellie set her supply tote on the bench behind their dining table. "I can't believe how good the great room looks after you scrubbed the walls," the girl said. "Reuben wants to paint every room in the house, but there is so much else to do, he had to decide what needed to be done most urgently."

"Like the roof." Ellie sorted through her supplies. "That makes sense. You never know when it will rain. Water damage is hard to fix." She pulled out a foaming spray, a roll of paper towels and window cleaner. "Your *bruder* knows what he is doing."

"I know." The girl sighed. "I wish I could do more for him. He hasn't been the same since Susanna died."

"I'm sorry. It must be hard for him having a son so young."

"'Tis. But at least I can be there for Ethan."

"Ja, but what about your plans?"

"I'm fine. Once Reuben finds someone to care for Ethan, or if he chooses to marry again, then I'll join my *eldre* in Ohio."

Ellie studied her with warmth and compassion. "You haven't been out of school long."

"I finished eighth grade last session."

She smiled. "You're a *gut* sister, Sarah."

The girl shrugged. "He's family. You do what you can for family and friends."

"Wise as well as compassionate," Ellie murmured with a smile. "I'm going to tackle the bathroom." There was no sign of Ethan. She looked around, wondering if someone had taken the baby to help out. "Where's your nephew?"

"Sleeping." Sarah grinned. "Hard to believe given the noise Reuben is making, but he's asleep in the other room. Last night Reuben made him a large cradle for the great room. I was able to feed him, then rock him to sleep."

"Then you'd better enjoy the moment. I'd say peace and quiet, but clearly you don't have that," Ellie said drily as she glanced toward the ceiling.

The teenager laughed. "That I don't."

When she entered the bathroom, she was surprised to see that it was amazingly clean.

Ellie sought out Sarah. "Who cleaned in here?"

"Reuben," the girl said. "My *bruder* likes a clean *haus*, which is why this—" she gestured all around her "—upsets and embarrasses him."

"I can help. He has enough to do." She was actually shocked that the man had done work that most of the men in their Amish community wouldn't touch because they considered it women's work. She must have spoken her thoughts aloud, because Sarah answered her.

"Reuben helped Susanna during her pregnancy. He doesn't mind doing women's work."

"An unusual man," she murmured beneath her breath. Ellie saw that Sarah looked much better today, with bright eyes, clean clothes and hair rolled and pulled back neatly into the style of Amish women. Reuben, she realized with an odd pang in the center of her chest, cared about his sister's well-being and probably made time for chores so Sarah wouldn't be overworked.

She swallowed hard. She didn't want to think well of him. Her sister Meg had mooned over him for a long time after she met him at a youth singing one summer a few years back. Reuben had belonged to another church district and hadn't come back to visit until nearly two years later. Then he'd finally shown an interest in her sister. He'd offered to take Meg home from the singing and she'd agreed. It had been a rainy night as Reuben steered his buggy along a back road as he drove her home. A speeding car had rounded a bend, forcing his buggy off the road, down an incline and into a creek. Reuben and Meg had ended up in the hospital; Meg's injuries were a concussion and a severely fractured leg. Reuben had suffered a worse concussion that had affected his memory of the crash.

Reuben's attention toward Meg before and after the crash had been caring and courteous. But Meg had realized early on that she'd fixated on him because she'd been trying to forget her feelings for Peter Zook. She'd continued to see Reuben, feeling as if she owed him after he'd saved her life, but then she realized that she couldn't allow Reuben to court her when she was in love with Peter. After Peter and Meg discovered they were meant for each other, her sister had realized that it was Peter, not Reuben, who had rescued Meg from the creek. Despite his foggy memory of that night, Reuben had known he couldn't swim and probably hadn't saved her. But when everyone had told him he had, he'd believed it because he'd wanted it to be true.

Once Meg ended her relationship with him, Reuben had no choice but to let her go.

Reuben as he'd looked years ago and the way he appeared now suggested he had suffered in the intervening years. Ellie didn't want to think about Reuben or his suffering. She forced him from her mind as she went upstairs to find the other bathroom as clean as the one on the first floor. She entered a bedroom where she began to dust furniture. Once finished, she picked up a broom, dust cloth and lemon polish, then left the room. And found herself blocked by Reuben.

She gasped. His imposing nearness stole her breath. She eyed him warily as he stood before her with perspiration staining his shirt and beading on his forehead. He smelled like man and hard work, and the scent wasn't unpleasant. "Reuben! You frightened me."

He didn't smile. Instead he narrowed his gaze and stared at her. "I thought I told you that I didn't need you." His lips firmed. "The *haus* is already clean."

"You cleaned the bathrooms."

He nodded. "And the rest of the *haus*."

"I'll just go over the bedrooms again lightly so you won't have to worry about them for a few days."

"Elizabeth," he began, and she jerked at the use of her proper name.

"Reuben, please," she pleaded, wondering why she was trying so hard. "Just let me do the work. It won't take up much time and then I'll be out of your hair and gone." She bit her lip. "And 'tis Ellie."

She was shocked to see a small smile settle upon

his masculine lips. "You are surprised I know your given name."

After a brief hesitation, she inclined her head. "My name could have been Ellen or Eleanor."

The good humor reached his eyes, startling blue in intensity, as he studied her. "But it's not. It's Elizabeth."

"How did you know that?" Then it hit her. For whatever reason, Meg must have mentioned it to him.

He shrugged. "Why does it matter?"

She stiffened. "It doesn't."

Reuben masked his expression as he took in the supplies she held. "How long will you be here?"

"No more than an hour."

He assented with a jerk of his head. "Fine. When you're done for the day, consider yourself absolved of doing anything more. You can tell Bishop John that you did your duty."

But what about tomorrow or next week? The man, like his sister, was stretched to the limit. Ellie had the strongest urge to convince him that it would be best if she cleaned his house on a regular basis. There was too much for him to do to worry about the inside of the house. He had his construction job—Meg had told her about it—and his work fixing up the house and a messy yard to clear. He might think she'd agreed because of her silence, but she would come back whether or not he liked it.

Reuben spun on his heels and left. Less than five minutes later, she heard him on the roof again. This time the sound was of him nailing down new shingles; the noise continued for the rest of the time she was there. When she went downstairs before leaving, it was to find Ethan awake and on Sarah's hip. The eight-month-old saw her and gave her a sloppy grin. When he extended a chubby hand toward her, Ellie took it and kissed the back of his fingers.

"All done," Ellie said to Sarah as she gathered up her supplies.

"Will you be back?"

Ellie glanced toward the back door. "I'll try. Your *bruder* doesn't want me here, but I think 'tis best if I return, don't you?"

Sarah bobbed her head. "*Ja*, please. I'll handle Reuben." She gazed at her surroundings. "Can you come back next week?"

"*Ja*, I'll have to check my work schedule, but I can always come after one of my other jobs." Ellie smiled at the girl as Sarah accompanied her to the door.

"Ellie?"

She met the girl's gaze. "*Ja?*"

"Can you teach me how to make a few recipes? I never cooked much while I was growing up. I have older sisters who did most of the cooking. I'd like to make Reuben something more than breakfast or sandwiches for supper. I'm sure he is especially tired of eggs, toast and sausage, although he never complains."

Warming to Sarah, Ellie grinned. "I'll find some simple recipes to start." She lowered her voice to a whisper. "And I'll bring the ingredients so Reuben will be surprised."

The teenager beamed at her. "*Danki*, Ellie."

"You are more than *willkomm*. I'll see you next week unless you're visiting on Sunday. 'Tis Visiting Day."

Sarah shook her head sadly. "Not this week. Reuben isn't ready to go visiting."

"I understand." And Ellie did. The man was going through a lot with having to raise Ethan on his own after losing his wife. She felt overwhelmed by compassion for him. He'd had a tough time, and he still had a long road to travel before he'd feel as if God had blessed him with a good and happy life.

"Any particular dishes Reuben likes?"

"Chicken corn chowder and strawberry pie."

"I'll see what I can do," Ellie promised before leaving.

Reuben had finished the roof. It was almost noon when he climbed down the ladder and headed in to wash up. He rounded the house and saw Ellie. She was loading her cleaning implements into the back of her buggy. She stepped back and untied her apron strings, then folded the garment neatly and placed it on the seat with her supplies. She turned to walk around to the other side of the vehicle and saw him. He saw her stiffen and raise her chin.

Reuben experienced a tightening in his chest. She was beautiful, and it wasn't the first time he'd noticed her. In fact, he'd thought her pretty as a young teenager. The shade of her light blond hair and her bright blue eyes were striking. But she'd been just a kid, younger than Meg, who'd been quick to smile at him and draw his attention. While he may have glanced occasionally Ellie's way, he'd known that she was too young for him. He'd wanted to get married, and Meg was the right age. And she was pretty like her sisters, although her coloring was different.

When he'd asked to take Meg home after the first singing he'd attended in their church district in years, he'd felt comfortable in Meg's presence. He'd liked her a lot. After the next singing, when she'd agreed to ride with him again, he'd felt as if he was on to something. He had easily imagined Meg as his wife...until it had all gone wrong, and he'd been forced to walk away and not look back. Not toward Meg, who he'd discovered was in love with Peter Zook. Not toward Ellie, who had still been too young to be a wife or mother.

Now, he was hungry and thirsty as he entered the house. Sarah turned from the kitchen counter with a sandwich on a plate for him. She smiled as she handed it to him. "'Tis just strawberry jam with peanut butter," she said.

He grinned. "Just what I needed." He looked around the room. "Where is Ethan?"

"Napping again."

"He's able to sleep through all the noise?"

Sarah nodded. "He's a sound sleeper."

Reuben took a glass from the cabinet and filled it with water. Then he sat at the table to eat his sandwich. "Have you eaten?"

"*Ja*. I decided to take advantage of Ethan's nap time."

"Ellie left?" he asked, knowing well that she had.

"*Ja*. She did a *gut* job with the house. Perhaps you should let her wash all the walls."

He tightened his jaw. "I'll buy the paint tomorrow so I can start on the rooms downstairs."

"Why don't you like her?" Sarah studied him curiously.

"I like her well enough. What makes you think I don't?"

"You weren't very pleasant to her. She only came to help."

"I don't need her charity, Sarah."

"She doesn't consider helping us charity, Reuben. She's a nice woman. She likes helping her friends." Sarah paused. "She's my friend."

Reuben softened his expression. "You're easy to like, Sarah. Everyone can't help but love you."

To his surprise, his sister blushed. "When do you have to go back to work?"

"Monday. Mike has a new job he wants us to start."

"I wish you didn't have to work so hard," she murmured.

"I don't work any harder than you do."

"*Ja*, you do, Reuben. I wish I could do more for you."

"You do more than enough, Sarah. I shouldn't have allowed you to stay. You're a young woman and you have your own life to live."

He heard Ethan whimper from the other room. Sarah went to check on him but was back within seconds. "He settled again," she told him.

Reuben rose and went to the sink, where he washed his dishes. "Why don't you take a walk?" he suggested. "'Tis beautiful outside."

She grinned. "I think I will."

He watched his sister leave the house with sadness. He shouldn't have allowed her to stay behind when his family moved. But he'd had no idea how he would manage without a caretaker for Ethan. He had to fix the house and to work to provide for Ethan and so he had the money for paint and building supplies. He glanced down at the kitchen floor with a frown. It was in terrible shape. When he selected the paint, he'd have to price new wood for the floor.

An image of Ellie settled in his mind. She was a hard worker. She'd gotten the house cleaned in a short time, especially considering how bad everything was. He'd tried his best to do what he could, but his work schedule mostly kept him from working on the house.

He hadn't meant to be rude to Ellie. The truth was it bothered him to have her near, although he had no idea why. She'd been kind to Sarah and good with Ethan. Why should it upset him that she had entered his house and won the hearts of his sister and his son?

He put away the clean dishes and filled up his water glass again. It had been hot working on the roof, but if he hadn't finished it now, he would have suffered worse temperatures as the summer lengthened.

Ellie hadn't agreed not to come back, he realized with sudden awareness. A small smile played on his mouth as he thought of her stubbornness. He had to make sure he sent her on her way if she returned. If she didn't listen, he would go to the bishop as she'd suggested.

Reuben continued to wonder how to handle Ellie Stoltzfus if she came back as she all but promised. Then his chest tightened with loss as he went into the gathering room to check on his sleeping son. It was wrong to notice another woman when his wife and the mother of his child, his precious Susanna, was dead.

Chapter Three

On Monday, Ellie returned to the Miller house to teach Sarah how to cook. "You'll need a large stockpot. I saw one in that bottom cabinet," she said, gesturing.

Sarah opened a door and grinned. "Here it is."

"*Gut.* First, we'll put in the chicken, then cover it with water. I bought chicken breasts because it's easier. You can use a whole chicken, but then you'd have to remove the meat from the bones. With the whole chicken, however, you'd get delicious chicken stock. I went to Whittier's and bought a container of chicken broth, which is easier and just as tasty. Just add a couple of tablespoons of the granules to the pot while you cook the chicken." She regarded Sarah with a pleased smile as she followed instructions.

The teenager beamed at her. "What next?"

Ellie went on to explain what other ingredients were necessary in making chicken corn chowder. Sarah followed her directions to the letter, then reduced the gas flame under the pot. She stood back and grinned. "I can remember that," the girl said.

"*Ja*, you can," Ellie said with approval.

"Now what?"

"I brought all the ingredients for making a straw-berry pie." She handed Sarah a recipe card. "Follow these instructions and you'll do fine." It was getting late. Ellie looked at her watch. "I need to get home." She had come well past noon after cleaning for the Brodericks. Reuben would be home from work soon and she didn't want him to find her here. She picked up her cell phone from the counter as she got ready to leave. She stared at Sarah a long moment. "Do you have paper and pencil? I want to give you my cell phone number. If you need me for any reason, call me. Will you do that?"

"*Ja*, I promise," Sarah said. "There's a pay phone across the road."

"*Gut.*" Ellie finished writing her name and cell phone number, then handed the paper to Sarah. "I hope Reuben enjoys his supper."

"He will." Sarah followed her to the door. "*Danki*, Ellie."

"'Twas my pleasure, Sarah."

"Will you come back to clean next week?"

Ellie agreed, then left the house. Reuben had pulled his buggy into the yard. Her heart started to race as he approached her. He didn't look happy. His mouth was tight and his eyes were cold.

"I told you that I didn't want you to clean house for us."

"I didn't clean." She lifted her chin as she glared at him. "I came to see Sarah." And his son.

He blinked. The tension left his expression and his blue eyes warmed slightly. "Have a nice night, then, Ellie."

Heart beating hard, she gave a jerk of a nod, then climbed into her pony cart and left. As she drove home, her thoughts went to Reuben, who'd surprised her. He didn't mind her visiting his sister? Apparently not. As long as she didn't clean. She could work with that, she decided. She wanted to be there for Sarah and Ethan. She'd visit early in the day if she could. If the house became a little cleaner while she was there, then all the better. Ellie frowned. She had a feeling that Reuben would make sure the place stayed spotless, even if he didn't get enough sleep.

She sighed and turned her thoughts to her parents. She'd be home in time to help Mam with supper. When she drove into the barnyard fifteen minutes later, Ellie smiled. She waved to her father, who was in the yard with Jeremiah, his beloved dog. She'd been shocked when Dat had decided to get a dog. Her sister Nell, the animal lover of the family who was married to a veterinarian, must have had more influence on their father than the family had realized.

Ellie heard Jeremiah bark as she climbed out of the buggy. Her father approached with his dog on his heels. "Dat," she greeted. "Taking Jeremiah for a walk?"

"*Ja.*" Dat regarded her with affection. "You're home early."

She nodded. "Finished with the Brodericks, then went to the Millers, a new family in Happiness." Her lips curving, she said, "I was teaching Sarah Miller how to cook. She never had much of a chance to learn with older sisters who did most of the cooking."

Dat's brows furrowed. "The Millers?"

"*Ja.* An Amish family who recently moved into

our church district." She glanced off into space, envisioning the vast amount of work that still needed to be done to Reuben's house. "The family moved into that old English place we've passed and commented on."

"Do they need help with the renovations?"

"*Nay*, the owner seems determined to handle the work himself."

"If he changes his mind, I'll be happy to gather a crew to help out."

Ellie smiled as she bent to pet Jeremiah. "I'll tell him." When the dog lay down and rolled over for a tummy rub, she laughed. She crouched and gave him some attention. "Where's Mam?" she asked as she straightened.

"At Aunt Katie's."

"Shall I plan supper?"

"I'm sure your *mudder* will appreciate it."

She studied her father carefully. "You feeling *oll recht*, Dat?"

"I'm fine."

Ellie stared at him. She didn't believe it. She'd caught his grimaces of pain too often in the last couple of months. "I'll feed the animals first."

"I'll feed them," he said.

"But I don't mind."

"Fine. Jeremiah and I will finish our walk, then." That her father gave in so easily only confirmed that he wasn't feeling well. "Charlie's marrying soon," he said. "Someday you'll find a man you'll want to wed, too. What will I do without you?"

She placed a gentle hand on his shoulder. "Dat, not to worry. I have no plans to get married anytime soon."

"But you'll marry and have children someday, *ja*?"

"*Ja*, someday."

"*Dochter*, you're twenty-one. You don't have forever." He smiled. "And I wouldn't mind more grandchildren."

"There's time enough," she insisted. "I'm not an old maid yet." After waving him on with his walk, she went inside to plan supper. She took chicken out of the freezer to thaw in the refrigerator for tomorrow. Ellie decided that tonight they'd finish the leftover roast beef. She'd make gravy so they could enjoy open-faced hot roast beef sandwiches. Then she made macaroni salad as a side dish before heading toward the barn to feed the animals.

Charlie pulled her pony cart into the barnyard as she crossed the yard. Ellie waved, and her sister grinned as she returned the wave. She jumped down from the cart, secured the horse, then joined Ellie, who stood watching her with an affectionate smile.

"Going to feed the animals?" Charlie asked. "Want help?"

"I wouldn't mind it." It was June, and in just five short months, Charlie would marry Nate and move into the farmhouse he was currently renovating. She would miss her sister when she was gone. She'd be the only one left at home with their parents.

"I had the best day," Charlie said. "You should see what Nate's done to the house. I'm going to love living there. We'll have plenty of room for a big family."

Startled, Ellie turned to study her as they entered the barn together. "You want a big family?"

"I do. You know how much I love *kinner*."

"I know." Her sister had always had a soft spot for children. It was why she'd agreed to babysit for Nate's stepmother and why she'd been eager to teach at their Happiness School. "I take it that Nate likes children, as well."

"Oh, *ja*! And he's so *gut* with them."

"A match made in heaven," Ellie murmured beneath her breath.

Her sister's sigh made Ellie grin. *"Ja."* Charlie filled up two feed bags and went to the horses first.

Ellie grabbed a bucket and filled it with chicken feed, then went out to toss the grain on the ground. As she watched the chickens peck at their food, Ellie heard her cell phone ring. Expecting one of her clients, she answered. *"Hallo?* This is Ellie."

"Ellie?" an anxious female voice said. "'Tis Sarah. Something happened. Can you come now?"

She knew instant fear. "I'll be right over."

"Danki," Sarah murmured and hung up the phone.

Ellie ran into the barn. "Can you finish with the animals? I just got a phone call and I need to go."

Charlie frowned. *"Ja*, of course. Is something wrong?"

"I don't know," she replied honestly.

Ellie ran to the pony cart. Within seconds, she steered her horse down the main road toward the Reuben Miller property. Had something happened to Ethan? Or Reuben? Fearful thoughts chased one another until the stress made her chest tighten.

No buggies were in the yard as Ellie drove up next to the house. She'd been gone only a short time. What had happened? She ran to the side door and it opened immediately, revealing a tearful Sarah.

"What is it?" Ellie asked with concern. "Is Ethan *oll recht*?"

Sarah bobbed her head. "Can you come inside?"

Ellie followed her into the kitchen and waited while the girl calmed down enough to explain. "Sarah?" she prompted softly.

"Dat called and left a message. Something happened to my *mam*. He has asked me to come home."

"Oh, Sarah," Ellie said with sympathy. "Did he say what's wrong?"

"Nay." The teenager shook her head. "But I know he wouldn't ask unless it was important. He knows Reuben needs me."

"Do they want your *bruder* to come home, too?"

"Just me. I have to go. I'm sorry. You told me to call if I needed you," Sarah said. "I need you, Ellie. I need you to take care of Ethan while I'm gone."

The pain in Ellie's chest intensified. "Me?"

"Ja, he likes you. He quiets down whenever you hold him. *Please* watch him for me. Reuben needs to work. He won't make any money if he has to stay home." She blinked back tears. "Will you do it, Ellie? Will you take care of Ethan for me?"

Ellie swallowed hard as she considered Reuben's reaction. *"Ja,* I'll do it. I'll take care of Ethan for you. When do you have to leave?"

Sarah looked away. "A car is coming for me within the hour. I've already packed."

Shocked, Ellie could only nod. "What time is Reuben expected home?"

"I'm not sure. He left about an hour ago after learning about a problem at his current job site."

She glanced at her watch. "'Tis nearly supper time. Do you want me to fix you something to eat?"

"Nay. I'm not hungry." In her anxiety, Sarah clasped

her arm. "The chicken corn chowder and strawberry pie I made are in the refrigerator for you and Reuben. Promise me you'll take care of Ethan no matter what. I know my *bruder* can be difficult."

Ellie briefly closed her eyes. "I can handle Reuben."

"Then you promise?"

She nodded. "I promise I'll take *gut* care of your nephew."

Sarah released a sigh of relief. "*Danki*, Ellie. I'll get word to you as soon as I can."

"Should I stay here until Reuben gets back?"

"I don't know how long he'll be gone. If it's too long, you can leave, telling him that you have Ethan at your *haus*," the teen suggested.

Ellie thought for a moment. "I'll do that."

Sarah hugged her. "*Danki*, Ellie. You are a true friend."

A cry from the other room announced that Ethan was awake. "Go get your bag, Sarah. I'll take care of this little man." While the girl ran upstairs, Ellie went into the gathering room, where Ethan sat up in his cradle. She picked him up and cuddled him. The smell of his diaper told her it needed changing.

"Well, little one...'tis you and me for a while. Let's fix your problem, then we'll spend some time together, *ja*?" The little boy was a beautiful child who resembled his father. What was Reuben going to say after learning she'd agreed to babysit indefinitely for his son? The man hadn't wanted her to clean his house. She could imagine what he'd have to say about watching Ethan.

What have I gotten myself into?

She needed to get word to her parents about what had happened. Using her cell phone, she made a call to their neighbors and asked them to let her family know that she'd be home as soon as she could.

School currently wasn't in session. Perhaps Charlie could help with Ethan's care until Ellie figured out a way to make time from her cleaning schedule for babysitting.

Less than an hour later, Sarah left. Ellie waited another hour and a half for Reuben's return before deciding to head home with Ethan.

Before leaving, she bathed and powdered Ethan, then wrote Reuben a long note, explaining what had happened and where Ethan was. She'd made sure she'd packed a bag with diapers, a bottle and food for the new charge. She hoped Reuben wouldn't be too angry that she'd left with his son. But she felt that she and Ethan were better off at her parents', since she didn't know how long Reuben would be gone.

Dear Lord, please help Reuben understand why I've taken his son home with me.

It was late when Reuben made it home after dealing with a plumbing emergency in the house they'd been building. He'd shut off the water, then had to figure out a way to clean up the mess while salvaging whatever he could in the rest of the house for his employer and the future homeowner.

It was close to nine when he drove his buggy into the yard. When he'd left the house earlier, he'd met an English driver hired by the construction company to transport their Amish crews. Reuben, newly promoted to foreman on this job site, had discovered that the plumber had failed to check his apprentice's work before leaving for the day. The flood of water from an improperly connected pipe had done an undeterminable amount of damage.

His body ached from stress as he climbed out of his vehicle and went inside. The house was silent, but he expected it to be. Ethan would have been put to bed earlier, and Sarah was probably in her room reading or fast asleep.

It was nearly dark outside and pitch-black inside, so he felt his way to the drawer where he kept a flashlight. He clicked on the light before he washed his hands at the kitchen sink and splashed water on his face. He was exhausted. The only thing he wanted to do was climb into bed and sleep for as long as possible before meeting up with his boss the next day.

After drying his hands and face with a towel, he tossed it into the washing machine in the back room. When he returned to the kitchen, he spied a piece of paper on the dining table. He read the note, then growled with frustration. His son and sister weren't at home. Sarah was no longer in Happiness. She'd gone to Ohio, summoned by their father. Ethan was with Ellie Stoltzfus at the woman's house. Ellie had written that she thought it best to take Ethan there to wait for his return. If he came in late, he shouldn't worry about coming to get him. She'd bring him home first thing in the morning. She knew he'd been working hard and he needed his rest.

Reuben growled with frustration. Ellie Stoltzfus had his son? He wasn't about to leave him with the Stoltzfuses. And he needed to know more of what had happened.

He sank into a chair to catch his breath and to summon the energy to get moving again. He scowled when he thought of Ellie and her nerve in taking *his* son home with her.

Anger gave him impetus, and he rose and grabbed his flashlight. He got back into his buggy and headed out to get his son. He'd have a few choice words with Ellie. He was more than annoyed. Having to make this trip was the last thing he needed, but he wanted his son safe and at home.

What was he going to do about Ethan now that Sarah was gone?

Reuben knew he had to find a wife and quickly. But first he had to contend with Ellie Stoltzfus and get the full story from her.

Chapter Four

After a last check that Ethan was asleep in a crib in her bedroom, Ellie headed downstairs. It was late and dark out. Was Reuben still dealing with trouble at work? Had he gone home and found her note?

She went into the kitchen to find her mother heating milk on the stove.

"He all settled in?" Mam asked.

"Ja." She bit her lip.

"Want a cup of sweetened warm milk?"

Ellie nodded. She felt terrible that she hadn't told her parents previously about cleaning house for Reuben Miller. She'd been afraid to mention him, considering what had happened between him and her sister Meg. Since arriving with Ethan, she had confessed everything. "Mam..."

Mam met her gaze. "Elizabeth Stoltzfus, I know what you're going to say," she scolded. "Don't you dare apologize for not telling us about Reuben. I understand your concern, but you're wrong. Dat and I have always liked Reuben. He was wonderful with Meg after the accident."

"An accident he caused," she pointed out.

"The accident wasn't his fault. The fault, if anyone's, belonged to the Englisher who hit Reuben's buggy, then left."

"They never found out who drove the car," Ellie murmured.

"*Nay*, but it doesn't matter. Meg and Reuben are both fine. Meg is happy with Peter and being mother to little Timothy." Her mother smiled. "Reuben moved on, as well."

Ellie nodded. "But life hasn't treated him as kindly. His wife died only minutes after giving birth to that precious little boy in my room."

"Is Reuben angry with his son?"

Ellie smiled, remembering the love in his gaze as Reuben had held his son. "*Nay*. He's a *gut vadder*. He loves Ethan."

Her mother filled three mugs of hot milk, then added sugar to each one. One for each of them and one for her father. "He's a fine man. I'm glad you can help him."

She was glad, too, but she doubted Reuben was. From what she'd encountered from him so far, he resented help—at least he did hers. He'd be here as soon as he read her note. He'd be angry, but she wouldn't apologize. She'd done the right thing in bringing Ethan home with her.

Ellie decided to drink her milk on the front porch. She murmured good-night to her parents, then took a seat in a rocking chair outside. How long before Reuben's arrival? For he would come. And he wouldn't be happy when he did.

It was a pleasant night. The stars were out in full

force, bright lights twinkling in a midnight sky. She caught sight of a shooting star and, despite her worries, she felt a moment's contentment. There was something wonderful in caring for a child. Ethan Miller was precious, and she loved spending time with him. The fact that he took to her quickly made her feel special and loved. She was able to quiet him easily when he was tearful. He clung to her as if she were his mother and not a stranger.

Ellie set her empty cup down next to her chair and closed her eyes, then continued to rock. She'd been cleaning houses for years. She wanted a husband and children, but she couldn't worry about that now, for she had her parents to think about. She would keep up her business until Charlie married, save her money for when she'd need it.

She rocked back and forth in the chair until she got sleepy. A rumble in the yard startled her awake, and she recognized the man who pulled up his buggy close to the house. Ellie inhaled sharply. Time to face Reuben Miller. The man had come for his son.

She stood as she watched him approach the house. He didn't see her in the dark at first as he climbed the steps.

"*Gut* evening, Reuben," she said from the porch railing. She saw him stiffen.

"Ellie," he snapped, "where's Ethan?"

"He's upstairs sleeping," she replied quietly.

"I've come to take him home."

"I don't think that's wise, Reuben. He's settled in for the night. Why can't you let him sleep?"

"You had no right to take him."

She froze. "I didn't kidnap him, Reuben. I brought

him here because I didn't know what time you'd be home. Didn't you see my note? I wrote that I'd bring him home in the morning."

"He needs to be home now."

She moved out from the shadows. The moon lent a glow to Reuben's face. She could read tension in his features, the pain of misunderstanding. "It's better if he's allowed to sleep." He looked exhausted, worried, and he probably needed the innocence of his baby son to ease his pain. She relented. "I'll get him for you."

His hand settled on her arm. "You're right," he said softly. "Don't wake him." He sighed. "'Tis been a long day. Do you mind if we sit a moment?"

"Please do." She softened toward him further. "Would you like something to drink? Hot cocoa or hot sweetened milk?"

He leaned back in the twin rocking chair and closed his eyes briefly. "Hot cocoa would be nice." He gazed at her, his expression stark and full of emotion. When she caught her breath, he closed off his emotions.

"I'll be just a moment." The water in the teakettle heated quickly. It took her but a moment to make him a cup of instant cocoa. She exited the house and handed him a mug, then sat down in the rocking chair. "It's instant."

He awarded her a slight smile. "It's perfect."

"Sarah left because something happened in Ohio," she said. "Your father sent a car. Whatever it was, your *dat* doesn't want you to worry. Sarah said she'd call tomorrow to let you know exactly what happened."

Reuben frowned. "As if I won't worry."

"I promised Sarah that I'd watch Ethan until her return."

He stiffened. "I'll stay home to take care of him."

"And miss work for how long?" She began to rock in the chair. His scent—earthy, male, pleasing to her sense of smell—reached out to her, intensifying her awareness of him. "I made your sister a promise, Reuben."

"And you always keep promises," he said bitterly.

"*Ja*. I do." She stifled her anger. "I know you don't want me at the house. If you prefer, I can ask Charlie to keep an eye on Ethan. She's *gut* with children. But I refuse to ask her to be at the house all the time, just because you have a problem with me personally. I will watch your son, so you might as well accept it." She paused. "I would never hurt Ethan."

He stared at her silently with eyes like sapphires in the dark. His gaze made her uncomfortable.

"Say something."

"What do you want me to say?" he asked. "You want me to admit that I don't want you in my *haus*?"

Ellie blanched at the direct hit. Ignoring the shaft of pain, she lifted her chin. "I don't care if you feel that way. It wouldn't change anything. I promised Sarah I'd take care of Ethan, and I will make good on that promise."

"With your sister," he said huskily.

She shrugged, though she felt anything but casual about the situation. "If necessary." She stood and went to the railing, giving him her back. "Since you seem fine with leaving your son here for the night, I'll make sure we get him home before you leave for work in the morning. Let's say by seven if not before. Will that work?"

He stood, handed her his empty mug. "*Danki* for the hot chocolate."

She nodded. "Reuben?"

The man released a tired sigh. "Seven tomorrow morning will be fine. No need to come earlier."

Without thought, Ellie placed a hand on his arm. She was shocked as she felt him tense, the muscle tightening. She withdrew quickly. He stared at her as if stunned that she'd touched him. A strange frisson of awareness cropped up between them.

Reuben looked away. "Good night, Elizabeth."

She watched him descend the porch steps and head toward his buggy. "Good night, Reuben," she murmured. He must have heard her, for he stopped and gazed at her for several long seconds before he climbed into his vehicle and left for home.

The next morning before seven, Ellie steered the buggy toward the Reuben Miller house. Charlie sat beside her holding Ethan. She flashed her a glance. "Are you sure you don't mind watching him this morning?"

"Not at all. You know I love children, and this little one," she said with affection, "is a sweetheart."

Ellie smiled at her sister. "I have one house to clean this morning. It won't take me long before I can relieve you."

"That's fine. I promised Nate I'd stop by to check on the progress of the farmhouse." Charlie grinned. "I'm excited to marry Nate. I never thought I'd ever be this happy," she confessed softly.

"You've liked him for a long time. It took him a while to see you for who you are." She recalled the difficulty the two had had getting together. "You're meant to be with him. You love him."

"I do." Charlie shifted Ethan so he could look out the window as Ellie turned onto Reuben's driveway. "Look, Ethan! There's your *dat!*"

The child made a sound of pleasure as he recognized his father. Ellie pulled the buggy close to the side door, where Reuben waited.

She climbed out and took Ethan from Charlie until her sister alighted and reached for the little boy. "*Gut* morning, Reuben," she greeted.

He nodded, his expression sober, until his gaze settled softly on his son. "Was he any trouble?" he asked Charlie.

"None," Ellie said tautly, refusing to be ignored. "He slept through the night and I fed him before we left the *haus*."

He studied her briefly as Charlie handed him his son. "Ethan," he murmured, his eyes soft, as he took him into his arms.

"Reuben," Charlie greeted as she skirted the buggy with a smile. "I hadn't realized that you moved into our district."

Ellie waited for his expression to darken, but to her shock, he grinned. "I have a lot of work to do to this place yet, but 'tis home." She watched her sister and Reuben converse easily. Hurt, she turned and climbed into the buggy. Why didn't he like her? Why was Charlie acceptable as Meg's sister but not her? Her attention skimmed over him briefly before she addressed her sister. "I'll see you later, Charlie." To her relief, her sibling nodded without saying another word.

"Have a *gut* day," Reuben told her gruffly, almost

reluctantly. Then, dismissing her, he kissed his son on the forehead before he waved Charlie toward the house. "Come in, and I'll show you around."

Swallowing against a suddenly tight throat, Ellie picked up the leathers, then left, heading to the Broderick household, her first and only cleaning job of the day.

The Broderick house was in the opposite direction from her house, but Ellie didn't mind the drive. The weather was nice and she needed the time to relax. Her brief encounter with Reuben had agitated her. That he could be so friendly to Charlie and not to her bothered her. A lot.

She drove up the Broderick driveway and parked her buggy near the garage. She tied her horse to the handle of the garage door, then grabbed her cleaning supplies before heading toward the house.

Ellie climbed the stoop and knocked on the glass outer door. Within seconds, the door opened, revealing Olivia Broderick. "Mrs. Broderick," she murmured in greeting.

Without a word, Olivia opened the door for her. Her gaze shot past Ellie to where she'd parked the buggy. "I don't want you parking your horse in the driveway," she said. "If he takes a dump on my pavers, you'll have to clean it up."

Ellie nodded. "Is there someplace else you'd like me to park?"

The woman sniffed. "I'd rather you not park anywhere near our property."

"Where, then?"

"I don't care, Eleanor," she said with disdain. "Just not here."

Drawing a calming breath, Ellie nodded. Her name wasn't Eleanor, but the woman continued to call her that whenever she was unhappy with her. Why had she agreed to continue working for these people? Did she need their money that badly?

"Upstairs today?" Ellie asked.

Olivia nodded. "The boys' rooms are a mess. If you could start with them, then head down to the main floor, that would be great."

Nodding, Ellie headed toward the stairs and climbed to the second floor, fearing what she'd find once she entered the woman's sons' rooms. In one room there were clothes scattered across the floor. She stared at them, then left the room and headed to a second bedroom. The floor was clean, the room tidy. She dusted the furniture, then went into a hall closet to get out the vacuum cleaner. After she vacuumed the rug, she put it away, then headed downstairs.

"That didn't take long," Olivia said.

"I did your youngest's room. Your other son's floor is covered with clothes. I clean houses," she said. "I don't do maid service or laundry."

The woman narrowed her gaze at her. "Perhaps you'd prefer to work someplace else."

"If you'd like." Ellie took her cleaning supplies and headed toward the door.

"Wait."

Ellie stopped and turned. She had a feeling that no one else would work in the house, that Olivia had never expected that Ellie—an Amish woman—would dare walk away from a job. "Yes?"

"If you leave," the woman said with a dark smile, "I won't ask you back."

A harsh laugh escaped from Ellie's lips. "Have a good day, Mrs. Broderick." Then she exited the house, feeling better about her day as she stowed her supplies on the backseat.

"Wait!" The woman had followed her outside.

Ellie turned and watched the woman's approach, her gaze anxious.

"I'm sorry," Olivia said. "I…" She blinked, looking devastated. "Please stay. I need your help. I'm sorry I've been grouchy. I just learned I have cancer." She bit her lip. "*Please.* You don't have to do John's room. Will you finish the rest of the house?"

Heart welling with compassion, Ellie softened toward her. "Yes, I'll finish." She grabbed her supplies from her buggy and turned…and saw gratitude in the other woman's expression. She followed Olivia into the house and went right to work.

Ellie finished the Brodericks' home by eleven thirty and headed to the Miller house to relieve Charlie. In the end, she'd gone ahead and cleaned John's room. How could she not? But to her surprise, Olivia Broderick had picked up the clothes and put them in a laundry basket while Ellie cleaned her son Robert's room. As she steered the buggy down the road, she felt pleased with how well her morning went. Before she left, she promised to clean for Olivia toward the end of next week.

The woman had apologized more than once for her behavior. Ellie learned that she had just started her chemotherapy treatments, and Olivia confessed she already felt weak. Ellie couldn't imagine dealing with cancer or the long road ahead that Olivia faced.

If she could help in any way, Ellie decided, she would be there for the woman. It was the least she could do when the Lord had blessed her with so much.

She caught sight of the Miller house and smiled. She would pray for Olivia Broderick. And she would live in the moment, enjoying little Ethan, who had quickly captured her heart.

Reuben was bone-tired. After a long day of work yesterday followed by a sleepless night, he felt exhausted. Alone with Ethan, how would he get any rest? He loved his son, enjoyed every moment he had with him, but today he felt awful. He worried that he wouldn't be the kind of father he should be.

He hadn't heard from Sarah. Had she called while he was gone? He was worried. It wasn't like his parents to call her home at a time they knew he needed her. Had something happened to his father? His mother?

"*Hallo!* I'm home!" he called as he entered the house through the side door. "Anyone here?"

Carrying Ethan on her hip, Ellie entered the kitchen from the great room. Expecting Charlie, he was taken aback to see her.

She smiled at him. "*Hallo*, Reuben, did you have a *gut* day?"

"What are *you* doing here?" he demanded.

"I'm watching Ethan, like I told you I would."

"I thought you had to work today." He heard the harshness in his tone and wondered why she brought out the worst in him. Because he found her attractive and didn't want to?

"I finished the job this morning. When I was done,

I came to relieve my sister." Her eyes narrowed, as if daring him to complain. "Is my presence here a problem?"

"Ja," he bit out, then felt terrible when her face fell. *"Nay,"* he revised. "'Tis not a problem. I know you take good care of Ethan…"

"Then why are you so angry with me?" she whispered.

He shook his head, unable to explain, and the sight of her blinking back tears floored him. "I'm sorry. I've had a lousy day. I shouldn't have taken it out on you." He gave her a gentle smile. "Will you forgive me?"

Ellie appeared surprised, then her expression softened with understanding. "I know what it's like to have a bad day," she murmured. Ethan shifted in her arms and patted her cheek with his chubby little hand. She grinned and ran a finger across his baby-soft cheek. "Are you hungry?" she asked Reuben.

"I could eat," he said. A funny feeling settled in his chest as he watched the two of them.

"Have you tasted the chicken corn chowder Sarah and I made yesterday? And there's strawberry pie."

He blinked, shook his head. "I didn't know there was soup and pie." He studied her through tired eyes. "I guess I've been too tired to look. You taught her how to make my favorite meal."

"Sarah made the pie. I just gave her the recipe."

His chest tightened and his heart pumped hard as he gazed at her. "I haven't been home much lately." He suddenly realized that he hadn't gone grocery shopping. There had been only sandwich fixings and a few breakfast foods left in the house. "You must have bought groceries. How much do I owe you?"

"Nothing." Ellie dismissed his concern. The room lit up with the warmth of her smile. "I picked up a few things but the rest I brought from home."

"Ellie—"

"Reuben, if you want to buy some groceries yourself, I can make a list for you."

She placed his son in his arms, as if she were the boy's mother and had done it many times in Ethan's young life. He didn't want to think about the implications of his thoughts. As he held and jostled Ethan, Reuben watched as Ellie opened the refrigerator and pulled out a bowl. Next she ladled a measure of the bowl's contents into a pan she took out of the cabinet. She then set it on the stove and turned on the heat. Watching her work, he was glad that the gas stove was new—it was the first thing he'd bought for the kitchen when he'd moved in three weeks ago.

As the soup warmed, Ellie turned toward him with a smile. "Would you like crackers with your soup?"

He stared at her, transfixed. "We have crackers?"

She laughed. "*Ja*, there are oyster crackers. Sarah mentioned that you liked them."

Reuben scowled. "What else did Sarah say?"

"That you're a pleasant fellow mostly," she quipped, her smile lingering.

He opened his mouth to retort, but her good humor made him grin as she turned and pulled out an iced tea pitcher from the refrigerator.

"I made sun tea," Ellie said. She poured him a glass, then reached out to caress Ethan's head. The brief maternal gesture affected him like a kick to his belly. "Soup should be ready soon." She held out her arms. "May I hold him while you eat?" She eyed him carefully. "You should sit. You appear about ready to keel over."

He wanted to argue with her but couldn't. She made him feel things he didn't want to feel. But how could he object to her babysitting when she was obviously good with Ethan?

She stirred the soup, then started to ladle it into a bowl she'd taken out of a top cabinet. "How much would you like? I know you're tired, but you need to eat to keep up your strength."

He'd been ready to tell her he wasn't hungry, but then he smelled her soup. The scent of chicken corn chowder wafted through the kitchen, and he suddenly had an appetite. His stomach growled.

She chuckled. "That hungry, *ja*?" She regarded him over her shoulder with a twinkle in her pretty blue eyes. She narrowed her gaze. "When *was* the last time you've eaten?"

"I had breakfast this morning. A sausage sandwich from Whittier's Store. I ate it in the car on the way to the job site."

"You didn't eat lunch?" she scolded.

Instead of annoyed, he found himself amused. "I had a bag of pretzels and a bottle of cola around midday."

She made a *tsk* sound. "Reuben, you need to eat better or you'll get sick."

He arched an eyebrow at her, and she blushed. "Sorry," she mumbled.

She turned her attention back to his soup bowl, setting it on the kitchen table, out of Ethan's reach. Then she opened the box of oyster crackers before reaching for Ethan.

He studied her a long moment, and she reddened. Was she feeling it, too? he wondered as he gave her Ethan. This odd tension between them?

Ethan whimpered as Ellie cradled him with his head on her shoulder. She soothed him with a kiss on his forehead and gentle rubbing down his neck and back.

Reuben stared at her, his soup untouched. He tried to imagine Susanna with their son but couldn't. He could only see Ellie, which made him feel angry and as guilty as if he'd sinned.

She froze, probably sensing his mood, and faced him. "You don't like your soup?"

"I haven't tried it yet."

A light furrow settled between her eyebrows. "Why not?"

He shrugged, then dipped his spoon for a taste. Reuben hummed with pleasure. The chicken corn chowder was delicious. He couldn't remember the last time he'd enjoyed a bowlful. He didn't think Susanna had ever made it for him. He'd eaten it after they were married, but it was his mother who'd made the soup. In fact, his mother had done almost all of the cooking, with Susanna helping to clean up afterward.

He met Ellie's worried gaze and smiled. "'Tis so *gut. Danki*."

She grinned, looked relieved. "You're *willkomm*. I enjoy cooking."

"You do?"

She narrowed her gaze. "You're surprised that I can cook?"

"I didn't think you had time to spend in the kitchen with your *haus*-cleaning business."

"I don't clean *haus* all day, Reuben. Or I wouldn't be here, would I? I worked this morning. One job only, which is how I prefer it. I may be asked to handle two jobs in a day, but it's on rare occasions that I agree."

He watched myriad emotions cross her face. "I see."

"I like to be available for my parents if they need my help."

Concern filled him. "Are they ill?"

"*Nay.* Nothing like that." She shook her head. "It just doesn't seem right not to pull my weight at home."

He'd been tired, but Ellie's soup had revived him. "Did you hear from Sarah today?"

"I'm afraid not." Without asking, she refilled his soup bowl. He didn't object. "I'm sure we'll hear from her soon." She smiled down at the child in her arms. "Do you own a high chair?"

"*Nay*, but I'll buy one tomorrow." His voice lowered. "I didn't think about it. I'm sorry."

Ellie looked at him. "What are you sorry for?" she said. "You have enough worries. We have an extra one at home that no one is using. Charlie can bring it with her tomorrow."

"I can buy one for my son," he said sharply, then looked away, immediately regretting his tone.

"I know you can," she agreed. "Why don't you borrow ours until you find the time to buy one?"

His lips firmed but he kept silent. He didn't want her chair. He could buy or make Ethan a chair.

Ellie left the room. He'd sensed when she stiffened and felt the tension emanating in the air. Closing his eyes, he sighed. He was overwhelmed with emotion that confused him. What was it about this woman that made him feel this way?

Chapter Five

With Ethan on her hip, Ellie went into the great room to grab the quilt that had been draped over a chair. Why was Reuben so determined not to accept her help? She understood that he was a man trying to come to grips with all of the changes in his life. But he was making things difficult for himself, and she didn't understand why.

Back in the kitchen, she spread the quilt on the floor before settling Ethan close to Reuben. She'd cleaned the floor earlier, adding a layer of floor wax to smooth out the rough spots. She grabbed a wooden spoon from a drawer and handed it to the boy to play with.

She straightened and found Reuben watching her. He didn't say a word about her choice of toy for Ethan. She was relieved when the odd level of awareness between them dissipated as he consumed his second bowl of soup.

There was still chowder left in the pan. She set it on a hot mat. When it cooled, she'd store the rest in the refrigerator. She knew the soup was good, as it was her mother's recipe, rich in chicken, corn, noodles and vegetables. She recalled Sarah's enjoyment in learning to cook. Thoughts of Reuben's sister sparked her concern. Why hadn't Sarah called as promised? What had happened that her *dat* needed to send for her?

She faced Reuben, who was eating a cracker. "There's some soup left in the pan. Would you like more?"

He met her gaze. "*Nay*, I've had plenty. *Danki*. 'Tis *gut.*"

Ellie found herself lost in his light blue eyes. "You've enough left for a couple of meals."

Reuben nodded but didn't comment. She checked on Ethan as she retrieved Reuben's empty bowl. She saw with a smile that the child was chewing on the tip of the wooden spoon. Aware of Reuben's study, she met his gaze. "I'll buy you another spoon."

His lips quirked with amusement. "He won't hurt it."

She felt her heart skitter in her chest as she noted his tender expression as he watched his son. The man was a good father. Had he been a good husband? She imagined he had been kind and loving to his wife.

The dark circles under his eyes told her how tired he was. Would he be able to sleep with Ethan in the house? Dare she offer to take him home with her?

She drew a steadying breath. "Reuben." When she encountered his gaze, she felt her attraction toward him like a shock to her system. "I don't mean to interfere, but I was wondering…would you like me to take Ethan home tonight so that you can sleep?"

His features tightened. "He's my son."

He'd reacted as she feared he would. "*Ja*, I know," she said quietly. She started to wash the dishes.

"Ellie." His soft voice and presence behind her gave her a jolt. His hand settled gently on her shoulder and turned her to face him. "I'm sorry."

"I'm not trying to keep him from you," she whispered. Her throat tightened and she fought tears. Her shoulder tingled where his fingers touched her.

"I know." He released her suddenly as if he'd just realized that he'd been touching her. He ran a hand through his thick blond hair. "If you don't mind taking him home with you for the night, I'd appreciate it." He sighed heavily. "I'm well beyond tired."

She eyed him with warmth. "Charlie can bring him home before you leave for work in the morning."

Reuben nodded agreeably. *"Danki."* His brow furrowed. "What time will you be done with work tomorrow?" he asked.

"About eleven," she said. "Why?"

"I'm planning to work around the *haus* tomorrow. If Charlie doesn't mind watching him at home, you can bring him here with you after you've finished work."

"I'm sure Charlie won't mind watching him," Ellie said easily, but inside her heart raced wildly. He wanted her to bring him home? Why the sudden shift in attitude? "Depending on how the morning goes, I could be as late as one. Will you need me to stay and watch him?"

He inclined his head. *"Ja.* If you don't mind."

She flashed him a smile. "I don't mind." She grinned at Ethan, who played happily with his spoon. She looked up, met Reuben's gaze with a lingering smile. She glanced away after she noted the man's shuttered expression. "I'll finish the dishes and then we'll leave." She bit her lip. "If you still want me to take Ethan."

"Ja."

She felt glad that he trusted her enough to take Ethan home. She took out the cold strawberry pie and spun to face him. "Would you like dessert?"

He grinned. *"Ja*, please."

Ellie cut him a huge slice and placed it on a plate with a fork. His face lit up like a little boy's when she set the dessert before him. "Enjoy."

She bent, picked up Ethan—spoon still in the baby's hand—then placed the boy on her hip. He fussed when she gently took away his spoon until she gave him a piece of mashed strawberry. "I'll pack Ethan's bag and then we'll leave," she said.

"Danki, Ellie." The warm look in his eyes made her breath hitch.

She climbed the steps to Ethan's room and packed his bag before she returned to the kitchen. Her cell phone rang, jarring the silence, as Ellie entered the room. Her gaze met Reuben's briefly. She gave him Ethan before she answered it. *"Hallo?"*

"Ellie?"

She immediately recognized Reuben's sister. "Sarah!" Reuben straightened and stared. "How are things in Ohio? We've been worried while waiting for you to call. What happened?"

Reuben stood and approached. "May I talk with her?" he mouthed.

She nodded. "Sarah? Reuben is here. I'll put him on."

"Danki, Ellie," he said as she handed him the phone. He flashed her a grateful smile.

"Sarah? What happened? Are Dat and Mam *oll recht*?"

Ellie tried not to eavesdrop during his conversation with his sister, but she couldn't help herself. She was curious and more than a little concerned. She reached for Ethan, and Reuben handed her his son without hesitation. She smiled at the little boy and took a seat at the table with Ethan on her lap. She waited patiently for Reuben to finish his call. Finally, he ended the conversation and handed back her phone.

"What happened?"

Reuben ran his fingers raggedly through his blond hair. "My *mudder* fell. She broke her arm and sprained her ankle. There is no one but Sarah to help her while she's recovering. It could be weeks before Sarah can come home." He hesitated. "My sister told my *eldre* that you're watching Ethan." His smile was apologetic. "I'm sorry, Ellie. 'Tis not right to impose on you. I'll look for someone to watch him for me."

"Why?" she said evenly. "I like spending time with Ethan—and so does Charlie. 'Tis no imposition to care for your son. Don't be in such a hurry to find another babysitter. I love spending time with him."

Warmth flickered in his light blue eyes. "Ellie…"

"Honestly, Reuben. 'Tis fine. Please don't worry about this." She stood and shifted Ethan to her hip before she retrieved the bag of the child's belongings from the table. "Do you want anything else to eat?"

"I'm stuffed." The warmth left his features, which suddenly became unreadable.

Ellie ignored his expression. "There are muffins in the pantry," she said. "I made them this afternoon so they'll still be fresh in the morning." She paused and attempted to gauge his thoughts. "I'll bring Ethan when I'm done. Or if you'd rather, Charlie can bring him first thing."

"*Nay*, after you've finished work is fine." He followed her toward the door. "I owe you, Ellie."

She stared, then scowled at him. "You owe me nothing, Reuben, so get that idea out of your head right now." Irritated, she swung open the door.

"Elizabeth," he murmured. "I didn't mean to upset you."

She froze and saw regret on his face. "I'll see you tomorrow," she said softly. "Get some rest. You look like you need it."

His lips twitched. "Is that a polite way of telling me I look awful?"

"Maybe." She returned his smile. He would never look terrible, she thought. He was too handsome and way too attractive to ever look bad to her. Shocked by her musings, she still managed to keep her expression neutral. "Sleep well, Reuben." Then she left and was conscious of his regard as he stood in the doorway while she climbed into her buggy and settled his son on her lap. With a wave, she led the horses out of the driveway and headed home.

Ethan was a sweet-natured baby. That night he settled in easily in the crib in her room, for which Ellie was grateful. After checking with her sister about watching Ethan in the morning, she decided to read awhile before getting ready for bed.

Early the next morning Ellie received a call from the client she was to clean for that day. Anita Moss had unexpected company for the week. Would Ellie clean for her after her guests left, next Thursday or Friday? Ellie told her she'd call to confirm the date after she checked her schedule. Then she gathered Ethan, who'd clung to her since he awakened, fed him, then started the drive back to the house.

Reuben woke at dawn after a good night's sleep, ate breakfast, then began to paint the interior walls of the first-floor rooms. After two hours he'd finished two coats on the kitchen and smaller rooms, then he moved on to work in the great room. The freshly painted walls made a difference, and he was pleased with the effect. A short time later, he eyed his handiwork in the second room with satisfaction. Ellie wasn't due to arrive yet with his son. The smell of paint would be nearly gone by the time they came. Next, he would tackle the bedrooms upstairs.

Reuben opened the kitchen windows before taking a breather outside with a glass of iced tea. He sat on the steps and studied the yard as he sipped from his glass. There was still so much junk in the back of the house. His stomach tightened as he envisioned the work entailed in getting rid of it—a rusted hollowed-out shell of an automobile. Two metal barrels that looked worse than the car, and too many other items in the back of the barn as well as inside.

And Ethan needed a high chair. He was ashamed that he hadn't thought of getting one before now. Sarah had fed Ethan while holding him. It was true his son was getting older, but did he have the money that would allow for the purchase of the chair? He had no idea how much one cost, but the last thing he wanted was to accept charity from the Stoltzfuses.

The sun felt warm but not overly so this morning. He finished his tea, set his glass aside, then leaned back on his arms and closed his eyes. A light breeze caressed his skin, and he could hear the sounds of nature. A bird in a nearby tree. The rustle of leaves. The sound of his own even breathing.

The spin of buggy wheels on his driveway had him opening his eyes. Charlie Stoltzfus steered the vehicle to a stop a few feet from where he sat. He stood as Ellie climbed out with Ethan in her arms. He saw Ellie lean into the carriage to talk briefly with her sister before she straightened and turned in his direction.

"*Hallo*, Reuben!" Charlie called with a wave and a smile. Then she left, leaving Ellie at the house without a way to get home.

He watched her approach. Ellie met his gaze and the smile left her face as she hesitated. "Reuben," she said cautiously.

"You're here early," he replied without emotion. He wasn't ready to see her. He'd wanted to finish inside the house before she and Ethan arrived.

"*Ja,*" she murmured. "I didn't have to work today."

"I didn't expect you until later."

Her mouth tightened. "Is there a problem?" she asked tartly.

Before he could explain, Ethan squealed with delight and extended his arms toward his father. His expression softening, Reuben reached for his son, and Ellie handed him the baby.

She stepped back to allow them time together. As he cuddled Ethan, he shifted his gaze to the woman who'd cared for his child during the night. She looked as if she felt she shouldn't be there.

"How was he through the night?" he asked, surprised by the huskiness of his voice.

Appearing to relax, Ellie smiled as she studied Ethan. "He was a *gut* boy. Fell asleep immediately when it was time for bed and slept through the night." She raised her eyes to meet his. "Did you sleep well?"

Reuben nodded. He had slept once he finally stopped thinking. He'd gotten up early to paint, but it had been worth it. He wondered how Ellie would react to the change. She stood a few feet away, looking uncertain. He shifted his son's weight to one arm.

"We'll have to stay outside for a little while," he told her.

She frowned. "Why? What's wrong?"

"Nothing. I painted the downstairs rooms this morning. I'd like them to air out a bit longer before we bring Ethan inside."

"Oh." Ellie looked relieved. "Are you pleased with how everything looks?"

"*Ja*, the rooms are white and clean."

"And you no longer need someone to come in to scrub them," she muttered.

He shot her a glance. "'Tis not about you, Ellie. 'Tis part of fixing up the *haus*. Painting is a part of the renovations. I need to replace the floor, as well."

She held his gaze silently as if to gauge his measure, then finally gave a nod. He moved on the step, giving her enough room to sit. Ellie hesitated, then took a seat next to him. They were silent. Reuben was aware of her clean scent and the warmth of her close proximity. He tried to concentrate on Ethan, but then his son reached for Ellie, drawing his attention back to the woman next to him. Reuben released him into her care. The sight of Ethan's chubby arms around Ellie's neck got to him, made him feel things he didn't want to feel. He stood abruptly. "Paint smell should be gone," he said.

He waited for Ellie to stand, then reached to open the door, letting Ellie and Ethan enter ahead of him.

She gasped as she caught sight of the room. "It looks beautiful. The bright walls make the kitchen look bigger." She shifted Ethan in her arms. "Did you say you did all of the first floor?"

He nodded. "The gathering room and the bathroom. I even painted the mudroom."

"You got a lot done." Her gaze narrowed. "I thought you said you slept."

Reuben grinned. He couldn't help himself. "I did, until right before dawn when I got up and decided this morning would be a good time to paint." He studied Ellie as she took in her surroundings. Today she wore a purple dress that brightened her pretty blue eyes. Her blond hair, more golden in color than his, was neatly pinned beneath her prayer *kapp*.

"I'd like to start painting upstairs this afternoon," he said. "Can you manage with staying downstairs with Ethan?"

Her lips firmed. *"Ja."*

He inclined his head. *"Gut."* He went to the refrigerator and looked inside. "Are you hungry? There is soup left."

"I wouldn't mind a small bowl." She handed Ethan back to him. "I'll fix lunch."

Reuben wanted to object. Ellie was already doing too much for him and Ethan, but he knew he would only upset her if he insisted on preparing the meal, so instead he sat on a kitchen chair and settled Ethan in his lap. His son smelled like baby powder and sunshine. He studied him a moment before focusing his gaze on Ellie. She'd taken good care of Ethan and he appreciated it. As much as it pained him to accept help, he knew he couldn't manage on his own. And she seemed to enjoy watching his boy…at least until Sarah returned. He frowned. If his sister returned.

He hoped Sarah would call soon to bring him up to date on his mother's injuries. Maybe he should have moved with his parents to Ohio, but Lancaster County had always been his home, and he hadn't wanted to leave it. He'd already suffered too many changes in his life. And with this house, there was a promise of a better future.

He watched Ellie dump the soup into a pan and set it on the stove. She didn't glance back as she turned on the gas burner and waited for the chowder to heat. Stirring the soup, she stared into the pot, obviously lost in thought.

"Ellie."

She startled, then faced him. *"Ja?"*

"I didn't mean to be rude this morning."

Her lips twitched. "You can't help yourself, I know."

He was shocked when he heard himself laugh. To his delight, Ellie chuckled. They shared a moment of amusement, but when it dissipated, awareness cropped up between them. Conscious of his attraction to her, he rose with Ethan, eager to escape her presence if but for a moment, and went into the great room to check on the drying paint. As he studied his handiwork, Reuben felt immense satisfaction for the way the paint had transformed the room's appearance.

Ethan patted his cheek, demanding his attention. Reuben gasped with exaggeration and his son giggled. He grew soft as he gazed at the little boy he and Susanna had made together. Life could have been near perfect, but her death had been like a kick in the teeth, which had made him reevaluate his circumstances. He blinked as emotion threatened to overwhelm him.

"Reuben, the soup's hot," Ellie called from the doorway and he turned. He heard her inhale sharply, her gaze intent on his features. "I'll take Ethan for you," she murmured softly. Then she left, as if she wanted to give him a few moments alone to compose himself.

Perceptive woman, he thought with a little smile as the dark sense of loss left him. Still, he didn't return to the kitchen immediately. He crossed the room to peer out the window, absently touching light fingers to the wall next to him and noticing that it was completely dry. He stared out into the front yard. The view was decent. He couldn't see the junk in the yard from here. Maybe he needed to tackle cleaning up the grounds next so Ethan could have a place to play. He'd build him a swing set. There were bills to be paid, but eventually he'd have enough money to buy the materials he'd need for swings.

His stomach growled, a reminder that he'd skipped breakfast. After a calming breath, Reuben felt peace settle over him. He entered the kitchen to see Ellie placing soup bowls on the table. Ethan sat on a quilt on the floor, playing with a wooden spoon. He studied his son and became amused when Ethan grinned at him, waved the spoon in the air, then put the tip of it in his mouth.

"It smells *gut*," Reuben said as he took his seat.

With a small smile, Ellie joined him at the table. "*Ach nay*, I forgot the crackers." She sprang to her feet.

He reached to stop her with a gentle hand on her arm. "No need to get them," he said quietly. "Unless you want some for yourself."

She shook her head. "We need drinks, though. Iced tea?"

He nodded. Their gazes locked and he became conscious that he held her arm. Her skin was soft and silky to the touch. Startled, he released her and focused on eating his soup. Ellie was silent as she poured two glasses of iced tea. He took a sip from the one she handed him.

"This tea is *gut*," he said with surprise. He drank more.

Ellie flushed with pleasure. "'Tis sun tea. The tea steeped in a large gallon jar I found in your pantry. I just filled it with water and some tea bags, then put it out in the sun to heat."

Reuben studied his glass before meeting her gaze. "It tastes sweet and has lemon in it."

She smiled. "While the tea was still hot from the sun, I added sugar and lemon."

"You know your way around a kitchen," he said with a smile.

Looking uncomfortable with his praise, she averted her glance. "Spent a lot of time in one."

Reuben watched her silently as she continued to eat. Eventually Ethan grew fussy.

Ellie jumped from her seat and scooped Ethan into her arms, and the wooden spoon fell to the floor. "What's wrong, little man, did you hit yourself with the spoon?" she murmured soothingly to him. "I'll rub it better for you." She smiled as she stroked the reddened area on his left leg. The child stopped crying and gave her a watery smile. "Are you hungry?"

"You'd make a *gut* mother," Reuben praised. He regretted the observation as soon as he caught her expression. "What I mean," he quickly added, "is that Ethan responds well to you." He'd instantly regretted his words. While Ellie might be the perfect mother for his son, his unwanted attraction to her compounded with his love for his late wife reminded him it was foolish to consider Ellie.

Chapter Six

Startled by his comment, Ellie was aware of Reuben's continued gaze on her as she cuddled his son. She would have thought he would blame her for Ethan's injury. After all, she'd given Ethan the spoon. But instead of complaining, he'd given her praise. Surprised, she couldn't look at him, preferring instead to focus on the child in her arms. Reuben already churned up enough odd feelings within her she found disturbing.

She hugged his son, smoothed a gentle touch across his sore thigh, then placed a kiss on his forehead. As Ethan laid his head on her shoulder, Ellie blew against his neck, the raspberry sound making him laugh. She grinned. The little boy giggled as she repeatedly blew against his neck until she was stopped by her own laughter.

Reuben stood, moved past her to put their empty bowls in the sink. Then he paused near her shoulder. She tensed but forced herself to meet his gaze. There was surprising warmth in his blue eyes. She relaxed briefly, only to become startlingly aware of the tension she felt. A soft smile curved the man's lips and suggested he enjoyed watching the interaction between her and Ethan. She returned his smile before bending to blow another kiss in the crease of his baby's neck.

Reuben ran a hand gently across her shoulder as he reached to tickle Ethan. Ellie's breath caught, but Ethan laughed, the merry sound infectious. She grinned. It felt wonderful to laugh. The little boy put his arms about her neck. When he placed his head on her shoulder, Ellie melted.

"Hey, little one," she said softly. "Feel better enough to eat?"

"What will you feed him?" Reuben asked.

"I brought a box of cereal."

"Dry cereal?" He looked surprised. "He can eat that?"

Her gaze went soft. "*Ja*. Didn't Sarah give him finger food?" She raised Ethan high and tickled him by rubbing her nose onto his belly. The boy giggled and clutched the top of her head, nearly pulling off her prayer *kapp*. Ellie gently caught the little hand in time.

Reuben was silent. He appeared troubled.

"Reuben?" she said softly. "What's wrong?"

"I don't know much about my son," he admitted with concern.

"You know enough." She hesitated. "You're a *gut vadder*. Ethan is happy and comfortable in your arms." She caressed the little one's cheek. "Children don't come with directions. We do the best we can." She smiled at him. "You've been working hard. You mustn't worry because you can't anticipate every one of Ethan's needs."

He stared at her with a frown. She saw emotion briefly flicker across his expression, then disappear.

His demeanor changed. "I must get back to work," he said crisply.

Then he left the house so abruptly that she gaped at the back of him as he made his escape.

Minutes later, Ellie heard footsteps going upstairs. He must have come in the front door with whatever supplies he needed. She tried to forget the awkward moment between them, concentrating on Ethan instead. She hugged the boy close before setting him on the quilt and taking his cereal from a cupboard. Reuben needed a high chair for Ethan, but until he bought one, she'd sit at the table with the child on her lap. She poured a small of amount of cereal on the table within Ethan's reach and was rewarded when he grabbed and shoved a piece in his mouth.

After lunch, she laid him down for a nap in the great room, then washed and dried the lunch dishes. Once Ethan fell asleep, Ellie took a moment to sit quietly before planning supper for Reuben so that he had something to reheat when he was hungry.

It was late afternoon when Reuben finally came downstairs. He entered the kitchen, then stopped abruptly, as if he'd forgotten she was there. "What are you doing?" he asked politely. "Something smells delicious."

Warmed by the compliment, Ellie turned away from the stove to face him. "I made chicken potpie to reheat when you're ready. If you're hungry now, you can eat it while it's hot."

He looked tired as he ran a hand through his blond hair. "I just need a moment to clean up."

She managed a smile for him. "I'll ladle you a bowlful. I take it you like chicken potpie?"

He nodded. "*Ja*, although I haven't had any in…"

"Since your parents moved to Ohio?" she guessed.

His brows furrowed. "Much longer than that." He narrowed his gaze. "What do you know about my parents?"

She shrugged, ignoring his terseness. "Just what Sarah told me. That they moved to Ohio to live closer to your *mudder*'s *eldre*. Your sister stayed behind to help with Ethan."

Reuben was silent a long moment. "'Tis true." He sighed. "But I should have made her go. She's too young to take so much responsibility."

"She loves you and Ethan. She's happy to help."

He approached and stared into the pot while she stirred. "I need a wife," he murmured. "My son needs a mother."

Ellie tensed. She picked Ethan up and gave him to his father. "You want to fall in love and marry again?"

"*Nay*, I'll marry but I won't fall in love."

"You'd wed without love?"

"I'd wed for Ethan." He combed his fingers through Ethan's fine baby hair. "But love? *Nay*. I don't want or need it."

What woman would agree to such an arrangement? "I see." She glanced out the window to see her sister pulling the family buggy close to the house. Ellie reached for her satchel on the other end of the counter. "I have to go. Charlie's here."

It was important that she be on hand to help her mother. Soon Charlie would be married and it would be up to Ellie, the only daughter who'd be left at home, to make her parents' lives easier.

She felt Reuben watching her as she picked up her

bag, was conscious of him as he followed her out of the house. Charlie waved and called out to him. Ellie glanced back briefly to see Reuben wave back. She studied father and son. His arms circling Reuben's neck, Ethan was happy to be held by his father.

She stowed her bag in the back of the buggy, then climbed onto the front seat. With a last look in his direction as Charlie pulled away, Ellie wondered how a man who obviously loved his son could dismiss love in marriage so easily. What woman would be happy to be married to such a man and not fall in love with him? And with his son? Her thoughts in turmoil, Ellie was silent as they headed for home.

"You're quiet. Everything *oll recht*?" Charlie asked.

Ellie managed a smile. "*Ja,* Ethan and I had a *gut* day."

"I can watch Ethan for you tomorrow if you need me to."

"*Danki.*"

Early the next morning Ellie drove her sister to the Reuben Miller house before heading to her first cleaning job. Reuben had to work on a new construction site, and he needed someone to stay with Ethan. She longed to stay but couldn't. Her cleaning business would keep her occupied until noon, if not later.

"Are you sure you don't want to stay and watch Ethan?" Charlie asked as she eyed her knowingly.

"I can't," Ellie told her. "I've two jobs to do today, but I'll come as soon as possible to relieve you."

Charlie smiled. "I don't mind watching him for the day if you can't get away."

But I mind, Ellie thought. She wanted to spend time with the little boy. She loved Ethan. It was hard not to fall for the sweet, delightful child. She wished she could stay. She was fast losing her desire to clean house for Englishers, but until she gave it up after Charlie married, she had clients to keep happy. "I appreciate your help, Charlie." She changed the subject. "How are the *haus* renovations coming?"

Her sister grinned. "*Wunderbor!* Nate's been working hard on them while still helping his *dat* on the farm." A dreamy look entered her sister's expression. "I'm going to love living there."

"Especially with Nate," Ellie said with a grin.

Her sisters were blessed to have found good men they loved and respected. Someday, she hoped to be as blessed. She wanted a man who loved her. A husband who wanted to be her life's partner and raise a family with her.

Not everyone was as lucky in love, she thought with sadness. Reuben had loved and lost. He'd suffered so much that he couldn't bear marrying for love again. But he'd marry for Ethan.

Ellie could never marry a man who didn't love her. Even if the man was handsome, kind and a good father. Something shifted inside her breast. Reuben Miller possessed all the attributes of a good life partner. But he would offer friendship only. For herself, she wanted more.

Thank the Lord that she was immune to such a man.

The house loomed ahead. Ellie switched on the battery-run blinker before she steered her vehicle onto Reuben's driveway. The spare high chair that had been left unused in what had previously been Leah's bedroom was on the backseat. Charlie had insisted they bring it despite Reuben's objection, and Ellie wasn't going to argue with her sister. Would he be angry?

She parked the buggy and got out while her sister climbed out the other side. Charlie took out the chair. Ellie looked toward the house but didn't see Reuben.

"You look nervous. He really doesn't want this chair?" Charlie said knowingly.

Ellie released a heavy breath. "*Nay.* He doesn't." Her lips firmed. "But maybe you can convince him otherwise." She studied the chair. "Do you need help with it?"

"*Nay*, I can manage it on my own."

Ellie watched Charlie cart the chair up to the side door, then set it down on the stoop to knock. The door opened. Reuben flashed her sister a smile. He saw the chair and quickly reached out to take it from her. Charlie waved at her, and Ellie turned to leave, but not before catching the thunder in Reuben's expression.

"So you're angry with me and not Charlie?" Ellie murmured as she climbed into her vehicle. *Learn to live with it*, she thought as she picked up the leathers and steered the horse toward her first cleaning job of the day.

Reuben carried in the high chair. "Where do you want it?"

"Close to the kitchen table," Charlie said, watching with unreadable green eyes.

"What?" he said once he'd set up the chair.

"You're upset with my sister. She said you would be." The young woman regarded him thoughtfully.

"I told her that I didn't want it. I can buy a chair for my son."

Charlie nodded. "I understand, but why not use this one until you do?" She left the room but came back within seconds with Ethan on her hip. "She didn't want to bring it and upset you, Reuben." She smiled at his baby as she buckled him into the chair and slid the tray close to his body. "I was the one who insisted."

Reuben felt his gut wrench. "You?"

She crossed her arms as she faced him. "*Ja*, me. Ellie wanted to honor your wishes, but I—we—need a place to keep him safe while we feed him. He's old enough to sit on his own."

"Charlie—"

"You owe her an apology," she said. "I don't understand why you dislike accepting help."

"I've accepted yours and Ellie's," he pointed out. "With Ethan."

Charlie gave him a smile. "*Ja*. You should probably get to work or you'll be late."

"I...*danki*, Charlie."

Her lips curved. "We'll take *gut* care of your son."

"I know." His heart ached with the mistake of misunderstanding. Reuben grabbed his hat and his tool belt, then waited outside for his ride. Today he would be working with Jed and Elijah Lapp—Ellie's cousins. He was still waiting on plumbing repairs on his other job. His crew was split up and working other sites until the repairs were finished.

Jedidiah arrived alone. Reuben approached the man's vehicle and greeted him with a nod. "Going to be a warm one, I'm afraid," Jed commented pleasantly.

"*Ja*, it is," Reuben agreed.

"Looks like you've got a lot of work to do here yet."

Reuben stiffened. "*Ja*."

"Let us know if you need a hand." The man met his gaze.

He nodded. "I will. *Danki*." But he wouldn't be asking for help. He had something to prove to himself—that he was capable of doing things on his own.

Jed steered his wagon onto the main road. "Heard you got a son."

"You heard right."

"Mam said my cousins have been watching him for you."

Reuben tensed. They were talking about him. "*Ja*, they have been."

Jed grunted. "*Gut*. They'll take *gut* care of him. Even guard him with their lives."

He went still until the man laughed. "Let's hope they don't have to," Reuben said with a chuckle.

The day went fairly quickly for Reuben, considering that the sun was hot and the labor hard. Jed had him home by four thirty. He climbed down from Jed's vehicle. "Appreciate the ride, Jed."

The man smiled. "Anytime. See you tomorrow."

He waited until Jed had left before he turned. He felt worn out from the heat as he approached the house. He was aware that his blue short-sleeved shirt was stained with sweat and his pant legs and shoes dusty with dirt from the job site. They were building a small shopping center between the villages of Bird in Hand and Intercourse. When it was finished, there would be room for three shops. All of them, according to Jed, would be Amish owned and run. While he had no desire to be involved in businesses that attracted tourists, he understood what these businesses meant to Amish families who wanted to make a good living. He preferred construction or farming.

Reuben tried to open the side door but it was locked. He frowned. Did one of the sisters take Ethan home with them? He rapped on the door and waited. He was in a lousy mood. The last thing he needed was to fetch Ethan. When no one answered his knock, he started to simmer. He knocked harder out of frustration. The door suddenly swung open, and he could hear a child's cry.

Ellie stood in the doorway and gazed at him with irritation. "You woke up Ethan, and I'd just gotten him to sleep."

He stared at her through narrowed eyes, but his anger vanished with the onset of relief. "'Tis nearly five."

The woman turned and walked away, leaving the door open for him to follow her. She went into the great room and drew Ethan into her arms, urged his head onto her shoulder, then rubbed his back to soothe his child. Ethan finally quieted and his eyelids drifted closed. "He's been fretful all afternoon. I hope he's not coming down with something."

Reuben approached and placed a hand on his son's forehead. "He's warm."

Ellie looked at him. "'Tis hot today. I don't think he has a fever."

He swallowed hard at the compassion and tenderness he saw on her features. Something moved deep within him. She was an astounding woman who would make some man a good wife and mother for his children someday.

Reuben looked away. He didn't want to notice anything about Ellie. She was a complication he didn't need. "How can I help?"

Her smile nearly stopped his heart. "There isn't much to do at this point. I'll hold and comfort him until he falls asleep again." Ethan opened his eyes and tried to lift his head. Ellie rubbed his neck, and he lay against her shoulder again.

"Do you need a break?" Reuben whispered. "I can hold him awhile."

"He's settled down some," she said softly. "Better not to move him." She regarded him with warmth. "Supper's ready for you. 'Tis just macaroni salad, sweet and sour green beans and some fried chicken I picked up on my way over this afternoon. Everything is in the refrigerator. Chicken is usually *gut* cold, but if you want, I can heat it up for you."

She carried Ethan carefully toward the refrigerator and opened the door.

"Ellie, I can get it."

She nodded, swung the door shut and stepped back. She looked hurt. He closed his eyes, wondering what to say to wipe that look from her eyes. "You've done so much and I appreciate it," he said softly. "Ellie—" She met his gaze. "I'm sorry for being stubborn about the high chair. Your sister said that it was her idea to bring it. I should have accepted your offer when you made it."

Ellie looked surprised yet glad. "You can give it back when you no longer need it."

"Your family doesn't need it?"

"Nay." She shifted Ethan in her arms. "Not any-time soon." She smiled at his little boy. "I think he's nodded off." Her voice was quiet, almost reverent. The

beauty in her features arrested him, and he was forced to admit there was something compelling about her that drew him in. Ethan was fast asleep with his head on her shoulder.

"Do you want to put him down?" he asked.

She shook her head. "Let's make certain he is asleep first. *Ja?*"

He nodded. "I'll get dinner ready. You'll join me once you put him down?"

Ellie blinked rapidly. "You want me to eat supper with you?"

"Ja." He searched her expression, saw her surprise. "Do you need to be home?"

"Nay. I like to help Mam, but Charlie's home so she can help her."

His relief startled him. *"Gut."*

Ellie was stunned. Reuben had invited her to stay to eat supper. The knowledge shook her. Earlier, he'd been angry with her. Was he trying to make amends?

His apology had shocked her. He'd said that he should have accepted her offer of the chair from the start. What an enigmatic man.

Ethan felt good in her arms. He smelled of baby powder and lavender baby soap that she'd washed him with earlier that afternoon. She'd been reluctant to put him down until Reuben had invited her to supper. She laid him gently into the cradle bed in the great room, then entered the kitchen as Reuben was closing the refrigerator door. He hadn't taken out any food. Had he changed his mind about her staying? "Reuben?"

He gave her a rueful smile. "I should clean up first before we have supper. It won't take long."

She eyed him, noting his damp shirt, his dusty pants and the blond hair that was plastered to his forehead. No man had ever looked better to her. *Ach nay*, she thought, *I'm in serious trouble*.

"I'll set the table," she said quietly.

He stared at her with an unreadable expression, before he nodded, then headed upstairs. She heard his heavy treads on the steps to the second floor, then the sound of water through the pipes.

She set the table and put out the cold fried chicken with the side dishes she'd made. Ellie had finished pouring two glasses of iced tea when she felt Reuben's presence. Detecting the scent of soap and clean male, she inhaled deeply, then faced him. Her heart beat hard at the sight of him. He wore a light green shirt with navy trousers. His hair was damp, and his feet were bare. "Do you feel better?" she asked politely.

"Ja." His smile made her stomach flutter. His gaze went to the table. "Dinner looks delicious."

"I didn't heat the chicken. Do you want it warm? It won't take long."

"I like cold chicken."

"Me, too." She fiddled with the silverware, then put them beside their plates. Ellie felt awkward, nervous. She should be home with her parents, not eating with Reuben. She swallowed hard and turned. "I should get home."

He frowned. "You're not going to eat first?"

She shook her head. "I know I said that Charlie's there to help. But then I remembered she was with Nate this afternoon. What if she isn't home yet? I don't want Mam to worry about making dinner on her own. If I leave now I can still be a help to her."

"I see." He approached and she detected the heat, the clean scent, of him. "*Danki* for taking care of Ethan. I shouldn't need your help for much longer." If he was disappointed that she was leaving, he didn't show it.

Ellie stiffened at the reminder that he wanted to get rid of her. "I forgot to tell you. I heard from Sarah today. It will be several more weeks before she can return." Giving him her back, she felt a headache coming on and absently lifted fingers to rub her forehead. "Until then, Charlie and I can take turns with Ethan."

Reuben was silent. As she faced him, she caught a strange look on his face. "Reuben?"

"I don't want to put you to any more trouble."

"Your son is no trouble," she said, meaning it.

He gazed at her. Whatever he read in her expression must have satisfied him. He finally nodded with a small smile. "How are you getting home?" he asked.

Ellie was startled. "I forgot! Charlie was supposed to come for me." She picked up her cell phone from the counter. "I'll call Nell." She felt his gaze on her as she dialed her sister. Once she explained to Nell what she needed, she hung up and turned to him. "My brother-in-law is close. He'll bring me home."

Reuben studied her without a word.

"Reuben?"

He shifted his attention to the table, where he sat and took a serving of macaroni salad, green beans and two pieces of the chicken.

She felt her stomach tighten as she watched him eat. Why wouldn't he talk to her? She could have—should have—stayed for supper, but it was too late now. James was already on his way.

Ellie checked on Ethan in the other room, then returned to find Reuben still eating. The tension between her and Reuben had become unbearable. She crossed the kitchen and exited out the side door. She'd rather wait in the yard for James than endure another moment inside.

She stood in the warmth of the early evening sun, but hugged herself with her arms. The chill deep inside wasn't physical.

She'd never been so glad when James pulled his wagon up to the house. She grinned at her brother-in-law, "I appreciate the ride."

"Charlie forgot, I take it," he said with an amused smile. "Too busy with her sweetheart?"

Ellie grinned again. "It would seem so."

He jumped down from the wagon and assisted her up before he returned to climb onto the driver's side.

As James steered the horse toward the road, she glanced at the house and froze. Reuben stood in the doorway with a strange expression on his face. He looked…anguished. She inhaled sharply and faced the front. Had she hurt him by leaving?

Nay. She was imagining things. Reuben wasn't upset.

She glanced back one last time and saw that Reuben had stepped outside to watch her leave. She didn't know what to think. The man confused her on many levels.

Should she return the next day? She would. For Ethan.

"How was your day?" James asked.

You don't want to know. "It was fine. How about yours?"

And she listened with interest as he told her about the vet visits he'd made that day and the problems he'd encountered with the animals. She made all the correct responses, despite that Reuben Miller was foremost in her mind.

Chapter Seven

The rest of the week went smoothly. Charlie watched Ethan in the morning while Ellie relieved her after work in the afternoon. Despite Ellie's concerns, her young charge seemed fine the day after she'd had trouble putting him to sleep. Ethan was in high spirits, giggling easily when she made faces or tickled him under the chin. His belly laugh was infectious. She burst out laughing each time he giggled whenever he decided something was funny.

Of Reuben, she'd seen very little. He left each morning after Charlie's arrival. When he came home in the afternoon, he was polite and infrequent with his smiles. Yet he behaved like a different person with her sister. He thanked her every morning for babysitting. When Ellie greeted him, he gave her a quiet nod, then traipsed upstairs for a shower. When he came down, she had supper on the table for him. Although she was annoyed with him, she'd continued to prepare it for him. It couldn't be easy for him to raise his child alone.

Her garden at home was doing well. This particular morning Ellie picked a number of vegetables, stored them in her buggy and brought them in with her when she relieved Charlie. During the last few days, she'd fixed a variety of meals for him with beef, ham and chicken. She guessed he liked her cooking because he always finished what she'd made him. Yet he'd never said a word.

At first she was upset with his reticence, but today she decided that she no longer cared. Better that there was silence between them than the exchanging of harsh words. Yet his stern, contemplative manner bothered her despite her decision not to care. She couldn't change the man. What he thought about her in his home with his son shouldn't matter. But for her, it did.

Surely he trusted her a little, or he wouldn't leave the house each morning knowing Ethan would be in her care every afternoon when he got home.

Ellie wondered why she bothered coming or cooking for him. And then she knew. She was trying to live like the Lord wanted her to. Feeling blessed, she wanted to help someone in need. And if that person—man—didn't want her help? It didn't matter. He needed her help if only temporarily, and that was good enough.

This afternoon she fixed a green bean and ham casserole, a dish easy to keep warm in the oven. The temperature and humidity, although it was summer, had eased off a bit, and there was a soft breeze sweeping the countryside. Ellie had opened the windows earlier to let in the fresh air.

Ethan played on the floor with a pot and the wooden spoon he loved. Ellie smiled down at him before she turned back to the stove to check on the simmering green beans she'd picked from her garden. Next, she took a ham steak from the refrigerator and cut it into small pieces to add to the green beans, along with dumplings she had yet to make. She'd bought the ham on the way after housecleaning for the Brodericks.

Thinking of Olivia Broderick made her feel sad—and blessed. The woman was undergoing cancer treatments, and she looked terrible. In such a short time, she'd lost weight and there were deep, dark circles under her eyes. Ellie had taken extra care this morning to ensure that the house was spic and span. Then she'd offered to make Olivia lunch. The woman had declined since she felt too nauseous to eat, but she'd thanked her with a smile, then handed her a wad of cash that was way more than Ellie normally charged. Olivia had been surprised when Ellie had insisted on giving her back the excess. Ellie had simply smiled and told her she'd be back in two weeks unless she needed her sooner. Olivia said she would call if she needed her before then. Ellie had left and stopped at the grocery store on her way. She'd bought not only the ham steak but also a beef roast and the ingredients for a number of easy casseroles. And last but not least, she'd purchased the ingredients for a chocolate cream pie.

Ethan napped peacefully for just over two hours before waking in good spirits. Ellie wished it was safe enough for her to take him outside to play, as the day was beautiful. But she couldn't, not as long as there was rusted metal and other junk in the yard. Instead, she gave him loving attention as she played with him on the floor in the great room where the floor was in better shape than in the kitchen.

The afternoon flew by. The next thing she knew, someone was entering the house. Picking up Ethan, she went out to greet Reuben after he turned from hanging his hat on a wall peg.

"*Hallo*, did you have a *gut* day?" she asked pleasantly.

He faced her, one eye clear but the other eye bloodshot and bright red.

"Reuben!" she exclaimed, hurrying toward him. "What happened?"

"Got a fragment of siding material in my eye." He regarded her carefully. "The doctor in the emergency room took out the sliver, but I have to put ointment in it for the next couple of days."

Feeling relief that he was okay, she nodded. "Would you like me to put some in for you?"

He didn't say anything at first, and she grew uncomfortable with her offer. He looked at her, then his son, before he returned his attention to her.

Taking his silence as a possible yes, Ellie went into the gathering room, picked the quilt off the floor and returned to the kitchen, where she laid it before she set Ethan down. The little boy cried out and held up his arms. She glanced at Reuben to find his blue gaze intent on her face. She gave Ethan the wooden spoon. "It won't take but a moment," she assured him, happy when Ethan finally settled down with his favorite toy. She held out her hand for the prescription ointment tube.

He gave it to her, then sat down and tilted his head back. Ellie stepped in close and was immediately aware of him as a man. His rugged scent. The warmth of his skin. The sound of his breathing. Her heart fluttered inside her chest as she unscrewed the cap. She felt the hitch in her breath as they locked gazes.

"Do you want to hold your eye open?" she asked.

"I trust you to do it."

She nodded, then reached for his bottom eyelid. She gently tugged downward and clicked her tongue in sympathy at the bright red that should have been the white of his eye. Ellie gently, capably squeezed out a single long bead across the bottom of his eye. She felt overwhelmed by being this close to him. "Blink several times," she instructed.

She stepped back, heart racing, as she concentrated on putting the cap back on the tube.

She sensed when Reuben straightened in the chair. She looked over and saw him blinking his eyes repeatedly. "Did I hurt you?" she asked softly. The last thing she wanted to do was cause harm to this man.

"Nay." He smiled at her. It had been so long since she'd seen his smile. The view was like a kick to her solar plexus. *"Danki."*

"You're *willkomm.*" She reached for Ethan, who'd been watching Reuben and her together. She smiled as she lifted the boy into her arms. "Want to give a proper *hallo* to your *dat*?"

As if he understood, Ethan turned in her hold and reached for his father. Reuben stood and tugged him into his arms. He hugged Ethan and rubbed between his shoulder blades before returning his attention to Ellie.

"Danki," he said quietly. "For everything."

She was floored by his thanks. Was this goodbye? Was he telling her that he no longer needed her?

He frowned. "You don't have to come if it inconveniences you."

His worried expression eased her mind. It would

have bothered her if this had been the end of her time with Ethan. *And Reuben.* "I don't mind watching Ethan. He's such a sweet boy who is easy to love." She gasped, shocked by her words, which revealed too much to the child's father.

She was startled to see only relief in his expression. "I'll see you tomorrow." She grabbed her cloth shopping bag that she'd used to carry in the groceries. "There's supper in the oven. 'Tis just green bean and ham casserole." She hesitated. "I made chocolate cream pie for dessert." She inhaled sharply as a thought occurred to her. "I hope you like chocolate..."

He smiled. "I do."

She released a calming breath. "*Gut.* Have a nice night, Reuben." She reached out to stroke Ethan's sweet baby cheeks. "Behave for your *vadder*, little one."

Then she left with a last look at the house. To her surprise and pleasure, Reuben had stepped outside with his son. He didn't look stern or angry. His expression was soft, friendly. Ellie drew in a shaky breath and continued on, for she found this man hard to resist. And resist him she must because he would marry without love in order to give his son a mother. When she married one day, it would be to someone who offered her more.

Sunday was here before Ellie knew it. She hadn't seen much of Reuben in the last two days. He'd asked Charlie to stay with Ethan for the whole day yesterday, and Ellie couldn't help but feel hurt that he hadn't been happy with the arrangement she and her sister had worked out.

Ellie put on her best Sunday dress—a royal blue tab

dress with white apron. She had washed and dried her hair the day before. After pinning her hair in place, she donned a black prayer *kapp*. She turned as Charlie entered the room.

"Mam and Dat ready?" she asked.

Charlie nodded. "*Ja*, they asked me to check on you."

"I'll be right down."

Her sister lingered. "I wonder if Reuben and Ethan will be at church," she said, startling Ellie.

"They haven't come yet."

"'Tis been difficult for him, I think." Her sister smiled. "He's settling in now. He worked with Jed again the other day."

Ellie blinked. "He did?"

"*Ja*. I saw Jed yesterday when he was at the house helping Nate." Charlie's gaze went soft at the mention of her betrothed, Nathaniel Peachy. "Reuben's been working on Jed's crew, but he'll be back managing his own construction site tomorrow."

"Reuben is foreman?"

"I got that impression."

She headed toward the door and her sister followed. "How's the *haus*?"

"'Tis *wunderbor*! I love it. I can't wait to wed and move in with Nate."

"You're eager for the *haus*? Or for Nate to be your husband?" She glanced at her sister, then grinned when Charlie blushed.

"I'm eager to marry Nate." Her cheeks remained a bright red. "I love him."

Ellie placed a hand on her youngest sister's shoulder. "I know you do, Charlie. Nate loves you, too."

Charlie's features lit up with happiness. Ellie longed to feel as Charlie did with Nate, but she would have to wait for some unknown future date. Helping her parents had to take precedence over finding a loving husband.

She descended the stairs with Charlie to join their parents. Mam smiled at them while she handed them each a cake to carry. Her mother held a large bowl of potato salad. All the dishes they brought would be shared at the midday meal after church service. The Peachys were hosting today, a fact that clearly thrilled her sister. Charlie looked excited, eager to see her betrothed, as Dat pulled their buggy onto the Abram Peachy farm. After her father parked the vehicle at the end of a long row of other buggies and wagons, Charlie jumped out with cake in hand and raced into the yard to look for Nate.

Ellie exited the vehicle more slowly. After laying the cake on the backseat, she helped her mother from the vehicle, then waited patiently for her father to join them. Ellie grabbed the cake, then accompanied her parents to the Peachy barn. The building was only a few years old, having been replaced after a fire caused by lightning. It was a nice structure with plenty of room for the congregation. In the summer months, members of their community often used barns for service. After a peek inside, Ellie took the salad bowl from her mother and headed to the house to set the cake and potato salad in the kitchen with the rest of the community's other food offerings.

It was as she was leaving the Abram Peachy farmhouse that she spied Reuben with Ethan. They must have just arrived, or she would have noticed sooner.

She was surprised yet pleased to see them. She'd prayed and hoped that he'd feel comfortable attending church in his new community one day. Now that he was here, she realized he was finally settling in.

Charlie and Nate chatted with him. Her sister held out her arms and Ethan appeared happy to go to her. She eyed father and son with longing. How would it feel to have this man's attention and love? To have Ethan as a son?

She brought herself up short. *Dangerous thinking, Ellie.* She pretended she hadn't seen him as she crossed the yard to the barn. She nearly made it to the barn door when Charlie raced to join her with Ethan in her arms. The little boy took one look at Ellie and held out his arms. She shouldn't be glad that he wanted her, but she couldn't help it. He was a baby, only eight and a half months old. And he gave her such joy just to be near him.

"Service is about to begin," Nate murmured, having approached from behind.

Charlie smiled at him over her shoulder. "I'll see you after church."

Nate eyed her sister with softness that tugged at Ellie's heart.

They entered the dark interior of the barn. Once their eyes adjusted to the light, the room didn't seem dark at all. Ellie led the way, still holding Ethan, into the women's section, where she saw her sisters Leah and Nell. Meg was out of town. She and her husband, Peter, had gone for an extended visit to see Peter's grandparents in New Wilmington. She smiled at her sisters as she slid onto the same bench. Leah had grown larger with her pregnancy. There was happiness and contentment on her face that hadn't been visible before she'd married Henry Yoder.

Ellie was happy for her sisters. Each one of them had found a good man. Now their love was expanding to include children. Nell had learned she was two months pregnant only recently. She constantly smiled and glanced with love at James, her veterinary English-turned-Amish husband. James beamed back at her, clearly loving his wife and his life.

Ellie made sure Ethan was comfortable. If the boy had been older, he would have sat with his father in the men's section, but he was just a baby who needed his mother. Though a female friend would have to do since his mother was dead. Ellie felt a moment's heartbreak for the woman who never got to know her own child. She offered up a silent prayer for the woman and her family. Reubén was still grieving. It had to be hard for him to see his little boy resemble his wife, the woman he'd lost.

Church started and Ellie was amazed how well behaved Ethan was. Service took most of the morning. After singing and sermons that ran for hours, the congregation dispersed and headed outside. Ellie was exiting the barn with Ethan when Reuben approached.

"I'll take him," he said easily.

She nodded. She had work to do. She would help to put out the food. Without meeting his gaze, Ellie handed him Ethan, then went to the house to join the other women in the kitchen.

"Who's the little boy?" Alta Hershberger asked.

Ellie stiffened. Alta, the community busybody, didn't need to know the circumstances of her relationship with Ethan or Reuben. "He belongs to Reuben Miller. He moved into the community with his son and his sister."

Alta frowned. "His sister? I haven't seen the girl."

She sighed. She didn't want to natter, but Alta would be relentless if she didn't. She tempered her words as she explained. "Sarah is with her parents in Ohio. She's due back soon."

"Who's been watching the boy while she's gone?"

"My sister and I."

The woman narrowed her gaze. Ellie kept her expression light and smiling until Alta was forced to nod and return her smile. "That's kind of you."

Ellie shrugged. She was eager to escape the woman. Thankfully, Alta had decided she'd heard enough and left to natter to anyone who would listen. Ellie exhaled sharply and sent up a silent prayer of thanks that Meg wasn't here to complicate the situation.

Once the food was put out, she joined her family as they filled their plates. Ellie couldn't help her glance toward Reuben to see how he was doing. There were a number of young women around him apparently eager to help him and his baby boy. The sight of Reuben surrounded upset her. Did he envision one of the women as his future wife? She took her measure of the situation but received no clue to his thoughts. The few times she'd caught him smiling at a woman, even laughing once as he conversed with two of them, made her chest hurt. Apparently, it was just her he had a problem with. Especially since she knew he got along well with Charlie.

Her gaze shifted to Charlie and Nate, who had eyes only for each other. The start of their relationship hadn't been easy. At first, Nate had decided that he was too old for her sister, but thankfully time and Charlie had changed his mind.

With a small smile, Ellie poured herself some lemonade, then took a seat next to Nell.

"How is the cleaning business?" Nell asked.

"*Gut*. Got plenty of work to keep me busy. I'm glad I've cut back to a half a day, though."

Her sister nodded. "It can't be easy working for Englishers."

Ellie recalled one particular woman she had no desire to clean for again. Mara Golden had treated her like a servant, expecting her to pick up after her family before she cleaned house. She'd been condescending and cruel. Ellie had quickly suggested that she find someone else to clean for her. Mara hadn't taken the news well, but there had been nothing she could do or say that would have changed Ellie's mind.

The afternoon lengthened quickly. Ellie tried not to look at Reuben but found it impossible to avoid him. On one occasion, he locked gazes with her and she felt her chest tighten while her belly filled with butterflies. When Ethan fell asleep in his father's arms, she wanted to rush over to take the little boy and hold him close. Watching the two of them together made her feel warm inside.

Reuben stood with Ethan still sleeping against his shoulder. She saw him speak briefly with the people nearest to him before he headed toward the lot where everyone had parked their buggies.

He's leaving! Unable to resist, Ellie followed him. "Reuben," she called as she caught up to him.

He halted and turned. And his eyes became shuttered. "Elizabeth."

Ellie blinked and tried not to feel hurt by his reaction. "Do you still want Charlie and me to come tomorrow?"

"I don't want to put you to the trouble," he began.

"'Tis no trouble. I enjoy spending time with Ethan, and so does Charlie." She managed a smile. "And 'tis better to have the same people watching him until your sister's return," she added.

She watched as the tension left his shoulders. "I'll see you tomorrow, then."

Ellie nodded. "Have a *gut* night," she said softly. "If you need us before…"

His lips quirked. "Call you?" he teased. "Not all of us own a cell phone."

She blushed. "*Ja.* Do you want one of us to stop by? To check if you need anything?"

"We'll be fine. Ethan's had a long day. I'm sure he'll fall right asleep."

"I'll see you tomorrow, then," she said as she turned. She started back toward the gathering.

"Ellie," he said, and she stopped, faced him. His expression was soft. "You are a *gut* friend."

Friend. Her smile hurt her cheeks as his face became shuttered. Feeling embarrassed that she'd sought him out, she rejoined her family in the Peachy backyard.

His thoughts were on Ellie as he put Ethan to bed, and remained on her throughout the night when he couldn't sleep. By Monday morning, he'd found a way to harden himself against her. The last thing he wanted was to fall for the young woman. And his guilt stabbed deep that he'd thought of her at all when his wife hadn't been dead a full year.

His son still slept as Reuben climbed out of bed and dressed. Forcing Ellie from his mind, he went into the kitchen for breakfast. He opened the refrigerator and froze. Besides leftovers, there were several days' suppers that Ellie had made for him. He chose the leftover egg casserole, then heated it up in a pan coated first with melted butter. Once it was hot, he sat down to eat, and the delicious taste brought his thoughts back around to Ellie. She'd make someone a good wife. She deserved someone who would love her. *Not someone like me.*

He finished eating just in time, as he heard his son's cry from upstairs. Reuben rose, put his dishes in the sink, then headed to fetch Ethan. Less than an hour later, Charlie arrived.

"*Gut* morning," she said with a smile. Her gaze warmed as it settled on Ethan. She held out her arms and the boy reached for her.

Reuben relinquished his hold, satisfied to see Ethan content in Charlie's arms. Once again, he thought of Ellie and the way Ethan had laid his head trustingly on her shoulder. The way she cuddled and rubbed his son's neck and back. His lips firmed. Why did it seem right for Ellie to hold him and not Charlie?

"Do you have everything you need?" he asked.

"*Ja,*" Charlie said. "I brought puffed wheat for Ethan."

He was quiet as he collected the lunch made from bread Ellie had baked and jelly she'd made fresh during strawberry season. He reached for his hat, then faced her. "Is Ellie coming to relieve you this afternoon?"

"She'll be here after she finishes work." She didn't meet his gaze as she answered. She was grinning at Ethan as she jostled him in her arms. His son's sudden laughter filled the room, making him smile.

"I'll be heading off," he said. She faced him then. "*Danki*, Charlie. I don't know how I would have managed with Sarah gone."

"'Tis our pleasure, Reuben. Ellie and I love children."

Ellie loves children. His heart thumped hard. "I'll see you tomorrow."

She nodded. "Have a *gut* day."

"The same to you," he said. As he steered his horse-drawn vehicle to Jedidiah Lapp's house, where he was to meet the construction crew, Reuben couldn't banish the mental image of a certain golden-blond-haired woman. Elizabeth Stoltzfus. She would continue to be a source of anxiety for him until he found a wife and married. Only then would he be able to move on with the future he envisioned for himself and Ethan, one with an uncomplicated wife, without the difficult feelings of loving someone.

Chapter Eight

"Ellie." Charlie stepped into the bedroom and regarded her sister. "I can't watch Ethan today."

Ellie turned from the window where she'd been fixing her hair as she'd admired the view outside. "I'll re-
schedule work," she said easily. She'd rather spend the
day with the boy anyway. "Better yet, I'll call Rebecca
Yoder to cover for me." And maybe she'd think about
finding someone to take over her business for a while.
Sarah still wouldn't be back for another few weeks yet.

"Are you sure?" Her sister appeared concerned.

"I'm certain." She smiled.

Charlie looked relieved. *"Gut. Danki."*

Ellie regarded her with surprise. "What are you
thanking me for? You're the one helping me."

Her sister grinned. *"Ja.* I forgot about that."

After she left the room, Ellie dialed Rebecca, who,
she knew, wouldn't mind taking over her work for the
day. After she had Rebecca's consent, she called her
two clients to inform them of the change. The first one
was livid until she explained that her fill-in for the day

was also Amish. The second one had no problems at all with the change.

She smirked. Why did Englishers think that Amish women were better at cleaning house?

Ellie glanced at her wristwatch and gasped. She needed to get to Reuben's before she was late. She grabbed the pie she'd baked for him from the refrigerator, then climbed into her pony cart and headed out.

She arrived five minutes later. She was early but not by much. Charlie was usually fifteen minutes early. As she headed toward the house, Reuben swung open the door, looking worried.

"I thought no one was coming," he said brusquely. He looked wonderful in a maroon shirt, black suspenders and navy tri-blend pants. She could see the muscles of his arms beneath his short shirtsleeves.

"I'm sorry. Charlie couldn't make it. I had to make a few phone calls before I came."

"If 'tis too much trouble…" he began.

"Nay." She tried to smile, but Reuben wasn't welcoming. Obviously, he preferred Charlie.

His eyes dropped down to the pie she held.

"Dried apple pie. I baked it last night. I hope you like dried apples."

His expression thawed. "I do."

She brushed past him and into the house. Ethan was in the high chair, and she immediately went to him. She caressed the top of his head, then bent to kiss it. The child looked up and smiled.

Reuben was silent. She could feel his gaze and spun. "Don't you have to work?"

He glanced at the wall clock and grimaced. *"Ja,* I need to go."

"You don't have to worry, Reuben. I'll take *gut* care of him."

"I never doubted that for a second," he replied sincerely. He grabbed his lunch bag from the counter.

"I'll see you when you get home," she said easily as he reached for his hat.

He stiffened. "You'll be spending all day with him?"

"*Ja.* Charlie is busy." She lifted her chin.

"Don't you have to clean house?"

"I made other arrangements."

He stared at her hard before he finally nodded. Then he left with mumbled words about being home at four this afternoon. Ellie watched him leave through the side kitchen window. Her heart was heavy as she realized that Reuben had hoped to see Charlie and not her.

She returned to Ethan, ensuring he had enough to eat. Today she'd teach him to drink from a cup, she decided. He was too old for a bottle. Ethan ate dry cereal by himself. Surely, he could learn to use a cup.

Ellie went to a cabinet to search for a cup for him. All she found were several glass tumblers and a small tin cup that she realized was a measuring cup.

"You and I will be going to the store today," she told Ethan with a smile. "I'm going to buy you a sippy cup."

Ethan kept eating, not understanding her or concerned with her decision to leave the house. While at the store, she'd also purchase a few groceries.

After breakfast, Ellie changed Ethan's diaper. She wished she'd brought the buggy. It would have been safer for Ethan to ride in. She called Nell on her cell. Nell was allowed a phone because of her husband's veterinary practice.

"Can we switch vehicles for the day?" she asked, explaining why.

"I can pick up what you need," Nell said. "I'm in Whittier's Store."

Ellie gave her a list over the phone.

"I'll be there as soon as I can," Nell promised.

After thanking her sister, Ellie hung up the phone and smiled at Ethan. "Wouldn't you like to be outside and enjoy this delightful summer breeze?" she asked softly. The boy laughed and she grinned. "What's so funny, little man?"

After she cleaned him up, she grabbed a quilt and took Ethan outside to play just outside the side door. On impulse, she brought the pot and spoon he loved. The summer breeze was pleasant. It had rained during the night, and the temperature had cooled down to the upper seventies.

Ethan loved being outside. He sat on the quilt, banging on the pot with the spoon. Watching him, Ellie got an idea. She stood and reached down for him. He looked at her and his lips quivered. "*Nay*, sweetheart, we're not going inside."

He appeared on the verge of tears, and she hugged him close. The sudden stark realization that she was here with Ethan when his young mother was cold in the ground made her feel sorry for Susanna. For Reuben, who had lost the woman he loved.

She closed her eyes as she held Ethan tight. The boy struggled in her arms, clearly wanting to get down. She crouched, set him on his feet, then, holding on to his hands, she kept him upright and urged him to take a few steps. Ellie took joy as Ethan tried, putting one foot in front of the other. He would have fallen if she'd let go, but she kept a close, loving eye on him as she held on to him. When she sensed he'd grown tired of the game, she set him down, then handed him his spoon and pot. She watched with a smile as he went back to hitting the bottom of the pot with the spoon handle.

A while later Ellie could tell Ethan was tired. Glancing at her watch, she was startled by the hour. "Lunch, Ethan, and then nap time."

She fed him cooked mashed carrots for lunch, which he clearly enjoyed, as he ate every bite. She then gave him a handful of Cheerios. Ethan devoured them, then leaned back in the high chair with heavy-lidded eyes. "Time for a nap," she said.

Ellie put Ethan in the bed in the next room. The child turned on his side and promptly fell asleep. With a smile, she returned to the kitchen, made herself a sandwich, then cleaned up.

Nell arrived and handed her the requested items. Ellie paid her, then waved as her sister left to join her husband at a nearby farm.

Knowing that Ethan would sleep for an hour and a half, at least, Ellie put away the groceries and set the blue-and-white child's sippy cup on the kitchen counter. Next, she took out a broom and swept the kitchen floor. Should she cook the beef roast? The day was cool enough for the oven. The breeze wafting through the open windows would help modulate the indoor temperature. Ellie then wiped down the countertops before she headed upstairs to collect dirty laundry. As she carried the clothes basket downstairs, she experienced the strangest feeling. Doing Reuben's laundry felt like something only a wife would do. But Sarah had done the wash, she thought. And so could she.

She frowned as she filled the washer with colored clothes.

Would Sarah call today? She hoped so. Maybe she should call and leave a message for the girl. It would be good to talk with her, to ask after Reuben's mother. Yet she hesitated about calling. If Sarah was returning, then Reuben would no longer need her.

She froze. The thought of leaving shouldn't bother her, but it did.

The downstairs chores complete, Ellie made a cup of tea, then sat at the kitchen table and sipped from it. She didn't want to think about the time she would no longer get to see Reuben daily. She didn't want to think about leaving Ethan, the sweet child who'd captured her heart.

She took a swallow of tea, then paused. She thought she heard the sound of running water. She didn't think much of it at first, believing it to be the washer in the back room. But then she heard the washer spin and realized that the steady sound of water flowing had continued when it should have stopped. She got up and went to check on the washing machine. The machine had stopped, yet the sound of water continued—and it wasn't coming from this room.

With a frown, she headed toward the stairs and paused at the bottom, where the sound of water was louder. She raced up the steps and found the source. Water sprayed from under the sink and flooded the floor. Heart racing, Ellie wondered how to turn off the main water line. The leak appeared to be from the other side of the sink's turnoff valves. She ran downstairs and found the main valve in the mudroom where the washer and drier were located. She turned it and was relieved when the sound halted.

Ellie hurried to check on Ethan, who stirred as he woke up. She gasped. Water had leaked through the great room ceiling not far from where Ethan had slept. *We can't stay here.*

She'd take Ethan home with her. They couldn't stay here without water. She'd make sure they were back before Reuben was expected home.

She would try to reach him first so he wouldn't worry. She dialed the construction company, but the call wouldn't go through. She waited a few minutes, then tried again.

She called her sister Leah at her store, Yoder's Craft Shop and General Store. Her sister and her husband, Henry, had recently started carrying groceries again. The shop had been a general store until Henry's parents had turned it over to Leah for a craft shop. Henry, a cabinetmaker, kept furniture items as well as sample kitchen and bath cabinets in the store, as well.

"Yoder's Craft and General Store," her sister announced as she answered the phone.

"Is Henry there?"

"Ellie! He's up at the house."

Ellie bit her lip. "Do you think he would mind trading vehicles with me? I'm watching Reuben Miller's son, and there's been a water pipe leak. I had to shut off the main water valve, and I'd like to take Ethan to Mam and Dat's, but I have the pony cart."

Leah chuckled. "I'll send Henry over with a buggy seat," she said.

"A buggy seat?"

"Just something Henry made with our future son or daughter in mind."

"And it will hold an eight-month-old?"

"Ja."

"Danki."

"I'll call up to the house and tell him."

"I appreciate it."

"I'll expect you to watch your niece or nephew when needed."

Ellie grinned. "It would be my pleasure." She loved children. She had yet to watch Meg's baby, and now with her two other older sisters pregnant, there would be more little ones to love.

Henry arrived twenty minutes later. He grinned as he saw her in the yard with Ethan. "Special delivery," he said.

She gave him a wide smile. "I'm happy to see you and your thing—whatever it is."

He took out a wooden seat, which he strapped onto the pony cart seat beside her. It was the perfect size for a child. Once it was in place, he met her gaze. "All set. He'll be safe in this."

"Danki."

"You're *willkomm.*"

"How is Leah feeling?"

He beamed at her. *"Wunderbor."*

"You'll be a *gut vadder.*"

"I hope so."

"No doubt about it." She shifted Ethan in her arms. "I should go. I want to get to Mam and Dat's and back before Reuben gets home. You know they're going to want one of these."

Henry grinned. "I'll be glad to make them one." He helped her onto her cart. "I'll see you on Sunday."

Ellie nodded, then watched him get into his own vehicle and leave. Minutes later, she arrived home. Her parents were surprised but happy to see her and Ethan.

"What's wrong?" her father asked.

Ellie explained the situation.

He listened carefully, then asked for the house key. "We'll get it fixed up for you."

She gave him the key, and he immediately left to get his brother-in-law, her uncle Samuel, to see if they could fix the leak.

Dat and Uncle Samuel returned an hour later. "We were able to fix the leak," her father said.

"And you turned the water back on?"

"*Ja*, we had to check to make sure the repair held, and it did."

Ellie released a sharp breath. "I should get back, then. I tried to call where Reuben works but I haven't been able to get through. The phone lines must be down."

"We saw a car accident between here and the house," her uncle said. "Looks like the driver hit an electric pole."

"I hope no one was seriously hurt." She murmured a quick, silent prayer that the driver and any passengers were well.

"There was an ambulance on the scene. I don't know how many were in the car."

Ellie nodded. "I'll be careful going back. Should I take a different road?"

Her father agreed that it would be best if she drove

back via a different avenue. He told her which way to go. She nodded in agreement before she picked up Ethan, then left.

Despite the seat that kept Ethan safe, Ellie steered her vehicle slowly back to the Reuben Miller house. She left the pony cart in her parents' yard, opting to take the family buggy instead. The wooden seat that Henry made fit well in the buggy, and she was glad she'd called Leah to ask for help.

It took her a little longer to get back to the house since she was forced to take a different route. She was relieved when she caught sight of the house ahead. She'd approached from the opposite direction, and she turned on the directional signal and pulled into the yard. To her shock, she saw a buggy parked near the hitching post. Reuben was already home.

She pulled in next to his vehicle and closed her eyes briefly in preparation for the coming confrontation. The man wouldn't be happy to have her gone from the house with his son.

Breathing deeply to calm herself, Ellie got out, then skirted the buggy to take Ethan from his seat. When she turned, Reuben stood outside near the side door.

She approached. "Reuben."

"Where have you been?" he demanded harshly.

"With my parents."

"Why? Because you can't manage to stay a whole day?"

She brushed by him to enter the house. He followed her but she refused to answer him.

"Elizabeth!"

She spun to face him. "I'm not a child, Reuben."

"You left."

"I had a *gut* reason." She felt Ethan struggle within her arms. She could sense his upset, and she quickly soothed him with a gentle caress on his head and back.

Reuben eyed her skeptically. "What reason?" He didn't look as fierce, but his expression hadn't softened either.

"You had a water leak. I had to shut off the water to the house. 'Tis hard to care for a child without water."

His blue eyes darkened. "Where?" His tone suggested that he didn't believe her.

"In the upstairs bathroom." She marched with Ethan into the gathering room and pointed toward the wet ceiling.

Reuben followed her. It was only after he saw what she meant that he frowned. He gave a heavy sigh. "I'll get my tools."

"No need," she said stiffly. "The leak is fixed. My father and uncle took care of it."

"What?" His tone was soft, as if he was trying to control anger.

"I said—"

"I know what you said," he cut in. "What right did you have to allow strangers into my home?"

"They're not strangers—"

"They're your family, not mine! You had no business inviting them into my *haus*. I could've fixed the leak."

She strapped Ethan into his high chair. "Reuben, they offered and I couldn't say *nay*," she said softly. "It took them less than an hour—and that with time to get here and back."

"The time it took is irrelevant. It's up to me to take care of my house. I don't need your interference."

"Why is it so hard for you to accept help, Reuben?" she cried. "I don't understand you at all. My father and Uncle Samuel were trying to help you. You have a lot on your mind. They thought they were doing a *gut* thing!"

"I can take care of my own!"

"Apparently." She sighed. "It's getting late. I should leave."

"Fine." His tone was sharp, the one word abrupt.

She released a cleansing breath, then turned to run a caring hand over Ethan's shoulder. "Take care, little man. I'll see you tomorrow."

"There's no need for you to come back tomorrow," Reuben said evenly, making her blanch.

Ellie nodded and left, wondering how a simple helpful gesture had gone so wrong.

She blinked back tears as she climbed into her buggy and headed home. She wouldn't tell her father about Reuben's reaction. Her *dat* had done a good thing, and no one was going to make him feel bad about it.

Hurt, she tried not to think of the near future. She would miss Ethan. More than she should, she realized. She had gotten too emotionally involved with him and his mercurial father. It was probably for the best that she didn't go back.

Yet a painful constriction in her chest told her differently. That she'd rather spend time with Ethan—and his father—than clean house. These last two weeks, she'd felt so alive.

Was this how Charlie felt when she was with Nate?

And Leah with Henry? Nell with James? Meg with Peter?

She thought of her parents. They had a good marriage. She saw the subtle looks they exchanged, which suggested a solid relationship. A partnership. That was what she wanted with a husband some day. She sighed. Was that why Reuben was a bitter man? Because he'd lost that time, that partnership, with his young wife?

That night, as she climbed into bed, she decided that it didn't matter if Reuben didn't want her to come. She would go anyway. The man and his son needed her, whether he liked it or not. With that decision made, she went to bed and slept well.

When she woke the next morning, she wondered if it was still a good idea—going to Reuben's as if he hadn't dismissed her the day before.

She was at the kitchen table eating breakfast when there was a knock at the back door. Ellie rose to answer it, her eyes widening as she saw Reuben with his son on her doorstep.

"Reuben?"

"I need to talk with you."

She stepped back and allowed him to enter.

Chapter Nine

"Ellie," he murmured as he stepped into the room. "Elizabeth."

She studied him carefully. "What's wrong?"

"I've been called in to work." Reuben looked sheepish, apologetic. "I can't take care of Ethan."

The man appeared anguished. She saw the pain in his blue eyes, the sorrow in his handsome features. "You want me to watch him?"

"I have no right to ask."

Ellie arched an eyebrow. "I don't have a problem with giving or accepting help, Reuben. You do."

He glanced away. "I know. I'm sorry."

She was stunned. "'Tis *oll recht*." She reached out for Ethan, and Reuben released his little son into her arms.

He wouldn't meet her gaze. She could feel the tension emanating off him, the confusion, his fear.

"I'll take *gut* care of him."

He nodded as he raised his eyes to lock gazes with her. *"Danki."*

"You should go before you're late."

"Ja." He shifted. "I would have come to apologize even if I hadn't been called to work. I was…ill-mannered and ungrateful."

"Your usual self," she quipped with good humor.

His features relaxed as a spark of amusement entered his blue eyes. "I've never met anyone like you," he said.

Ellie frowned, unsure if it were a good or bad thing that he thought her different. Vaguely, she wondered what he would have thought if she'd marched up to his house this morning, despite his unwillingness to have her in his home and with his child.

"I'm one of a kind," she finally agreed.

He smiled. "I'll stop after work to pick him up unless…"

"I'll be happy to take him home in a little while," she said. "As long as you don't mind me in your *haus* again."

Regret flickered in his gaze. "That would be fine."

Ellie was surprised when he hesitated before leaving. "Don't you have to get moving?"

Reuben blinked. *"Ja.* I will see you after work."

"Ja, you will."

Since she'd already called Rebecca to cover for her today, Ellie brought Ethan inside to have some breakfast before she took him back to the house. It must have taken a lot for Reuben to come and apologize. It said a lot for his character. He did it because he needed her, but still, it couldn't have been easy. She recalled the regret in his blue eyes. He felt bad about the way he'd treated her, though she found it easy to forgive him.

An hour later, Ellie and Ethan headed home. She used the key Reuben had given her to unlock the door.

She stepped inside and took stock of her surroundings. The kitchen was sparkling clean. Had Reuben eaten? There was no sign of dishes, either in the sink or drying in the drain rack.

Why am I worried about him? He wouldn't appreciate it.

The day went quickly. Ellie cleaned the rooms upstairs while Ethan napped downstairs. She stopped what she was doing often to check on him, but the little boy continued to sleep. Then she heard a sound at the side door announcing Reuben's arrival. She was on the great room floor changing Ethan's diaper when Reuben walked in. *"Hallo,"* he greeted pleasantly. He sounded friendly.

"Reuben, *hallo*. Did you have a *gut* day?"

He nodded. "We got a lot done."

"Gut," she murmured as she fastened Ethan's clean diaper. Holding him by the waist, she stood Ethan on his legs. The baby laughed with delight and reached out a hand toward her prayer *kapp*. She chuckled. *"Nay,* you don't, little man!"

She felt Reuben's intense regard and glanced at him. Ellie was surprised to see a soft expression on his face. She stood and held Ethan out to his father. "Would you mind?"

He took his son easily and without hesitation, holding him in one arm while he watched Ellie, who picked up the wet diaper to dispose of in the diaper pail to be washed later.

"Are you hungry?" she asked as she returned. "There are potatoes and sausages in the oven. I hope you like them."

He gazed at her a long time with what looked like awe. "I do. I haven't had them since I was a child."

Ellie beamed at him. "I hope these are as *gut* as those you remember." She collected her bag, rubbed Ethan's back where he lay cuddled in his father's arms, then headed into the kitchen. "I'll see you tomorrow."

Reuben had followed her. "Don't you have to work?"

She shook her head. She had asked Rebecca to cover her workload for the entire week. Thankfully, Rebecca had agreed. She'd stop by Rebecca's house on the way home to confirm. "I'm available to watch him."

He nodded. "I'll see you tomorrow, then." He no longer appeared to mind her in his house, spending time with his son. She sighed with pleasure. Being friends with Reuben was better than being at odds with him.

As she steered her buggy home, she tried not to think about why it was wrong to cook for Reuben, care for his child and clean his house. She found she enjoyed babysitting better than cleaning Englishers' houses. And therein lay the problem. She was filling in for Reuben's sister until her return or until the man found himself a wife. A wife he wouldn't love. A woman he wanted only as a mother for Ethan.

For the next few days, Ellie went to Reuben's after her morning chores. It was more or less an amicable arrangement. The tension of those early days between them had dissipated. She and Reuben were friendly to each other, and the time flew by quickly until she realized with amazement that it was already Friday afternoon. As Ellie had thought, Charlie was happy to spend time with Nate before school started again and she would be back teaching in the classroom. Her sister came home each night with a goofy smile of love and affection for her man still on her face.

Reuben greeted her warmly at the end of each workday, and she felt something blossom inside. She wasn't sure what she was feeling, but it felt good. Tomorrow was Saturday, but he still wanted her to come. She would go after she did what she could to help her parents. And she'd make sure Charlie was available to help while she was absent.

The next morning, she rose early and went to take care of the animals, as usual. As she fed the goats, she was happy to see her sister enter the barn. "Charlie, did you sleep well?"

Charlie smiled. "Like a baby."

"Not a crying newborn, I hope," she teased.

Her sister laughed. *"Nay."*

"Charlie," Ellie said, her tone serious, "will you be home today?"

"Ja, why?"

"Reuben wants me to watch Ethan, but I want to make sure Mam and Dat have the help they need."

Charlie frowned, as if puzzled. "I'll be here. Nate may stop over later. He can help Dat if he needs anything."

Ellie felt the tension leave her frame. *"Danki."*

"You love that little boy, don't you?"

She nodded. "He's a sweet baby."

"And the father isn't ugly either," her sister teased.

"Reuben has nothing to do with this," she insisted.

Charlie narrowed her eyes but said nothing. She

turned back to grooming one of the horses as Ellie went outside with a bucket of chicken feed.

When she was done with the animals, Ellie went to the house to collect her bag and the chocolate cake she'd baked for Reuben. As she took it off the washer in the back room, she wondered why she'd baked for him again. Her sister's words came back to jolt her. *And the father isn't ugly either.*

It was true. Reuben was an extremely handsome man and she was attracted to him. But she knew better than to think that anything could happen between them. Especially given his decision to marry not for love but for Ethan.

"I'm leaving, Mam," she called as she came out of the room. Her mother turned from the kitchen sink, where she'd been washing the breakfast dishes. "I should have helped you with those," she said apologetically.

"I can handle the dishes, Ellie," her mother replied with a smile.

Ellie noted that her *mam* looked well today. The dark circles that she'd seen under her mother's eyes were gone, as if a good night's sleep had erased them. "I feel like I haven't been around much to help out," she said softly.

"With what?" Missy Stoltzfus looked confused. "I manage fine without help."

"But Charlie will be home today, *ja*?"

Mam smiled. "*Ja.* And Nate. She loves that young man. 'Tis *gut* to see them together."

She nodded. "They are eager to be man and wife."

"I want the same happiness for you."

"Mam…"

"You work too hard. I think you like caring for Ethan Miller because you love children." Missy eyed her silently. "You'd make a *gut mudder* to Ethan."

"*Nay.* I'm just helping until Sarah comes back."

"You seem happier spending time with the child than you are cleaning *haus* for Englishers."

"Mudder…"

Her mother shrugged as she smiled. "Just a thought." She reached into a cabinet and pulled out a box of baby cookies. "Take these for Ethan. I'm sure he'll love them."

Ellie blinked, stunned that her mother had purchased something for Reuben's son. "Mam, I'm not marrying the man. Ethan will not become your grandchild."

Mam chuckled. "With God's blessing, one can always pray and hope."

His son was still sleeping after Reuben had been up well over an hour and a half. He needed to get work done on the house, but he didn't want to disturb Ethan's rest. A quick glance at the wall clock in the kitchen made him wonder what time Ellie planned to come. It was nearly eight thirty. Had they arranged a time? He frowned. He didn't think they had.

Once Ellie arrived, he'd ask her whether or not it would be wise to wake Ethan. He'd hoped to replace the flooring downstairs. He'd purchased linoleum for a reasonable sum, and would install the same pattern in the kitchen and great room. It was an unusual pattern for linoleum flooring. Made of heavy vinyl, it resembled wood. Linoleum was best kept clean with a damp mop, and a lot of Amish families used it in their houses.

He opened the side door to allow in air. The day looked promising. Not too hot or humid, with a light breeze wafting in from outside. He put the coffeepot on to perk, then went outside to sit in the morning sun. The sound of carriage wheels drew his attention as Ellie steered her pony cart toward the barn and parked. She hopped out, tied up her horse, then skirted the vehicle to head toward the house.

She froze, faltering, when she saw him. But then she approached with a smile on her face. "Reuben, *gut* mornin'. Have you had breakfast?"

He shook his head, noting how pretty she looked in a pink dress with black apron and white head covering. Her blond hair was neatly pulled back and tucked underneath her *kapp*. "Just put a pot of coffee on the stove."

"And Ethan?"

"Still sleeping." He studied her with a frown. "That's *oll recht, ja*? That he's still sleeping?"

She smiled in reassurance. "'Tis fine. He's a little boy who needs his rest. He had a busy day yesterday." She went to the counter and set down the chocolate cake she'd brought. "I made chocolate."

He grinned. "Sounds *gut*."

"Would you like eggs and bacon?" She reached into the refrigerator for the carton of eggs and package of bacon.

Reuben stared. He hadn't gone shopping lately. Were the eggs from when Sarah was here? He must have said something aloud, because Ellie answered.

"I brought a few things with me yesterday." She paused. "I hope you don't mind."

He opened his mouth, then closed it. To object would make him ungrateful. They were just eggs and bacon, after all. He watched her get out a frying pan, then add a pat of butter. The coffeepot had finished perking, and Ellie turned off the gas burner, then grabbed him a mug and poured him a cupful. She silently handed it to him, then turned her attention back to making his breakfast.

"Aren't you going to eat?" he asked when he saw she'd made enough for only one.

"*Nay,* I ate before I came."

"You don't have to cook for me, Ellie."

"I don't mind. I like cooking."

He felt himself smile. *"Oll recht. Danki."*

In a few short minutes, she had heated the pan, cooked his bacon and eggs and dished them onto a plate. He sat down at the table and was about to suggest that she sit with a cup of coffee when he heard his son cry out.

"I'll get him," Ellie said with a grin. "I'm sure the little man needs to be changed before he eats."

Reuben watched her leave, marveling at the easy way she had about her. She made him feel relaxed, content. It was only as he remembered Susanna and his decision to marry for Ethan rather than love that he stiffened his spine and hardened his heart.

When she came into the room a few minutes later with Ethan, he had the mind-set to ignore the fact that she was pretty. Or that he'd been attracted to her for a minute. *Or fifty.*

Ethan smiled, obviously happy to be up, as Ellie set him in the high chair.

"Would you like more coffee?" she asked.

He rose from the table. "*Nay*, I should get to work."

She took a box of cereal out of the pantry and dumped some onto Ethan's tray. "What are your plans for today?"

"I'd like to install flooring here and in the great room, but since you and Ethan are here…"

"I can take him home with me if you'd like."

He jumped at her offer. If he didn't, he was afraid he'd find himself thinking about how pretty she was again. "I'd appreciate that."

She blinked. "How long do you need us to be gone?"

"Until this afternoon? About three or so?"

Ellie nodded. "Come, little man. You can finish your breakfast at my *haus*."

Without meeting his gaze, Ellie packed a bag for Ethan, then reached for her purse. "Help yourself to the cake. I think there is still lunch meat if you'd like a sandwich later."

And then Ellie left, taking Ethan with her. The house suddenly seemed empty and silent. Too silent. The afternoon, when they would return, seemed a long way off. There was just one thing to do—get to work. He would start in the kitchen, then move into the great room. Once he laid the flooring, they would have to stay off it until the glue set well. And if he got it done soon, he could head over to the Arlin Stoltzfus house-hold to invite Ellie and his son home. Maybe he could offer to buy her supper.

He scowled. What happened to keeping his mind-set about women and marriage?

Reuben released a huge sigh and went out to get the rolled linoleum he'd purchased a while ago out of the barn.

Ellie was disappointed and she didn't know why. She enjoyed taking care of Ethan. It had nothing to do with Reuben Miller. Or did it? It bothered her how quickly he'd accepted her offer of leaving with Ethan.

Her mother grinned as Ellie entered the house with the boy. "What a nice surprise!" She held out her arms and Ethan reached for her.

With a chuckle, Ellie relinquished her hold on the little boy. "He feels comfortable with you, Mam."

"He is a sweetheart."

She watched her mother hug and love on Reuben's child and wondered whether she'd been disappointed that she'd had five daughters and no sons. Ellie asked her.

Mam looked at her with frown. "*Nay.* I've never been disappointed. Neither has your *vadder*. You girls have given us great joy. You were sweet youngsters and have grown up to be fine young women."

Suddenly misty-eyed, Ellie gazed at her. "I love you, Mam."

Her mother regarded her with warmth. "I love you, *dochter*."

"Ethan hasn't finished his breakfast."

"Let's make sure he has plenty to eat, then, shall we?" Mam ran a gentle finger along Ethan's baby-smooth cheek.

Ellie worked in the kitchen with her mother and Charlie while Ethan played on the kitchen floor. When it was time for lunch, the three women ate sandwiches and fixed a plate for Dat. Ellie held Ethan while she gave him some cooked carrots that had cooled off enough for him to pick up and eat. The little boy enjoyed them immensely, eagerly grabbing up another one, then shoving it into his mouth. For dessert, she gave him a cookie especially made for babies. Holding it with both hands, he chewed on it with a grin, then held it up for her inspection. Ellie smiled and praised him until she was sure he had eaten all that he wanted. She then cleaned him up and put him down for a short nap.

At three o'clock, she grabbed her market tote and Ethan's bag and put them in the backseat after settling Ethan in his buggy seat up front. She, her mother and Charlie had baked five loaves of bread and two butter pound cakes today. Her tote carried a loaf of bread and one cake for Reuben. As she steered the buggy toward his house, she eyed the passing scenery, glorying in the sunny afternoon. She wondered how Reuben had made out with the flooring.

The man was outside with a cold drink when she drove up to the hitching post. She got out, then reached in for Ethan, but left their bags in her vehicle. Straightening, she glanced toward the house and encountered Reuben's intense blue gaze.

Heart skittering in her chest, she approached and managed a smile. "Reuben," she greeted with a nod.

"Elizabeth."

She frowned. When he used her given name, she felt as if he was putting her in her place. What had she done wrong now? "Did you finish the floor?"

"*Ja*. We should be able to walk on it now." He

smiled, and the change made her catch her breath. "Want to see?"

Filled with excitement, she followed him into the house. She stepped in the kitchen and halted. Her eyes widened. The floor looked beautiful—shiny wood that added to the appeal of the room. "You put this wood down in one afternoon?" she asked, astonished.

Pleased by her reaction, Reuben grinned. "'Tis not wood, El. 'Tis linoleum. Here. Feel." He felt the warmth of her skin as he took her hand, then pulled her down to touch the floor. Ethan squirmed in her arms.

Reuben reached for his son. "Come here, little man. Now you can sit and play on this new floor without a blanket." He set his son carefully in the middle of the kitchen and straightened.

"It looks lovely," Ellie murmured as she walked farther into the room. The soft, awed way she said it smacked him hard in his chest.

He reined in his feelings. Ellie Stoltzfus churned up something inside him he didn't want or need. "'Tis a floor," he said with less warmth.

She glanced at him, her blue eyes wide. "Is something wrong?"

Reuben felt immediately contrite. It wasn't as if she'd done anything to upset him. He had done that entirely on his own. "*Nay*, everything is fine." He managed a smile. "I appreciate you taking him with you this morning. I wasn't sure how I'd get all this done with him here."

Ellie nodded. "*Ja*, I can understand that." He sensed her sudden discomfort as she turned away. "I should get our bags in from the buggy."

Definitely uncomfortable, he thought. It was as if she was using an excuse to escape. He allowed her to leave, watching with pleasure as Ethan scooted across the floor on his hands and knees. *When did he start doing that?*

The thought came that he should pick Ethan up, then follow Ellie to help with the bags.

The door opened and Ellie entered with two bags, one he recognized as belonging to his son. The other one was hers. He'd seen it before. With a brief smile in his direction, she went to the table and set down both bags. She opened her bag and pulled out two wrapped loaves of bread and a large round plastic container. "I brought bread and cake." She picked up the bread loaves and set them on the counter close to the refrigerator. "Are you hungry? I can cut you a piece of cake."

"You brought me bread and cake," he muttered, floored. She was always doing something nice for him and Ethan. Was it any wonder that she'd been the focus of his thoughts a lot lately? She was a friend. A helpful friend, and while he didn't like taking help from anyone, he didn't mind that she was helping Ethan. He had simply benefited from her presence and care of Ethan.

She was eyeing him warily. "You don't want my bread and cake?" she asked quietly.

He made a quick decision. "I'll have a slice of each."

When she grinned, looking pleased, he knew he'd made the right choice. After all, he had to think of Ethan. If he upset his caretaker, then where would he be?

He simply ignored the niggling inside that suggested he was fooling himself to believe his only concern was Ethan.

Chapter Ten

Ellie returned, expecting to find Reuben busy working somewhere in the house or outside in the yard. Seeing him on the front porch, relaxing, made her stomach flip-flop and her breath hitch. He was so handsome, and she didn't want to notice. Worse yet, she liked him, and she couldn't afford to have feelings for him, for he only wanted a woman in his life who was uncomplicated, a mother for his child—and nothing else. She would watch Ethan until Sarah returned and then continue her life without them.

It was heartwarming to see Reuben enjoy the bread she'd made, sliced and buttered for him. She found more enjoyment from watching him eat her pound cake. When he was done, he stood and excused himself to work upstairs, and Ellie cleaned up the dishes, then fed Ethan dinner. She had picked up a few jars of baby food, although she preferred to mash vegetables that she'd grown and cooked herself. But she hadn't given it a thought until she was on her way over when she'd stopped at the store for a quick purchase of baby green beans, squash and turkey with vegetables…all smooth and easy foods for this little boy to eat.

After Ethan had eaten, she cleaned his face, then changed his clothes and his diaper. By then, it was getting near suppertime at home. She went to the bottom of the stairs and called up to Reuben that it was time she headed back.

He appeared seconds later at the top of the stairs. "'Tis that late?"

She nodded. "*Ja*. I fed Ethan and he's ready for bed whenever you're ready. Unless you want me to put him down now?" She waited a heartbeat.

"*Nay*," he said. "I'll come down and spend some time with him. I can't do any more up here right now anyway." He came down the steps, and Ellie moved back as he reached the bottom stair. She could detect his scent. He had washed up earlier, and the lingering odor of soap and male that belonged only to Reuben reached her senses. She drew a sharp breath as she waited for him to precede her into the gathering room, where Ethan played on the floor with a wooden toy.

Reuben grinned when he saw Ethan, and Ellie noted the resemblance between father and son, which reached out to tug on her heartstrings.

"There is some leftover ham and lima beans with dumplings in the refrigerator for you for supper," she said. "So I'll be off." Ellie picked up her bag. "Will I see you tomorrow?" she asked. "'Tis visiting Sunday and my family is hosting. I hope you will come." Feeling herself blush, she turned. "Have a *gut* night, Reuben."

"Have a pleasant evening, Elizabeth. I'll see you tomorrow," he murmured behind her.

His soft tone drew her gaze to his face one more time. His expression was warm, easy, and Ellie knew she was lost. *Ach nay!* She cared deeply for this man.

She left hurriedly to get home in time for supper. She'd helped her mother make sides for a roast beef dinner before she'd left to bring Ethan home. She forced her thoughts to the meal and spending time with her parents and her sister. But Reuben's attractive features and smile kept returning to her thoughts.

She swallowed hard. She should find someone to take over watching Ethan, but she couldn't bear not to spend time with him...and his father.

She thought of the day she'd had. She wouldn't have left if there had been some place for her and Ethan to go while Reuben installed the flooring. While it was good that she'd been at the house for her mother, today had been one of those times when she wasn't needed by her parents. Charlie was still in residence and she'd spent the entire day there, with Nate arriving just as Ellie left to take Ethan back to Reuben.

Ellie thought of the yard. If not for the rusted junk on the property, it would be a fine place to take Ethan outside to enjoy the warm balmy days of summer and the upcoming fall. An idea came to her while she parked her vehicle next to Nate Peachy's. She could enlist her family to clean up the yard while Reuben was at work on a construction site. He no longer worked with any of her cousins. He was foreman again on another job. A perfect opportunity to get the work done, as long as her cousins could afford to take the time. *I'll ask them. If they can't, they can't, but maybe they will be able to help him.*

She was afraid that Reuben wouldn't be open to the

idea, but she would go ahead with her plans anyway. Although he tried, the man couldn't handle everything on his own. He was only one person, and he had a full community of workers at his disposal. But she would ask only her family. And pray that he wouldn't be too angry once he realized what she'd done.

With that resolve, Ellie went into the house to enjoy the evening with her family. It was only as she was alone in her room later that her feelings for Reuben came back to haunt her.

She'd have to call Sarah to see when she might be returning. She had to protect her heart. Although it might be too late.

Sunday morning Ellie got up early and went downstairs to help get ready for their company. She wondered if Reuben would come with Ethan. He'd been to church, but he hadn't come visiting on Visiting Day since he'd moved into their church district.

She watched all day for Reuben but he never came. She frowned. Why not? He'd said that he would see her today. Why did he keep himself isolated from the company of friends and neighbors?

Reuben had planned to visit the Stoltzfuses, but Ethan had woken up crying, and it had taken everything in him to soothe his son. His boy had felt warm to the touch, and he'd realized that his son had a fever. Was it because he was cutting teeth? Some didn't believe that teething caused a fever, but he knew better. He remembered when Sarah was a baby and teething. She'd cried and cried, and she'd run a fever. Mam had put her in a cool bath to try to bring it down, but she'd continued to cry as she sat in the cold water. Reuben had felt bad for his baby sister.

Was Ellie upset that he didn't go? He hadn't known what else to do. His son didn't feel well, and his health and happiness had to come first.

Ethan had fallen asleep about an hour ago. His baby cheeks were red from crying, and Reuben's heart broke every time he went in to check on him. He loved his little boy. It had been tough after his wife had died, but he and Ethan were fine. And he was glad to have Ethan in his life. Despite his loss, he had the most precious gift Susanna could ever have given him—their son. It was up to him to make sure Ethan was loved, fed, clothed and well cared for.

His thoughts centered on Ellie, as they had so many times these past couple of weeks. She was good for his son. For him. She'd make a fine wife, but would she accept that he wanted to marry her for Ethan's sake? He couldn't possibly marry for love. He and Ellie were friends. That was a good basis for marriage, wasn't it? But would it be fair to ask her to marry without the prospect of future children?

A lead weight settled in his chest. No, it wouldn't be fair to her at all.

Ellie drove to Reuben's house the next morning. Although it hadn't been discussed, she'd decided that he still needed her to babysit. Yesterday afternoon, she'd approached her father, uncle and cousins about cleaning up Reuben's property. She'd told them she wanted to surprise him, so if any of them were available, would they come and do the work?

To Ellie's discomfort, Jedidiah had stared at her

while she'd explained. And after Daniel, Joseph, her father and her uncle had agreed to come at ten Monday morning, Jedidiah had cornered her alone to talk about her plans.

"Do you think 'tis a *gut* idea to do this, Ellie?"

Ellie had frowned. "Why not?" She drew in a steady breath. "Reuben has too much to do, Jed. If we can do this for him, it will reduce some of the stress in his life."

Jed had eyed her thoughtfully. "You like him."

"He's my friend."

"Is that all he is?" her cousin had asked softly.

It was all it could ever be. "*Ja*, just friends."

He'd continued to study her a few seconds longer. "*Oll recht.* We'll do what we can to help your...*friend.*"

The sight of Reuben's house brought her back to the present. She drove into his driveway, tied up her horse, then approached the house. Would he tell her why he didn't come over yesterday?

The door opened as she drew closer. "Reuben. You did want me to babysit today, *ja*?"

He nodded. The man appeared exhausted.

"What's wrong?" she asked.

"Ethan's been running a fever. All day yesterday and through the night. I don't know for certain, but I think he may be teething."

Ellie nodded. "*Ja*, teething can be hard on a little one." She studied him thoroughly, then blushed when he held her gaze. "Did you get *any* sleep last night?" Then she felt her face heat even more as she realized how she'd sounded.

"Once he fell asleep."

"Did you give him something to ease his pain?"

"I wasn't sure what to give." He looked regretful, troubled. Helpless.

She smiled. "Don't worry. I'll take care of him for you while you're at work today."

She was happy to see him relax, as if her words had calmed him. "I should go, but…"

"'Tis fine, Reuben. You have work to do. The little man and I will be fine." She walked to the doorway of the great room. "Where is he?"

"Upstairs sleeping. It was a long night."

She handed him a bag. "I fixed you lunch with left-overs from yesterday."

The surprised look on his face warmed her. "*Danki*, Ellie."

"Do you know what time you will be home?"

He stilled. "Do you need to leave at a certain time?"

"*Nay*, I simply wondered, as I thought I'd make a pot roast for supper."

Reuben blinked. "About four or four thirty."

She smiled. "I'll see you then." Ellie watched him through the kitchen window as he climbed into his buggy and left. After he drove away, she went upstairs to check on Ethan.

At nine thirty, two wagons, a buggy and a huge truck drove into the yard. Ellie started. She'd expected everyone at ten. What if Reuben had still been in the area? She stepped outside with Ethan in her arms as Jedidiah climbed down from his wagon.

"You didn't see Reuben, did you?" she asked.

Jed smiled. "I saw him an hour ago but didn't get the chance to speak with him. I stopped by Whittier's Store this morning for some drinks and snacks, and he was there, climbing into the company car that would take him to the job site."

Ellie released a relieved sigh. "What's all this?"

"These are your workers, and this—" he gestured toward the truck "—is a roll-off."

She frowned, then understood as she and Jed watched as the truck released a huge rectangular container near the side of the barn.

"It's for garbage," the young driver said after he'd hopped from his truck to have Jed sign a document attached to a clipboard.

Jed's brothers Daniel and Joseph joined them. Another wagon pulled into the yard that carried her father and Uncle Samuel. To her surprise, her brothers-in-law, Peter, Henry and James, also came to help.

"Danki," she told them.

Her father dismissed her thanks with a wave of his hand. Jedidiah stepped up to be the man in charge. Satisfied that the yard would be cleared before Reuben got home, Ellie headed inside. She had food to prepare—lots of food. Just as she wondered what to make, the side door opened and her cousins' wives, as well as her mother and two of her sisters, entered with a variety of snacks, lunch dishes and desserts.

Ellie beamed at them. They had come because she'd asked. She loved and was grateful for every single one of her family members.

After the work was done, she began to worry about Reuben's reaction when he got home. She tried not to think about how angry he might be once he realized that her family had invaded his kitchen. The room looked wonderful with its new paint and floor. The entire interior was something to be proud of. Reuben had done a great job.

By three thirty everyone had gone, and the roll-away container filled with debris and garbage had been removed. It had been a nice afternoon. Her cousins Daniel and Joseph had finished painting the trim on the front side of the house. Ethan had enjoyed the day, too, she realized. No longer feverish, he had gone willingly to each woman, grinning his baby smile, displaying his two bottom teeth and one up top that recently had broken through. She'd put him down for his nap at one thirty, and despite the commotion out in the yard, he'd fallen asleep immediately.

She heard him in his room now, cooing and making little happy noises. Smiling, Ellie went up to get him. He grinned at her and patted her cheek as she lifted him from his crib. "Did you have a nice nap, *bebe*?" She changed his diaper, then brought him downstairs to help him drink from his cup, then took him outside into the yard to play. She smiled as she kept him company, focusing her attention on him rather than the upcoming confrontation she feared she'd be having with his father. The sun felt warm but the air wasn't humid. She set Ethan on his feet and began to walk him around the yard, held up by her hands.

Reuben was tired. Exhausted, actually. It had been a good workday, but a long one. All he wanted to do was get home, sit down and enjoy a glass of Ellie's iced tea. He'd visit with Ethan, then eat whatever Ellie had left him for supper.

She was an unusual, giving woman. He vaguely wondered what might have happened if he'd courted and married her first. It would have been awkward, he realized, since her older sister Meg had broken off their relationship. But what if he'd never spent time with Meg? What if Ellie had come first? He hadn't realized that Ellie was only a year and a half younger than Meg. He'd thought her much younger.

Would he and Ellie have married? Would Ethan have been Ellie's child? Would they have been happy? Had more children? Because it felt as if Ellie was stronger than Susanna had been at the same age.

Thoughts of his late wife gave him pause. It still hurt to think of her taken from this earth so young…

As he steered his horse home, Reuben looked forward to seeing Ethan and Ellie. It wasn't far to the house. He'd be home by four fifteen.

The first thing he noticed when he pulled into the driveway was Ellie and Ethan seated on a blanket in the yard. Ellie looked breathtaking in pink in the sunlight. Her blond hair looked golden under the summer sun's rays. His son giggled as she tickled him, and her answering laugh was girlish. The sound hit him right in the center of his heart.

And then he saw the yard. He narrowed his gaze. What had happened to all the junk, the garbage, on his property?

Ellie, he thought. Ellie had done this. And after he'd told her he didn't like anyone interfering in his business, in his home. His heart hardened as he headed in her direction. As if sensing him, she glanced over, smiling, until she saw his expression. Her features became shuttered. She lifted Ethan into her arms, propping him on her hip, as she stood. Like she was his mother.

"Elizabeth."

"Reuben," she said. "You're home."

"Obviously."

"And you're mad."

"I'm not happy," he said, his tone even, cold.

"Reuben—"

"You knew how I'd feel about people in my house... *in my yard*." He marveled at the amount of work that had been done in his short absence. *"Helping me."* His gaze wandered to the house. Someone had finished painting the outside window trim. "You're responsible."

He heard her draw a sharp breath. *"Ja."*

Something hurt him inside, cut him deep. "Why?" he snapped.

"Because you have so much to do," she breathed. Her face turned pale. "I wanted to help. My family wanted to help."

"Your family." Surely it had taken more than her father and uncle to accomplish the task.

"My *dat, onkel* and cousins," she confessed. She raised her chin in defiance, as if ready to face the brunt of his anger.

The longing he felt for her infuriated him all the more. He had no right to have feelings for her, to notice how pretty she looked or how well she handled his son and had slid easily into his life.

"You should go," he said.

He saw her swallow hard. She nodded. Ellie approached and handed him his son. Then without another word, she walked to her buggy, climbed in and left.

His heart pounded in his chest, making it difficult

for him to breathe. She'd meant well, he supposed. She'd known how he felt about accepting help, yet she'd arranged for workers to clear his yard and paint his house.

He grew suddenly anxious as he watched her leave. He called out her name to stop her. Running with Ethan in his arms, he chased after her but she didn't stop. A truck rumbled down the road, drowning out his cries with the loud roar of its engine.

"Ellie!" he cried. He halted, out of breath. She must have heard him, but she'd chosen to ignore him.

Ethan started to cry as if he sensed something was wrong, and Reuben turned his attention to soothing him. "*Ja*, little *soohn*. I know you miss her." *I do, too.*

He had failed too many times in his life. He'd failed and felt helpless when he and Meg had been involved in a buggy accident that had ended up with both of them in the hospital. Ellie's sister had been thrown into the creek. He'd suffered a knot on his head that he later learned was a concussion. He hadn't known how to swim then, and the fact that he hadn't been able to rescue Meg from the water showed him he was a failure.

He'd failed to save his wife, who'd died after giving birth to Ethan. He'd failed to build a new house for him and Ethan. He should be able to handle the renovations to this house and take care of his son, but he'd failed again. He must have, since Ellie had felt the need to step in with her relatives to work on his house and clear his property.

He'd tried. He'd done everything he could to become a better person but his wife had died and his parents had moved away.

It wasn't Ellie's fault that he had trouble accepting

help from people. He'd overreacted and hurt Ellie, a woman he cared about, in the process. He'd accepted her help with his son, so what difference did it make if others had come over to assist?

If his life were different, he'd ask Ellie to marry him, but he couldn't. Because of his growing feelings for her. He would always think of Susanna with sadness. She'd had such a short life, and she'd never been able to hold their baby. Yet having Ellie in his life had lessened the loss, had made it bearable. But he wasn't worthy of her.

He should leave Ellie alone. It wasn't fair to her that he couldn't offer her anything but friendship. But yet he couldn't seem to let Ellie go. He would apologize and explain why he felt the way he did.

I can only hope that she understands and forgives me. Because although he didn't deserve her love, he wanted—needed—her friendship.

Chapter Eleven

Ellie went to her room, then placed a call on her cell phone to Sarah. She had to know when the girl was coming back. As much as she cared for Reuben, she had a hard time handling his changing moods. They had been getting along well…until the moment he'd realized what she'd done. She'd known she'd be risking his anger when she arranged to have the work done without his consent. But she'd hoped that afterward, he'd realize a lessening of his burden. She'd only wanted to make his life easier. *Wrong move.*

Someone picked up the phone in the store where Sarah used the phone.

"Hallo?" She gave her name and asked the person to have Sarah call her. The man at the other end of the line agreed to give Sarah the message.

Ellie rattled off her cell number, then hung up. She sat on her bed, feeling hurt and lost. She would no longer be caring for Ethan. *And his father.*

She lay back and closed her eyes. The image of Reuben's livid expression made her gasp and roll over to bury her face into her quilted bed covering. *What have I done?*

Her cell phone rang, startling her. She sat up and answered.

"Ellie!" It was Sarah. Ellie felt relief at hearing from her friend. "How are you? How are Reuben and Ethan? Is everything *oll recht*?"

"*Ja*, Sarah, everything is fine. And your *bruder* and nephew are well. How are you? How is your *mudder*?"

"I'm well, Ellie. Mam is doing better, but she still needs my help with cleaning and with my *grosseldre*." She paused. "I'm sorry, but I can't come back yet."

"That's fine, Sarah. You stay and be there for your *mam* and your grandparents." She knew what it was like to worry about a parent. She worried for hers, wanted to be there for both parents after Charlie married Nate.

"Tell me more about Reuben and Ethan."

"They are both well. Ethan got a new tooth! That makes three, and there's another trying to break through. The house is coming along. Reuben painted the walls and installed new flooring in the kitchen and the gathering room."

Sarah made a sound of pleasure. "I bet everything looks nice."

Ellie couldn't help but smile. "It does."

"Give them my love? I just stopped in for a few things for supper and discovered you'd called. I need to get back to the *haus*."

"I hope your *mudder* feels much better soon, Sarah. Take care."

"I will, Ellie, and *danki*. I feel better knowing that you are there for Ethan and my *bruder*."

Ellie hung up the phone, her thoughts in turmoil. She had promised to take care of Ethan and to help Reuben, but the man was angry and no longer wanted her help. What was she going to do? She'd have to arrange for someone to care for Ethan. It would be difficult knowing that some other woman would be caring for Reuben's son, making the man his dinner.

She fought the urge to cry. It was her own fault. She lay back on her bed and stared at the ceiling until her eyes blurred with tears.

Reuben was nervous as he raised a hand to knock on the door to the Arlin Stoltzfus residence. Would Ellie agree to see him? Or would she turn him away? Would her parents glare at him with irritation or worse for hurting their daughter? He rapped hard twice.

The door opened, and to his amazement, Missy Stoltzfus's eyes lit up at the sight of him. "Reuben!" she cried. "And Ethan. Come in. Come in! You must be here to see Ellie."

He nodded. "*Ja*, I'd like to speak with her if I may."

"Of course." She gazed at him and Ethan with warmth. "Ellie is in the barn. May I watch Ethan for you while you visit?"

His eyes widened. "You don't mind?"

Ellie's mother held out her arms. "Why would I mind taking care of this precious boy?"

Reuben handed her his son. "*Danki*. I won't be long."

Missy smiled. "Take your time. Ethan and I will get reacquainted."

He headed out to the barn. Inside the light was dim, but he knew exactly where she was. He could detect her sweet scent, felt her presence as his breathing spiked. Would she see him, then send him away? Or would she listen to his apology and forgive him?

Reuben approached without her notice, watching as she lovingly groomed a horse. She looked pensive, wistful. And sad. Because of him? She was beautiful. He loved everything about her. He stiffened with the realization, briefly closed his eyes, then moved to the door of the stall.

"Ellie."

She gasped as if she'd recognized his voice but didn't immediately turn around. "Why are you here, Reuben?"

"I need to talk with you."

She spun, speared him with a hostile glance. He drew a sharp breath as he felt the sting of her anger. "Where's Ethan?"

"With your *mudder.*" He saw her mouth gape open in shock. "Ellie, I've come to apologize. To explain." He heard her draw a calming breath.

"Explain what?"

"Why I have trouble accepting help from others." He didn't like admitting his failures, but he would because Ellie meant something to him. It scared him, these sharp, painful feelings he had for her. He gazed at her with longing. She had turned back to grooming her horse. "I've felt like a failure for a long time," he began.

Her hand holding the brush stilled. She faced him and regarded him with a soft expression. "Why, Reuben?" she asked quietly.

"You know that Meg and I were in a buggy accident. I didn't save her. I couldn't have saved her. I didn't know how to swim." He looked away, unwilling to see her censure, but she had to know the truth. That her sister would have died if Peter hadn't arrived and rescued her.

"You didn't cause the accident," she murmured.

He shot her a glance. To his amazement, she didn't appear to be upset by his admission. "And my wife... she died, Ellie, because I wanted a family. There was nothing I could do for her. Nothing."

"You felt helpless." She gazed at him with blue eyes filled with emotion.

Pity? He didn't want her pity. But he realized that she didn't pity him. It was compassion he recognized in her gaze.

"*Ja*, I felt helpless." He paused. "I wasn't a *gut* father to Ethan after Susanna died. I was wrapped up with anger and feeling sorry for myself so I let my mother and sister care for him."

He saw something shift across her expression. A look of sadness? Disappointment? She couldn't be any more disappointed in him than he was in himself. *I'm not gut enough for her.*

"Grief, Reuben. You were grieving." Her study of him made him glance away. He needed to go on and couldn't bear to see her face change.

"I've watched you with Ethan," she continued. "You're a *gut* and loving *vadder*."

"I wasn't."

"But you are now," she replied, once again surprising him. She gazed at him thoughtfully. "You need to get past the determination that you have to do everything yourself. You belong to a community. We help each other. There is no shame in asking for or accepting help. If you don't accept help from your fellow church members, how can we ask for yours?"

Reuben was startled. "You think someone would want my help?"

She frowned. "Didn't members of your former church community help each other?"

He'd been so wrapped up in the things that had happened to him in the last few years, he had forgotten, but he must have. "I'm not a *gut* man."

"Reuben Miller, you don't get to judge you. Only the Lord can judge, and I believe He loves you and looks upon you kindly. I believe you are a *gut* man." She stepped closer. Terrified by his feelings, he instinctively backed away. She didn't follow. The hurt look on her face twisted something painfully inside him.

"You have friends who want to help you," Ellie said huskily. "Learn to use your friends. They won't mind. I can promise you."

"*Ja.* I've been worried for so long that I haven't been able to see past the work and my need to be self-reliant. I've pushed everyone away." He hesitated. "Except you." He flashed her a twisted smile. "Actually, I have pushed you away a bit," he admitted, "which is why I'm here. To change that."

"You're willing to accept my help," she murmured, her tone off, as she spun back to grooming the horse, slow even strokes of the brush against the animal's chestnut coat.

"Ellie," he said, "I know that I have much to be thankful for. My son. A place to live—although it still needs work. But not as much anymore thanks to you." His voice trailed off and he felt something close to…

despair. She didn't turn, wouldn't meet his gaze. Had she given up on him? Had she decided that she'd had enough and washed her hands of him? He couldn't go until he made her understand. "I overreacted," he whispered. "I'm sorry."

Her hand stopped mid brush stroke. She faced him. "I understand that things have been hard for you, Reuben, but we—my family and I—weren't trying to undermine you. We just wanted to help. You shouldn't have to do everything on your own."

His chest tightened as he held her gaze. If only things were different...if he'd married her first, there wouldn't have been a problem, he thought again. Unless she'd died the way that Susanna had after giving birth to his child. The thought made him shudder and sent a shaft of pain into his chest and his heart. "I know."

"Do you?"

He inclined his head. "I do." He debated whether to tell her more and decided that he owed it to her. "I once told you that when I marry again, it will be so that Ethan can have a mother." He paused. "I still want that."

She blinked without saying a word.

He was silent for several seconds as he continued to stare at her. "What I never admitted to you was that I noticed you first. Before I became involved with Meg." He hesitated before continuing. "I avoided you because I felt you were too young for marriage. You had years to enjoy before becoming a wife and a mother. Meg's attention was flattering at a time I wanted to wed." He saw disbelief then pain in her eyes before she shut down her expression. "I liked Meg, and I was hurt when she broke things off to be with Peter."

"I don't want to hear—"

"Ellie, please," he pleaded. "Let me finish."

Closing her eyes, she gave a nod. She obviously didn't want to hear about his feelings for her sister. Which lifted his spirits. And gave him hope.

"Susanna and I met not long after your sister and I parted ways. We liked each other immediately. We became friends." He watched Ellie carefully to gauge her reaction. "We wanted the same thing—to get married and have a family and a home…"

"Why are you telling me this?" she asked sharply.

"I need you to understand why I've been determined to do things on my own."

"Reuben—"

He gave her a tentative smile. "Ellie."

"Why do I need to know?"

"So that you'll know the truth…and maybe forgive me?"

Ellie didn't want to hear about the other women who had been in Reuben's life. She already understood why he had difficulty accepting help, but she meant it when she told him he needed to get over it.

He'd noticed her before Meg? *Unlikely.* Or could it be true? Why was he telling her this? Wrapped up in her thoughts and the pain of his rejection, she felt her mind drift and she withdrew from him as she tried to protect herself.

"Ellie?"

She met his gaze. "You want me to continue to

watch Ethan," she said crisply. He would allow her to watch his son, cook his meals and clean his house. *Like a stand-in wife.* She'd be useful until he found a woman he decided to marry, then she'd be on her own.

He blinked as if stunned by her tone. *"Ja."*

"I'll come back to watch your son, but under my terms."

Looking wary, Reuben tilted his blond head as he studied her. "What terms?"

"If I want to bring Ethan here to the house, I should be allowed to take him."

He nodded in agreement, and a little smile tilted up the corners of his mouth.

Ellie narrowed her gaze. "If I want my cousins to help with your house, then you need to be amicable." His brow furrowed. She could tell he didn't like that.

"Fine," he said reluctantly, quietly. But she knew he felt uneasy with the idea.

"Gut." Her head ached, and Ellie lifted a hand to rub one temple. "Why tell me about Meg and Susanna? So I'll feel bad enough to return?"

"Nay. I just wanted you to understand…" He shifted and looked away.

She tried to gauge his thoughts. "Reuben?"

"I care about you, Ellie."

She jerked. "As friends," she murmured. "I know."

He nodded. "I wish it could be more."

So did she. Ellie had had enough of this conversation. It hurt when he confirmed he was unwilling to pursue a relationship with her. *I'm gut enough to be his friend but nothing more.* She swallowed against a suddenly tight throat and changed the subject. "I spoke with Sarah today. Your *mudder* still needs her help for a few more weeks." She watched him closely. "Did you talk with her?"

Was that why he'd wanted to apologize? So that she would help him until Sarah returned? Her lips twisted. She'd been pushing him to accept help, and now that he was willing, she wanted more from him.

"*Nay*, we haven't spoken," he replied quietly. He gazed at her with an odd look in his beautiful blue eyes that made her heart race. "Ellie, it doesn't matter if my sister is coming back or not. This isn't about Ethan or Sarah."

"Then what is it about, Reuben?"

He looked suddenly uncomfortable. "I was wondering if…"

"I told you I'll take care of Ethan. Isn't that what you want?"

Reuben's face turned red. She frowned. She'd never seen him embarrassed before, but now she knew she was right in believing that he'd come to make sure he had a babysitter for his son. "Ellie—"

"I'll see you tomorrow, Reuben." She turned her back on him to finish grooming the mare.

"Ellie, you were too young years ago," he whispered, "but you're not now."

She froze but didn't face him.

"I've thought about asking you to marry me—not for Ethan but for me."

She couldn't help turning then. His expression was anguished. She had the strongest urge to take him into her arms and hold him tightly. Reassure him that they would be wonderful together. But, of course, she didn't. "Reuben—"

"I can't, though. Don't you see?" He ran his hand

raggedly through his blond hair. "I care too much for you. If we wed, I'll lose you, too."

"Reuben—"

"*Nay*, Ellie," he breathed. He touched her arm, and she felt the warmth of him beneath the fabric. "I wish…"

"What do you wish?" she breathed huskily.

"*Nay!*" he gasped. Then he turned and hurriedly left, as if he couldn't bear to stay.

Ellie watched him, her heart racing wildly. Everything in her longed to run after him. But she didn't. Because she knew that he meant it. He would never marry her because he wouldn't marry for love.

She frowned. He'd never actually admitted loving her. If he had, she would have chased him until he gave in to his feelings. But he didn't love her. Ellie closed her eyes and released a shuddering breath. She had fallen in love with him. With him and his son. And except for a temporary babysitter for Ethan, she would never be anything more than a fellow church member. She didn't think they'd remain friends after Sarah's return when he no longer needed her. And that hurt and felt wrong.

She stood for a moment, her heart aching. She was empty inside, and the void hurt. She would be his friend, watch his son and find someone to take her place as the boy's caretaker before her heart broke beyond repair.

Again, the sudden urge to run after him overtook her. Ellie put away the brush and raced toward the house, but Reuben had gone. He must have rushed in to grab his son and escaped.

She would see him tomorrow. She'd promised that

she'd be there for Ethan. Ellie would take her cue from Reuben then. If he acted like they'd never had this conversation, then she would pretend that she hadn't been affected by it. She blinked back tears, then entered the house.

"Ellie," her mother said warmly. "Ethan is such a sweet boy. No wonder you enjoy taking care of him."

Ellie nodded. "He is. Did you see his newest tooth?"

"I did." She frowned. "I'm sorry Reuben had to leave so quickly. He said he had things to do, but he thanked me for watching the boy while you talked." Mam narrowed her gaze as she studied Ellie. "What did you talk about?"

"About Ethan. He wanted to make sure I'll be there tomorrow," she said truthfully. There was no reason for her mother to know everything they'd discussed. "Do you need me to do anything for you tomorrow before I go? I know you wanted to can tomatoes."

"Meg and Leah will be here. There is nothing to stop you from helping Reuben."

"Meg's home." Ellie managed a smile. "I hadn't realized she and Peter had returned from New Wilmington."

"They'll be staying for supper, so you'll get a chance to visit with them then."

"If you change your mind and need help tomorrow, let me know. I can always bring Ethan home with me."

"As much as I enjoy seeing him, Meg will have her little one, and I'll want to focus on having time with him." She grinned. "But if you decide you want to come home tomorrow, please do. But not to work. We'll be done by then."

"Ethan usually naps in the afternoon, but maybe I'll

bring him another morning." *If I'll still be watching him then.* "May I help with supper?" She managed to distract her mother away from talking about Reuben or Ethan any further.

Her conversation with Reuben had left Ellie aching and confused. And longing for something that would never be.

Chapter Twelve

The next morning Ellie filled her buggy's backseat with food supplies. As she started to climb into the vehicle, she heard the sound of wheels on the dirt drive to their farmhouse. She recognized the pony cart's driver immediately.

"Ellie."

"Rebecca!"

Rebecca Troyer, the young Amish woman who'd been handling her clients for over a week, approached with a look of regret that gave Ellie a bad feeling.

"I'm sorry for the early morning visit, but I had to tell you I can no longer work at your clients' homes for you. I've been feeling overwhelmed."

Ellie nodded. "I appreciate all you've done. Can you handle today's?"

"There are none today. The Broderick woman canceled, and the Smiths didn't like the way I cleaned for them last week, although I spent extra time at their house and I never charged them for it."

The Smiths had been difficult on occasion, and Ellie thought she'd cut them loose, but they must have gotten Rebecca's number. "The Smiths are no longer my clients."

Rebecca frowned. "I didn't realize. When the woman called, I thought she was one of yours."

"Used to be, but to say the family is difficult is an understatement." The only client she was worried about was Olivia Broderick, the woman fighting cancer. "*Danki* for what all you've done."

The young Amish woman smiled. "The extra money was appreciated. I wish I could still help. It's been tough meshing the schedules since some of yours wanted me to come when I already had others scheduled that day."

"I understand," Ellie said. "I'll make other arrangements. Nothing to worry about."

Her friend looked relieved. "Enjoy your day, Ellie."

"The same to you, Rebecca." Ellie watched her leave before she left for Reuben's. She had to decide what do. Did she find someone else to clean for her or find another caretaker for Ethan? Would Reuben be relieved if she found another caretaker for his son?

She thought of their conversation in the barn. He had confessed that he was drawn to her, but she didn't believe he felt anything but gratitude toward her.

She had liked her housecleaning business, but she hadn't missed it recently. Sarah wouldn't return for a long while yet. *Do I want someone else to take care of Ethan?* She inhaled sharply. *Nay, I don't.* But if she gave up her business, then what happened when she was no longer needed by Reuben?

She frowned. It wasn't as if she needed the money. She'd been saving for years now. She had a nice nest egg in the bank. And Charlie was getting married in

November. She wouldn't be housecleaning outside her parents' house then. Did it matter if she gave it up now rather than later? A little boy needed her. She wanted to be there for him. And for Reuben. She'd always known that it was a temporary arrangement. He wouldn't need her once his sister returned.

Ellie sighed. She had the distinct feeling that after their conversation last night, Reuben would look harder for a wife. Someone safe, who didn't mind a marriage of convenience.

She shuddered out a breath. "If he falls in love with the woman he marries, I'll have to watch." *Brokenhearted.*

Ellie had made up her mind. She would shut down her business. She'd ask Rebecca if she wanted her clients permanently. The woman could change the schedule any way she wanted to make it work out for her.

Ellie realized that she felt slightly afraid of her decision, but she wouldn't change her mind. There was much to do at home, and if she was to be there for her parents after Charlie married, she would be ready.

She caught sight of Reuben waiting at the side door for her when she arrived. Her heart began to thump hard. Would she ever get over this heightened sensation of expectancy whenever he was near?

She took care of her buggy and grabbed her things from the back, then headed toward the house. Ellie felt like a bundle of nerves by the time she reached the house. When her gaze locked with Reuben's, she offered a tentative smile. He grinned as if happy to see her, and she relaxed and returned his grin.

"Ellie," he murmured as he opened the door for her and stepped aside for her to enter. Reuben looked wonderful in a blue short-sleeved shirt, black suspenders and black tri-blend pants. As she entered, she noticed his bare feet, and something inside her shifted.

Ethan was in his high chair and she immediately went to him. "*Hallo*, little one."

The little boy looked up and his small mouth split in a drooling smile. He made a gurgling sound of delight. Ellie unstrapped him from his chair and tugged him into her arms. She hugged him and nuzzled her nose into his neck. Ethan giggled and she nuzzled again. Each time she did it, the child laughed, clearly delighted with her attention.

She felt Reuben's presence behind her. She faced him and was stunned to see warmth and caring in his beautiful blue eyes.

"You're great with him, Ellie," he said softly as he sat in a kitchen chair to put on his socks and shoes.

"He's an easy child."

"*Nay*, I think 'tis you." The affection in his gaze changed the color of his eyes to deep blue.

"Reuben—"

"*Danki*, Ellie," he breathed.

"There's no need—"

"I've been thinking all night," he admitted. He stood and closed the gap between them. His physical nearness caused a tiny fluttering in her belly. "I've been thinking about you…and me. And there is something I'd like to ask you." He hesitated. "Ellie Stoltzfus, will you marry me?"

She started. *"What?"*

"I would like you to be my wife," he said softly. "You'll make Ethan a wonderful *mudder* and me…"

Mother. Every other word he'd said after that one

was lost. Because she could focus on only one thing. Reuben needed a mother for his son, and he'd decided that it should be her. Because she was good with Ethan. She felt the blood drain from her face. He wouldn't have asked her if he loved her. Which meant he didn't.

Ellie swallowed hard. She loved him. If he'd loved her even just a little, she would have happily married him. But she wouldn't—couldn't—be a mother and not a real wife.

"That's…unexpected." Ellie put distance between them. She drew in a sharp breath, then released it. "*Nay*, I'm sorry but I can't marry you."

He blinked. "*Nay?*" He appeared stunned. "You don't want to be my wife?" He looked upset. Defeated. As if her refusal had shaken him. Roughly.

She opened her mouth to tell him she loved him but then closed it. He was grateful for her help. His proposal had been impulsive, she realized, sprung from his gratitude.

He looked stunned. Then, as if coming to his senses, he wiped his face of all expression.

"Do you want to know why I can't marry you, Reuben?" she asked, watching him closely. When he nodded, she said, "I want a family with someone who loves me."

Reuben paled.

She nodded. "Just as I thought. I'm sorry but I won't marry you. The man I marry will love me and want to have children with me."

Darkness descended on his features as he took a step closer. "Ellie… I can't."

Ellie smiled weakly. "I know. Let's keep things how they've been. Leave our arrangement as it stands until

Sarah gets back." She felt her words like knife stabs into her heart. She wouldn't accept anything less than what her sisters had with their husbands—men who loved and wanted babies with their wives.

He gave a sharp nod. As he turned away, he ran a hand through his blond hair, mussing it into gorgeous disarray. Her heart hurt as she watched him. She wanted a life with him, but she wouldn't accept anything less than a life with love and a passel of children.

He grabbed a paper bag off the countertop. His lunch, she realized, that he must have made himself. He wouldn't need her for much longer. In a few weeks, his sister would return and she'd be back at home with her parents.

She stood in the doorway with Ethan on her hip, watching Reuben as he left for work. He headed toward his buggy, then paused midstride to glance back at her. There was nothing in his expression to give away his thoughts. "Not to worry, Reuben Miller," she said with what she hoped was a smile, "Ethan's safe with me."

He gave her a nod. Minutes later, he met her gaze and waved briefly as he steered his buggy off the property. Ellie felt her composure slip as she fought back tears.

Yet she managed a smile for Ethan. "'Tis just you and me, little man," she murmured as she opened the door and slipped inside. It was only after she put Ethan down for his nap that she allowed herself to cry. After a few minutes, her tears drying on her cheeks, she cleaned Reuben's house while his son slept.

He couldn't do it, Reuben thought as he drove to work. He couldn't marry and get her with child. There were ways to prevent children, weren't there? He cared for Ellie more than he'd cared for anyone in a long while. But to wed, then get her with child? *Nay.* How could he?

Did he want to marry Ellie? *Ja.* Because he wanted a mother for his son? Yes, she was wonderful with him. But that wasn't the only reason. He loved her. He thought about her all night long and knew he was hopelessly in love with Ellie Stoltzfus.

He knew now he couldn't have her. She wanted children. She loved Ethan. It was easy to see how much in her blue gaze. But she wanted more. And he couldn't give them to her. Because if he did, then something might happen to her. And he couldn't risk it. He wouldn't survive if anything bad happened to Ellie. He'd have to look for a woman who didn't want children, who'd be content with Ethan. Someone older who couldn't have children, perhaps.

Even if it wasn't Ellie.

He inhaled sharply as he was hit by a fresh wave of pain.

Ellie was a good friend. He had to be satisfied with her friendship.

Reuben arrived at Yoder's Craft Shop and General Store, where he'd be meeting his crew. They would be driven via car by their English crew member. As he went around the back of the store to where Henry and Leah Yoder allowed them to park their buggies, he saw that Rob Brandon was already there, waiting with the Suburban the construction company provided for their transportation. The three other Amish workers were there, getting their tools out of their buggies. Reuben pulled in his wagon, then got up, secured his horse and reached in for his tool belt. He addressed Rob. "Everyone here?"

The twenty-year-old driver nodded. "All here and accounted for, boss man."

Reuben sighed at the young man's irreverence. Rob was a careful driver and a hard worker. He didn't have any real problems with him. "Let's move."

While everyone got into the car with their tools, he couldn't keep his thoughts from Ellie. A band of pain tightened around his chest. He breathed through it, and the constriction faded.

The job was a new one. They would be building a house for a client of the company, starting from the bottom up. Last week, the basement was dug and footers poured. Today Reuben would be overseeing the masonry work. The property was large, and Reuben told the driver to park away from the building area. He climbed out with his crew, grabbed his tools and went to work.

The end of the workday came faster than he thought it would. He stood for a few moments, talking with the crew, deciding what they wanted to accomplish the next day. Afterward, as he climbed into the vehicle, he was left alone with his thoughts of Ellie. He'd tried fighting them all day, but her image—and her rejection—wouldn't let go of him.

While Ethan slept, the day dragged on. Everywhere Ellie looked in the house, she saw Reuben. Reuben eating at the kitchen table. Reuben in the great room holding his son. The images, the memories, were painful. She decided that she'd take Ethan to see her parents. She'd hoped that her mother and sisters would have finished canning by the time they arrived. She had to get away from the Reuben Miller home. The morning had started well, but then after the man's marriage proposal, things had ended badly.

She loved Reuben, she did, but she would not marry him with the knowledge that he'd never love her in the same way. It was good that she'd said no. It was the only thing she could do under the circumstances, but it devastated her.

By the time she arrived home, her sisters had left and her mother was enjoying a cup of tea alone at the kitchen table. "Mam," she greeted.

Her mother smiled. "Ellie! And little Ethan."

"I'd hoped that I wouldn't be interrupting."

"As you can see, you're not." Mam gestured toward a chair at the kitchen table. "Sit. Tea?"

Ellie nodded. "*Ja*, please." She pulled a high chair from the corner of the kitchen to the table and strapped Ethan in. She sprinkled the tray with cereal.

Without asking, her mother filled a child's sippy cup with apple juice, which she silently put on the table. Ellie smiled, then gave it to Ethan. She grinned as the boy put the cup to his lips and drank. He gave her a sloppy smile as he set it down, then grabbed a handful of cereal.

After enjoying tea, then lunch with her mother a little while later, she headed back. Reuben and his marriage proposal had been on her mind all day. She was nervous about facing him. The last thing she wanted was for him to realize that she had deep feelings for him.

Ellie glanced at her watch. She'd get home before Reuben's return.

As much as she loved the little boy in the seat beside her, she wanted children of her own. *At least three more.* She thought of the women within the community. Any number of them could marry Reuben, especially the older spinsters. Drawing a painful breath, Ellie realized she hated the thought of him with anyone but her. But how could she complain if he chose another when she'd said no? Which gave her something to think about, something bound to keep her up in the nights ahead.

When they arrived, Ellie was surprised to see Reuben's buggy in the yard. Her heart raced and she felt sick to her stomach. Heat filled her cheeks, and she had the strongest urge to flee. But then Ethan made a sound, and she realized that she couldn't escape, not with the man's son.

There was no sign of Reuben in the yard or inside near the window as they approached the house. Forcing herself to relax, Ellie turned the doorknob, only to have the door pulled from her hand. Reuben stood on the threshold, looking tired and disheveled. She fought the strongest urge to hug him.

"Reuben," she greeted. "We went on a little trip to see my *eldre*."

"Did you have a nice visit?"

"We did," she said as she smiled at the child in her arms. "Didn't we, little man?" When she turned back to Reuben, a strange look passed across his face. "Are you hungry? I thought you'd be home later or we would have come back sooner."

"'Tis fine, Ellie." He stepped back and she lowered Ethan to the new kitchen floor to play.

"I made chicken potpie earlier, enough for you to

have dinner for two days. And there is a cherry pie in the pantry. I remember Sarah said that you liked it. If not, there are cookies in a tin beside the pie." Ellie knew that she was babbling but was unable to stop herself. Her love for him made her nervous. "I can make you something else if you'd like."

"Ellie."

"There is plenty of meat in the freezer, and I took out ground beef earlier to make you something different for dinner tomorrow."

"Ellie." His quiet voice drew her up.

"Ja?"

"'Tis all fine. I appreciate all that you do for me." He smiled. *"Relax and breathe."* He looked amused, which only added to his good looks and angered her that she felt embarrassed.

"I should go." She bent down and placed a gentle kiss on little Ethan's head. When she rose, she found Reuben watching her with strong emotion in his eyes. She glanced away, because she had to be reading him wrong. It looked as if he didn't want to lose her. But she knew that couldn't be true—he only wanted to marry so that Ethan could have a mother. Any woman who was good with children would do. "I'll see you tomorrow, Reuben—" She stopped. "Unless you arranged to have someone else come in my place?"

He shook his blond head, his blue gaze continuing his perusal of her. The feelings churning inside fueled her need to escape. After a smile for the child on the floor, Ellie opened the door and stepped outside. She made it to her buggy before she glanced back toward the house. Reuben was there. "Ellie!" he cried.

She froze.

"Please think about it. Marrying me. *Please* reconsider and think about it."

Ellie nodded, for what else could she do? She felt a pang in her heart as he held her gaze. Her thoughts were filled with his marriage proposal as she headed home.

That night while lying in bed, Ellie stared at the ceiling. She loved Reuben. Should she have agreed to marry him? Wasn't it better to marry someone you loved than not marry at all? Would she ever find love with another? Or was Reuben *it* for her? She covered her eyes with an arm. What was she going to do? She loved Ethan, but to be a wife and mother without love? The thought was too painful, and she tried to push it away.

Chapter Thirteen

Ellie received a call from Olivia Broderick the next morning. The woman's plea for her to clean her house this morning aroused her sympathy for the ill woman, and she agreed. After she hung up the phone, she went in search of her sister and asked Charlie if she could watch Ethan.

"*Ja*, I can babysit for him this morning," Charlie said, her expression soft after hearing about the woman's situation.

"*Danki*," Ellie murmured. "I'll relieve you as soon as I'm done."

Ellie headed to the Broderick house, aware that she'd miss seeing Reuben before he left for work. What would he think when Charlie showed up in her place? That she was purposely ignoring him?

Ellie had to hide her shock when Olivia Broderick opened the door. The poor woman looked awful, with sunken cheeks and deep, dark circles around her eyes. She had lost a lot of weight, judging by how thin and bony she appeared.

"Mrs. Broderick," she greeted softly. The woman

stepped back and Ellie entered with her cleaning supplies. "You're not feeling well."

Olivia shook her head. "The chemo treatments have been hard, but I'm hanging in there." She tried to smile. "Thank you for coming on such short notice." She frowned. "I didn't know this Rebecca who called to schedule."

"She's a friend who does a good job. You can trust her with your house."

"You want to get out of the business," the woman said astutely.

Ellie inclined her head. "My sister's getting married soon, and I want to be available for my parents."

"Are they ill?"

"No, but they're getting older, and they can't do as much as they used to. I'll be the only one home to help." Ellie hesitated. "And I've been helping a friend with a child. The friend works and I babysit."

Olivia seemed to understand. "I'm sorry if I pulled you away. I trust you. I can't keep up with the house at all anymore. I need someone to clean frequently."

"I think you should give Rebecca a try, but I'm here now, and I'll come back next week until you are satisfied with my replacement."

"You'll call Rebecca for me? Ask her to stop in to talk with me?"

"I'll be happy to." Ellie paused. "Perhaps we'll clean together next week and you'll see what I mean."

Four hours later, Ellie finished the Broderick residence and left to relieve Charlie. She'd done more work than usual, with Olivia unable to do the simplest household tasks.

She arrived two hours before Reuben was due home.

Charlie grinned as Ethan leaned out of her arms and reached for Ellie. "He loves that you're here. I think he's becoming attached to you."

Ellie frowned. "That might not be *gut* for him."

"Why not?"

"Sarah will be back soon, and I won't be coming anymore."

"You could stop by to clean for them," Charlie said.

She shook her head. "I think not."

"Why not?"

"It just wouldn't be wise," Ellie insisted.

Charlie fixed her with a look, but dropped the topic of conversation. She gave Ellie an overview of her time with Ethan.

"Was Reuben upset that I hadn't come?"

Her sister shrugged. "I think he was surprised to see me, but he seemed *oll recht* after I told her you had to work this morning."

Ethan patted her cheek, and Ellie grinned at him. "Did he nap?" she asked her sister.

"*Ja.* Had a nice one this morning. He just woke up from a shorter one this afternoon." Charlie reached out to caress the little boy's cheek. "I think he wants a snack. He didn't eat much for lunch."

"I'll make him one." She smiled her thanks. "I appreciate your help."

"I didn't mind. Nate is shopping for building supplies out of town this morning. I'll head over to the *haus* to see if he's back."

"I'll see you at home later," Ellie said.

Charlie assured her that she would, then she left. With Ethan firmly on her left hip, she went to the pantry. Ethan seemed to have grown a great deal in the last two weeks. His second upper tooth had broken through, leaving him with four teeth total. It was time to introduce him to new foods. She eyed the pantry shelves as she debated what to give him.

The sound of the side entrance door drew her from the food closet. To her shock, Reuben was home early. He stopped and stared when he realized that she and not Charlie was holding his son. "Ellie."

"*Hallo*, Reuben. I didn't expect you home for a while yet."

"I didn't expect to see you today." An odd, undecipherable look flickered across his expression. "Charlie said you had to work."

Ellie nodded. Was he upset with her decision to take the job? She debated whether to explain, but when his lips firmed, she decided not to bother. She had the right to choose what she wanted to do for the day. It wasn't as if she'd left him without a babysitter. She'd arranged for Charlie to take her place.

She sniffed and turned away. "I was going to get Ethan a snack," she said stiffly. "Do you want anything?"

Reuben didn't answer. He stared at her as she strapped Ethan into his chair. When she met his gaze, she shifted uncomfortably under his steady regard.

"I'll get Ethan a snack, then I'll leave you two alone."

He seemed to come out of a trance. He reached out to snag her gently by the arm. "Don't leave yet. I'm sorry if I seemed rude. 'Tis been a rough day…"

She felt herself soften. "Why don't you sit and I'll get you a tall glass of iced tea and a piece of cake?"

The man smiled. "That would be nice. *Danki*." Ellie

tilted her head as she looked from the boy to his father. "Keep him company?"

He nodded. As she poured him some iced tea, she heard Reuben chatting with his son, telling him about his day.

Ellie felt his eyes on her, assessing, before she entered the walk-in pantry. She grabbed an unopened bag of cereal and returned to father and son.

Reuben was silent as she opened the bag and spread a handful of puffed rice on his son's tray. Ethan picked up a piece of cereal, put it in his mouth and chewed happily.

She cut Reuben a piece of cake. "Will you be fine on your own? If so, I'll leave—"

"Please don't go." He caught her arm again, and she froze as the warmth of his touch radiated along her skin.

"Reuben."

"Spend some time with me, Ellie. *Please.*" His eyes begged. "You said yourself that you didn't expect me home. Please stay and keep me company."

Gazing at him, she debated. She wanted to stay with a strength of will that shocked her, but she was afraid. She'd already fallen for this man. To spend more time with him could ultimately wound her deeply in the end.

Her will overcame her protective sense. "I can stay a little while," she murmured. The relief on his features was startling. "Are you hungry?"

He shook his head. *"Nay."* He watched her as she put away the cake. "Would you go on a picnic with me and Ethan?"

"Reuben—"

"Please."

She couldn't resist him. It was already too late. Her heart was involved and would suffer later. Until then, she'd enjoy every second with her two favorite men outside of family. "I don't think we have picnic food in the refrigerator."

"You'll come? Stay for supper?" He looked hopeful, like a little boy.

Ellie smiled. "I'll come, but—"

"I'll go to the store. What would you like? Fried chicken? Potato salad?"

She laughed. "Get whatever you'd like. There's nothing I won't eat."

Reuben rose with a pleased look. "I'll be right back."

"I thought you said you weren't hungry."

"I suddenly got my appetite back!" He opened the door to leave.

"Reuben!" she called. He shot her a look as if he expected her to change her mind, and he anticipated disappointment. "You didn't eat your cake. I brought it this afternoon. If you're okay with the chocolate cake, we'll have it for dessert."

He grinned. "I love chocolate cake," he said.

Then he left, and Ellie found herself grinning, surprised with how eager he seemed to be about spending time with her.

Reuben was excited as he drove his horse and buggy to Whittier's Store. Ellie had agreed to go on a picnic with him! He'd never before felt this wild expectancy. He shouldn't have asked her to marry him the way he had. He wanted her for his wife and Ethan's mother. He should have courted her before asking. He knew the problem of children still hung between them, but they'd figure it out.

The memory of the first time he'd seen Ellie came to mind. She was sweet and young, with a pretty face and lovely blue eyes. She'd worn a pale blue dress that heightened her coloring. He'd fought his attraction to her because he'd thought her too young. Her older sister Meg was warm, open and dark-haired. The complete opposite of Ellie in looks but not in temperament. Meg's interest had buoyed his spirits and bolstered his self-esteem at a time when he'd needed it. Until the accident and Peter Zook.

He sighed as he pulled into the store parking lot. Things happened for a reason. Reuben prayed daily for strength and guidance. He believed that he and Ellie were meant to be together, that their relationship was blessed by God.

He bought fried chicken that looked crispy and smelled delicious, a quart of potato salad—Amish style—some broccoli salad, a half-dozen freshly baked rolls and a six-pack of root beer. He hoped she liked root beer. If not, they'd bring iced tea. He paid for the items and headed for home, eager and excited.

Worry set in as he drove closer to the house. He'd have to be careful; he didn't want to scare her off. He prayed he could convince her that he cared, that his intentions were honorable. He wanted Ellie for himself as much if not more than he wanted her for his son.

It was a perfect evening for a picnic. The temperature was warm. There was a gentle breeze and little humidity. He made Ellie wait inside with Ethan as he chose a spot in the backyard, then spread out a quilt. He retrieved his purchases from his buggy—paper plates and plastic utensils along with a small bouquet of flowers he'd paid for at the last minute. He set out supper and used an old canning jar from the barn for the flowers. He filled it with water from the outside hand pump in the backyard, then carefully arranged the daisies. He placed her flowers along one edge of the blanket, then headed in to get Ellie and Ethan.

She was seated at the table near Ethan's chair showing him different shapes with her fingers when he walked in. Ethan had no idea what Ellie was doing, but from his giggles, his son clearly loved it. Or he loved her attention.

"Ellie."

She met his gaze with a twinkle of amusement in her pretty blue eyes. "Is supper ready?"

He beamed at her. "*Ja*. Come and see."

She picked up Ethan. As she approached, Reuben held out a hand to her and was surprised when she took it. He led her carefully outside, conscious that he was with his two most precious people.

"Fried chicken, potato and broccoli salad and freshly baked yeast rolls," he announced as they reached the blanket. "But no dessert, for you brought chocolate cake, and I like chocolate cake."

Her smile reached her pretty eyes. "Sounds delicious." Still holding Ethan, her eyes widened as she spotted the flowers. She shot him a surprised look. "Daisies?"

"I thought you would like them." He frowned. "Was I wrong?"

"They're my favorite flower. How did you know?"

He grinned. "I didn't, but you are bright and cheery like a daisy. When I saw them, I immediately thought of you." He heard her sharp intake of breath. She was beautiful, and she'd captured his heart. "Have a seat," he instructed. He reached for Ethan so that she could get comfortable on the quilt, close to the flowers, he noted with delight.

He sat down and set Ethan between them. "I'm glad you stayed," he said huskily.

"Reuben—"

"No pressure, Ellie. I'd simply like to enjoy a meal outside with you."

She was silent a long moment. "Me, too," she whispered so softly he almost didn't hear her. When he realized what she'd said, he felt a rush of warmth and affection. It took all of his control to keep from scooting closer to her. But he stayed where he was. He'd promised he wouldn't pressure her. He'd go slow and take it one step at a time.

They ate companionably, enjoying their meal. Ellie stopped eating frequently to feed Ethan dried cereal and pieces of cut-up peaches that she'd retrieved from the house, along with a baby cookie. She fed him easily, naturally, as if she were his mother. She smiled at his son when she saw that he had peach juice in the corners of his mouth. She picked a napkin and proceeded to wipe his little mouth. Ethan squirmed a bit but allowed her to finish. She rewarded him with a grin and the cookie.

Reuben chatted with her about the weather. Ellie told him about her parents, her sisters and her father's dog. "I never thought I'd see Dat with a dog of his own. After Nell married James and took her dog, my *vadder* seemed lost. He perked up after he decided to get one of his own. It was doing some renovations in a stall for his new dog that helped to bring my sister Leah and her husband Henry together."

"You have four sisters," he said with interest.

She nodded. "We're all close. We enjoy each other's company. We don't spend as much time together as we used to, but when we do, it's *wunderbor*."

All too soon for Reuben, they had finished their picnic and it was time for Ellie to go home.

"*Danki* for the picnic," Ellie said as she gathered up the remnants of their meal. "And the daisies."

Reuben picked up the empty paper plates and stuffed them inside the paper bag the chicken had come in. "*Danki* for keeping me company…" He wanted to say more but couldn't.

She was quiet. The intensity of her gaze speared through him. "I enjoyed myself." She stood, then reached for Ethan. "I should be able to come tomorrow morning, if you still want me to."

Nodding, he said, "I do." As he followed her toward the house, he felt the strongest urge to ask why she'd chosen work over watching Ethan this morning. Her choice shouldn't bother him, but it did. Yet he kept silent. They'd shared a delightful evening, and he didn't want to ruin it.

Ellie bathed and dressed Ethan, readying him for bed. Reuben poured them each a glass of iced tea with the hope that she'd stay a few extra minutes after his son was settled in bed.

She arched her eyebrows when she came downstairs and saw the tea. "I'm sorry, but I can't stay. I didn't expect to be this late. My parents will be worried."

He nodded. "I didn't think. I apologize."

"No need," she said with a smile. "I had a nice

time." She stepped away from him, left the room for the food pantry and returned within moments with a slice of chocolate cake. "You didn't have dessert."

"Neither did you."

"I know." She set the slice on the kitchen table, then went back to retrieve the entire cake and took out another plate, a knife and two forks. "I can stay a few moments longer for cake."

Reuben chuckled. "I'm glad. Cake and your company—it doesn't get any better than this." And he meant it.

Chapter Fourteen

Ellie was already smitten, but her love for him grew during the evening. The man had been attentive since he'd asked her to supper. The fact that he'd bought the meal, set up the blanket and bought her daisies made him all the more special to her. She cut herself a small piece of cake, then sat down to enjoy the treat with the man seated across from her.

It was as if they were friends who found pleasure in each other's company. Ellie wished they could be more than friends, but she would enjoy whatever time she had left with him—while dreaming of things that could never be.

They ate their cake and drank their tea. When they were finished, Ellie rose and placed the dirty dishes into the wash basin in the sink. She turned on the water and reached below the cabinet for dish detergent, but Reuben stopped her. He came up from behind, gently removed her hand and closed the cabinet door. Then he reached over her shoulder to turn off the water.

"I'll take care of the dishes." His voice rumbled near

her ear, making her tingle where his breath touched her skin.

"I don't mind—"

"This is my night to do something for you. 'Tis the least I can do. You've done so much for me."

He stepped back and she could breathe again, but she was still hyperaware of his scent, his nearness. She turned. "If you're sure…" He nodded, and she said, "I'll go, then."

She grabbed her bag and left the house. Ellie was aware that he followed her closely, escorting her to her vehicle to see her safely inside. It was that time of night when dusk was beginning to settle and darkness was soon to follow.

Ethan was sleeping only a few yards away in the house. Ellie experienced a hitch in her breath as Reuben reached for her hand. She felt the warmth of his fingers against hers as she was assisted inside her buggy.

She felt her face heat as she reached for the leathers and hoped he didn't notice. She breathed evenly, then faced him. "*Danki* again for a lovely night."

"I had a *gut* time."

"Me, too."

"I'll see you tomorrow?"

She inclined her head. "If for some reason I can't make it, I'll make sure Charlie comes in my place." She sensed when he stiffened. "What's wrong?"

He gave her a rueful smile. "Just tired," he said. His smile widened.

"Enjoy the rest of your night."

"The same to you, Ellie Stoltzfus. I'll see you again

soon." The way his eyes warmed as he studied her made her feel happy inside.

As she pulled away, she knew she was in deep trouble because she seriously wanted to marry that man. And if she didn't discover a way to change her affections, there was every chance there'd be a broken heart in her future.

For the rest of the week, Ellie babysat for Ethan. Each day, while he was napping, she made phone calls, first to Rebecca to offer her clients, then to help her find someone else to handle the ones the girl couldn't take. Most of her clients were accommodating. They simply wanted someone to clean for them and do a good job. Rebecca took five of her clients, and the rest were divided between others who cleaned house for a living. The Broderick household Ellie kept for now until she could introduce Olivia to Rebecca. She knew the two would get on well.

Since their picnic supper, Reuben had started to come home for lunch. The first time he'd entered the house, she'd gaped at him in shock. She had cooked sliced carrots for Ethan and run them under cold water to cool them down. Ethan was in his high chair, eating the carrots, content with his new food. She'd filled his sippy cup with milk, and he drank from it easily.

Apparently noting her reaction, Reuben apologized for coming unexpectedly.

She scowled at him. "'Tis your *haus*, Reuben. You've a right to come home for lunch."

"The job we started today is just up the road."

"You'll be home for lunch every day, then?"

Reuben hesitated before replying. "*Ja*, if you don't mind."

Her expression softened. "I don't mind."

Reuben continued to come home at noon every day, and Ellie looked forward to his midday visits. She liked figuring out what to make him, and enjoyed his company for the forty-five minutes he had to spend with her.

Friday morning, she was downstairs while Ethan napped in his room when she received a phone call from Olivia Broderick, who pleaded with her to come this afternoon.

"I have company coming, and I need to get the house ready. There's so much to do and I have no energy."

Ellie thought longingly of her anticipated lunch with Reuben. "I can be there at two."

"Thank you, Ellie," Olivia expressed warmly. "You don't know how much this means to me."

After she hung up, Ellie finished cleaning the downstairs, then went into the kitchen to prepare lunch. Ethan would be getting up soon. He'd already outgrown the cradle that Reuben had made for him. She didn't mind going upstairs periodically to check on the little boy. It was easier to get things done around the house when Ethan wasn't sleeping in the great room.

She decided to make BLT sandwiches, but as she looked inside, she saw only two strips of bacon, and she didn't want to give something to Reuben that she wouldn't also be eating. He would be the gentleman and insist that she eat the BLT while he settled for a peanut butter and jelly sandwich. She knew he'd had way too many of those while Sarah was here.

Ellie hadn't had a chance to grocery shop for Reuben. She called her sister Leah, whose craft shop now included a small general store. The building that housed Leah's craft shop had once been a general store owned by her in-laws.

The phone call to Leah at the store went through immediately. When her sister picked up, Ellie explained what she needed. "I know you're busy, but do you think you could find someone to bring them to me? Ethan is napping…"

"I'll bring them," Leah said. "Henry is here, and I could use a break. He'll watch the store for me."

"I don't want to cause you any trouble. I can come after he wakes up." She'd be tight for time if she did that, though—she needed to have lunch ready for Reuben, then she'd head over to the Broderick home after he left. She'd take Ethan to her parents and Charlie could watch him. Then she'd pick him up on her return to the house, and get back before Reuben's arrival in the afternoon. She told Leah of her plan.

"I can stay with Ethan," she offered. "I'm having one of my own. I'd like to spend time with the little one."

"Henry…"

"He won't mind," Leah assured her. Her voice lowered to a whisper. "He loves me."

Ellie smiled. "*Ja*, he does," she said, then paused. "Leah, Reuben will be home for lunch."

There was silence on the other end of the line. "You don't want me there when he comes."

She felt her face heat. "'Tis not that I don't want you here." She drew a calming breath. "Reuben doesn't know I have to work this afternoon."

She could envision her sister's eyes widening. "Why not?"

"Because he wants me to be here, and I will be again...after I finish at the Broderick *haus*."

"He wants you." There was a pregnant pause. "Does he like you?"

Ellie's mind raced to formulate the right words. "I don't know, but he might."

"I think that's *wunderbor*!"

"Please, Leah. You can't tell anyone. Not even Henry." Her stomach burned. "Especially not Meg."

She could sense her sister's disapproval. "I don't keep secrets from my husband, and I don't like keeping them from my sisters."

"'Tis not your secret," she told her. "'Tis mine, and I don't think anything will come of it."

"Fine," Leah said sharply, and Ellie closed her eyes. The last thing she wanted to do was upset her sister. "I'm sorry."

"No need to apologize." Her sister's tone had softened. "I understand."

Leah told her when she could come, and, relieved, Ellie decided she'd make Reuben custard for dessert since she already had the ingredients on hand. She'd placed the last of the custard cups into the refrigerator when her sister arrived.

Leah looked wonderful, and Ellie told her so. Her sister entered the house with a bag of groceries, and Ellie scolded her for carrying them. "Does Henry allow you to carry in the groceries?"

Leah blushed. "*Nay*. But 'tis only one bag. There are more in the buggy."

Ellie suspected that Henry had wanted to be the

one to make the delivery, but Leah had insisted that it be her.

"Please sit down. Would you like tea? I can put the kettle on, then get the rest of the groceries." She hoped that Ethan continued to sleep while she was outside.

She was back in less than a minute with two shopping bags. She paid her sister for the groceries, then put them away. Leah had turned off the stove and was preparing two cups of hot tea. "I see you found the stash of tea."

Leah grinned. "In the pantry, where we keep tea at home."

Ellie nodded. She had done some rearranging in the pantry earlier this week.

The sisters talked about Meg, Charlie and Nell.

"Everyone seems to be doing well. Happy and content in their marriages," Ellie said.

"They are. We all are." Leah eyed her thoughtfully, and Ellie was afraid she'd bring up the subject of Reuben, but she didn't. Ellie offered up a silent prayer of thanks.

Leah glanced at her watch and stood. "I need to get back. Henry will worry, and Reuben will be home soon," she said, adding the last bit with a mischievous smile. "Why don't I stop by Mam and Dat's and ask Charlie to come and watch Ethan for you."

"I don't know if she's free to come."

"I'll call you if she can't make it. If she's busy, you can take him for Mam to watch him. She'd love it."

Ellie worried that she'd be imposing too much on their mother and said so.

"*Nay*. She watched Meg's baby one afternoon before they left for New Wilmington." Leah smiled. "She made out just fine."

Ethan cried out from upstairs.

"Get him. I can see myself out." Her sister grinned at her. "I'll call you to let you know if Charlie can't babysit. If not, maybe you'd like to bring him to the store. 'Tis closer, and Henry and I can both keep an eye on him. It will be on-the-job training for when our baby arrives." She patted her stomach.

"Danki," Ellie murmured.

She went up to get Ethan and smiled when he started babbling when he saw her. She thought she heard him say "da," as if trying to say Dat, but she couldn't be sure. Still, she beamed at him, choosing to believe that he'd called out to his father.

After she changed his diaper, she fed him downstairs. A quick glance at the wall told her it was nearly noon. Reuben would be home any minute. As she sat close to his son, watching him eat, she felt anticipation. She liked spending time with Reuben. She couldn't wait for him to come. With that thought, she rose and grabbed the bacon that Leah had brought for her and what was left in the older package, then she began to make lunch. She fried the bacon until it was crispy but not overdone, then took out the lettuce and tomato and the jar of mayonnaise. She sliced homemade crusty bread, ready to toast on the stove. And she waited for Reuben.

Noon passed, then twelve fifteen. She had to leave after lunch. How late would Reuben be? Finally, she heard his buggy through the open kitchen window. She smiled, pleased, her heart beating with nervous excitement. She turned on the gas, buttered the bread lightly, then set about making toast. Reuben came through the door as she was putting together their BLT sandwiches.

"Ellie," he said warmly. His smile lit up his blue eyes. "Something smells delicious."

"I made BLTs."

His blue eyes brightened. "I love BLTs. I can't remember the last time I had them."

She gestured toward the table. Reuben stopped to ruffle his son's light cap of soft hair. "What would you like to drink?" she asked.

"Is there iced tea left?"

"*Ja*, I made a fresh batch this morning."

"I'll get it," he offered, and he surprised her once again as he took the iced tea pitcher from the refrigerator, then started to reach over her shoulder for two glasses as she turned with plates in hand.

Ellie froze as she found herself face-to-face with Reuben, and so close she could detect his scent combined with soap and water. He must have washed up outside before coming home.

Home. How would it feel if this were her home as Reuben's wife? He hadn't mentioned marriage again. Had he changed his mind? The thought saddened her. But then she recalled the picnic they'd shared at the beginning of the week. He'd been kind, almost romantic. The evening hadn't been arranged by someone who didn't care.

Was he silently courting her? Trying to change her mind? Brightening, she experienced warmth in her heart. There were still problems to work out. He had difficulty accepting help for one, and the other, the big one—he didn't want more children, and Ellie desperately wanted a large family.

She put the sandwiches on the table. Reuben had sat down after fixing each of them a glass of iced tea. It was almost as if they were married. The feel in the kitchen was of a family—father, mother and son—eating together. Only Reuben wasn't her husband, nor Ethan her son. A longing rose up in her that nearly stole her breath.

Reuben narrowed his gaze on her after apparently noting the change. "What's wrong?"

She gave him a genuine smile after fighting back the myriad emotions she felt. "I'm worried about my parents," she said, because it was another obstacle in her marrying.

"Are they ill?" he asked with concern.

"*Nay*, but I can see them aging. Mam needs my help in the kitchen and with doing chores." She looked down at her plate, unwilling to be drawn deeper into her attraction toward him. "Dat is doing well enough, but he still worries me."

"Why?" Reuben's voice was soft.

She glanced up at him briefly. "I don't know. 'Tis something that I feel."

He was silent, but she could feel his gaze. She transferred her attention to Ethan, smiling as she gave him another carrot slice and watched as he bit into it.

"Ellie."

She locked gazes with him. *"Ja?"*

He shook his head. "Never mind."

She frowned. "What is it?"

"I think you may be worrying more than you should. 'Tis *gut* that you want to help your parents. I'm glad of that." His voice became husky. "I'm grateful you've given up time with them to be here. For Ethan." He paused. "And for me."

Ellie blinked. She couldn't let him see what was in her heart, especially if he was no longer interested in marriage. But he wasn't looking at her like she was just a friend. She was confused. She knew what she wanted to do, but she was worried her choice would lead her down a spiraling path to heartbreak and unhappiness. Not that Reuben wasn't an honorable man. She was sure if she married him he would treat her right.

She pushed everything out of her mind. She was here with Reuben, and she needed to enjoy his company before Sarah came back. She looked at his plate and smiled at him. "You liked your BLT?"

He nodded, his smile a little slower in forming. "Delicious."

"Do you want another one?"

Reuben shook his head as he stood. "'Tis getting late. I need to get back to work."

Ellie watched as he bent to place a gentle kiss on his son's forehead. Her heart melted. He loved his son. Now if only he would love her.

She watched as he grabbed his hat from a wall peg before he headed toward the door. After a quick glance at Ethan to ensure he was fine, she followed him to the door and outside. He started toward his vehicle. Suddenly, he halted and faced her.

"I hope you're still thinking about my marriage proposal," he said.

Ellie drew in a sharp breath as she nodded.

His face lit up as he spun back to continue to his buggy. He climbed in and steered the horse back to the road, then glanced at her and waved as he continued on. Ellie felt breathless and excited and worried and scared as she reentered the house.

Ethan babbled to her, and she lifted him from his chair and hugged him. "I'd love to be your *mam*, little man, but I don't know if I can. While I love you—and your *vadder*—I want you to have brothers and sisters. But your *dat* wants you to be an only child."

A quick glance at her watch had her gasping with stunned disbelief. She hadn't heard from Leah so Charlie must be on her way. She needed to gather her cleaning supplies and get ready for her arrival. She had a cleaning job to do for a sick client, and she didn't want to upset her by being late.

The image of Reuben's expression after she confessed with a simple nod that she was still considering his proposal warmed her from the inside out. How she loved that man and his little boy! Yet that didn't mean she'd settle for less than she wanted, needed. She'd have to come to a decision soon, and she feared either choice would be a difficult road to travel.

Chapter Fifteen

Reuben finished his workday and was eager to get home. To Ellie. The fact that she acknowledged that she was considering his marriage proposal gave him hope. He loved her. He never thought he'd fall this hard and quickly in love with anyone, but he had with her. He knew there were problems to overcome, solutions to discuss. She wanted another child. Could he go through the worry and fear again while waiting for her to give birth?

He would. For Ellie. He loved her too much not to give her what she wanted. And the thought of their tiny baby in his arms brought him joy. As long as nothing went wrong during the baby's birth or shortly afterward—he couldn't imagine raising two children on his own. If something happened to Ellie, he'd never marry again. Even to have a mother for his children. He'd just have to rely more on help from the community. *Accepting help.* Something else he had to work on.

The more he thought about his life with Ellie, the more he wanted it. He would give her children. He would love them and Ellie. But he knew she had concerns—his Ellie. He just had to convince her that it would be all right.

He pulled into his driveway and up to the house. He hurried inside, eager to see her, talk with her and confess his change of heart. Would she believe him? Would she look at him with joy? He caught his breath as he secured his horse and approached the house. Would she gaze at him with love?

What if she didn't love him? He realized then that he wouldn't marry her if she didn't. As he reached for the door, he offered a silent prayer to the Lord. *Please, Lord, let Ellie love me. I want to marry her and I need Your blessing. And Your guidance to do the right thing when the time comes.*

He stepped inside the house, his gaze searching. He heard sounds from the great room and went inside. But he didn't see the blond-haired woman he loved. He found someone else instead—her red-haired sister. He experienced a burning in his belly as he studied Charlie, who was changing his son's diaper.

"Charlie," he said.

Her gaze rose as she regarded him with a smile. "You're home! *Gut.*" She lifted the soiled diaper and set it in the diaper pail. Then she turned to face him.

"Where's Ellie?"

"She had to houseclean for a client, so she asked me to watch Ethan."

Reuben nodded, keeping his expression polite, but inside he was struggling to understand why Ellie had left again. Because she couldn't bear to face him after their parting words?

Charlie, unaware of his turmoil, picked up Ethan, then handed his son to him. "I think he misses his *vadder.* Ellie heard it and so did I—your *soohn* was calling you today. We're sure we heard him say *Dat.*" She grinned. "See? Even while you're at work, he thinks of you."

He held Ethan close to his chest, studying Charlie as she got ready to leave. "Will Ellie be back tomorrow?" he asked casually, attempting to hide his feelings.

"I'm sure she will. What time do you need her?"

"Does she need to help your *mudder*?"

Charlie shrugged. "She likes to help her, but I doubt she'll need to tomorrow. I'll be there, and my sisters are coming. We'll be cooking food together for Sunday."

"I'll see her tomorrow, then. She can come when she likes. I have a few things I need to fix around the house, and I'd appreciate it if she'd watch Ethan while I work."

Charlie studied him thoughtfully. "I'll tell her," she said. Then she left.

Reuben couldn't help wondering if Ellie was avoiding him again, even though he thought their lunches together had gone well. Every moment they'd spent together had been good.

He would ask her tomorrow for the truth. If Ellie sent someone in her place, then he'd know what her decision was.

"Da. Da. Da." Ethan patted his cheek and repeated his sounds.

He gazed at his son, saw that Ethan had his eyes on him as he continued to say, "Da. Da. Dat." He distinctly heard the *t* on that last word. He grinned. His baby had just spoken his name.

* * *

The next day he got up early, showered and dressed. Would Ellie come at the regular time? Or send someone else?

He hoped not. He wanted her to come, but more than that, he wanted to spend time with her.

Shortly afterward, after he'd taken Ethan from his crib, then gone downstairs ready for the day, Reuben heard the sound of buggy wheels. He resisted the urge to peer out the window. If it was Charlie instead of Ellie, he'd find out soon enough. He heard the door-knob rattle, then turn.

Ellie entered the house with her head down, unaware that he sat at the table watching her.

She was lovely in a bright purple dress with white apron and prayer *kapp*, her blond hair golden. He realized that she was struggling to carry in two huge bags. He immediately went to her.

"Ellie, let me help you."

She gasped and jolted. "Reuben, I didn't see you."

He regarded her with amusement. "You were busy trying to carry too much at one time." He tugged on one bag, and she released it into his care. He lifted it to test its weight. "What do you have in here?"

She blushed, avoided his glance. "Just a few things."

He stared at her. "What things?"

"I cooked last night. I brought food to share." Her gaze met his, then skittered away. "And I stopped for a few groceries."

Her thoughtfulness made him feel warm inside. "Picnic food?" he teased.

She carried the other bag and lifted it onto the

kitchen counter. "That depends," she murmured, "on what you consider picnic food."

Reuben carried the other bag and placed it next to the one she'd set down. "Picnic food is anything we can eat outside."

Ellie turned then, and he felt the impact of her beautiful blue eyes. "Then I guess we have picnic food." She bit her lip. "You're not angry?"

Reuben stilled. "Because you shopped for me?"

She bobbed her head.

"I want to pay you for the food."

"You may pay me for the few groceries but not what I cooked."

"Oll recht," he said agreeably. She was wonderful. It took all he had not to ask her again to marry him. He wanted, needed an answer. He stood for several minutes, watching her put away the food. He could sense that she was growing tense. He frowned.

She shot him a glance. "Don't you have work to do?"

"Ja, I thought I'd install new flooring in the bedrooms upstairs."

She arched an eyebrow. "All of them?"

"I'll start with the largest room, then go from there."

"Did you eat breakfast?" she asked.

He nodded. "I ate a bowl of cereal."

"I'll fix you lunch when you want it. Just let me know." She bent to kiss Ethan's smooth baby cheek.

Seeing them together reminded him of Ethan's recent words. "He said *Dat,*" Reuben said with a wide smile. "He said *Da-da* first, but then I heard the *t* sound at the end of the last one. He said *Dat.* He said my name."

Ellie regarded his son with a softness that Reuben yearned to have aimed at him. As if she'd heard his inner thoughts, she met his gaze, her eyes crinkling with enjoyment, her lips curving into a soft smile. "Congratulations, Dat. Your son recognizes how special you are to him."

Am I special to you?

"Go to work. Ethan and I will be fine." She went to the refrigerator for a cup with two handles containing milk.

"I didn't know he could drink out of that." His lips twisted. "He's growing fast."

Ellie nodded. "Now will you go to work?"

"Are you trying to get rid of me?"

She blushed but didn't say anything. Why? Because it was the truth?

"I'll be upstairs in the master bedroom," he said gruffly, then he left her before he said something he didn't mean. She hadn't stayed yesterday afternoon because she'd worked. He wanted to ask her why the sudden need to houseclean. But he didn't. He didn't want to be at odds with her. It was all right to have disagreements, but he didn't want them while he waited for Ellie's decision about marriage. Until then, he'd try to woo her so she'd realize how deep his feelings were for her. And hope that she'd begin to feel the same way.

He had brought up the flooring yesterday after Charlie had left and Ethan was in bed for the night. He went upstairs and got to work. And tried not to wonder why Ellie had found it more important to houseclean for somebody than spend time with Ethan. *And me.*

* * *

Ellie frowned as she watched Ethan eat his breakfast. She had put away the food she'd brought and made herself a cup of tea, then grabbed a fresh muffin before she sat next to her charge.

"Da-dat!" Ethan said.

She grinned. "*Gut* boy!" She broke off a piece of sweet muffin and placed it on his tray. He'd already eaten his cereal. She eyed him fondly as he picked up the broken-off bit and put it in his mouth. As he chewed, his eyes got big. Ethan loved the new food.

She wasn't sure what to do while Reuben was upstairs working. There was a new added tension between them. She urged him to work because she'd needed some space. He'd reminded her of his marriage proposal. She wasn't sure what to do. She loved him, but should she marry him? There was still so much between them—the memory of his late wife, his avowal that he would marry only for Ethan, her parents' well-being. She no longer worried about her business, having decided that she'd had enough. And then there was Meg. The fact that he and her sister had once had a relationship, if a short one. Would Meg be upset if she accepted Reuben's marriage proposal?

There was only one way to find out. She'd visit Meg and ask.

There was also the fact that Reuben didn't accept help well. Her family would want to be there for her new family. They would want to pitch in whenever there was a construction project or if they needed someone to watch their children.

Ellie closed her eyes and had a mental image of what it might be like to marry Reuben. It would be wonderful if he loved her. She could see herself large with child, Reuben's concern as the midwife arrived to deliver their baby. He would look anguished but he would kiss her, tell her he loved her, and he would wait downstairs with her father and other family members while her baby was born. It would be hard giving birth, but Ellie could see her joy after the midwife placed a little girl into her arms. No, wait! There was another one—a baby boy. Twins!

She gasped and opened her eyes. Why on earth did she envision twins? Because it would mean less stress if Reuben had to worry through only one pregnancy and birth?

She loved him. She wanted a life with him, but she couldn't decide what to do.

Ellie took Ethan outside after breakfast. It was warm, but it was still early enough to enjoy the day. She studied the backyard. Green filled the empty spaces left by the rusted junk after it was removed. Reuben had put up a clothesline, and Ellie decided that she'd do the wash later in the afternoon. *Just like a wife,* she thought.

She took Ethan for a walk about the property. Carrying him on her left hip, she showed him a honeysuckle bush with its rich fragrance, keeping him far enough away so the bees wouldn't bother them. It was quiet, peaceful. A good day to think about the future. To silently pray to God.

The morning flew by as she explored the grounds with Ethan. She glanced at her wristwatch and gasped. It was nearly noon. She had been teaching Ethan to walk by holding on to his hands, a great way to strengthen his legs for when he could walk by himself.

As she entered the kitchen, she saw that Reuben had come downstairs. He seemed harried, upset. It looked as if he'd run his hand through his hair, for it was tousled.

"Where were you?" he asked sharply.

Ellie stiffened, not liking his tone. "We were outside, enjoying the day."

"You could have told me." The tension had left his frame.

"I didn't want to disturb you." She looked away and carried Ethan to his high chair. He had missed his morning nap. He was sleepy. Ellie debated whether to feed him or put him to bed. "Is Ethan's room done?" She met his gaze.

"*Nay*, but the other rooms are."

She nodded. "After lunch, I thought I would take Ethan to my parents' for a nap."

Reuben narrowed his gaze. "He can sleep here."

"Actually, he can't. He doesn't sleep well with noise anymore." She went to the refrigerator and took out a piece of American cheese, then broke it into pieces, which she set on the little boy's plate. "Do you want lunch? I brought cold roast beef. I can make you a sandwich."

He was silent, so Ellie turned. There was an odd look in his expression, which he quickly masked when he caught her gaze. "I could eat."

She nodded, then prepared lunch for the three of them. She made sandwiches for her and Reuben after asking if he wanted mayonnaise on his. She took potato salad and pickles out of the refrigerator and set them on the table, poured them each a glass of iced tea and gave Ethan a serving of cooked cold peas.

As the three of them ate their lunch, Ellie thought it felt as if they were a family. Reuben had let go of his sour mood. He ate with enjoyment, praising her for the food, thanking her again for caring for Ethan.

"I don't mind if you want to take Ethan to your parents' *haus*."

Ellie was surprised at his change of heart. "We don't have to go. I just thought it would be quieter there for his nap."

"Ja," he agreed. "By the time you get home, I'll have finished the flooring." He hesitated. "What time do you think you'll be back?"

She thought of Ethan's usual nap time and factored in that Reuben's son had forgone his morning sleep. "Three thirty? He didn't nap this morning so I don't know how long he'll sleep."

"Three thirty is fine." But there was something in his gaze that made her wonder if, despite his agreement, he was disappointed that she and Ethan were leaving.

"If he wakes up sooner, I'll bring him home," she said.

His expression warmed. "That would be *gut. Danki.*"

After she cleaned up, she and Ethan left while Reuben went back to work. The thought occurred to visit Meg before heading to her parents'. Peter and Meg's house was a little out of the way, but not by much. Her belly burned and she was nervous. How would Meg react to Reuben's proposal to her?

She turned onto the dirt drive leading to the house. Her heart started to hammer hard. This was her sister. How could she consider marrying Reuben if Meg had a problem with it? And that was assuming she knew that she wanted to marry Reuben, despite the problems that seemed insurmountable between them.

Her breath hitched as, with Ethan in her arms, she climbed Meg's front porch. She lifted a hand to knock but the door swung open, revealing her sister, who grinned at her. Then her blue eyes dropped to the child in her arms and her expression changed.

Chapter Sixteen

"Ellie!" Meg exclaimed, her gaze shifting from her to Ethan. "Come in!" With her young son on her hip, she stepped aside to allow them entry.

"How was your trip to New Wilmington? Was his family there nice?"

"I had a great time. Everyone fussed over Timothy."

"*Gut*, *gut*, then you enjoyed yourself."

Meg nodded.

"We're on our way to our *eldre*," Ellie said. "I thought I'd stop by and maybe have a cup of hot tea with you."

"Sounds *wunderbor*. Timothy just got up from his nap."

Ellie frowned. "I can't stay long. Ethan hasn't slept yet." She sensed her sister's curiosity as she followed Meg down the hall to the kitchen in the back of the house.

Meg went right to the stove and put the kettle on. There was a high chair in the corner of the room. Ellie's nephew was too young to sit in it yet, but it was there for when he got just a little bit older. Her sister set her son into the baby seat that sat on the table. "Watch him for me?"

She nodded, and Meg pulled over the high chair. "I could have done that."

"I'm not helpless."

"I know," Ellie said as she placed Ethan in the chair.

The kettle whistled, and Meg fixed two cups of tea, then handed one to Ellie. Her sister sat across from her. "Something's bothering you."

Ellie inhaled sharply but nodded.

"Does it have something to do with this little one?" Meg asked softly. "Who is he?" She narrowed her gaze. "He looks familiar."

"His name is Ethan Miller. He's Reuben's son." She saw her sister's mouth drop open. "I've been watching him for nearly three weeks now." She bit her lip. "Reuben's a widower. He recently moved into our church district."

Meg didn't say anything at first. Ellie felt her chest tighten.

"That's why he looks familiar. Ethan looks like his *vadder*."

Ellie nodded. "Meg… I wanted—needed—to talk with you." She explained how she came to be cleaning house for Reuben, who hadn't wanted her there at first. About his grief over the death of his wife. "I became friends with Sarah, his sister, who was baby-sitting for him until he could marry or hire someone else to watch Ethan…"

She noted the changing expressions on Meg's face before she continued. "Reuben's *mudder* got hurt and their parents needed Sarah. Sarah asked me to take care of Ethan until her return, but that was weeks ago and she's still not ready to come back."

"How did you manage Ethan with your housecleaning business?"

"At first, Charlie watched him in the mornings for me, and I took over in the afternoons. Now I take care of Ethan full-time."

"So what's the problem?"

"I'm in love with Reuben." She saw the startled look on Meg's face. "And he asked me to marry him, but I haven't given him my answer yet."

"I don't understand. If you love him, why won't you marry him?"

Ellie felt her throat tighten. She blinked back tears. "He wants to marry so his son will have a *mudder*. He doesn't want love. He said he'd already loved and lost and won't go through the pain again."

"*Ach nay*, Ellie!" her sister said quietly. "What are you going to do?"

"The idea of me with Reuben doesn't bother you?"

"Why should it? I have a husband whom I love with all my heart. I was infatuated with Reuben years ago, but once I was with him, there was nothing there. My heart always belonged to Peter. Reuben with you or anyone else won't affect me one way or another."

"But if I marry him, he'll become part of the family."

Meg smiled. "As would this precious young man here." She locked gazes with Ellie. "You love Ethan, too."

Ellie nodded. "*Ja*, I adore him. He's so smart. Do you know he said *Dat*? Reuben was thrilled."

"You will marry Reuben, then?"

"I don't know," she whispered. "Meg, he thinks Ethan is enough. He doesn't want more children."

Her sister's features softened with compassion. "And you've always wanted a large family."

"Ja." She turned to Ethan, ran a finger gently down his arm, enjoying the smoothness of his baby skin. "You know Reuben better than anyone. What should I do?"

"I don't know him as well as you do. He took me home a couple of times from singing and once wc went on an outing with Peter and…" She smiled ruefully, shook her head. "Then the accident happened, and Peter and I were asked to plan a Christmas birthday celebration for his mother and our *dat*, and everything changed." Meg reached across the table and placed a hand over Ellie's. "You have to decide what means more to you…being Reuben's wife or a mother of a large family."

"But there's more. I'm worried about Mam and Dat. If I marry, then how will I help with the chores? I've caught Mam struggling with a heavy pan, and Dat needs help with the animals. I don't know what to do!"

"Ellie, our parents have three daughters who are married to strong, healthy men. And Charlie's Nate is always willing to lend a helping hand. What makes our parents your responsibility alone?"

"I don't know. I've just felt that way."

"Well, stop it. Mam and Dat will be upset to know that you've felt this way. They have all of us to help them. Don't make them an excuse for not marrying Reuben. If you love him, marry him. You need to decide one way or another."

"I know." Ellie noted that Ethan was nearly asleep

in his chair. She stood. She had a lot to think about. "I should get to the *haus*. This little boy desperately needs a nap." She moved to unstrap him from the chair. "Meg, if Peter hadn't wanted children, would you still have married him?"

Meg frowned. "*Ja*, because I loved him too much to live without him."

Pressing Ethan's head against her shoulder, Ellie exchanged smiles with her sister. "You'd be *oll recht* with it if I say *ja* to Reuben?"

"As long as you're happy, I'm fine with it."

"*Danki*, Meg. For the talk and the tea."

Meg stood at the door while Ellie set Ethan in his buggy seat. The child woke up crying and out of sorts. "Don't fret, my little man. You'll be cozy and asleep once we get to Mam's."

Ellie put Ethan to bed at her parents'. He fell into a deep sleep immediately, and she went downstairs to see what she could do for her mother.

The rain started midday. It continued as a heavy downpour that seemed like it wouldn't stop anytime soon. Ellie was due to bring Ethan home at three thirty, but because of her stop at Meg's, Ethan hadn't gone down for his nap until late. After missing his morning sleep, the little boy would probably be out for more than two hours yet. At three fifteen, Ellie decided to drive to Reuben's to explain the situation. Her mother agreed to keep an eye and ear out for Ethan sound asleep in her room. Ellie prayed that Reuben wouldn't be mad at her.

Reuben finished the floor in less time than he'd expected. In an hour or so, they would be able to walk on the floor, and next time Ethan wouldn't have to go to the Arlin Stoltzfus's *haus* for a nap. And Ellie would be here. He made his lunch at noon, then went back to work. Once he'd finished the two rooms, he cleaned up downstairs and took a seat at the kitchen table. The house seemed empty without Ethan. *Without Ellie.* What if she didn't want to marry him?

It was getting late. Past three thirty. Maybe Ethan was sleeping late and she didn't want to wake him. But she knew he expected her home at three thirty. He began to pace. It had started to rain. As the clock struck four, he became afraid. The rain was a heavy downpour, and the memory of his buggy accident late at night during a rainstorm made him uneasy. Should he drive over to the Stoltzfuses'? See that they were still there and all right?

The rain beat hard against the roof. Reuben peered out the kitchen window, saw water pooling on the driveway and on the lawn, running off the roof of the old barn. A crack of thunder startled him, and he decided at that moment that he couldn't stay any longer. He left his hat and ran to his buggy, silently apologizing to the animal for the rain. He drove onto the road after twice checking both ways for traffic. The last thing he needed was for a car to zoom up behind him and drive him off the road.

His hands were shaking as he held the reins and spurred the horse into a fast trot. *Please, Lord, keep them safe.* He was scared. This day reminded him of another. He had a baby son he loved…and the woman of his heart whom he loved and wanted to marry.

The rain was blinding, and he had to slow the horse down. Just a little farther, then he'd be at his destination. And that's when he saw a buggy off to the side of the road, close to a pond on the far side of an English farmer's property.

Nay! He pulled his buggy over and ran toward the vehicle. It was on its side, leaning toward the water. *Ethan! Ellie! Lord, please let them be all right!*

There was no one inside the vehicle. He saw the wooden child's buggy seat. It had tipped over inside. "Ellie! Ethan!"

He heard a soft moan. He skirted the front of the buggy and saw her lying on her back in the water. He could see a small cut on her forehead. He stared, knowing that he would have to go into the pond to get her. "*Gott*, please help me," he murmured over and over like a litany of prayer.

Ellie's life and perhaps that of his son relied on his getting to the woman he loved as quickly as possible. He knew how to swim. It wasn't like the last time. He'd taken swimming lessons, for he never wanted to feel helpless near the water again. He stepped in, lowered his body into the water and did the breaststroke until he reached Ellie's side.

Reuben offered up a silent prayer of thanks when he reached her.

"Ellie."

She opened her eyes. "Reuben?"

"*Ja*, dear one, 'tis me." He surrounded her with his arms and started toward the shore.

"I'm sorry."

His pulse raced with fear. "Are you *oll recht*?" He saw her nod. "Where's Ethan?"

"Safe. He's with Mam. I didn't want to be late… needed to tell you why. Late to nap. I'm sorry."

Near the shoreline, he picked her up in his arms and cradled her against him. "Nothing to be sorry for, El. 'Tis me who's sorry. I love you. I should have told you sooner."

But Ellie's eyes had closed. Alarm tensed up his body. "Ellie?"

She drew and exhaled a sharp breath. "I'm fine."

"You need a hospital."

"*Nay*. Take me back to Mam and Dat's. Please?"

He couldn't deny her anything. He set her gently in his buggy. He would see to her safety and have someone fetch her vehicle. He retrieved her horse and tied him to the back of his buggy.

The downpour had eased as he climbed in and drove down the road, moving slowly to protect the horse tied up behind his vehicle. Ellie sat next to him. She leaned against the back of the seat with her eyes closed.

"Ellie," he said urgently. "Dear one, open your eyes. Let me know how you feel."

Her eyes flickered open. "Reuben?"

"*Ja*, Ellie. 'Tis me." He regarded her with concern. "You're almost home. Do you hurt anywhere?"

"My head a little, but I'll be fine."

"Are you certain? We can call the ambulance."

"*Nay*, Reuben. I just want to go home."

"Almost there."

He carried Ellie as he climbed the steps and knocked hard. Twice. The door swung open, revealing Missy, who cried out when she saw Ellie in his arms. "Is there someplace I can put her? She said her head hurts, but otherwise I don't think she's seriously injured. I still think she should see a doctor, though." He laid her gently on the sofa, grabbing a pillow from a chair and placing it carefully under her head.

"What happened?" Missy cried as Arlin entered the room. Ellie's father took one look at his daughter on the sofa and turned pale.

"I was worried when she didn't come back. I started over here to make sure they were safe. I found her in Prescott's pond. She was floating on her back. I was able to get to her and bring her to shore. Your horse is tied to the back of my buggy." He hesitated. "I drove slowly."

Missy regarded him with tears in her eyes. "*Danki*, Reuben."

"Don't thank me. She must have been on her way to see me. I know she was worried about bringing Ethan home late. 'Tis my fault that she had the accident."

Arlin stepped up close to him. "Now see here, Reuben Miller, you are not responsible for this accident. It was Ellie's idea to go out in the rain in the first place. Don't you beat yourself up over this, do you hear?"

Taken aback by her father's tirade, Reuben could only nod. "You've all done so much for me. I can't put into words how grateful I am."

The man flicked his hand in the air, dismissing his gratitude. "You saved my daughter. I'll never be able to thank you enough."

Reuben felt the warmth and love of this family as it surrounded him. His eyes stung and he blinked. "Ethan sleeping?"

Missy nodded. "He was extra tired. Ellie felt bad that she didn't get him down for a nap earlier."

He regarded Ellie's mother with a soft expression. "Ellie has nothing to feel bad about. She's been *wun-*

derbor. I don't know how I'd have gotten along without her." *In fact, I love her.*

"Arlin," he said to her father. "May I have a word
with you?" He hesitated. "Alone."

The man nodded. "We can talk in the kitchen. Charlie's at Nell's. 'Tis just us here."

Reuben gave one last look of longing toward Ellie
where she rested on the sofa, eyes closed. "Is it *oll
recht* to leave her?"

"*Ja,* her mother will stay with her."

She was soaked through, but her parents hadn't hesitated at having her on their furniture. "Thank the Lord
that it's not winter," he murmured.

"Amen," Arlin whispered.

The two men entered the kitchen and sat down
across the table from each other.

"What's on your mind, Reuben?"

"Ellie."

"What about her?"

"I'd like permission to marry your daughter if she'll
have me." He felt his face heat as he looked away
briefly. "I asked her, but she's not made up her mind.
If she won't have me, I'll understand and leave her
in peace. But if there is a chance she wants to be my
wife, then I'd like to know that I have your blessing."

Arlin frowned. "You came to me instead of the
bishop?"

Reuben nodded. "*Ja,* I know 'tis unusual, but after
what just happened, I felt I had to confess how I feel.
I love her. I know 'tis only been nine months since Susanna died, but Ellie…she makes me feel alive. She's
strong and wise, and I've never met a more generous

and loving woman. I desperately want her to be my wife."

Ellie's father eyed Reuben thoughtfully, as if to gauge his measure. "She may not have you."

He experienced pain in the middle of his chest. "I know."

"But then again, she may be stubborn and strong enough to take you on."

Reuben looked at the man with hope. "Arlin?"

"If my daughter wants to marry you, then you have my blessing. But there are things that need saying between you two, I imagine, since she hasn't made a decision yet."

"There are," he agreed.

Missy entered the room and went to the cabinet to take down a box of what Reuben recognized as headache powder. Grabbing a glass from a different cabinet, she filled it with water, then disappeared into the next room.

"Do you think she needs a doctor?"

"I don't know." Arlin looked worried. "I've had worries over Meg, but this one rarely gets sick or hurt."

"I'm responsible for your worries," Reuben admitted. "Over Meg."

"Nonsense, *soohn*. We've never for one moment cast blame on you. It was an accident, nothing more, and by the grace of the Lord, all came out well."

"Still… I didn't know how to swim then. If Peter hadn't stopped…"

"But he did, so don't fret over it. I don't, and after I heard what you told Missy, you must have learned to swim since then."

Reuben nodded. "I'm so thankful that I did…or I wouldn't have been able to pull Ellie from the water."

Arlin regarded him with respect. "I think you'll make a *gut soohn* if the girl will have you. We already love your little one."

He smiled. "He's a *gut* boy. Do you know that he says *Dat* now?"

The older man laughed. "Does he, now? 'tis a thrill, isn't it?"

"*Ja!* Ellie told me he said it, and now that I've heard it for myself…"

"You enjoy being a *vadder*."

"I do." But he'd lost his wife to childbirth. "I'd have liked to have more, but my wife…she died within minutes after giving Ethan life."

"The Lord must have been ready to welcome her home."

"*Ja*, but…" He thought of Ellie. He didn't want anything bad to happen to her, yet, she'd had an accident. He couldn't protect her from life. She wanted children. He wanted more children. It would be worrisome and scary, but he wanted Ellie as his wife and the mother of his children. More than anything, he realized. If he told her, would she believe him?

"I have to confess," he told Arlin, "that I thought to marry only for Ethan's sake. I wasn't looking for love. I was grieving for my wife, and I couldn't bear the thought of falling in love again only to lose the woman I love."

"You're afraid something will happen to my *dochter* like it did to your Susanna."

Reuben nodded. "*Ja.*"

"You can't stop life and the will of the Father, Reuben. If 'tis one thing I've learned, it is that things both *gut* and bad happen to families, to people. You have to accept the bad with the *gut* and enjoy every moment of this precious life that God has given us."

"I know that now. I understand."

"Well, then what are you waiting for? Go see the woman you love and get her to agree to marry you."

"*Danki*, Arlin."

"What for?"

"For giving me a wonderful example of a *gut vadder*."

To his surprise, Arlin looked embarrassed.

Reuben pushed back his chair, then after a nod in his prospective father-in-law's direction, he went to see if his girl—the woman he loved—would have him.

Her head hurt. She couldn't believe she'd lost control of her vehicle. It had been pouring heavily and difficult to see. When the dog ran across the road, she'd tried to steer her horse to avoid him. The next thing she knew, she had run off the road and her buggy had tipped to the side after throwing her outside it. She'd landed with a splash in the pond. She knew how to swim, but her head hurt and it took all she had just to turn to float on her back until someone stopped to help.

Reuben. It had been Reuben who'd pulled her from the water, murmuring gently all the way, picking her up as if she were precious cargo and settling her gently inside his buggy.

Her mother had brought her something for her headache. The powder wasn't a favorite of hers. It tasted nasty, and she had to quickly swallow a full glass of water to chase it down.

She was sore, but except for a slight headache, she wasn't hurt. Reuben had been so kind and caring. Did he love her? Had she been worrying over nothing?

The man in her thoughts entered the great room and moved to her side. She saw her mother exchange looks with him before Mam excused herself and left the room, leaving the two of them alone.

"How are you feeling?" he said huskily.

"My head aches, but I'm fine. I took something for the pain. I'm sure I'll be right as rain in the morning." She laughed at the mention of rain before the memory of the moments before the accident sobered her.

Reuben pulled a chair up close to the sofa where she lay. "Ellie, I have to tell you something, but I don't think you'll believe me…and I'm not telling you now because of your accident. I've been trying to come up with a *gut* time to say what's on my mind."

Ellie eyed him warily. Was he going to admit that he'd proposed for all the wrong reasons? And just when she'd decided to say yes?

"Ellie. Elizabeth Stoltzfus, I've asked you to marry me and you've been thinking about it. I gave you the wrong idea about my reasons—"

"Reuben, you don't have to tell me. I understand that you've changed your mind."

"Changed my—*nay*! I haven't changed my mind or my feelings for you. Ellie, I love you. I want to marry you because you're everything I've ever wanted as my partner in life. I've tried to give you time, but I… in this, the accident might have something to do with it… I can't wait anymore. If you don't want to marry me, please just say so. If you do, you'll make me the happiest man alive."

Ellie couldn't believe what she was hearing. "But there are things we don't agree on…such as children."

"I want children with you. I've realized that I can't stop bad things happening in my life, but I can enjoy the *gut*. And Ellie, you are all that's *gut* and wonderful to me. I love you. I want you to be my wife. Will you marry me?"

She studied him with affection. "You're going to let my family help you when we need it?"

Reuben nodded. "*Ja*. And I'm eager to lend a helping hand back."

"And you think you can put up with me for the rest of your life? I can be challenging."

"I can. I want to." He eyed her with hope.

"*Ja*."

He blinked. "Are you saying—?"

"*Ja*, I will marry you and be your wife. I will be a *mam* to Ethan and any future children we may have." She touched his cheek above his beard. "And I'll love you forever."

She was shocked to see tears fill her beloved's eyes. "Ellie," he whispered. He bent close and kissed her softly on the lips. She loved being close to him. She was blushing when he lifted his head. "I love you, Ellie."

"I believe you. And I love you." She smiled. "I guess you won't be needing Sarah to return. Except for our wedding."

"When will you marry me?" he asked.

"I have an idea, but I'll have to talk with my sister first. Would you mind marrying in a double ceremony with Charlie and Nate?"

"This November?"

"*Ja.*"

"I'm a widower. We don't have to wait until November. 'Tis only the end of August."

"We can talk about this later," she suggested. "When I'm feeling better?"

"Now that you agreed, I'm eager to make you mine."

Maybe they could marry in September, she thought. She'd suggest it later. "I am yours, Reuben Miller."

"Praise the Lord," Reuben murmured.

Her parents entered the room. Ellie saw her father and husband-to-be exchange glances. Reuben gave a little nod. Her *dat* grinned.

"I take it that little boy asleep in your room is soon to be my grandson?"

"Do you mind?" Ellie asked, pleased at the ease between her parents and future spouse.

"I'm always happy to welcome new members of our family."

They heard a sound from upstairs. "Ethan," Ellie murmured, starting to rise.

"*Nay.* Stay where you are. I'll get him," her mother offered. "I imagine he's hungry. You're staying for supper, Reuben, *ja*?"

"I will, *danki*."

Ellie locked gazes with her husband-to-be, and they shared a secret smile. "Go get our precious boy, Mam."

Epilogue

A year later

Ellie breathed through the contraction, then sighed with relief as it eased. The pains were coming more frequently now. Childbirth hurt, but she was fine. She was strong and she could do this. She couldn't wait to hold the baby—hers and Reuben's—and to calm her worried husband.

"You're doing fine, Ellie," the midwife said.

"Is my husband downstairs? I want to see him."

"He is, but I don't think it's a *gut* idea to have him come in."

"Please? Just for a moment."

"Just for a moment, then."

The midwife left and Ellie was overcome with another sharp contraction. She breathed through the pain, and once again it dissipated. Soon, there would be no relief as her labor progressed.

Reuben burst into the room, looking anxious. He leaned in close. "What's wrong? Are you *oll recht*?"

Ellie smiled and waved him closer. "I just have a

moment but I wanted—needed—to tell you that I love you, and I'll be fine."

"I love you, Ellie." There were tears in his eyes.

She reached up to caress his cheek. "I love you. Now stop worrying and go back downstairs. Mary will come get you as soon as our baby is born."

He left but only after glancing back over his shoulder at her several times. And not a moment too soon. Her contractions began in earnest. Less than an hour later, she gave birth to a beautiful baby girl. She smiled at the midwife, then gasped as she felt another sharp pain in her abdomen. "What's wrong?" she asked Mary. If something happened to her, Reuben would take the blame and never forgive himself.

"This is a surprise, Ellie. Looks like you're having twins, as there is another baby about to make an appearance. Your baby is in the right position. Go ahead and push."

Three pushes later and out came a baby boy. "You have fraternal twins!" Mary said with a grin. She opened the door. "Missy, can you come in here?"

"What's wrong?" her mother asked.

Ellie smiled at her mom. "Nothing. But we need your help."

Mam looked confused until Mary handed her Ellie's daughter. "Your *dochter* has given birth to twins."

"Twins!" Missy smiled. "Our family's been doubly blessed."

Mary cleaned and wrapped up the babies, then placed one in each of Ellie's arms. Mary and her mother left the room.

A few minutes later, Reuben entered, looking anxious. *"Hallo, vadder,"* Ellie said. She had a tiny baby cradled in each arm. He blinked, then gazed at her with wonder. "Come say *hallo* to our babies."

"Twins," he breathed. His blue eyes filled with love and happy tears. "You're well?"

"I'm fine." She smiled. "Never better."

"Praise be to *Gott*!" He placed a gentle kiss first on his wife's forehead, then on his babies. "I love you," he whispered. "So much."

"I love you, husband. Forever. I hope you're ready for a busy life."

"Absolutely."

Ellie laughed. "You sound so sure."

"I am." He grinned before he bent to kiss her. "Time to share our babies with the rest of our family." He gazed at her sharply to make sure she was ready for visitors. "A short visit only."

Her father and mother came into the room first. After expressing their happiness, her father said, "I was thinking, *soohn*. What do you say you and I exchange houses? You need the room that we have, and we'd like a smaller place as we're getting older now. Your house will suit us better."

Ellie glanced at her husband, who looked thoughtful but not upset. "Reuben?"

He smiled at his wife, the mother of his children, before turning a grin on to his in-laws. "Sounds like a fine idea to me."

Their visitors left. Ellie gazed at her husband, overwhelmed with love for him. She saw him blink back tears as he cradled their tiny babies. "Are you *oll recht*?"

He lifted his gaze, his blue eyes shining with joy and love.

"You've given me everything, El. I love you so much."

Emotion made her voice hoarse. "I love you, husband. You've given me all I've ever wanted and more."

* * * * *

AMISH COVERT OPERATION

Meghan Carver

To the Amish friends the Lord has brought into my life recently. I am grateful for your kindness and generosity in answering my questions and opening yourselves to me. You know who you are.

I will bless the Lord at all times:
his praise shall continually be in my mouth.
—*Psalms* 34:1

Chapter One

The steady rhythm of the bicycle did little to calm her nerves. Ominous dark blue clouds propelled Katie Schwartz forward. Faster. Her twin girls, Ruth and Rebekah, were safely ensconced with friends, and the adrenaline pulsing through her cemented her resolve to see this through.

A slight breeze ruffled the leaves, sending a few skittering across the road. But then it died, leaving an unnatural stillness in the hush of the oncoming storm. The only things still fluttering were her skirt around her knees and the ties of her prayer *kapp* flying behind her. They tickled her legs and her neck, like ants at a summer picnic, but she didn't dare let loose of the handlebars. Beads of perspiration dotted her forehead.

As she rounded a curve, the blue-black clouds chasing her, her *bruder*'s house and woodworking shop appeared. The white-sided house sat silent, not even the rocking chair on the front porch daring to move. She steered her bicycle around the house and to the barn door.

Should she call out? Announce herself?

What had her *bruder* been up to? What was keeping him from his family, from her and her daughters? It had been two months since she had seen him, and in their tight-knit Amish community, two months seemed like an eternity. Not even the bishop had been able to compel a meeting with him.

She wanted to call out a greeting, but her voice stuck in her throat before she could form the words.

She leaned the bike against the porch railing and stepped silently to the barn door. Her hair prickled on her neck, and she spun around to scan the nearby fields. By midsummer, the corn was tall enough to hide a man. Was someone there? She surveyed the adjoining field and woods, but the stillness revealed no one. Instead it settled on her shoulders like a heavy cloak. Not a bird or a cicada ventured to sing. She couldn't hear any animals scampering around or even automobiles on the nearby road.

She knocked on the door, the sound ricocheting around the silence of the yard, and then it swung open under her knock. Katie stepped inside, pausing to let her eyes adjust to the dim interior.

"Timothy?"

The volume of her own voice startled her in the eerie quiet. Yellow light from outside filtered through the rafters, and she closed the door behind her. She rubbed her forearms, but the goose bumps persisted.

A horse snickered from the stall. Wherever Timothy had gone, it wasn't far enough to take his horse and buggy. The sound of hay scraping on the floor sifted through the quiet, followed by a scurrying sound. She grasped her skirt. Her *bruder* needed a cat who was a better mouser.

Before she could reach the door to the workshop, the sound of a steady pounding reached her. Or was it footsteps?

"Timothy?" But anxiety's stranglehold on her throat made it come out as a weak squeak.

She clutched her apron in her damp palms as she inched closer to the door. Lightning suddenly flashed through the window, illuminating the stall, the animal and a pair of black shoes peeking out from under the bottom board. A fistful of hay flew in her direction. She pulled her arms up to protect herself, desperate to stifle a sneeze that tickled her nose. Thunder crashed a split second later, at the same time as the clatter of the back door.

The next moment, all was still again.

Katie rushed to the woodworking room and thrust the door closed. She leaned against it, gulping deep breaths to steady herself, clutching the neck of her dress, her eyes closed in a vain attempt to calm herself. Gradually her heartbeat returned to a rhythm that felt almost normal, and she loosened her grip on the smooth fabric.

She slowly opened her eyes. A small, rectangular piece of paper was staring back at her from the floor near the workbench. As she bent to pick it up, another flash of lightning struck, making the words on the front of the card clearly visible. *SOCIAL SECURITY* arched in capital letters across the top. The name on the paper was one she didn't know, and underneath were nine numbers that were meaningless to her.

She had heard of several *Englisch* laws from which the Amish were exempt. Social security was one of them. Their Amish faith forbade insurance, which was what their bishops said the government program was. So if they weren't going to benefit from it, they didn't have to pay into it. She had never had a card that looked like that, and she was fairly certain that her *bruder* had never had a card like that either. So why was this little piece of paper here, in his woodworking shop?

Another crash of thunder shook the barn, but this time it was paired with a crash from within the barn, as well. Katie jumped back against the door, her fingers releasing the little bit of card. It fluttered to the floor, and she grabbed the knob, jerked the door open, and rushed to the exterior door. She grabbed her bicycle from the side porch of the house, unwilling to stick around and find out who was there.

The memory of the hunting cabin in the woods rose up in her mind as she pedaled hard down the asphalt road. She felt desperate to talk to her *bruder*, her abdomen clenching from the exertion and a fair dose of fear. The bishop was kind and caring, and Sarah was a *gut* friend. But there was nothing like family, and with both their parents gone, he was all she had. Perhaps he would be at the cabin they had played in as children. Sometimes Amish woodworkers harvested their own lumber for special projects. In the past, Timothy had also spent a fair share of time there sketching new furniture designs.

A few days ago, some of the Amish teens from her church district had told her that they had seen something suspicious in the woods, but whoever or whatever it had been had disappeared before they could catch up. They thought perhaps it had been hunters, but deer season didn't start until November.

A fresh ache coursed through her with longing for her husband. If only he were here with her, he could talk to Timothy. Find out what was wrong. Help restore her brother's relationship with *Gott* and with his sister and nieces. Of course he would have protected her, too. But she had been tougher than he had realized. Or had that toughness emerged out of necessity and desperation in these last two years since his death?

She pedaled hard into the afternoon's yellow stillness, replaying the events of the past few months. Timothy had begun acting strangely not long after her husband was killed. A tear coursed down her cheek, and she removed a hand from the handlebars just long enough to swipe it away. Wasn't life difficult enough already without her husband? That aloneness had been a new sensation and one to which she still hadn't grown accustomed. But to also lose her *bruder*, her only remaining family apart from her girls, with his odd behavior? It seemed more than she could bear.

A dirt road veered off the pavement to the right, and with just a few more minutes of concentrated pedaling and praying, she came within view of the cabin. It seemed safer, somehow, to leave the bicycle propped against a tree, where it would be out of sight. From a position where she was concealed behind a bush, she surveyed the area. The eerie stillness had followed her from her *bruder*'s property, a yellowish haze of the impending storm permeating the clearing. But no one was in sight, and even the squirrels had ceased their chattering.

With a deep inhalation of the scent of pine trees and summer soil, she stepped into the clearing, keeping to the edge until the last moment. Eight paces brought her to the corner of the structure, where she grabbed a wooden crate and placed it in front of a window.

Gingerly she stepped up, clutching her full skirt in one hand and the window trim in the other. Through her shoes, her toes gripped the edge of the rickety crate. Desperation to stay upright and not teeter off sent a surge of adrenaline coursing through her as she swiped a hand across the grimy window of the hunter's shack. The crate dipped, and Katie grasped the frame of the window again. A splinter of wood pierced her skin, the sting of penetration barely registering as she focused on the task at hand.

"Timothy?" she whispered to herself. "Where are you?"

The boys who lived on the other side of the woods had to be right. They had told her they had seen Timothy going into an old shack in the woods, their description matching this one exactly. It had been months since she had seen her brother, and many more months since that day that had made her a widow and changed the course of their family, but it hadn't even been a week since she had cried herself to sleep. Even now the familiar tears threatened to blur her vision.

With the crate stabilized, she swiped over the glass again and squinted inside. But all that stared back at her was more grime. *Ach*, if only she weren't so short! But at a mere five feet four inches, she knew she needed a step stool for nearly every endeavor, especially for an old cabin elevated on cement blocks and with tiny windows. A bee buzzed around her face, and she waved a hand to shoo it away. The crate tipped again, and she grabbed at the window trim before she could tumble off.

Movement inside snagged her attention, although she couldn't make out figures. It was like looking through the bottom of a glass bottle, with only large blobs moving around. Voices filtered through the window, one louder than the other. What was going on in there? And was Timothy involved?

"*Gott*, help!" The whispered prayer flew from her lips heavenward. "Restore Timothy to the only family he has left!" He needed love and rest and plenty of good, nutritious food. He needed the strength within the Amish community, the salvation in Jesus Christ that the bishop preached and the productive life of a man of faith who worked with his hands. He needed family, a cornerstone of any Amish person's life.

Her nose touched the glass in her efforts to see inside. A face suddenly appeared in the window. It was distorted by the cracks in the glass, but it appeared to be her *bruder*. A moment later, the face disappeared.

She jumped from the crate and headed toward the corner of the cabin. Now that he had seen her, he had to come out and explain himself and return with her, stopping whatever this clandestine meeting was all about. Yet despite the warm summer air, a chill crept up her arms as she rounded the corner. The sour scent of the humidity in the woods tingled her nose and seeped into her brain, beginning the light pulse of a coming headache. Was she relieved that she had found him? Or was she apprehensive of who he was with and what he was doing? The emotions warred within her.

A man dressed in plain clothing, homespun pants and a light blue shirt stepped out through the door.

"Timothy!" But the wild look in his eyes stopped her from speaking further.

And then she saw it. A gun was pressed into his back. But the man with the weapon didn't step out.

"Katie! Run! Go!"

She jerked backward, an instinctual reaction to the presence of the deadly weapon. Panic gripped her throat, her mouth suddenly chalky. What should she do? Could she help him? But there was no way she was going to advance any closer to the door and that gun.

"*Dabber schpring!* Run quickly!"

She stepped backward, her gaze trained on the weapon. With another step, she saw her *bruder* pulled back inside the cabin. The gun reemerged, and she turned to run.

She was five steps away when the weapon fired, an explosive sound that hurt her ears. She pushed herself farther and faster, but her legs were burning. It seemed to take too many steps to reach the tree line. Voices sounded behind her, louder and harsher, as if they were exiting the cabin. She hiked up her skirt, desperately grabbing at the fabric with her sweaty palms, and crouched low as she continued to run.

Another explosion fired nearby, and a sapling splintered to her right. How close was the shooter? Was he following her? She glanced back over her shoulder to check his position, and her foot caught on something. Air rushed past her as she fell face-first into the leaves and dirt.

The ground slammed into her midsection, forcing the air out of her lungs. As she fought to get a breath, a hand clamped onto her shoulder. She struggled to turn over, but all she could see out of her peripheral vision was what she assumed was the man's other hand. He held a gun.

That was it, then. This would be the end.

"Are you all right?" Adam Troyer kept his voice to a low whisper. He glanced back to check the position of the men who had been in the cabin. The one with the weapon continued to advance. Whoever this Amish woman was, he needed to get her out of there. "Can you breathe? Can you run?"

Her answer was a scream.

Oh, that wasn't good. "Shh, shh. I'm not with them. I'm law enforcement." Another shot struck a nearby tree. "Come with me if you want to live."

The screaming stopped as he grasped her upper arm and pulled her to her feet. She grimaced, but if they didn't hurry, they might both be killed. He broke into a jog, the woman running alongside him, trying to brush dirt and leaves off her skirt with one hand and holding on to her *kapp* with the other.

"Danki." The thank-you puffed out with a breath as they hurried further into the woods.

He nodded his acknowledgment. She certainly sounded like a real Amish woman, but was she? It could be that she practiced the accent. Was she an innocent bystander? Or was she in league with whoever was in the cabin, just dressed to look Amish so as not to attract attention?

The sounds of their pursuer crashing through the underbrush grew louder. They would never be able to get away, especially with this woman encumbered by her full skirt and *kapp*. It was time for concealment.

Adam pulled her toward a thick stand of poplar

trees. "I called nine-one-one. It's the fastest way to get reinforcements here. Right now we need to hide."

She nodded and stepped in front of him as quickly as she could, a look of panic mingled with determination etching fine lines around her eyes. Scanning the forest growth around them, she whispered without looking back, "We go up."

It was brilliant. From a tree, not only would they be hidden but he could survey the area and, hopefully, find the man who had chased them from the cabin. A few more steps took them to the base of a thick tree with low-hanging branches.

"Here?"

Katie nodded. "Not for long, I pray."

But by the time he had holstered his weapon and cupped his hands together to provide a step up for her, she had gathered her skirt tightly around her legs with one hand. With the other, she grasped an upper branch. In a few seconds, she was several feet up the tree. Apparently climbing trees was not a new activity for her.

Adam followed behind until they came to a spot where two thick branches ran parallel and provided a sort of bench for them. He settled her in the seat and then lowered himself beside her. Branches full with leaves fanned around them, so thick that he had to pull a branch aside to be able to peek out. This would do well.

He couldn't see anyone below, but that didn't mean it was safe to emerge from their hiding spot. He turned to the Amish woman, her face startlingly close to his in their tight surroundings. "I'm Adam Troyer, by the way." He kept his voice to a whisper. "Immigration and Customs Enforcement special agent."

She turned to him. "Katie Schwartz." Her dark blue eyes flashed in the dimness of their cover as she pierced him with her gaze. "What are you doing here?"

Wait a minute. He was the one who should ask the questions. "Surveillance." He would answer that one, though, hopefully to build rapport, and then fire his questions at her. From his position earlier, he had seen her approach the cabin, acting suspicious and watching over her shoulder. Yes, she looked Amish. Even sounded Amish. But he had no way of knowing, at this point in time, that she actually was Amish. What if she was part of the criminal ring he was seeking, perhaps sent out for an errand, innocent-looking in her Amish garb, and now she was returning? He would stick close to her until he knew for sure who she was. In the meantime, though, there was no harm in her knowing he was ICE. He would not tell her any more.

"I heard a man in the cabin tell you to run away. Why are you here?" He peeked through the leaves again. Still no one had approached the tree. This was not the time or place to question her, but he could gather a little bit of information. If she was one of them, then she would be arrested. If she wasn't, then perhaps she had some insider information that would be helpful to the investigation. So much about her seemed suspicious and made the hair on the back of his hands raise up.

"I am looking for *mein bruder*." She scrunched her eyes and rubbed at them, a tear squeezing out and running down her cheek. She sniffed, a sound too loud for their concealed location.

A crashing sounded somewhere below, and Adam parted the branches to see the man with the weapon several yards off. He was looking straight ahead, and Adam couldn't see his face, only the top of his head, which was covered with a baseball cap.

Katie sniffed again, and Adam raised his finger to his lips to shush her.

"Allergies," she whispered. She wrinkled her nose and held a finger underneath.

Oh, no. This wouldn't help at all.

In a split second, she tilted her head back as if a sneeze was imminent. Adam grabbed her with both arms and, with his hand on the back of her head, pulled her into his shoulder. Her sneeze was muffled in his shirt, but she instantly pushed away from him. He cast what he hoped was an apologetic look in her direction and shrugged his shoulders, but he didn't dare speak. A peek between the branches revealed that their hiding space remained secure.

Without knowing how many men were in the cabin or how much firepower they had, he couldn't take them on all by himself. It was very likely he was outmanned and outgunned, and the best thing to do was wait for local law enforcement to show up. Still, despite the softness of the Amish woman next to him, or perhaps because of it, the hiding place was growing more uncomfortable by the second.

The woman sniffled again, and he pulled her into his shoulder as the second sneeze erupted. He wanted to shush her, but sneezes were uncontrollable. It wasn't her fault. Plus he didn't want the man somewhere below to hear him. They were like sitting ducks up here in their perch.

As the shuddering of the sneeze subsided, Katie pushed away. She seemed as uncomfortable as he was.

But her push must have been too hard, for she wobbled on the branch, her hands grasping for anything to keep her steady. She finally found traction with one hand on the branch and one hand on his arm. Once settled, she let go and straightened her *kapp* and her skirt.

"*Danki.* You have saved me two times."

Before he could whisper his response, the tree trunk exploded next to him.

"Ach!" Katie cried, her hand flying to her leg, obviously in pain but still trying to keep quiet.

Instincts kicked in, and he grabbed her close and pulled her down, trying to shield her from any other gunshots. Did the shooter know where they were, or was he the type to shoot randomly? Adam peered through the branches, but he couldn't see a thing.

"Are you hit?" he whispered, but he knew the answer already.

Katie drew her hand away from her leg. There was blood on it. "Is that what has happened? My leg burns terribly." Tears sprang to her eyes as she clutched the spot on her leg.

"Let me see." After one more look through the branches, he gently removed her hand from the spot and separated the folds of her skirt. The fabric was torn and bloody around the edges, but the injury was not bleeding profusely. She whimpered in pain as he touched the spot and then gathered the folds of her skirt to apply direct pressure to the wound. "Hold this here. We have to get out of here."

But was it safe to descend? He gingerly pulled the branches apart, but he couldn't see anyone. A squirrel chattered nearby. Could that have been what drew the attention of the shooter? At least there hadn't been another shot. Could Katie wait until law enforcement arrived? If they left the tree now, they could put themselves directly in the path of the shooter.

As Katie applied the pressure, her face grew pale, a sheen of perspiration breaking out over her forehead. "I have never been in danger before."

Suddenly she didn't look steady enough to sit on the branches. "An ambulance should be coming with the police any minute now. Can you make it?"

She moaned and clutched her stomach. "I do not know. Can we get down now?"

It wasn't the best idea, considering he still hadn't figured out the whereabouts of the shooter. But the alternative, Katie fainting and both of them falling out of the tree, wasn't any better. Down it would be.

"Sure. Let's go." He stepped down a couple of branches and then turned to hold her around the waist and help her down. They stairstepped down to the bottom branch before a loud rustling sounded from brush nearby.

His heart thrust itself against his chest, and he turned back to signal Katie to be quiet. But with a look of dismay, she stared at her fingers, bloody from her leg wound, her face even whiter than before. He grabbed her around the waist. "Katie?"

Another shot rang out, tearing through the branches around them.

Surely they had been found. That shot had been aimed more directly at Katie.

She stared at him with glassy eyes. Time seemed to stand still in the nanosecond before she closed them. Then she pitched forward, off the branch, and plummeted to the ground, her lifeless body pulling him with her.

Chapter Two

The pierce of sirens slowly circled in her mind as she became aware of the trees, the clouds and even the ground spinning around her. She grasped for something to steady herself with so that she wouldn't fall off. But off what? Where was she?

The sirens stopped, and the buzz of summer insects filled the silence. Something tickled her forehead, and with great effort, she lifted a hand to brush it away.

"Katie?"

Whatever was tickling her sprang back, and she brushed it away again.

"Katie, can you open your eyes?"

It was a low but strong male voice, and she forced her eyes open to find that this man was the one tickling her forehead, brushing and smoothing her hair away with his hand. She closed her eyes again, wanting to lie there and rest. But the man squeezed her shoulder. "Katie, you fainted. Can you wake up? Are you all right?"

Adam. That was his name. The events of the afternoon came rushing back—looking for her *bruder*, finding him at the cabin, climbing the tree with the ICE special agent.

Her head rested on a soft surface, and she noticed he now wore only a navy T-shirt with his khaki cargo pants. His button-down shirt was gone. He must have used it as a pillow for her.

Where is Timothy? With her abdominal muscles, she pulled herself to a sitting position. The sky and trees began a violent spin around her, and she swayed against Adam. With eyes closed, she leaned against him until the spinning subsided.

Slowly she opened her eyes. "Are we safe now?"

"Yes. The police are here. They found the cabin cleared out."

"*Mein bruder?* Timothy?"

"I'm not sure who your brother is, but everyone was gone. I would guess they scattered when they heard the sirens."

"Who are they? What are they doing here?"

"First let's get you some medical care. The para-medics are here. Can you make it to the ambulance? They drove off the country road and into the grass, but they're going to have a tough time getting through the trees to us." He scanned the horizon behind her.

"*Jah,* I think so. But will you stay close? Just in case?" It felt like a weak smile that she offered him, but he smiled in return, a kind look in his eyes that hadn't been there before.

It seemed a long way through the trees to the spot where the ambulance had pulled up into the clearing. Katie breathed with relief to see that the paramedic was a woman. She looked barely older than Katie, with dark hair knotted into a bun. As she helped Katie lie down on the cot, she smiled warmly, and Katie had instant faith in her.

As Adam leaned against the open door of the ambulance, the paramedic quickly assessed the situation, taking her temperature and blood pressure, as well as asking a dozen or more questions. Then she removed solutions and bandages from various bins and boxes in the vehicle. "Special Agent Troyer was correct. The first bullet grazed your outer thigh. It didn't go anywhere close to your femur, your upper leg bone. It just skimmed the soft tissue, so I'm going to clean and bandage the wound. You might be hobbling for a week or so, but there won't be any lasting effects. If you need them, you can buy crutches or a cane from any local drugstore."

"Praise *Gott* for His protection." She closed her eyes for a quick prayer, but when the darkness began to spin, she popped them open again. *Gott* would hear prayers with eyes open, as well.

Adam had stepped away from the door of the ambulance, but he soon returned with a long, stout stick. He dug out a pocketknife and began whittling one end of the stick.

With a gentle touch, the paramedic cleaned and bandaged her forehead. "You have some minor abrasions, probably from your fall from the tree. They will also heal up with time. I don't expect you to have any scars."

"Did I faint? Is that why I am so dizzy?"

"Yes. It's called vasovagal syncope. Do you faint at the sight of blood?" She nodded toward Adam. "Special Agent Troyer told me you found your injury first by the blood on your skirt."

Katie glanced at Adam, but he was studying his

stick. Surely he was listening. "*Nein*. Not that I know of. When one of my twins scrapes a knee, I do not like that she is hurt, but the blood does not bother me."

"Extreme emotional distress is probably your trigger then. You've been shot at twice. That makes for a difficult afternoon. In response, your heart rate slowed and your blood pressure dropped. That made you faint."

The paramedic made it sound so matter-of-fact, but that was her job. Still Katie pressed the back of her hand to her forehead, an effort to wipe away the stickiness of anxiety.

"Would you like to go to the hospital? They can do a more thorough examination there."

"Do I need to?"

"Not necessarily. It's completely up to you."

Concern for her *bruder* was pushed aside by thoughts of her twins. The sun was slanting lower and lower, and the four-year-old girls must be anxious for her return. Her friend Sarah would take *gut* care of them, feeding them supper and probably too many treats. But Katie didn't like to be away too long. A mother needed to be with her children, and children needed to be with their mother. A trip to the hospital would most likely extend into the nighttime hours.

"*Danki*, but *nein*. I am sure I will be fine with some rest." How much would an ambulance cost, anyway? For sure and for certain, it was expensive, a cost with which she did not want to burden the community.

"I'll take you home." Adam looked up from his whittling. It wasn't even a question. It was a statement, and a shiver stairstepped down Katie's spine. Was it from the richness of his baritone voice or the insinuation that he had more questions for her?

An hour later, with the help of the paramedic, Katie scooted off the cot. A strong twinge of pain shot up her leg from the site of the wound. In the couple of steps toward the ambulance door, though, she determined that she could make it. But Special Agent Troyer was there with hand outstretched, and she willingly leaned most of her weight on him to get out of the vehicle.

Once both of her feet were firmly planted on the ground, Adam held the stick out to her. "It's a rough job since I didn't have much time, but I think it will serve its purpose." His voice sounded apologetic.

She took the walking stick from him and touched the simple spiral handle he had whittled at the top. It fit in her hand perfectly. Without letting go of his arm, she leaned into the cane. It held her weight comfortably. "*Danki*. You have skill. That is *gut*."

Between the cane and Adam's arm, she hobbled to his vehicle, a large black monster of an SUV called a Tahoe. The Amish Taxi that she used was a simple minivan. She had traveled in a van that had carried fourteen of them from their community in Northern Indiana for shopping in Fort Wayne several years ago. Most likely, vehicles like this had passed her buggy many times on the roads, but she had never noticed. Why would she when she had little use for or interest in cars?

"I'll get your bicycle." He left her leaning against the side of the vehicle, retrieved her bicycle from the trees and loaded it into the back. Without breaking a sweat, he returned to her.

At the door, she stared up at the seat. *Ach*, how would she ever get up that high?

As if he had read her thoughts, Adam leaned in and

pointed. "Lean on me to get your good leg on the running board. I'll help you up."

A moment later, with Adam lifting on her elbow, she was perched in the SUV. Adam jogged around the front and quickly seated himself behind the wheel. He didn't start the vehicle, though, but turned to her with his eyebrows scrunched into a questioning look.

Apparently he wasn't just going to take her home. She would have to answer more questions first. Her heart thrummed within her chest.

"Why don't you tell me about your brother. What's his name? When did you last see him?" He tapped one finger against the steering wheel.

From this height and location, she had a clear view of the cabin. Several officers were working at various tasks, including one putting yellow tape around the perimeter. What *had* Timothy been doing there? She couldn't imagine, but it hadn't involved sketching.

She closed her eyes and took a deep breath, but everything began to spin. With her eyes open, it wasn't much better. Anxiety overwhelmed her, and her hands began to shake in her lap. Her brother was still out of contact, she sat in the vehicle of a law enforcement officer who had saved her from two bullets and she wasn't sure when she would see her twins again. She grasped one hand with the other, an act of will to stop the trembling, but it only worsened until tears cascaded down her face. She swiped at her cheeks, desperate to get some control over her emotions and be strong for her daughters, but it felt hopeless. Her parents were gone, her husband had been killed two years ago and now she seemed to have lost her *bruder*, as well.

Was she in custody? What were the intentions of this

agent? When would she get to Jed and Sarah's house to see her twin girls again? With no husband to step in for her, she would have to have a special reliance on the care of *Gott*. Her leg throbbed, and although the officer was kind enough to make a cane, how would she keep up with the household chores?

Her world was crashing down, and she had no family to which to turn.

The Amish woman sucked in a deep breath and let it out slowly, lifting a dainty finger to wipe away a stray tear.

She was lovely, wholesome, innocent-looking. But Adam couldn't let that influence him. Until he found out exactly what she was doing there and confirmed it with someone reputable, he would consider her a person of interest.

He shifted in his seat to get a better look at her. As he waited for her to begin answering his questions, he noted her light green dress with the white apron, which was soiled from the tree and the shooting. Her dark blond hair was pulled back into a bun, but her *kapp* now sat askew.

Stray thoughts wandered unbidden through his mind. Where would he be right now if his own father hadn't rejected his Amish upbringing? Adam knew a little of the Amish from his infrequent visits to his grandparents, but the faith and lifestyle he had seen in them hadn't saved them from difficult circumstances, including outright rejection and scorn from their own son, Adam's father.

He shook his head to force himself back to the present task, a responsibility that had nothing to do with his own Amish heritage, a generation removed.

Katie stared out the front window, not blinking, and said, "*Mein bruder* is Timothy Schwartz."

Okay, that was a start. Silence stretched between them, but Adam could sit for as long as it took.

"I last saw him on Easter. I do not know where he is or what he has been doing. That is why I was looking for him today." She paused, but he waited patiently. "I found a social security card in his shop, but I do not know the name on it."

Adam hid his surprise. He tucked that valuable piece of information away for later examination as he quickly completed a mental calculation. "So, it's been over two months since you talked to your brother. Isn't that unusual for the Amish? Unless you don't live near here?"

"*Jah*, it is quite unusual. Since I am widowed, I was accustomed to seeing him every day, when he would come to care for my animals. I live close by. I have looked for him many times at his house, but this is the first I came to this cabin." She gestured toward the back of the SUV, where her bike rested. "One person can travel only so far by bicycle."

"Do you ride your bike often?" He felt his eyes narrowing into what felt like his customary expression during interrogations, and he quickly forced what he hoped was simply an inquisitive look. He knew from his grandparents that the Amish were not fond of law enforcement, and he didn't want her to stop talking. At least not until he had all the information he needed.

"*Jah*, it is easier sometimes than hitching up Molly, my horse. I live over on Five Pines Road, a couple of miles from here."

"How long have you lived in Northern Indiana?"

"All my life."

"And you said you were widowed? What about other family?"

"*Nein*. My *daed* and *mamm* died about three years ago, just a few days apart. *Daed* died of a massive heart attack, quite suddenly. A few days later, *Mamm* died of a broken heart. That is what the doctor said." She took a deep breath and stared out the side window, seeming to refocus. "My husband was killed in an accident at work. That was two years ago. Now I only have my twin girls, Ruth and Rebekah. They are four."

"Where are your twins now?"

"They are with my friend Sarah and her husband, Jed. I left them for a little while so I could go to *mein bruder*'s house. I needed to talk to him. To find out what struggle keeps him from his family and the church."

He studied her profile, the drooping prayer *kapp*, the hair that had escaped and now trailed across her cheek, the fine lines around her eyes. She looked tired, exhausted even. Everything she said seemed genuine, and Adam relaxed in his seat ever so slightly. She may not be in cahoots with the shooter, but she still might be a helpful source of information. "Tell me about Sarah and Jed. Who are they, and how do you know them?"

"Sarah has been a *gut* friend since she moved here from Lancaster County several years ago. She was a widow also and had a little girl, and we would help each other out. A few months ago, she married Jedediah Miller. He used to be a police officer from Fort Wayne, but now he is Amish. He works at the same sawmill where my husband did."

He felt a muscle spasm in his jaw, the same one that ticked when he was trying to figure out a case, and he rubbed to soothe it. "If he's Amish, then there's no way I could call him. Or does your church allow telephones?"

"*Nein*. There is a phone shanty not far from their house, but if you are taking me home, you can meet him. I need to pick up my twins, if you are willing."

"Fine. I need to check in with the sheriff, and then we'll be on our way."

He slipped out of the car and closed the door gently, so as not to shake her up further. Katie seemed to be made of tough stuff, but everyone had a limit to their endurance. The slamming of the heavy car door would only add to her jitteriness.

The scene in and around the cabin was intense and busy, but that was the way Adam liked his work. He leaned against the driver's side door and pulled his pocketknife and a small piece of wood out of his pocket. Whittling helped him think, and right now he especially needed to concentrate. A ring of smugglers out of Chicago had expanded, ICE believed, toward Cincinnati. That would take them right through the Amish communities of Northern Indiana. He hadn't had much success in his investigation thus far, and now this Amish woman landed right in the middle. What should he think about it? Where did she fit?

"Troyer!" Sheriff Moore, a man with a thick torso and a jovial demeanor, sauntered toward him. The sheriff's easygoing attitude seemed to be appreciated by the Amish, who apparently had had some difficulty with their last sheriff, but he was a little too laid-back for Adam's preference. Still, the man was well-liked and got the job done. "Find out anything?" He nodded his head toward Katie in the SUV.

"Not much. You know her?" Adam took a few steps toward the sheriff as he scraped his knife over the little piece of wood. It would soon be a squirrel, a twin to the one that already resided in his pocket.

"No. Haven't met her yet."

"She says she's friends with a Sarah and Jedediah Miller. Says Jed's former law enforcement from Fort Wayne."

"Yeah, he's out of it now. Decided he wanted the plain life."

"How'd he end up Amish?" Adam could appreciate a lack of complication as much as the next guy, but leaving electricity behind seemed a little drastic. Why couldn't he just have a sticky bun with his Saturday-morning coffee and old-fashioned newspaper?

"From what I've heard, he was working undercover and about to testify against a ring of counterfeiters when he was found out. Had a snowmobile accident, hit his head on a rock and woke up with amnesia. Sarah found him and took care of him. He's fine now. A real upstanding guy." The sheriff swiped a hand across his brow and adjusted his hat.

The more he heard, the more Adam thought Katie's story was legitimate. There didn't seem to be any other way to explain her presence at the cabin. If her brother was involved in whatever nefarious activity was occurring in the area, she could be a helpful asset. She certainly seemed concerned enough about her brother, despite his wayward ways. He had to take her home anyway, so he'd have a few words with this Jed.

Adam nodded back toward his SUV. "The bullet

grazed her leg, so she won't be riding her bike anytime soon. I'll take her to her friends' house to pick up her twins and see if I can get a private word with Jed."

"He'll tell you what he can." The sheriff plucked a long piece of foxtail grass and stuck the stem between his teeth.

"Good. I'd appreciate being kept in the loop with what you find here."

"We don't hope for much. So far we've pulled a bullet out of a tree trunk. We'll look for a match, but I'm doubtful at being able to find the weapon. I'll keep in touch."

"Thanks." Adam turned back to the Tahoe, determined to get a little more of Katie's story from another law enforcement officer, even if he was Amish now.

Chapter Three

As the crow flies, the drive would probably have been only a few minutes, and that certainly would have been safer. But the back roads through the hills and hollows of Northern Indiana Amish country took a bit more of a winding route. Adam found he couldn't get over thirty miles per hour in most stretches. Slowing down for a couple of buggies didn't help either.

The painfully slow speed also didn't help his anxiety at the shooter still being on the loose. Would he come back for Katie? Why was he shooting at her in the first place? Would he go after a law enforcement officer? Some criminals did, and some didn't. Adam just didn't know enough about who this shooter might be to be able to determine his probable next move.

He tore his attention from the rearview mirror and checked both side mirrors. Through the drive, all had been clear. As he crested a hill, an Amish homestead came into view.

"There. On the right." Katie leaned forward as if it would help her get to her children faster, her hand on the cane.

The property wasn't large, but the whitewashed house was sizeable, the barn a cheerful red. Colorful flowers—marigolds, maybe—dotted the edge of the house and the barn. A large vegetable garden filled a back corner. As he approached, a malamute bounded forward, tail wagging and tongue lolling.

Memories of childhood time spent with Amish grandparents struggled to free themselves from the dusty corners of his mind. His *grossmammi* with a plate full of oatmeal cookies and a pitcher of warm milk that was fresh from their dairy cow. His *grossdaadi* sitting on the porch, showing him the finer points of whittling, while his cousins swung from the hayloft. Adam swallowed hard and shoved the memories back to their places. His father's *rumspringa* and continuing alcoholism had altered not only his father's life but the lives of his future children, as well. And after his father's and brother's untimely deaths in the automobile accident, those remembrances didn't deserve the freedom to roam unhindered through his thoughts. The only way to assuage the grief was to maintain his laser-like focus on his job and the justice for victims that he sought every day.

Adam pulled into the lane, and a man emerged from the house, placing a straw hat on his head as he approached the vehicle. Adam opened the car door and hopped out. He smiled as warmly as he could and raised a hand in greeting, palm open and facing out, as he jogged around the front of the Tahoe. The man's countenance was expressionless until Adam helped Katie down from the SUV. As she emerged from behind the door, a wide smile split the man's face, and a woman with three girls, all in identical blue Amish dresses and white starched prayer *kapps*, stepped out of the house.

"Katie, are you all right?"

"*Jah*, Jed." She leaned heavily on Adam's forearm. Grasping the cane, she stepped toward Jed but still held on to Adam's arm.

The woman who must have been Sarah flew toward them. The three girls followed on her heels, all chattering at once.

"*Ach*, Katie! Where have you been? You are injured!"

"*Mamm!* Are you all right?"

"What happened, *Mamm*?"

Sarah frowned in Adam's direction and took Katie's arm from him as twin girls threw their arms around Katie's waist. Both had the same shade of dark blond hair and the same pert nose, although one appeared to have a few more freckles than the other. *Adorable* seemed too blasé of a word to describe them.

"*Liebchen!* My loves!" Katie smiled broadly and shrugged at Adam as she tried to hug both twins with Sarah hanging on. "I will be fine, Sarah. I will tell you everything inside."

He felt himself begin to trust her a little bit more as he observed Katie's affection for her girls. She gently pulled her arm from Sarah, and, leaning on the cane, she tucked a stray hair back into one girl's *kapp* and then ran her finger down the cheek of the other girl. A smile played about her lips as she seemed to relax. With a reflex honed from training and experience, Adam glanced around the yard and down the lane to make sure all was quiet. Then he stepped toward Jed.

"You must be Jedediah Miller. Sheriff Moore told

me you're retired from Fort Wayne PD." He extended his hand, and they shook. "I'm Adam Troyer, special agent with Immigration and Customs Enforcement, Homeland Security."

"Call me Jed. And yes, retired police officer."

Adam felt his eyebrows scrunch together. "You don't sound Amish, like Katie and Sarah."

Jed smiled. "No. Most of my growing-up was in the *Englisch* world. I just took my vows to join the Amish church a few months ago, so I'm still learning. I imagine it'll be a lifelong process." He looked Adam up and down, the smile sliding off his face. "What's your business here?"

Before Adam could respond, Sarah called from the house. Jed turned to wave and then spun back to Adam. "Before you can answer that, we're required to head in the house for cookies and coffee. Or tea. Or milk. Whatever's your pleasure. It's the Amish way."

In the house, Adam squeezed into a place at the long table and gobbled down three of the most delicious oatmeal cookies he had ever eaten. A twin leaned on either side of Katie as she told of going to her brother's house and then to the cabin. All eyes widened at the mention of the gunman, and Jed nodded an acknowledgment to Adam.

"You must leave Ruth and Rebekah here overnight, then." Sarah leaned forward to run a hand down Katie's arm. "You will rest better."

Katie paused before answering. "*Danki.* That would probably be best for my recovery."

As he reached for a fourth cookie, Adam's phone rang, the ringtone a loud gong in the quiet Amish house. "Excuse me," he said softly and stepped outside the back door before answering.

The late afternoon sun was beginning to cast sleepy shadows across the property, shadows that, to Adam's way of thinking, could hold danger. But Sheriff Moore's voice filled his ear, and the best he could do was visually survey the perimeter.

"Yeah, Troyer? We got nothing. You said you wanted to be kept in the loop, but there's nothin' there. We pulled the bullet from the tree."

"I knew that before I left the site."

"Yeah, and there was nothing worth fingerprinting inside the cabin. Pretty bare in there. All rough wood surfaces, way too porous and too recessed to collect fingerprints. Even if I could find a print, it wouldn't stick to the lift tape. There's no way to lift a print in a wooden cabin."

"So, we got nothing."

"That's what I said."

The door closed behind him, and Adam turned to see Jed step outside. "Thanks anyway, Sheriff." He pocketed his phone.

"Sheriff Moore is a good guy." Jed hesitated. "Learn anything you can share?"

"No. Didn't learn anything at all. I don't know anything more about what happened today than Katie does, and you know that means the investigation is at a standstill." Adam couldn't share anything more with Jed, but he walked slowly around the house and toward the lane, surveying, as Jed fell in step beside him. The night air cooled his skin as he breathed deeply. "You might be able to help, though. What do you know about Katie's brother, Timothy?"

"Probably nothing more than she told you. He's a stand-up guy and an excellent furniture-maker. Then, a couple of months ago, he stops coming around. He's not caring for his sister's horse anymore, not coming to church services or visiting on the off Sundays. Basically he's nowhere to be seen."

"What about his customers? His business?" Adam looked up and down the road and then turned to walk back up the lane.

"I don't know. I haven't seen him to be able to ask him. I know that's not helpful, but I don't have any further information. It's like he just disappeared."

"But he didn't leave the community? Quit being Amish? Did he and Katie have a falling-out?" The sun dipped behind the tree line, and the first fireflies of the evening began to flash. Darkness was fine when it worked in his favor and hid him, but it could be deadly when it concealed the enemy.

"No. He's still around. There's evidence of that. When I stop by, his dog is obviously cared for. His yard is kept. I've even seen wash on the line. But he's never there." Jed crossed his arms over his chest, a sign of resignation. "He's there but not there."

"So, he knows that you're coming and takes off?"

"It seems so. I've thought of contacting an old buddy of mine in Fort Wayne, but I don't have anything to tell him. There doesn't seem to be any evidence of wrongdoing. He just doesn't come around."

"You're still in contact with people from your…former life?" Adam just couldn't wrap his mind around the idea of leaving law enforcement to be a farmer or to build furniture, or whatever it was that Jed did to earn his living.

"Sure."

"How did you ever decide to—"

"Join the Amish church?" Jed chuckled. "I had amnesia."

"And then you remembered you were Amish?" Adam couldn't keep the sarcastic tone from his voice. But to give up a career in law enforcement, a job that righted wrongs and fought for justice? He couldn't understand that.

"No, but as I worked through the difficulties of my loss of memory, including my run-in with the guys who were after me, I realized I'd been wanting a more relaxed and slower pace to my life. I was ready to settle down, spend time raising a family, eat pie." An easy smile stretched across his face.

It still wasn't anything Adam could understand, although he begrudgingly admitted to himself that he admired the peace Jed seemed to have. He was ready to move on to the next topic. "What about Katie? All she told me was that her brother is her only family left."

"That's probably about all you're going to get as far as information goes. I haven't known her long, but Sarah tells me Katie's husband was killed in an accident at the sawmill. It's been a struggle for her since, but we help as much as we can. And her brother has always been helpful, until just recently. The Amish take care of each other, especially families."

"Would she be helpful in the investigation?"

"The Amish don't like to mix with law enforcement. They keep to themselves as much as they can. Considering what the former sheriff was like, I can't say I blame them all the time." Jed shook his head and smiled. "I should say *we* keep to ourselves as much as possible. It's only been a few months since I joined the church, and it's going to take a while to get used to. With Katie, though, I think she honestly doesn't know anything about her brother. Just give her time. The Amish believe patience is a virtue."

Adam touched his weapon in its holster, his fingers rubbing on the smooth leather, and scanned the perimeter again. For too long he had been investigating a suspected ring of identity-document smugglers. Counterfeit passports and social security cards had been leaching out of the Chicago area and turning up all over the Midwest. Katie's brother had been missing in action for two months, there but not there, and now it seemed that someone was willing to shoot at Katie. Patience may be a virtue, but he didn't have time to wait. The sooner justice could be administered, the better.

Katie might be Amish but that didn't mean she was naive. She noticed things. A lot of things. Facial expressions. Unspoken words. Nearly imperceptible gestures. She had clearly seen Adam's skeptical look in her direction when he had stepped out to take his telephone call. His brown eyes had clouded with uncertainty. The man doubted her, and to some extent she could understand why.

Her own *bruder*, her only *bruder*, was a person of interest. What was that phrase? Guilt by association.

But she wasn't guilty. She was scared and doing her best to trust in the goodness and divine will of *Gott*.

Katie sipped her coffee and forced herself to make conversation, trying not to stare out the window. Eventually Adam returned, and although he didn't exactly smile at her, it seemed that his clouds of doubt had cleared. Perhaps whatever private conversation he had had with Jed had satisfied him.

He grabbed another cookie and bit off half. "Ready to go?"

"Jah." She hugged her twins tightly, cherishing the softness of their cheeks against hers, planting kisses on their foreheads, engraving their cherub faces in her mind's eye.

As she stood, Sarah gathered the twins to the folds of her skirt. Sarah's daughter, Lyddie, stood nearby, just a couple of years older and a *gut* friend to her girls. "It is only for tonight," Sarah reassured her. "Tomorrow you will be together again."

After Adam had checked the front yard, she hobbled back to his SUV and allowed him to help her in. Her leg was feeling better, but she still appreciated his assistance, as well as the cane he had whittled. After Katie waved one last goodbye through the window, the vehicle roared down the road.

With Adam's driving speed, it did not take long to reach home. Of course she had ridden in a vehicle, but Adam seemed to drive much faster than other drivers, with trees and bushes and homes whizzing past at a tremendous pace. As he pulled into her lane, she grasped the door handle to keep herself upright.

When he put the vehicle into Park, she turned to him. His eyes flashed in the dim interior of the vehicle, seeming to reflect the moonlight, and she forced her gaze toward her house and away from him. His handsomeness was not something upon which she should dwell. *"Danki,* Special Agent Troyer. I have much for which to thank you. Saving my life, whittling the cane, driving me home. You have protected me, and I am grateful."

He retrieved a business card from his wallet. "If your brother contacts you or you think of anything that might be helpful, can you get to a telephone and call me? Or if your leg does not heal well and you want to get to the hospital, call me and I'll come for you. Is there a phone nearby?"

Shadows played around his angular features when she glanced at him. "*Jah*, a couple of houses down the road." It would not do for her to find him handsome. There was nothing that could come of it. If she ever did remarry, it would be to an Amish man, not a brooding, weapon-carrying *Englischer*.

He simply nodded and hopped out of the vehicle, jogging around the front to offer her assistance. "I'll get your bicycle and then wait until you get inside and turn on a light."

"*Danki*. Just lean the bicycle against the porch railing." She stole one last glance at his strong profile. "Good night."

"Good night," he called over his shoulder as he parked the bicycle.

She opened the front door, stepped inside and closed the door behind her. By the light of the moon, she stepped toward the propane-powered lamp in the living room, running her hand along the top of the easy chair. If she had come in the back, there would have been a battery-powered lantern at the door. But she hadn't expected to be dropped off in a government agent's vehicle after dark.

On her third step, she paused, the skin on her arms rippling into goose bumps. Was someone else in the room? It didn't feel right somehow, and her heart slammed against her chest. Slowly she turned in a circle, peering into the darkness. The moonlight that had seemed so bright outside suddenly seemed extinguished within the house.

She spied a figure at the back door, and adrenaline spiked through her arteries, her fingers digging into the chair back. But it was only her winter cape hanging on a hook at the back door. Now that warm weather was here for the summer, she ought to store it away.

Her mind was playing tricks on her. That was all. She straightened her apron and inhaled deeply, then took the last few steps to the lamp. With her hand on the knob to regulate the propane, and her other hand reaching for the lighter, a voice hissed at her from the darkness.

"Katie, no."

As if acting independently, her hands jerked back from the lamp and clutched the bodice of her dress. She knew that voice.

A tall figure stepped out from its hiding place, pressed against an armoire near a particularly dark edge of the living room.

She gasped. "Timothy!" Dizziness threatened her, but she gulped air to fight it.

"Shh." He grasped her shoulders and pulled her into a tight hug. A moment later, he pulled away with a quick glance out the back window.

"I have been looking for you. Where have you been? Are you well? Are you in trouble?"

"I cannot stay." He pulled her hand toward him and pressed a folded piece of paper into her palm.

Instinctually she closed her fingers around it.

"Whatever you are involved in, turn yourself in before you are caught. I will help you."

"I am innocent. Whatever they tell you, believe that." He paused, the intensity of his gaze drilling into her. "What I do is for you. For the twins."

A car door sounded from outside, and Katie jerked her gaze toward the front window. Adam had been waiting for her to turn on the lamp. But Timothy's hands slid away, and with a few long-legged strides, he was at the back door. As if she were made of stone, Katie couldn't move. Should she run for Adam, tell him she was safe and that she had found Timothy? Or run for her *bruder*, her only family? Then, without a word, Timothy slipped away.

The corner of the folded paper poked into the flesh of her palm, and she unfolded it and scanned it quickly. It was simply a series of numbers. There was something familiar about the groupings of the numbers, but she couldn't quite put her finger on it. Whatever it was, it must be important, considering the clandestine method of conveyance.

There was no time to decipher it now. Adam knocked softly at the door. Her heart still pounding, Katie quickly refolded the note and tucked it up inside her prayer *kapp*. Right or wrong, there wasn't time now to examine her motives for keeping the secret a little longer, until she had opportunity to figure it out.

She opened the door, and Adam stepped in, scanning the living room. "Are you all right? You never turned on the light." Then his eyes seemed to stop at the open back door.

"I am fine." She swallowed hard. "But *mein bruder* was here. He is gone now. Out the back." As she spoke, she spied a figure running through the side yard and into the adjoining cornfield.

"Stay here. Light the lamp. Lock the doors." And Adam was gone, running through the back door and after the figure in the cornfield.

Katie pressed a hand to her chest as if that could slow her heart rate to normal. At least she had seen her *bruder*, and he had appeared to be well. But what was going on?

At the back door, she grasped the knob to close and lock it, when a man appeared in the shadowed doorway. Forcing down her surprise, she opened the door farther. "*Danki* for returning, Timothy. It will be better for you if you come forward."

But as the man stepped through the doorway and out of the shadow, she saw he wasn't Timothy. This man was taller, bigger, with an unkempt beard and a look of malice in his eyes. A scream stuck somewhere in her throat, and she turned to run for the front. That door was still unlocked. It would be her escape.

But as she turned, the man grabbed her from behind, pinning her arms to her sides. "It's not Timothy." His whisper blew sour breath in her ear. "But I know he was here."

Katie squeezed her eyes shut, as if that would block out his horrible threats of how he would harm her if she didn't tell him everything that had just happened. "How did you know we were at the cabin? Did he give you anything? Where did he go?" The man's hands slid into her apron pockets but came out empty. She pictured the folded piece of paper tucked securely in her *kapp* but immediately forced it from her mind. She didn't fight back, but she certainly wasn't obligated to tell him anything.

He pushed her farther into the house, kicking the door shut behind him.

Herr Gott, help me! The pain from the bullet wound seized her leg, and she stumbled. He cursed her, and she longed to cover her ears. But he held her arms tightly.

Over the sound of his raspy breathing, she heard the door open again and tossed up a quick prayer that her attacker hadn't heard it. But as quickly as she could utter the words, he let her go and turned toward the sound. Adam rushed the man, barreling straight at him. Together, they fell into a wooden chair. The sound of splintering wood filled the room, along with the struggle of the two men.

Alarm filled Katie. She grasped one hand in the other in a vain attempt to stop her trembling. What could she do to stop this? To restore order to her simple world? But her mind could barely comprehend the fighting in her home, let alone figure out a way to stop it.

With a punch to the attacker's jaw, Adam subdued the man. Adam jumped up from the floor and drew his weapon, pointing it at the intruder. "Up. On your feet." Adam's voice held an austerity that Katie hadn't heard before. "Now, let's get some answers."

The man slowly stood, his hands on his knees as he pushed himself upright. As he straightened, he jerked to the side and grabbed a kitchen chair with both hands. In an instant, the chair was airborne and flying toward Katie.

The room seemed to stand still for a split second,

the chair suspended in midair as it hurtled toward her. All breathing stopped. Could this really be happening?

Then all was moving again. She lunged to the right to dodge the chair, placing her weight squarely on her injured leg. Overwhelming pain shot through her body. Her leg collapsed underneath her. As she fell, she glimpsed the two men struggling over the gun, her attacker with his hands on the weapon and turning it to point at Adam.

Her head hit the floor as she heard the gun go off. A moment later, darkness swallowed her.

Chapter Four

Katie! Adam's heart and mind screamed. But as his consciousness absorbed the fact that his opponent's gun had discharged, the only sound he emitted was a grunt as he lunged for his attacker.

The gun had gone off, but was he shot? No zing or ache of injury threatened him. Of course adrenaline would mask it for now, especially as he barreled toward the man in the dark. With a thud, he had the man pinned to the wall. The only thing he would notice now would be a gaping hole in his chest. He would check better later.

The man tried to kick him, but Adam twisted to the side, keeping the man's shoulders pressed against the wall. "Who are you?" He managed to utter the single question through teeth clenched with physical effort.

The man remained completely silent, his eyes burning with fury. His only response was, with apparent great effort, to push Adam's arm back. He brought the gun up to point at Adam's midsection.

No way. Not on my watch. In his peripheral vision, Adam saw Katie begin to move on the floor, a low

moan issuing from her. He longed to check on her, see
that she would be all right, but if he let her attacker
go, it most likely wouldn't end well for either Adam
or Katie.

Doubling his efforts with what felt like the last of
his strength, Adam brought up his knee to kick the
man's gun hand. He missed, and his attacker thrust
the weapon into Adam's ribs. Pain pierced his side.
Doesn't this guy ever get tired?

Adam tried to study the man's features to be able
to identify him later, but his vision was clouded with
pain and the moonlight wasn't bright enough. With
a quick twist, Adam released his grip on the man's
shoulders and spun to grab for the gun. But the man
moved, and the weapon flew from his hand and skittered across the floor, toward the kitchen table and the
remaining chairs.

With a growl, the man dove for the gun as he thrust
his hand backward. He made contact with Adam's
shoulder. Adam staggered but quickly recovered his
balance. He also charged toward the attacker and his
weapon, dodging his legs and shoes. If he could get
this guy, then Katie's difficulty, her brother's problem
and perhaps even the entire investigation could be done
and over. Case solved.

But Adam was a few seconds too slow. Instead of
stopping the lowlife, he only got the heel of the man's
shoe pressed against his cheekbone. The man scooped
up his gun but fumbled it, and the weapon slid away.
A split second later, he grabbed another chair from the
kitchen table and swung it low toward Adam. Adam
ducked, only to see him release the chair and let it fly
in Katie's direction.

Even as his mind registered that it was merely a distraction technique, Adam's body sprang toward the chair in an effort to catch or stop it before it hit Katie. The man's aim was high, though, and the chair sailed over Katie's head. An instant later, the chair crashed into the armoire, heralded by the sound of fracturing wood. Splinters from the chair rained down on Katie. The armoire wobbled upon impact, toppling dangerously forward.

Katie lay right in its path.

Adam rushed forward as it began to fall and caught it on his back and shoulders. Pain cut through his upper body, but he held steady. His teeth ground together as he pushed back against the piece of furniture, maneuvering it back to its place against the wall. Katie fluttered her eyes open, a look of terror seizing her as she realized her situation. With pain etched across her face and her jaw set in a grim line, she dragged herself away from the armoire. Once the cabinet stood upright again, Adam ran to the open back door. Their attacker was just disappearing into the cornfield and out of Adam's line of sight.

Adam drew a long, deep breath, forcing his pulse to slow and his nerves to steady with the inhale of oxygen. He closed the door and locked it with both the knob lock and the dead bolt. If the man was running away, he probably wouldn't be back right away. For the very immediate future, at least, he could see to Katie's injury.

It only took a moment to cross the kitchen and the sitting room, dropping to his knees and sliding the last few inches on the wood floor. He grabbed a pillow off the couch and tucked it under her head. Her alertness at the danger of the armoire had been temporary, and she had quickly slid back into unconsciousness.

Now he rubbed her upper arms. "Katie? Wake up. You're all right now."

She tossed her head to the right and then to the left with a moan.

Adam pulled a strand of hair off her cheek, trying not to notice the softness of her skin. "Katie? Come on."

"Mmm?" A raspy cough worked its way out. Her eyes opened again and then immediately widened as she seemed to realize that she was on the floor, with Adam hovering over her. "Is he gone?"

"Yes. For now." He held out his arm.

She pulled herself to a sitting position. "My leg hurts. Again."

"It's bleeding a bit. Can you get to the armchair if I help you?"

"*Jah.* I will try." She lifted herself with the help of his arm, and he gently pulled her into the easy chair. She scooted to lean against the back and breathed a sign of a relief. "*Danki.* Please forgive my complaining about the discomfort."

"What complaining? Your previous injury has been aggravated. You're only human." Fresh blood had appeared on her skirt. "Can we take a look? I think the wound is seeping again."

He looked at the lamp next to the chair. "How do I light this thing?"

She pointed toward a lever on the outside of the lamp. "Turn that lever there. That turns on the propane. There is a lighter in the drawer below. Just light the mantle."

With the lamp lit, she found the tear on her skirt and pulled it open to reveal the bandage the paramedic had applied. A fresh redness saturated the edge of the gauze. "Perhaps just a new bandage and some aspirin?"

"That would probably do it. Then we'll just keep an eye on it. Do you have a first-aid kit?" He turned toward the kitchen, waiting for her instructions.

"Look in the cupboard under the second sink, the one for washing up near the back door."

"Second sink?" He detoured to the back porch area.

"*Jah.* It is what we call the sink and counter area right close to the back inside porch. It is where we wash hands and faces after working in the garden or the barn, but before coming into the house properly. It is also the place for tending to wounds, but it will be easier if you bring the items to me. Look for a blue tackle box. It is filled with medical supplies."

He quickly found the box in the lower cabinet and brought it back to her, setting it on the chair's side table and opening it for her. He lifted out the top trays to reveal stacks of bandages, ointments, tweezers, rubbing alcohol, cough drops and a thermometer. "You have nearly an entire drugstore in here."

She sighed but smiled at him. "*Nein.* Not quite."

But his teasing had the desired effect. At least momentarily, her mood had lifted and her mind had been elsewhere. Right now she didn't need to focus on the danger that waited outside the house. She only needed to redo the bandaging and feel better.

She twisted to reach the tackle box of medical supplies but quickly sat back in the chair with a grimace. "I cannot sit that box on my lap, not with the discomfort of the injury. Could you find the gauze and the medical tape, please? *Danki.*"

With the proper supplies at hand, Katie quickly replaced the bandaging. "The bleeding has stopped. I think it will be fine, in time."

"That's good. No need for an ambulance?"

She grinned, but it was tinged with a touch of discomfort. "*Nein.* Not this time."

As she returned the supplies to their appointed slots, Adam dialed the sheriff and told him of the attack. He said he would dispatch a deputy and be there himself in a few minutes.

Adam put the tackle box back in the cabinet. "I hate to have to ask you to remember him, but did you recognize the man who attacked you?"

"*Nein*, I have never seen him before."

"I've been investigating for several months, and I don't think I'm any closer to the truth than I was when I started, except that I know there is smuggling of identity documents through Northern Indiana and now we have the counterfeit social security card you found. But a good smuggling ring usually takes several people to operate smoothly. And this ring is good."

"*Gott* reveals truth in His timing and when it suits His purposes."

God? She had just been attacked by a violent man, and she was talking of God's purposes? Her calmness in the face of danger floored him. But the memory of his Amish grandparents and their peacefulness struck him, sending goose bumps along his arms. Their steadfast trust in God and the calm that it brought to their lives and their home was something he hadn't fully appreciated as a child. Now, though? Now he could use an extra portion of peace and calm.

Katie's leg throbbed, but she refused to give in to complaining or grumbling. That bad attitude hadn't worked well for the Israelites wandering in the wilderness for forty years, and she was determined to learn from their mistakes. Still, though, a little painkiller would help.

She pushed herself to the edge of the chair, her palms on the armrests, prepared to push herself up. The acetaminophen was in a kitchen cabinet, and as kind as the ICE agent had been, she didn't want to ask him for anything more. But before she could push herself to standing, he was there, holding out his arm to steady her and help lift her up.

"Going somewhere?" He smiled down at her, crinkles around his light brown eyes, the flecks of gold glittering in the lamplight.

But the smile didn't quite reach to his whole face. He was trying to cheer her up, to get her to forget about the danger, to not be scared. Warmth seeped through her at his thoughtfulness, but it was tinged with the chill of fright at who might be lurking outside her door.

"*Jah*, to the kitchen. *Mein* acetaminophen are in a cupboard, and I will make us some tea. Chamomile is soothing, which helps with anxiety. And it is anti-inflammatory, which helps with injuries, as well as aches and pains." And with the tea, she would retrieve her brother's note out of her *kapp* and show it to the special agent.

"Then make us a gallon." He grinned as she reached for his arm.

With his help on one side and the cane on the other, she made it to the kitchen. There she released his arm, and he moved to straighten the kitchen table and remaining chairs. She rummaged around in the end cabinet, moving aside various odds and ends before producing a small bottle. One step to the side brought her to the sink, where she filled a glass with water. As she popped two tablets in her mouth and swallowed, she caught Adam's surprised expression.

"What is it?"

"I have never seen my grandparents take pain pills or even vitamins or any kind of supplement. Granted it's been a while since I've seen them. And they were—are—very conservative, even for being Amish. I just didn't think Amish took any kind of medication."

"Your grandparents are Amish?" That was an interesting bit of information she would tuck away to examine later. A thousand thoughts pinged in her mind, but her throbbing leg overrode them.

"Yes."

Katie put her glass on the counter and reached for the kettle. "*Jah*, some church districts are so conservative that they do not call the doctor. I am grateful that our district is not like that. If *Gott* has been so *gut* as to allow us to discover a way to relieve physical pain, then I am thankful." She held the bottle out for him to peek inside the almost-full container. "I do not take it often, as you can see. But I have it just in case."

She returned the bottle to the cabinet and then filled the kettle. *Jah*, she sought normalcy and comfort in the routine of making chamomile tea, her favorite. But it would take a lot more than tea for her to feel the least bit normal again. Her hands began to shake at the thought of an intruder in her home, a man who attacked both her and Adam, the agent who was spending his evening protecting her.

Gott, help me! Help mein bruder! A tear strayed down her cheek, but she quickly dashed at it with the back of her hand before Adam could see it.

The tea was put on hold, though, with the arrival of the sheriff and a deputy. As Adam stayed with her, the two men searched her yard and the surrounding area. Sheriff Moore examined the living room and kitchen while the deputy took her statement and Adam called his supervising agent.

"I wish we had more information, ma'am, but your attacker didn't leave anything to go on." The sheriff held his hat in his hands. "My deputy is on duty through the night, and I'll have him drive by and walk around the yard several times, to keep an eye on you."

"*Danki*, Sheriff. I appreciate it."

"I'll stay, as well," Adam said, "in my SUV out front and patrol the perimeter every hour or so."

The sheriff put his hand on her arm with the warmth of a father. "Try to get some rest." He turned to Adam on his way out the door, his deputy following. "Call me if you need me."

Adam walked them to the door, locking it behind them. The headlights of the sheriff's vehicle flashed through the window as he turned onto the road.

"Now, why don't you sit down and let me make the tea? I might need some instructions, but you need to rest."

"*Nein.*" She limped to the propane stove and put the kettle on, ignoring the ache in her leg. The acetaminophen needed to do its work soon or she would be forced to sit down. "I do not want this injury and attack to slow me down or defeat me. *Gott* is good, and He will help me." Without moving her feet, she reached to the cupboard to retrieve two mugs. "See? If I just bend and twist enough, I can get it done."

Ten minutes later, she set two steaming mugs of chamomile tea on the table, along with a tin of sugar cookies. As Adam bit into his cookie, she retrieved the coded note from her prayer *kapp* and unfolded it on the table. She wasn't sure, even now, that she wanted to show him the piece of paper. She certainly had not been comfortable showing the sheriff and his deputy. The Amish separation from the world and the community's distrust of law enforcement had been taught and modeled through all her life. But surely her *bruder* had had a purpose in risking his life to give it to her. What did he want her to do with it? Right now the most she could manage was to trust this man who had saved her life.

His eyes widened as a myriad of emotions played across his face. He quickly finished his bite. "Where did you get that?"

"From *mein bruder*. He did not explain anything. Just pressed it into my hand before he ran out."

Adam leaned over the paper, examining it as he chewed another cookie. "The numbers seem to be grouped into threes. Is it a secret message? A code of some kind? Is he trying to tell you something without being discovered by someone?"

Katie sipped her tea. Perhaps the chamomile would calm the erratic thumping of her heart. After months of no communication with her *bruder*, he reappeared and gave her this. It must have some meaning, and hope in a restored relationship blossomed within her chest before she could tamp it down. "*Jah*, I think so. I hope so."

"It's meaningless, though, until it's deciphered. What is the code?"

"*Ach*, I do not remember. I have been so tossed around today that I cannot think straight. *Mein bruder* was always secretive, always coming up with different ways to communicate so no one else could understand, always reading about spies and their secret codes." After the day she had had, she could puzzle over it all night and probably not have an answer in the morning.

"Of course." He sipped his tea as he continued to examine the paper. "I'll have the agency's cryptographers take a look at it tomorrow. Right now, let me get a digital copy." He retrieved his phone from his pocket and took a picture of the piece of paper, then tapped a few more buttons on the phone. "It's on its way. I'll get the local guys on it as well, first thing in the morning. If it's meaningful, we need to know sooner rather than later."

She nodded and examined the note again. *What are you trying to say, Timothy?* Of course the law enforcement officers were intelligent. But her brother was also pretty bright. If they could decode the secret message, she would be impressed.

"What else can you tell me about Timothy? The more I know about him, the more information I have to figure this out."

And get me out of harm's way... He didn't say it, but by the way his voice trailed off, she knew that's what he meant.

"All I know is what I saw and what he said more than two months ago. It seemed he had changed some of his business practices, like using a different supplier for some of the hardware for his woodworking business. I saw a company name on a box, a company that the Amish do not usually do business with. One time I stopped by his workshop and saw a different man there with him. Timothy explained that the man was a new hire, but the man was not Amish. He was dressed in Amish clothes, and he had a beard like Amish men that covered his face. But he was wearing a baseball cap, pulled down low over an *Englisch* haircut. I tried to greet him, but he hurried away to the back of the workshop. *Mein bruder* was quick—too quick—to explain that his new hire worked best alone and was a little shy of strangers."

"Did you get his name?" Adam stood to pull back the window shade slightly and peer outside. Seemingly satisfied, he sat again and selected another cookie from the tin.

"*Nein.* Now that I think on it, Timothy was rather hesitant to tell me anything at all. He spoke in that slow way he gets when he is trying to think what to say as he is talking." She sipped her tea, that day and that meeting fresh in her mind. Her brother had seemed odd then, but it had never occurred to her that something was *this* wrong. If she had persisted then in finding the truth, could all of this danger and these attacks and the shooting have been avoided?

"Do you think he was lying?"

That very word, *lying*, made Katie sad, a bit of grief pinging in her midsection, but perhaps he had been. Still, she couldn't tolerate the idea. "We are taught not to lie from the time we are small children. Lying is a sin."

"Perhaps he feels so threatened that he thinks he must lie. He believes he has no other choice."

"*Ach*, I cannot imagine that much danger." With her hands hidden in her lap, though, she wrung them together. Was Timothy's situation that bad? Most likely so, judging by the attacks she had suffered that very afternoon and night. Adam just didn't want to scare her.

She appreciated the carefulness of the agent sitting across the table from her, but she could see the facts, as well. Her brother just didn't come around anymore like he used to. He hadn't attended church services in more than a month. He always had some excuse like illness, which she would see in a note he would leave for her now and then. Was he distancing himself deliberately from their Amish ways? It seemed as if he wanted nothing to do with her, but he was feeding her just enough information to make everything look normal so she wouldn't question him or examine the situation any further.

Sleepiness began to overtake her, and she wrapped her hands around the warm mug. A glance at the clock on the wall revealed the lateness of the hour.

"You need to rest." Apparently Adam had noticed her fatigue, as well.

"*Jah*, and wash and put on clean clothes." A fresh change of garments always made her feel better. It was too bad that she couldn't change her emotions as easily, from fear and trembling to confidence and calm. "What about the intruder? Will he come back?"

"The deputy will drive by, remember, and walk the yard. And I'll be here, in my SUV out front and patrolling the perimeter every hour or so. Will that help you rest?"

The generosity and thoughtfulness of this *Englischer* surprised her. He would give up his sleep so that she could sleep? "*Danki.* And I will try to think some more on the secret code."

"We'll tackle that in the morning, at the sheriff's office."

But as she rinsed the mugs and put them in the sink, she couldn't help but wonder if they would even survive the night.

Chapter Five

Adam had pulled all-nighters before, but usually with several cups of coffee. Why hadn't he asked Katie to fill a thermos before she had turned in for the night and he had retreated to his SUV? He rubbed his eyes and walked the perimeter of the yard again as the sun rose, stopping to peer through the trees at a scampering noise that turned out to be a chipmunk. Despite his sleepiness, at least they were still safe, thanks in part to the vigilance of the deputy through the night. Perhaps Katie's relief at getting some much-needed rest would override any upset that he had worn a path in her yard.

An hour later, he had had two cups of coffee and a helping of scrapple, a delicious Amish pork breakfast dish that summoned up pleasant childhood memories of his Amish grandparents. Two hours later, he was in the driver's seat of his Tahoe, speeding back toward Jed and Sarah's house so that Katie could check in on her twins. He hadn't been sure it was a good idea to drop in, but the desperation of a mother to hug her children was difficult to reason with.

"*Danki* for returning to Sarah's house. The sher-

iff's office is not a place for children, is it? I will ask
Sarah to keep Ruth and Rebekah a while longer." Katie's lilting voice filled the SUV as Adam checked all
the mirrors.

So far, on this road, he hadn't seen a single vehicle.
"Yeah, that would be best. We need to concentrate on
deciphering the secret message. And they would be safe
with Jed and Sarah." He didn't add that they would be
more safe there than with them, but Katie could probably guess the unsaid words.

She nodded and held her breath, as if she were afraid
to say something.

He glanced at her profile as she stared out the windshield, biting her lip. If she knew something, he needed
to know also. This was no time to be scared to speak.
"Something on your mind?"

She exhaled and rotated toward him. "I was so tired
last night, and overwhelmed by what all happened, that
I was dozing off before I could ask you. With all the
physical activity of yesterday—bicycling, running, getting injured—as well as the mental exhaustion of puzzling over *mein bruder*, all the police and then leaving
my twins, I was worn out."

"Are you feeling better now?"

"*Jah*, I am. My leg aches a little, but it will heal."

"What did you want to ask?" Or did he not want to
know? It sounded personal, and he'd guarded his private life and his background so much in his job as an
ICE special agent that he wasn't good at talking about
anything except his work. Yet this beautiful Amish
woman was so much more sincere and honest about
herself than anyone he'd ever met that the prompting
came out before he knew what he was saying.

"It is about your last name, Troyer. It has been puzzling me since that moment outside the cabin yesterday, when you introduced yourself. I know there are many who have names that were originally Amish even though the person is not Amish, but you said something about your grandparents. What is the connection?"

Adam glanced in the rearview mirror and scrubbed a hand over his face. She was clearly just curious, but he wished he didn't have to talk about it. His family history was not one he was proud of. Yet one look at Katie and her wide blue eyes, and he knew he would answer anything she asked.

He shifted in his seat and hitched his grip on the steering wheel. That wasn't a good position for a special agent—to be ready to tell all. He hadn't known her long, but something about her wholesomeness and innocence had seeped into him, acting like a truth serum on his hardened outer shell. He liked to do his job and focus on that—seeking justice—not his painful past.

Apparently he had been silent too long, for she broke his contemplation with another question. "Should I not have asked?"

His throat seized, and he cleared it, then grabbed the bottle of water that rested in the console. Perhaps if he shared his past, explained that they did have some common Amish ground, it might help Katie to remember whatever she needed to decipher the coded message from her brother.

"No, no, it's fine." He gulped again from the water bottle and then returned it to the cupholder. "My grandparents were Amish, so I inherited the name through my father."

"*Ach*, I do remember now that you said that last

night. Maybe I know them. Do they live nearby?" A smile lit her face.

"No, they're several communities away, closer to the Michigan state line."

"Do you see them often?"

The Tahoe crested a small hill, and Adam slowed to pass a horse and buggy. "My job keeps me too busy." It was a weak excuse, but it was all he could offer at the moment. "I remember just a few visits to my grandparents in all of my childhood years. I think my father took my brother and me to visit because he felt guilty about leaving before his baptism and his complete rejection of the Amish faith. But then, after a visit..." Did he have to finish the sentence and tell her about the despicable behavior of his father? How he had longed, over the years, for more of the love and encouragement of his grandparents.

She placed her hand on his arm, her touch gentle and reassuring. "Why did he leave the church?"

"His running-around time."

"*Rumspringa?* What happened?"

"He got in with the wrong crowd. Started drinking. It took him over. In his addiction, though, he was still functioning. Got married. Had me and my brother. But we were never a real family. We were what the shrinks like to call dysfunctional. Eventually my parents divorced. My mom disappeared. She had had enough, I guess, and I never heard from her again. Then both my dad and my brother were killed in a car accident while my dad was driving drunk." He was unwilling to admit that he had struggled with alcohol, as well. He had overcome it, but the guilt of his poor choices still hung heavily on him. How could God love him, a sinner?

She bit her lip and looked out the window. "I am sorry, Adam. Alcohol is a powerful evil."

Her sympathy warmed him in a way no one else's had. Perhaps it was the sincerity she exuded. Jed and Sarah's house came into view, and he instinctually checked his mirrors to see if anyone was around. All was clear as he pulled into the drive. Before he turned off the SUV, he rotated to her. "My dad wasted his life, but I'm determined not to waste mine. That's why I'm with ICE. I want to do something significant. Something productive and helpful." He turned the key and opened his door. "Are you ready to crack that code and get this case solved?"

A surprised and somewhat sorrowful look crossed her face, but with a visual scan of the property, he hopped out of the Tahoe and hurried to her side, helping her down without making eye contact. Why was he sharing so much of his past? This was just a case. Besides, how would acknowledging his Amish roots improve his life? How could one man working a field, or doing whatever it is Amish men do to earn a living, improve the world? The Amish were hiding from the world, and Adam Troyer did not hide from anyone or anything.

Katie's twins burst from the front door, one of them sporting an adorable milk mustache. They must have arrived in the middle of breakfast. Katie hugged both daughters as one told her mother about the other hogging the bed last night. "*Ach, mein liebchen, Gott*'s Word tells us not to complain." But a large smile stretched across her face, and she hugged her twins closer.

"Go on inside, Katie, and I'll be in in a minute." He withdrew his phone from his pocket. It was time to check in again with his supervisory special agent.

A moment later, the door closed on Katie and the twins as his supervisor answered his call. Adam quickly told him of their safety through the night.

"And you think the Amish woman will be helpful?" His supervisor's voice seemed loud in his ear compared to the quiet of the country morning.

"Definitely. Her only brother is involved, so she's invested."

"Well, keep her safe at all costs, until that message is decoded and she is no longer in danger. We can't let an innocent Amish woman be harmed. That's not the way the agency operates."

"Of course, sir." Adam peered around the yard.

"What about taking her out of the Amish area? Hide her somewhere?"

"I think she's an important part of decoding this message first, sir. And wouldn't she be more conspicuous in her Amish clothing outside the community?"

"Have her change. Buy her some jeans and a sweatshirt."

"It isn't that simple." What he knew of the Amish from his grandparents rose strong in his mind. "A faithful Amish believer would never put on worldly clothes. She has already mentioned trusting God with her safety."

"Okay, fine. She does seem to be an important part of this case. But do whatever you need to do to keep the two of you safe."

Adam pocketed his phone and headed inside with one last examination of the area. The aroma of freshly brewed coffee assaulted him, and at Sarah's urging, he accepted a second breakfast, consisting of a sticky bun and a mug of coffee, his third cup already that morning.

"Is everything all right with your supervisor?"

He took a sip of his coffee. "I've been tasked with keeping you safe until this can all be resolved. We don't want any more attacks like yesterday. And we have agents examining the card you found, as well as the message from your brother. Those pieces of information could be helpful in ICE's search for the document smugglers." Somehow his words came out more briskly than he had intended. It wouldn't be a burden at all to protect this pretty Amish woman. Adam tried to soften his tone as he added, "If you'll have me." Not that she had much of a choice.

Katie nodded, a somber expression on her face.

As he bit into the bun, Sarah seemed to size him up. "I think Jed's clothes would fit you."

Had he missed something? "Why?"

Sarah stacked a couple of plates and carried them to the sink. "I was remembering the time Jed wore Amish clothes because his were torn, and it helped him not be recognized because he looked Amish."

Katie wiped off one of the twins' mouths with a wet cloth. "*Jah*, that is a *gut* idea. You could disguise yourself by wearing Jed's Amish clothes."

Wear Amish clothes? Wasn't this going backwards? He would look like his grandfather. "What about driving my SUV? Yesterday, at the cabin, I had hidden the Tahoe down the road. It was unlikely anyone saw it. And, obviously, I might be more noticeable if I look

like an Amish man but I'm driving an automobile."
Were they serious about this?

"You could just remove the hat when you are driving. Then you would look *Englisch* with your *Englisch* haircut and clean-shaven face." Katie tilted her head and looked at him as if she were studying his haircut and facial hair.

Under her gaze, suddenly the idea didn't seem so crazy. "I suppose I could still carry my weapon. I have a holster that fits at the small of my back. And for as long as I'm here, in the Amish clothes, I would be perceived differently by the non-Amish, so that might give me an advantage in a pinch. An *Englisher*, as you call them, wouldn't be as careful with information around an Amish man they think is just going about his business." If dressing Amish would allow him to move around the community incognito, then that could only help to keep Katie safe and catch the smugglers. "It would also help disguise you, wouldn't it? Would you be more noticeable if you were seen with an *Englisher*?"

"*Jah.* Definitely."

Before he changed, he dug the little whittled squirrels out of his pants pocket. As he presented one to each of Katie's twins, their eyes widened with wonder at the tiny wooden creatures. *"Danki,"* they murmured in unison.

It didn't take long to don the Amish clothing, the dark trousers and blue shirt, although the suspenders would take some getting used to. As he buttoned the shirt, he remembered his grandmother explaining that the straight pins a woman used wouldn't be practical for a man's shirt. The twins, Ruth and Rebekah, gawked at him, probably unaccustomed to seeing a man in Amish clothing without the bowl-style haircut. Katie said her goodbyes to her children, looking uncertain about when she might see them again, and soon they were speeding toward the sheriff's offices.

The one-story redbrick building that housed the local law enforcement sat in a remote and quiet corner of Nappanee. For that, Adam was grateful. He would have enough trouble explaining his Amish dress to the sheriff without encountering citizens on the street.

But inside, the Sheriff greeted him with an offer of coffee or tea and expressed approval of his disguise—his blue shirt, broadfall trousers, suspenders and straw broad-brimmed hat. Adam brought him up to date on the prior evening's events, and when he saw the coded message, he picked up his phone to summon a deputy.

A uniformed officer with thick glasses and an even thicker mustache appeared in the doorway before Adam could sip his fourth cup of coffee for that morning.

"This here is Deputy Cravens," Sheriff Moore said. "He's had extensive training in ciphers. Let's see what he can do."

Adam shook his hand and introduced Katie. "Glad to have help."

The deputy opened his laptop, and as it booted up, he examined the note. "As you probably know, Agent Troyer, a cipher, to operate correctly, usually depends on a key. A key could be anything. It's just a piece of supporting information that is needed to unlock the code. But the cipher cannot be decoded without knowledge of that key."

"So we find the key, we break the code." Adam knew all this.

"Right. But there's no telling how detailed the key could be. And without the key, we will not be able to decrypt the cipher."

The deputy peered at the screen of his laptop and pecked at the keys. "I'm going to enter a few of these numbers into my cipher program, and we'll see what happens."

The only noise in the room was the inner whirring of the computer. Katie looked down at her hands in her lap, seemingly uninterested in the deputy's technology.

"Nothing. The program isn't putting together anything that makes sense." The deputy looked at the note again. "Let me try a few other combinations of the numbers."

But even after several more attempts, the computer hadn't solved anything.

Deputy Cravens stood and walked around the room, as if thinking. "What do we know about the person who wrote this message? Sometimes knowledge of the person who wrote the message can help figure out the key, especially if it's something personal."

Katie leaned forward and studied her brother's note again, her eyebrows creasing. "When you use the word *key*, could that be a book?"

"Definitely. A book cipher is actually brilliant because both the person writing the message in code and the person reading it need the same book. And since it's a regular book, neither look suspicious." Deputy Cravens pointed to the numbers on the slip of paper. "See how these numbers are in groups of three? They could point to a specific word in the book. Then the first would be the page number, the second would be the line number and the third would be that number word in that line."

"And eventually, with all the words, you have the message." Adam watched Katie finger the paper, a myriad of emotions in her expression.

She held her breath as she turned the paper over and ran her finger over a few letters printed on the back side, near the torn edge.

He leaned toward her, the hair on his arms standing at attention with anticipation. "What is it? You're remembering or realizing something." It was a statement, not a question. He could tell that she had figured it out. "You know how to crack the code."

It really was true. It was that simple. Her brother had used their old method of sending secret messages. All those years ago, when they were scratching pencils on paper in the dark of the night, hiding under the covers of their respective beds with a flashlight, so as not to be discovered by *Daed* or *Mamm*, she never imagined their secret code would be used in such a dangerous situation.

She took a deep breath to steady her hands. "*Jah*, it is a book code, as you call it."

"What book?" The deputy had moved to the edge of his seat, but Adam held out a hand to shush him.

With her finger, she pointed to five letters printed on the back side. The rest were missing because the paper was torn. "These are the last five letters of the name of a publisher of the *Ausbund*. That is the hymnal that all Amish use. My brother must have torn this piece of paper out of a copy of the *Ausbund* and used the hymnal as the book key."

"That makes sense." Adam touched her forearm, a gesture that calmed her. Sitting in the sheriff's office with two men in uniforms was not an everyday occurrence for her, and her nerves had been on edge ever since being in the woods the day before.

The sheriff pierced her with his stare. "And you and your brother have communicated like this before?"

"*Jah.* When we were children. A long time ago. It was just for fun."

"But why would a little girl know the name of the publishers of the hymnal?"

Katie shifted under his scrutiny. "I was bored sitting through three hours of sermons every other Sunday. *Mamm* would make dolls out of her handkerchief and do her best to entertain me, but there were still moments of overwhelming boredom. So I read the hymnal from cover to cover. Every single page, over and over."

Sheriff Moore leaned back in his chair, apparently satisfied that she knew which book was the key. "So, what words do all these numbers correspond to?"

She tucked a stray piece of hair back inside her prayer *kapp* as she reminded herself to be respectful of his authority. "I do not know. That was a long time ago." She added in a lower tone, "I do not recall ever knowing exactly what words fell on which page."

"That's a great breakthrough." Adam leaned back as if to relax the others and reduce the tension between the Sheriff and Katie. "Let's run back to your house and get one. We can get this solved and get you safe."

"It is not that simple, unfortunately. Amish households do not typically have hymnals on their shelves, at least not the hymnal we use for service. The hymnals stay with the benches and are delivered to the house that will host church."

Deputy Cravens leaned toward Katie, his forehead wrinkled with confusion. "Benches delivered to a house?"

"*Jah*. We do not have church buildings. We worship in each other's homes or barns. But no one has enough seating for the entire congregation, so there are benches that the bishop keeps. On the Saturday before a church Sunday, he delivers the benches and the hymnals to the home wherever church will be."

"So, you don't have a copy of this *Ausbund* at your house?"

"*Nein*."

"What about a friend?"

"*Nein*."

Adam held up a hand. "Okay, Deputy, she doesn't have one." He stared at the floor for a moment, then looked back at Deputy Cravens. "Let's get online. Everything is online, right? Bring up Google and search the text of the *Ausbund*." He flashed a smile at Katie, but it looked insincere. Nervous, even. "How do you spell it?"

"A-U-S-B-U-N-D."

As the deputy tapped on the computer, Katie picked at a fingernail, eventually forcing herself to stop by placing her hands under her white starched apron. If Adam was nervous, then she didn't have the slightest idea how to handle her emotions. She didn't know much about being online, although she had seen a little from *Englisch* acquaintances at the market and the other patrons at the public library. But why would anything Amish be online? That seemed to fly in the face of what the Amish were really all about.

Adam continued giving instructions as the deputy stared at his screen, scrolling and clicking on his mouse. "If we have to pay for a pdf download, fine. I'll give you my credit card number to charge it." He stood and crossed the room, joining the sheriff to look over the deputy's shoulder.

Several minutes passed in relative silence, broken only by the click of the mouse or a question of *What about that?*

"There's nothing here." The deputy exhaled noisily. "I can keep looking, but I don't know where else to look. There's some history about the Amish. A slew of bloggers and websites with photos and information about how the Amish live. But there is no full text of the *Ausbund* available online."

The sheriff ran a hand through his graying hair. "Seriously?"

Adam just chuckled and returned to his seat. "Well, they are Amish. No technology." He scrubbed a hand over his chin and looked at Katie. "What else can you tell us about the hymnal?"

"It dates back to the 1500s, and it is written in Pennsylvania German."

"German?" The sheriff frowned. "Well, this just keeps getting better and better."

Katie stiffened at his comment but said nothing. She had not written the book. It wasn't her doing. And she had not written the message either. She was trying to help them as best she knew how. "It is our language." It was the only comment she could muster.

Adam looked at her with kindness radiating from

his rich brown eyes. At least she had one ally in the room. "That means then, gentlemen, that the book key must be in German. An English translation wouldn't have the same words in the same order for the book code to decipher the message properly. Deputy, try an online-bookseller's site. Perhaps we can get an ebook version or order an original."

A few clicks later, the deputy had more bad news. "I see two versions available, neither for ebook. Both are used. One is temporarily out of stock, with no notice for when it might be available. The other is over one hundred dollars and would take five days to arrive by mail."

"Five days? We can't wait that long. Is there a way to contact the seller and expedite shipping?"

"No."

Katie summoned her courage and cleared her throat, shrinking slightly back into her chair when the three law enforcement officers all turned to look at her. Law enforcement had not always been kind to the Amish, but she was stuck now. There was no way out except to help find a copy of the *Ausbund*. "*Mein bruder* and I had access to the hymnal when we were children because our father was the bishop. But when *mein daed* died, another bishop was appointed. All the hymnals were passed on to him. *Mein bruder* probably thinks I have an old copy at home. The church purchased new hymnals a few years ago, and those would be a different version."

"Why couldn't your brother have just written English words on the piece of paper?" the deputy asked. "It would be so much easier."

"And so much more dangerous for him if he was

caught," Adam replied. "So, where do we get a hymnal?"

"We could check the Amish bookstore. That would be faster than ordering through your computer and waiting for the mail."

"Yes, the Amish bookstore." The sheriff was quick to agree with Katie, looking as if he wanted to swipe his hand across his brow in relief. "That would be quick and easy, and we could get this wrapped up."

Adam slid a hand up and down one of his suspenders, then let it slap against his chest, wincing slightly with the impact. "Let's do it. We'll grab a copy of the hymnal from the Amish bookstore and get that cipher cracked today. The sooner, the better. Katie can direct us." He grabbed his straw hat from the desk and put it on. "Thank you, Sheriff. Thanks for your help, Deputy. I'll keep you posted."

But as Katie said her goodbyes and let Adam usher her down the hallway and toward the door, she couldn't help but wonder how Adam would be received in the Amish bookstore. The owners knew every Amish resident within miles of their store. What was that *Englisch* saying? Would he be perceived as a wolf in sheep's clothing?

Chapter Six

Back in the passenger seat of Adam's Tahoe, Katie was gradually getting used to the roar of the automobile. But she prayed to *Gott* she wouldn't ever need to get used to a special agent checking all the mirrors and scrutinizing the surrounding area so constantly as they traveled. And with the speed at which he traveled, she wondered, each time she climbed into the vehicle, whether they would make it to their destination alive.

Gratitude for her simple lifestyle flooded her, and even as Adam checked the rearview mirror again, she observed the teaching of the Psalms and blessed the Lord, trying to keep His praise continually in her mouth.

But did Adam really want to live like that? Constantly checking and being hyper-vigilant of his surroundings? Surely he would be happier, more satisfied, more at peace with himself and his life if he could slow down, relax, and believe in the goodness of his fellow man again.

Katie pushed a hair back into her *kapp*. My goodness, she was becoming philosophical. Did it have anything to do with the handsomeness of the agent and the comfort his presence brought her—comfort she hadn't felt in a really long time? *Ach*, she was better off not thinking such thoughts.

A buggy traveled on the right side as they crested a small hill, and Adam removed his hat and placed it on the console between them. He moved the Tahoe to the other side of the road and slowed, but Katie's palms slicked with anxious perspiration to think of the speed he still maintained. It was an entirely different sensation, and not one she cared for, being in the vehicle that was passing the buggy rather than being in the buggy that was being passed by a vehicle.

"You need to turn at the next left." Katie released her grip on her skirt to gesture to the next road. "Then we will drive past the large market building, and about a mile down the road, you will see the grouping of five shops."

Adam only grunted in response and shifted his hands on the steering wheel. Katie glanced at him in her peripheral vision. His nervousness filled the vehicle, and she felt her legs becoming jittery as they approached the bookstore. She had known the owners, Paul and his wife, Penelope, for nearly her whole life and had many good memories of her *mamm* taking her to the bookstore on a Friday afternoon. While her *mamm* would visit, she had been free to wander the aisles, staring longingly at the candy or running her fingertips across the book bindings, wishing she could take home every single one.

As they passed the market, Adam slowed as a four-door sedan turned into the parking lot. He peered ahead, down the road, then shot a quizzical look at Katie. "Is the bookstore in the middle of a bean field?"

She couldn't contain a nervous giggle, even as Adam scanned the market parking lot for potential threats. "*Jah*, sort of. The bishop from the neighboring church district sold a bit of his land on the outskirts of Nappanee to allow a few of our business owners to build shops. He thought it would help Amish from both communities."

He sped up as they pulled past the market, and from behind the building ominous dark clouds approached from the southwest. "Looks like a storm is coming."

"Mayhap. But it is Indiana, so we may never see rain. The clouds could glower at us and the wind pick up until it drives us off the road, at least if we were in a buggy, but we may never actually see any drops. That has frustrated many a farmer and gardener." She pointed down the road to the right. "There it is."

"Most county roads run parallel and perpendicular to each other so that you can drive in a square around a piece of land. Is that the way it is here?"

"*Jah*. Keep going and turn right at the next opportunity." She paused. "Is this for surveillance?" She snuck another glance, and his jaw was set in a firm line, shadows filling in his stubble that had formed from sleeping in the Tahoe to protect her the night before.

He didn't look at her but continued to scan the bean field and surrounding area. "Yes. I need to make sure of where a person might be able to hide, and it'd be mighty tough for a grown man to hide in those short soybean bushes. There are a couple of trees on the far edge of the field but anyone hiding there would be too far away to accomplish any sort of attack. In my line

of work, I always need to be thinking of how to anticipate my opponent's next move."

As they drove the country roads that formed a
square around the grouping of Amish shops, Katie
could see clearly across the tops of the soybean plants
to the stores and the owners' buggies parked out back.
"Does this look safe?" It was nearly impossible to
imagine any sort of danger in her sleepy little Amish
community or a man with a gun in a bookstore, especially an Amish bookstore. But her leg still ached from
yesterday's trouble, reminding her that danger was here
whether she could imagine it or not.

"As safe as can be expected, I suppose. I'm glad
it's removed from the market building and all of that
traffic and noise. It's quieter here, and that's the way I
prefer it. It's easier to detect a threat."

The tires squealed on the hot asphalt road as Adam
guided the Tahoe back onto the main road and toward
the shops. With one more glance toward the market,
he was apparently satisfied with their current safety.
He pulled the SUV into the frontage road that ran the
length of the five shops.

The road and each parking lot were bordered by
mulched flower beds blooming with the color of yellow
marigolds, pink zinnias and purple petunias. An asphalt sidewalk connected the few stores, but otherwise
the shopping area really was on the edge of a soybean
field. As they drove past, Katie admired the vegetable
plants and pots of flowers in the nursery, as well as
the bolts of material and sample quilts in the window
of the fabric supply store. She quickly powered down
the window a couple of inches to inhale the tantalizing
aromas emanating from the coffee shop and waved to

the wheelwright who was setting a buggy out front of his shop with a For Sale sign.

Adam parked in front of the store and followed Katie closely through the screen door. The dim and relatively cool interior of the bookstore was a welcome respite from the sun and humidity of outside. The owners still ran their business the Amish way, without electricity, so there was no *Englisch* air-conditioning. But without the sun beating down on her head, Katie felt cooler immediately. A few gaslights swung from the ceiling, but they were not lit. They would only add heat to the inside, and there was plenty of light from the carefully placed windows and skylights.

"Does anyone work here?" Adam whispered, his breath close to her ear.

"*Jah*. Paul and Penelope are husband and wife. But it is close to time for the noonday meal. They are probably in the back, making sandwiches." She turned to smile at him and his *Englisch* impatience. But his handsome face was startlingly close, and she quickly stepped away to finger a child's purse that hung on a spinning rack filled with goodies for little girls. Some blank journals with pictures of flowers and birds were displayed nearby, but she didn't have time to shop for trinkets for the twins.

Voices sounded as a door at the back of the shop opened. Adam stepped in front of Katie. She peeked over his shoulder to see Paul, the store owner, emerge, wiping his mouth with a napkin. He stopped short at the sight of Adam and frowned. "*Wilkom?*" It came out as more of a question than a greeting.

His wife Penelope quickly followed, and Katie stepped out from behind Adam, plastering a smile on her face. "*Ach*, Katie, how are you?" The woman's face blossomed with a smile, and she gently pushed her husband forward. "It has been a long time since I have seen you."

The man stopped again and stood near the battery-operated cash register, looking down his nose, through his glasses, which were perched precariously there, at Adam. Paul appeared to eye Adam's haircut, at least what was visible from under his hat, as criticism oozed from Paul like the perspiration dotting his forehead on the warm summer day. Surely Paul could tell Adam was an *Englischer* by his fancy haircut. He pulled on his scraggly beard as he examined Adam. But Adam glowered back, plenty capable of holding his own in the staring contest.

Katie turned her attention to Penelope, who watched her husband with amusement for a moment and then looked at Katie. Her hands spread wide, she asked, "Where are Ruth and Rebekah?"

"They are with Sarah for today."

"*Ach*, I adore Sarah. She has come through some difficulties and emerged as a stronger woman, *jah*?" She patted Katie's arm. "Well, you understand those difficulties, dear. I cannot believe Sarah found herself an *Englischer*. But then he turned out all right, *jah*?"

There was nothing for Katie to say, so she just nodded her head in agreement. But then Penelope looked away, and Katie followed her line of sight to Adam. She seemed to look him up and down for several seconds and then turned her attention back to Katie with a satisfied smile. "What can I help you with?"

"I need a copy of the *Ausbund*. Do you have any?"

"*Ach*, my, of course we do. That is one book we will

always carry, although why more do not buy one for their personal use, I do not understand. Perhaps it is because we have so many hymns memorized already."

As the woman prattled on, Katie caught Adam's eye and nodded for him to come with her. With one last glare at Paul, Adam quickly followed, a strange mixture of frustration and relief clouding his features.

Penelope walked them to the Bible and hymnal area, even though Katie had been coming to the bookstore since she was a little girl and already knew where everything was. They passed stacks of school paper, mason jars of brightly colored pencils and pens, games, flashlights of all sizes, and the always-enticing candy section.

And with each window passed, Adam made sure to step to her side, shielding her from exposure to the glass as he peered out to survey the bean field.

"So, here are the Bibles, in case you need one." Penelope stared at Adam, her gaze taking in his haircut as if he were a heathen, and yet a playful smile curling on her lips. She pointed back to the shelf. "And we have a couple of hymnals, so you can take your pick. Is there anything else I can help you with?"

Adam immediately reached for the closest copy of the *Ausbund* and leafed through it.

"Nein, danki." Katie turned her attention to the book as well, but a small cough from Penelope returned Katie's attention to the store owner. The woman raised her eyebrows at Katie and then looked pointedly at Adam, tilting her head in his direction.

Ach, no. Katie felt heat rise to her cheeks. She didn't need someone acting as matchmaker. Perhaps she was done grieving her husband, but even if she did marry again, it would only be as equally yoked…to a good, upstanding, peace-loving Amish man.

Katie shook her head *nein* so vigorously that the ties to her prayer *kapp* slapped her cheeks.

But Penelope would not leave. "Those twins are growing up fast, are they not?"

Katie nodded as she tried to look over Adam's shoulder at the *Ausbund* selection. "*Jah*, for sure and for certain." She tossed the woman a small smile.

"Are you going to begin teaching the hymns to the little girls? They are a might young, but with only the two children, you probably have the time to begin early."

"We do sing together sometimes as we do our work."

"That is *wunderbar*." Penelope clasped her hands together. "And your friend? Does he help you with the barn chores? Your garden?"

Adam exhaled noisily and cut his eyes at Katie. Frustration danced across his face.

Katie quickly selected a different hymnal from the rack, ignoring Penelope's nosy question. It looked more familiar than the one that Adam was holding, but she couldn't be sure if it was the proper version until she could check it with the encrypted message. Adam looked at the book she was holding in her hands, his eyebrows arched into question marks. She nodded for him to put his book back on the shelf.

"This one will be fine." Katie showed it to the store owner. "*Danki* for your help."

She hurried back to the register, with Adam on her heels. A hand-lettered sign declared CASH ONLY, and she turned to see Adam pulling the necessary bills out of his wallet.

With a final goodbye to the store owners, Paul still frowning at Adam as he stepped outside before Katie so he could survey the sidewalk and parking lot for threats, they escaped back into the Tahoe.

Another sigh erupted from Adam as he settled into the driver's seat. "I was never allowed to utter a single word in there." He locked the doors. "Perhaps that was for the best. That man didn't like me much, did he?"

Perhaps Adam had been uncomfortable in his clothes? He looked just like all the other Amish men she came into contact with, but it must be odd for him to be dressed so differently. "Paul has never been a friendly sort. That could be why he married Penelope. She has enough friendliness for the both of them. But maybe it was your *Englisch* haircut."

He shrugged and didn't answer. Now that they had what they needed, he probably didn't care what the Amish couple thought of him. He had a job to do, and that was all. He wasn't trying to fit in with the Amish community, a realization that struck Katie with a sudden sadness. When Timothy was found and all were safe again, Adam would go on to his next assignment. She gripped the brown paper sack that contained the book. She couldn't—wouldn't—think about that now. Or ever.

Adam started the engine and pulled out of the spot only to pull into an opposite spot that faced the road. Katie must have had an inquisitive expression, for he explained that he wanted to keep an eye on the traffic going past. He left the Tahoe going with the air-conditioning on high, and Katie suppressed a shiver.

She retrieved the *Ausbund* from the sack as Adam found his photo of the note on his phone. The console in between the two front seats was wide enough to hold the text open as she laid it on the leather.

Adam glanced at the book and then at her. "Considering that it's in German, I think you're going to have to manage this." He smiled sheepishly, a crooked grin slanting across his stubbled jaw.

Ach, he is handsome. Katie quickly stared down at the *Ausbund*, reminding herself that she ought not consider any man who wasn't Amish. Her heart longed for a life's companion, but she knew an *Englischer* could never be *Gott*'s will for her.

She cleared her throat and focused on the image on his phone. "All right, so the first number is the page number. That's forty-two." In her nervousness, she flipped and crumpled pages, taking what seemed like an eternity just to find the proper page. "The second number is the line. Three." She ran her finger down the page. "The third number is the word in that line."

Sliding her finger across the words, she found the word *heart*.

Adam leaned in to look at the word in German. "That means *heart*? I can't imagine a message starting with a word like that, but let's keep going and see what we find."

At Adam's direction, she found a pad of paper and a pen in the glove compartment, and a few minutes later, the entire message was translated. The words didn't make any sense, though.

"I cannot understand it. The words are a jumble." She had let herself be hopeful that this would bring her *bruder* back and all would be well again. But with this nonsensical grouping of words, her heart seemed to stop beating for a moment. Would she fail at helping her only sibling?

Adam stared at the paper in her hand. "I don't see any sort of message there. Are you sure it doesn't mean anything to you? Anything that relates back to the childhood you shared with him? A place or a person, or an activity you did together? Anything?" Desperation tinged his tone.

"Nothing. I am sorry." She looked again at the spine and the information at the front of the book. "I do not think it is the same as the hymnal we had when we were children."

Adam stared out at the bean field. "That's probably why the message doesn't make sense. It's not deciphered correctly because we have the wrong key."

"If it has to be the exact same book, then I am not sure what to do. Our old hymnals were falling apart, and the bishop ordered new ones." A car approached, driving past the grouping of shops slowly. Katie watched it go, scrutinizing the driver. *Ach*, she was beginning to pick up Adam's habits.

Adam exhaled as if he'd been holding his breath through her explanation, a tightness around the edges of his eyes and mouth. The bishop was their community's senior spiritual leader, a man of *Gott*, intent on living life God's way, as he interpreted it, but also a tall, imposing man with a rare smile. Katie clutched her dress over her thumping heart. If the Amish bookstore was not a help, what else could they do? "Perhaps we need to ask the bishop? Maybe he would know where we could find a copy of the old hymnal." But how would the bishop receive Adam, a federal law enforcement office masquerading in Amish clothing?

* * *

The bishop? Adam knew full well that the Amish didn't generally like law enforcement, especially in their homes and affairs. Would the man even be willing to answer a few questions?

Adam pulled his cell phone from his pocket, his hand gripping it until his knuckles turned white. "Before we rush right over there and interrupt the man's day, since I'm assuming we can't call the bishop and make an appointment, let me update the sheriff. It's professional courtesy. He's been helpful and has a stake in all of this since it's happening in his county." He cleared his throat to mask the feeling that he was going to choke, thinking about sitting in the bishop's living room, letting the man scrutinize him and see right through him to his evil, sinful past. Somehow the bishop would know that Adam could never measure up to the purity and wholesomeness of the Amish.

That was an agony Adam wasn't sure he could bear, and he'd had to deal with a lot of agony in his life. And yet, was he foolish to hope for that peacefulness that seemed to come with faith? Where could he find it?

"Whatever you think is best." Katie looked out the window as if to give him some privacy for his phone call.

A moment later, the sheriff's deep voice boomed through the phone. "How'd it go?"

"The book doesn't work. We're going to have to—"

"Tell me in person, son. I thought I better stay close to you two, just in case you needed some backup. So I'm at the coffee shop just a couple doors down from where you are. Stop in and we'll talk."

Katie tilted her head as if she could hear the sheriff's invitation, but she remained silent.

"I think we'd better keep going—"

"Son, the Amish make the best coffee and the best sandwiches this side of the Mississippi. Probably the other side, as well. Get on down here and get a cup. You can tell me then." The sheriff hung up before Adam could reply.

If he had had any doubt about what to do next, now there was no choice. They would go see the sheriff. He plastered on a smile for Katie. "Hungry?"

"I suppose, *jah*."

He twisted in his seat to check every direction, but all was well. They had been stationary for long enough, and he was ready to move the vehicle. But the coffee shop was just a couple of doors down. It seemed there was no right answer. With an armed man on the loose, perhaps more than one man, looking for Katie, no place was truly safe.

"The sheriff is at the coffee shop and wants us to stop there to talk to him. He hung up on me, insisting that we have a sandwich."

Adam decided to leave the Tahoe parked where it was, outside the bookstore. If their predator did find them, perhaps Adam would see him first if he thought they were in the bookstore.

Adam turned to Katie with what he hoped was a reassuring look. "Ready?"

"You would know better than I would. Are we ready?" She tried to smile, but it only slanted across her pretty face. Perhaps his look wasn't as comforting as he wanted, but she certainly was perceptive.

"Let's go."

She met him around the back of the Tahoe, and he stepped around her so that she was on the inside, near the stores, and he was on the outside, near the road. He put on his straw hat and then took it off and put it back on, angling it slightly to see if it could have a more comfortable fit.

"Stop fidgeting with your hat. You look fine in your Amish clothing."

"Is my discomfort that obvious?" But his discomfort wasn't really with the clothing. It was with the life he had been leading and its juxtaposition with Katie's simple life.

She simply nodded and looked at the buggies as they passed. He had the sudden urge to take her arm, but this was not a companionable moment. It was a job, an assignment, and soon he would move on to the next assignment and then the next and then the next. It was the nature of his position, a job he enjoyed and from which he derived great satisfaction.

Until now. What was it about Katie and the Amish faith that made him want to shrug off the burdens of the world and be plain? He had enjoyed the little amount of time spent with his Amish grandparents. That was true. There had been a simplicity and a peacefulness that he hadn't ever found elsewhere. He certainly had looked for it, including at the bottom of a bottle. But when he hadn't found that calm and tranquility there, he had managed to overcome his alcoholism. He did like his electricity, but was that enough to keep him tied to his current life? Perhaps not.

He shook his head to clear away the ridiculous

thoughts. With his past problem, he wasn't good enough for God, for Katie or for the Amish people.

As they approached the door of the coffee shop, the tantalizing aromas wafted toward them, and Adam's stomach growled in response. Perhaps a bite to eat was the right thing, something to keep up his strength and help him think clearly. The only way to find the attacker and make Katie and her brother safe was to decode that message. Timothy had risked his life to get that information to Katie, a message that should ultimately keep her safe.

Two steps from the door, tires squealed on the asphalt, a screech that drove his hand to seek his weapon in the holster. His other hand found the small of Katie's back, ready to push her down and cover her with his own body. With another shriek of the tires, he thrust her into the doorway, heading her toward what he hoped was safety as he scoured the street for the speeding vehicle.

Chapter Seven

Adam nodded a fast thanks as the sheriff pulled Katie inside the coffee shop. He must have heard the squeal of tires, as well.

With his weapon drawn, Adam spun back to the parking lot. He ducked as best he could behind a tall potted plant, praying it would provide adequate concealment. A white cargo van swerved close. A shot hit the cement step below him, sending small chunks of concrete flying. Adam crouched lower, his eyes squinting out of instinct to keep the flying debris out, but preventing him from getting a clear look at the shooter.

The van jerked back toward the road. Adam stepped out from behind the plant, prepared to fire back, but the vehicle sped away too quickly. With dismay, he saw that there was no license plate. With no tag number, the sheriff would probably be unable to identify the van.

Sheriff Moore stepped out from behind him. "Katie's safe, and everyone's staying inside. What happened?"

Adam didn't stop his scan of the area. "Warning shot. I think the driver could see that he wouldn't get

Katie, but he wanted to make sure we knew he was here."

"I radioed my deputy. He's on his way."

A few moments later, the law enforcement vehicle arrived, and the deputy began processing the scene.

Adam stepped inside the café, behind the sheriff. At least he knew his senses were alert. Now he needed to make sure they stayed that way.

More coffee would help with that.

He took a deep breath and willed his pulse to stop pounding as he confirmed that Katie was unharmed.

"You're doin' fine, son. Let's sit down and catch a breath. You can fill me in while the deputy searches outside." Sheriff Moore clapped him on the shoulder and led the way to a table near the back. Adam had been an ICE special agent for enough years to develop some maturity in his skills, yet the sheriff's words of encouragement were a balm to his nerves.

Katie smiled demurely and said, *"Danki,"* and then followed the sheriff to his table. Wide-eyed, she nodded to a server she seemed to know, an Amish woman with the same style of white starched prayer *kapp*, as she sat.

Adam selected a chair on the side of the table, from which he could see both the front and the back of the little café. Instinctually he visually scanned and made mental notes of the exits, the customers and what he could see through the kitchen door. "Not many customers now?"

"No, and that's a blessing."

"But now the step out front is damaged."

"Everyone's just glad no person is damaged. We'll get the cement fixed."

The Amish server approached and poured coffee

for Adam and Katie, and then brought chicken-salad sandwiches with a pickle and a side of potato chips.

"So, the hymnal from the bookstore isn't the key to the cipher?" The sheriff took a large bite of his sandwich and washed it down with a drink of coffee.

"No. We figure it's a more recent printing."

"The copy of the *Ausbund* that *mein bruder* and I used seemed to be old even then, when we were children. It could have been printed a half of a century ago. It probably is no longer being printed." Katie added sugar to her coffee and stirred.

"So, we can't find one online." Adam recapped as he took a sip of the strong black coffee. The sheriff had been right. It was the best he had ever tasted. "There's no time to order one. And the Amish bookstore doesn't sell one that will break the cipher. I think Katie's brother must have thought she had one of the old hymnals, otherwise he wouldn't have made cracking his code this difficult."

Sheriff Moore wiped his mouth with a napkin. "What about the bishop? Maybe he can help."

The bishop. Adam's pulse spiked. "Okay. Sure."

"Maybe he still has a copy of the old hymnal."

"That's what Katie wondered." Adam's leg began to jiggle underneath the table, a nervous habit he thought he had conquered in school. He was a federal agent of some experience and caliber of skill. Meeting an Amish bishop shouldn't be intimidating. But it most definitely was. "I guess it's worth asking. And I'm eager to get this resolved before someone gets hurt."

"I would be happy to go with you. Perhaps my presence would make the visit seem more like official business. Of course there's no guarantee that would help, but most likely it wouldn't hurt."

Katie folded her napkin and laid it on the table. "It is true that the Amish do not usually care for law enforcement. But this is a simple request about a book. I do not think the bishop will take issue with that."

"If it's any help, son, I've met the bishop. I've had a piece of his wife's fabulous strawberry pie, and he seemed to be an upstanding guy."

Somehow Adam couldn't see an Amish bishop taking kindly to being called a term so casual as *guy*. And good pie didn't make for a pleasant visit, necessarily, but since the sheriff had met him and Adam hadn't, Adam would take his word for it. At a loss for an intelligent reply, Adam stayed silent.

"*Danki*, Sheriff Moore," Katie said in the gap of silence, "but we will go. Bishop Zook worked with and studied under my *daed*, and *Daed* always spoke of him fondly. That relationship, to my *daed*, as well as to *mein bruder* and me, will soften him to both the visit and the request. Then *Gott* will handle the rest." She smiled at Adam, dimples deepening that he hadn't noticed before. "All Agent Troyer needs to do is get us there."

And keep her safe, she didn't say. But from the look of peace on her face, perhaps she hadn't even thought it. What would Adam give for that kind of calm about life? That level of trust that the best would work out, that Someone was watching over him?

The realization hit him square in the chest. He would give everything.

Adam gradually became aware of the sheriff and Katie staring at him as he gazed at his half-empty cup of coffee. "Ahem, yes. We'll take care of it. Do you think this Bishop Zook will see me as making an effort, due to my Amish clothing? Or will I be perceived as an imposter?"

Katie gently touched his hand. "It will be fine. *Gott* is *gut*, and He looks after us."

The sheriff made eye contact with Adam, his gaze penetrating to Adam's soul. Then he turned to Katie with a gentler look around his eyes. "Would you like to visit with your friend who's working here? Why don't we see if she can take a break?" He looked to Adam. "I'll take her back to the staff break room and make sure the area is secure."

He returned a moment later and took a sip of his coffee. "Want to tell me what's going on, son? Your shaking leg is about to upset everything on this table. There's something more here than just pursuing a lead in a case."

The sheriff's gaze softened, reminding Adam of the few good times he had had with his father. Adam had been forced to be strong for so long that he wasn't sure what to say or how to respond to genuine interest and concern. To buy himself some time, he took a gulp of his coffee, but he choked on it and sputtered into his napkin. The sheriff clapped him on the back, a knowing look in his eyes.

"I'm just nervous about meeting the bishop. Someone who is harsh and critical of outsiders."

"What makes you think he'll be harsh and critical?"

"My dad always thought so. That's why he left his Amish roots. My grandparents were kind people, but that only caused me more confusion about the Amish and religion in general. I mean, isn't the Amish life one that someone is usually born into? You don't just join them like you join a health club." Why was he saying all of this? Was he that desperate for someone to talk to? He had stuffed his past down for so long and moved into the future as if the past hadn't existed, that now, here in this Amish world, he felt like he was going to explode with questions and confusion.

"Grandparents, huh? I thought Troyer sounded like an Amish name."

"Yeah, but I didn't spend time with anyone other than my grandparents and a neighbor every now and then. Certainly not a bishop." And if the bishop knew of his past? Well, the man wouldn't want to be tainted by close proximity to such a sinner as Adam.

"Obviously I don't know your grandparents, but I think you'll find that most Amish are more like them—kind, generous, thoughtful. They're good people."

"Too good to be around someone like me." Adam toyed with his coffee mug, unable to look the sheriff in the eye.

The table creaked as the sheriff leaned forward. "Well, I don't know about that. The Amish have their share of problems, as well. No one is perfect, not even the Amish."

"Okay, but they still haven't had the problems I've had." And in response to the empathetic look in the sheriff's eye, before he could even think it through, Adam found the rest of the confession tumbling out uncontrolled. "My dad started drinking in his running-around time. Got involved with the wrong crowd. So he was never baptized into the church. He got married. Had me and my brother. But he never could conquer the drinking, and my mom left him." He grabbed a glass of water and gulped. "Well, isn't there a verse about the sins of the father? It wasn't long after my dad and my brother were killed in a drunk-driving accident that I succumbed, as well. Stupid, wasn't it? I had barely buried them, they were killed because of my dad's drinking and I chose to bury my guilt in the bottle."

Sheriff Moore sat silent, giving him room to talk and breathe.

"I kicked the habit eventually. I've been sober for three years now. But don't you see? I'm not good enough for the Amish. Not good enough even to be around them. Not good enough for God." He swallowed hard at the bitterness that rose in his throat.

"Now, son, it sounds to me like you know a little bit about your Bible. And so you know that God forgives, if we ask Him to. It's that simple." The sheriff scrubbed his hand through his hair. "As far as the bishop goes, remember that this is only for the hymnal. It's no big deal. The bigger issue here is the way you look at Katie and the way Katie looks at you."

A sudden heat smacked Adam in the face. Had it really been that obvious, his admiration of her simple beauty? She didn't wear a bit of makeup and wasn't bedecked in jewels like other women he knew, but she radiated an appealing wholesomeness.

"Is something brewing here?"

Adam scooted his chair back to get some distance from the idea that Katie might be looking at him. "N-no, sir. Not that I know of."

"Okay. Well, there's still time. The important thing to remember is that what's in the past needs to be left there—in the past. The Amish—and the Lord—are a lot more forgiving than you might think."

* * *

Katie peered through the round window in the swinging door, her hand paused before she pushed it open to return to the table. Adam and Sheriff Moore seemed to be in an intense conversation. Whatever their topic was, it had made Adam red in the face. He had a finger crooked into his collar, as if trying to loosen its stranglehold on his neck. Was he really that nervous over meeting Bishop Zook? She could understand that. Considering the circumstances, she would do most of the talking. Perhaps that would calm him.

Her friend, the server, walked up from behind and pushed the door open for her. "Is everything all right, Katie?"

"*Jah. Danki* for the Danish."

"Come back anytime. And I will pray that *Gott* would protect you."

Katie nodded and stepped through the door. She quickly approached and smiled, what felt like a feeble attempt to reassure him. But before she could sit, he glanced at the sheriff and reddened with whatever look the sheriff had on his face. What about her could possibly make him anxious? So far as she understood his job, this was routine. Seeking out bad guys, protecting innocent parties—it was all part of his position with ICE.

Was he worried that if something happened to her, it would not look good for him in his job? Or was he bothered that he was tasked to protect her, because he had other, better, things to do? She glanced at his place at the table. The remains of half of a chicken-salad sandwich sat on his plate. Perhaps the mayonnaise wasn't settling well in his stomach.

"Did you have a good visit?" the sheriff asked as she sat down.

Adam was silent, barely able to look at her. He reminded her of a boy in sixth grade who had sat behind her at school and couldn't even utter her name when she said hello. She had eventually heard through the grapevine that the boy was sweet on her and excruciatingly shy. That couldn't be Adam's problem, could it?

She focused on the sheriff, suddenly unsure what to say or do around Adam. *"Jah, danki."*

Adam stood abruptly. "Ready to visit the bishop?" Without waiting for an answer, he headed for the register, retrieving his wallet as he walked and visually scanning the exterior through the windows.

Katie reached the front as he received his change. His Adam's apple bobbed up and down with what looked like a hard swallow as he put on his straw hat. Then he turned toward the sheriff, who had followed him to the register.

"Thank you, Sheriff." Adam shook Sheriff Moore's hand. "I'll keep in touch."

"No problem, son. Anything you need." The sheriff laid his bill on the counter and reached into his jacket pocket for his money clip, nodding to the server behind the register. "My deputy's cleared the area, but go out the back. I'll go ahead of you and double-check."

A few minutes later, as Adam and Katie waited in the kitchen, Sheriff Moore unlatched the back door and signaled that they could leave.

Adam opened the door, but Katie paused to turn back and wave to her friend. There was no way to know when she might make it back for a quiet cup of coffee with her. *If ever, depending on how this situation*

with Timothy might turn out. She immediately stuffed
that idea to the back of her mind, refusing to give in
to worry and doubt.

She took the door from Adam, allowing him to step
out first. He looked to the left and then to the right,
toward their vehicle, which the deputy had brought
around. When he seemed satisfied, he half turned his
head to nod at her and proceeded down the three steps
to the parking lot. With one last glance at the cozy
café, Katie let the door close behind her and fell into
step beside Adam, careful to be between him and the
shops, as she had been before.

In Adam's fast SUV, it wouldn't take more than a
few minutes to get to the bishop's house. She would
use that drive time to pray for Adam and his comfort
with the bishop, as well as for a final conclusion to
their entire situation.

The cooled air of the coffee shop had been refresh-
ing, but now the heat and humidity of the Indiana summer settled on her with a vengeance. For the sake of
safety, they needed to get to the Tahoe quickly, but
Katie couldn't seem to force her feet to move much
faster than the slugs she found on the hostas in her
flower garden.

Adam was a full step ahead as they reached the
wheelwright's shop. Her *mamm* had always said she
was the peacemaker of the family, trying to make sure
everyone was happy and content. Even now she tried to
formulate some words of assurance for Adam in his apparent anxiety. Conflict had always been something to
be avoided, and now that danger came with it, she was
nearly at a loss for what to do or think or feel. At least
she had a protector. But now that he seemed to strug-

gle, she couldn't bear it. If she could just find the right words, perhaps all would be well between them again.

Before Katie could articulate the proper sentence, a vehicle skidded through her peripheral vision. She turned to see a van rushing toward her, gunning the engine and coming seemingly from nowhere. She froze. It felt as if her shoes were stuck in the hot asphalt of the parking lot. The cargo van careened over a strip of grass and tore through the flower bed that separated the fenced-in trash receptacles from the rest of the parking lot.

"Katie!" Adam lunged for her as the van veered back onto the pavement.

She screamed, a primal sound from the depths of her being, as Adam shoved her in between two buggies at the back of the wheelwright's.

"Go!"

But she couldn't move. The safety of the shop was a few steps away, but she couldn't turn from Adam. As she stood rooted to the spot, Adam drew his weapon and pointed it at the driver as the van continued to race toward them.

Chapter Eight

Adam stood rooted in place despite the recoil of his weapon. The discharge was earsplitting, but it didn't distract him from rushing out into the parking lot and firing again into the back of the retreating cargo van.

It only took a moment for the van to disappear into the haze of humidity. All seemed quiet except for the ringing in his ears and the sheriff's boots on the pavement as he ran to Adam's side.

"I heard the tires squealing and the shouting. What happened? Was it the same vehicle?"

"I think so. And he turned before I could shoot, so I only hit the side of the van." Adam turned to check the crowd, but the sheriff must have told everyone to stay inside.

Katie huddled next to a buggy, her arms wrapped around her middle as if trying to make herself as small as possible. A dazed look was etched across her face.

He rushed to her, patting the sides of her arms as if that could reassure him that she was uninjured. "Are you all right? Are you hurt?"

She slowly focused on his face. "I am unhurt. But

may I sit down?" Her legs wobbled, and he grabbed her before she fell, leading her to a bench near the back door of the wheelwright's shop.

After making sure she was settled, he returned to the sheriff to survey the damage. Huge grooves sliced through the grass and mud from the van's tires as it had torn toward him and Katie. Mulch had been thrown all over the wheelwright's back parking lot. Flower petals were scattered everywhere.

The sheriff tipped his head toward Katie. "She need an ambulance?"

"No. The van didn't get close to her. What she needs is for this case to be solved and the danger to end."

"I'll get my full team down here and see what we can do to find the driver. It looks like he left a little more evidence this time. We'll get imprints of the skid marks and the acceleration scuff marks. You said he spun out and changed course when he saw your weapon?" He removed his hat and wiped his sleeve over his brow as he had Adam repeat the dynamic movements of the van. "I'll check whatever imprints we find against the FBI's Footwear and Tire Tread Files database. Maybe we can connect it to the suspect's vehicle."

"That's a long shot, though, isn't it?" Adam pointed to the grooves in the mulch and the tire tracks on the asphalt. "Looks awfully smeared."

"Maybe. Don't know until we try."

Adam crossed his arms over his chest. "Do you know how easy it is to change tires? The driver could just jump the fence of a junkyard or steal them off the rack at a tire shop a couple of counties over. You'd never be able to find him."

"That may be true, but my department is going to do our best to find this guy. I can't have this happening in my sleepy little county. Tourism is growing here, and tourists want to come see the Amish. They should be able to stay in a bed-and-breakfast and buy a quilt or some homemade jam without fear of being run over. I also have a responsibility to the Amish who live here. They should be safe in their buggies as they share the road and not be afraid of being run over by a crazy English driver."

Adam held up his hand. "Of course, Sheriff. I'm just being realistic."

As the sheriff got on his radio to summon his team, Adam walked around the path of the cargo van, careful not to disturb a single blade of grass or a bit of mulch. As he examined the evidence, he glanced at Katie. She seemed to have relaxed a bit, loosening her grip around her middle.

Wasn't there anything more he could do to find her attacker? Sure, he had been pessimistic with the sheriff. In his experience, no suspect had ever been caught by something so simple and easy as a tire imprint. But the sheriff was right. It was worth the effort. Anything that could help end this danger for Katie would be worth it. She had done nothing wrong except care for her brother. And whatever her brother was involved in, she had had no choice in that either. Increasingly Adam didn't think that even Katie's brother had had much choice in the matter. Whatever he had done, it had been against his will.

The Amish were a peaceful group, doing their level best to separate themselves from the world. Adam knew that well enough from the tranquility of his grandparents, as well as the angry comments his father had made on occasion. Timothy had most likely not chosen this clandestine life of illegal activity.

But if that were true—and Adam had no way to know for sure since it was a hunch at this point—then there were two people here who needed rescue—Katie and her brother.

Adam bent to look more closely at the tire tracks on the asphalt, strengthening his resolve to protect Katie and find this suspect. He would do all he could to bring an end to these attacks.

He visually checked on Katie again as she sat on the bench. Her head was bowed, and her lips were moving ever so slightly, probably whispering a prayer. His chest tightened as a new sense of purpose washed over him. He should do a bit of that, as well—praying. If Katie thought it was a good idea to seek the help of an almighty God, then he would join her. It certainly couldn't hurt or make their situation any more desperate.

God, help! Adam fisted his hands. Wasn't he supposed to say more than that? But what else? This was more difficult than he thought it would be.

He inhaled fresh oxygen and began again. *God, I know we haven't spoken for a while. Quite frankly I'm not sure why You'd want to listen to me. But I need Your help. More importantly a devout and faithful Amish woman needs Your help. If not for me, then protect her. Help me to keep her safe and put an end to the danger.* He mumbled an *amen* and returned to his examination of the tire tracks.

An hour later, both Adam and Katie had given their statements when the sheriff approached with a look of fierce determination about him. "There's nothing more you can do here. It'd be more helpful if you got to the bishop's and asked if he still has an old hymnal. The sooner we can figure out that message, the sooner we can catch the suspects, and the sooner I can get my little town safe again. All right?"

"I agree." Adam clenched and unclenched his fists, that same fierce determination washing over him as he glanced at Katie. He needed to get his anxiety under control and do his job to the best of his ability. That meant protecting Katie from being trampled like the delicate flowers that now lay on the ground, flattened by the attack.

The drive to the bishop's house was quiet, save for the hum of the Tahoe's engine and the one time Adam tried to reassure Katie that everything would be fine. But how did he know? Wasn't he offering simple platitudes that were meant to make her feel better and make him feel like he was actually doing something? But had he truly accomplished anything?

He halted that line of thinking as they pulled into the bishop's lane. An older man wearing broadfall trousers, a dark green shirt and a scowl stepped out the front door at the first crunch of their tires on the gravel. He stood on the porch that wrapped around the two-story white structure and waited for them to approach.

"Good afternoon, Bishop Zook." Katie stepped onto the porch and Adam followed, fingering his suspenders. "We have a favor to ask of you."

The door opened, and a gray-haired woman with a plum-colored dress swept out. "*Wilkom.* Good afternoon, Katie. Come on up and sit on the porch for a while. We have heard of the danger from yesterday. How are you?"

Adam inched forward, his mouth open to speak, but with a glance back, Katie held out a hand to stop him. "Actually, Elizabeth, could we sit inside?" Adam suppressed a smile at how quickly the Amish woman had picked up on the appropriate precautions to keep them both safe. Sitting on the porch would leave them exposed to whoever might drive by on the road. Yes, the Tahoe was in the driveway, but inside, there would be a literal wall of protection around them.

The bishop's scowl deepened, but his wife simply said, *"Jah,"* and led them inside. Bishop Zook followed closely behind Adam, so closely that if Adam stopped abruptly, the bishop would surely run into him. Even though Adam was in Amish clothing, it seemed clear to him that the bishop knew Adam was simply masquerading and was actually one of those dreaded law enforcement *Englischers*. But was he still pretending? The Amish clothing was becoming physically comfortable, and he wondered if this was the spiritual life for him. Perhaps his grandparents were right.

Elizabeth gestured to a chair at the kitchen table and busied herself in the kitchen. A few minutes later, there was a slice of peach pie and cup of hot tea in front of Adam. The aroma tantalized him, and his stomach rumbled in response. A window was open just a few feet from the table, and as Adam forked a bite into his mouth, he surveyed the Tahoe, the lane, and the bit of road he could see through the opening.

Katie fingered the handle of her teacup. "Bishop Zook, do you still have a copy of the *Ausbund*, one of the hymnals that were cared for by my father? We need to borrow one, and it would be just for a few days. We will return it quickly."

The older man took a long swallow of his tea before he spoke. "I have a few still, but those hymnals belong to the People. They are under my explicit care, along with the benches used for Preaching Sundays. Why can you not buy one for yourself?"

"We, that is, I did. But it will not serve my purposes. I need one that Timothy and I used when we were children."

"And what are your purposes?" The bishop leaned back in his chair and stroked his long gray beard.

Adam checked out the window again and then leaned back on his chair to peer out a side window as Katie explained the note from Timothy and their need to decode the secret message. He sliced through the pie with his fork for another bite, studying the wood grain on the table before returning his gaze to the window.

"*Ach*, young Timothy. He has been a mystery these past months. And you believe this particular copy of the *Ausbund* will be helpful?"

"*Jah.* Definitely."

The bishop cleared his throat forcefully, and Adam turned to find the older man's penetrating gaze lasered on him. "Young man, is there a reason you cannot focus on the conversation?"

Adam ran a hand through his hair—his short, spiky hair that was most definitely not Amish. "I'm watching through the available windows in case there's trouble. I need to protect Katie from any harm, and if her attacker finds us again, I'd like to get a jump on him."

The bishop continued to stare. "You mean you want

to know if he is coming so that you may adequately prepare."

"Exactly." Maybe the bishop understood more than Adam thought he did.

The bishop was silent for a moment while the only sound in the room was the chirp of the sparrows from outside the open windows. "Young man, it must be a difficult and stress-filled life you lead, always on the lookout for danger. Do you have any faith in the Lord, Jesus Christ, in the sovereignty of God, in His guidance and protection? Does anything within you yearn for the simple life? A life that God ordained, of working with your hands and living in community with other like-minded believers, trusting *Gott* with everything?"

Adam shifted in his chair, heat rising within his chest. On the other hand, maybe the bishop didn't understand anything at all.

Katie ran her finger around the rim of her teacup and watched the handsome agent squirm. The bishop was asking Adam everything she herself had wanted to ask him, but she had not thought it her place to be so forward. The bishop, on the other hand, had the courage, as well as the authority, to ask anyone anything.

With one last sip of the tea, she admitted to herself that she had found herself thinking of Adam more and more throughout the day. His bravery. His light brown eyes that seemed to have specks of gold. His broad shoulders that had such strength to protect her.

Ach, but she ought not be unequally yoked. He was not Amish, and she was. The conflict was clear. Would she be willing to leave the Amish faith behind for him? Face the shunning and turn her back on all she had ever known just to be by his side? Drag her twins away from all they were growing up with and all the people they loved? No. She couldn't see that ever happening.

There was an alternative. Could he leave his *Englisch* lifestyle, his automobile, his electricity, his fancy phone, and become Amish? It was highly doubtful. It was, in fact, so preposterous, that she ought not even entertain the notion. And what would he do to earn a living? There was no place in the Amish community for a special agent.

Why was she thinking such thoughts to begin with? There had not been any indication that he was developing feelings for her. Sure, there had been a glance, a touch on the arm, that seemed to be something extra, like a show of affection or caring. But had she been imagining it?

Was she really this lonely?

She shook her head and forced her mind back to the conversation at hand. Adam still had not come up with a suitable answer to please the bishop. Even though he was cute when he was nervous, his cheeks pink from the scrutiny, compassion welled up inside her. "Bishop Zook, the hymnal? I appreciate your fervor for righteousness, but I am also concerned with my brother. If decoding this message will help, I am eager to give it a try."

With one last glare at Adam from under his bushy gray eyebrows, he looked at Katie with a half smile. "I am not sure you ever explained how this particular copy of the *Ausbund* will help you."

Katie blinked several times, but the bishop continued to examine her. "*Ach*, I guess it is confession time. *Mein bruder* and I, when we were children and *Daed* was the bishop, would use the hymnal for a book cipher and write secret messages to each other. I saw Timothy last night, at my house."

The bishop and his wife leaned forward with the news. "You did? How was he?"

"I only saw him briefly, and it was dark. But he gave me a note written in a secret code we used as children. Agent Troyer and I believe that if we can figure out the code, Timothy's message will be helpful in finding both him and my attacker."

"How could this note have meaning or be helpful at all?" The bishop leaned back again, his arms crossed over his chest. "Your secret messages were the play of children. Naughty children taking a sacred hymnal and using it for their own deceitful devices."

Elizabeth placed a hand on her husband's arm. "But if it helps Timothy?"

The bishop hesitated, and then he nodded. "*Jah*, I grieve for the boy, as well. If a hymnal might help bring a wandering one back into the community, then you may borrow one. I will get it."

Katie helped the bishop's wife wash the dishes while the bishop retrieved the hymnal. "You will let us know how this message comes out, *jah*?"

"*Jah*. And keep praying for Timothy."

"Of course."

At the door, Katie hung back as Adam stepped outside first and checked the perimeter of the bishop's property. When he nodded that all was safe, she turned to the bishop. His grip on the *Ausbund* was firm, but he slowly let it go.

"*Danki*. I will be careful with it."

"I know. Please let me know how the situation progresses."

Bishop Zook and his wife walked alongside as Katie hobbled to the Tahoe with the help of her cane. "*Jah.* For sure and for certain."

But as the vehicle door closed behind her, and the bishop and his wife returned to the porch, a bit of doubt wiggled its way down her back. What if this copy of the hymnal didn't help and they couldn't decipher the message?

Chapter Nine

"My house would be the quietest place to work on the secret code, and I should change my bandages." Katie waved one more time to the bishop and his wife, and then stared out at the nearby cornfield as Adam backed down the lane and into the road. The corn was just about ready for detasseling—the removal of tassels from every fourth row of corn—but would she live long enough to see the harvest in the fall? How terrible it would be to miss the cooler temperatures, fall foliage and *wunderbar* aroma of pumpkin pie. "May I see my twins again?"

"I'm not sure that's best, but we'll see."

In the short time they had been forced together, apparently Adam had learned enough of the country roads that he didn't need directions back to Katie's. The drive passed quickly in silence, with Katie offering up continued prayer for her safety, for Adam's safety and for her twins.

As the Tahoe turned into her driveway and she surveyed the yard, making a mental note to water her marigolds, goose bumps pricked at her flesh. Something was wrong. She rubbed her arms, a reassuring gesture meant to flatten the bumps, as she scanned the area.

Adam turned off the engine, but when he moved to open his door, she stopped him. "There is something not right, but I cannot tell what it is." Her voice came out only as a whisper.

She continued to scan, feeling like she was looking for what was missing in a child's search-and-find game.

Adam's whisper broke through her concentration. "It's your front door. It's ajar."

Katie's hands flew to her throat, where she could feel her pulse thrumming. "Someone has been in my house?" Visions of the attack from the night before rose up unbidden, and she grasped the door handle to steady herself.

"Whoever it is may still be there." He retrieved his weapon from the holster at the small of his back. "Stay here and lock the doors behind me."

Once he was out of the Tahoe, the clunk of the locks falling into place seemed to ricochet around the quiet vehicle. Katie sat in the passenger seat, her hands bunching and releasing her skirt fabric as she watched Adam creep around the house and peer into the windows. In what seemed like a few heartbeats later, he emerged through the front door. A stricken look stretched across his face. The despair in his eyes forced her from the vehicle, rushing forward toward the front door as fast as she could with the cane to help her.

"What is it?" She couldn't keep her voice low any longer. "What is wrong?" She could imagine all sorts of terrible things happening, but all the people she loved would not have been nearby.

"Your house." His voice was hoarse with some unidentified emotion. He laid his hand on her arm as she came close. "Someone's torn it up."

A gasp erupted. She hobbled to the door, still standing open from Adam's exit. The sight from the door was one of utter destruction, and she felt herself leaning heavily against the doorjamb, perspiration breaking out across her forehead despite the cool of early evening.

Adam stood behind her, his hand on her shoulder, a weight of strength and comfort that gave her a different sort of goose bumps. "Whoever it was is long gone." His breath tickled the back of her neck and the few hairs that she could never get caught up into her bun and prayer *kapp.* "I've cleared the house and the yard. I'm going to call the sheriff. He'll want to send a team over."

Katie could only nod as she sagged in the doorway and listened to Adam talk on the telephone about statements and dusting for fingerprints and setting up a perimeter.

Ach, another statement? How much longer, Gott? How much more? She was sorely tempted to begin a mental list of her woes, beginning with the death of her parents and continuing with the untimely death of her husband in an accident at the sawmill. But she stopped herself before she could go on. Instead she would choose to bless the Lord. At all times. She blinked furiously, but she couldn't stop the tears once they began. Soon they were cascading down her cheeks and dripping onto her dress, despite how much she tried to thumb them away.

And then, as quickly as the tears had started, they dried up. She refused to wallow in self-pity but determined instead to count her blessings. Adam was still talking on the telephone, so she stepped inside.

It took several moments to absorb the depth and breadth of the destruction of her personal belongings, many of them sentimental and irreplaceable. It seemed that every drawer and every door had been opened. Some looked as if they had been ripped off their hinges in a violent fit. The armoire that Adam had heroically saved just the night before was now on the floor, smashed into a dozen pieces. A quilt her *gross-mammi* had made that Katie had hung over a chair had been slashed, its fluffy fill falling out. Katie took two steps farther in, peering into the kitchen. Another tear leaked out as she saw that even her canisters of flour and sugar had been dumped. It looked as if the monster—whoever it had been—had stood at the cabinets and pulled everything out, not caring whether or not it smashed on the floor. Several pieces from a set of dishes her husband had given her had been destroyed and scattered over the floor.

More tears sprang to her eyes, but this time they were mixed with something different. It was something a good Amish woman shouldn't feel, and her fists began to shake and her arms began to quiver with the desire to throw something for herself. She was a widowed woman, responsible for two little girls, with no family to help. *Jah*, she had friends, but they were not the same. She forced her fists to unclench and she inhaled slowly as she turned to glance at Adam, who was still on the telephone. Now, to add to that burden, she had no choice but to traipse around the county with the *Englisch* law enforcement officer.

But as she watched him, his eyes met hers. He

smiled slightly, just enough to indicate that he knew she was overwhelmed and that he would do whatever he could to help her. *Ach*, so much trouble and danger could *ferhoodle*, truly confuse, a person. Her shoulders relaxed as she chided herself. What was it the *Englisch* Christians liked to say?

Gott is *gut*. All the time. Even with her house torn up, she knew that *Gott* was with her. It was all in His will, and she had no place to question His goodness.

She bent to pick up a chair and set it to rights, but Adam's strong grasp on her arm stopped her.

"Don't touch anything. We need to leave it all as it is for the crime-scene photographer. The sheriff will dust for fingerprints, as well. There could be evidence here, if we can just find it, that would lead us to whoever did this."

Katie sniffed and swiped away another tear, her heart thumping a rapid beat. "Who, though? Was it the same man as last night?"

"That's my guess. It was probably your attacker from yesterday, looking for something. Remember he seemed to suspect that your brother had given you something, perhaps some kind of communication? He could have been looking for that note or maybe that social security card you found at Timothy's." He ran his hands down her arms. "Whatever it was, I'm glad you weren't here when he returned."

Katie shivered and wrapped her arms around her middle at the memory of the foul man who had pressed himself upon her the night before. But the warmth and comforting pressure of Adam's hands on her arms soothed her.

But as she stood as still as possible, not wanting

the moment to end and Adam to draw away, another thought struck her. When this was over, how could she return to so-called normal life without Adam's comforting presence?

Gingerly, afraid he would scare her away, Adam pulled Katie all the way into his arms. Even as he wondered if that was proper law enforcement behavior, he knew he couldn't just leave her standing there by herself. He couldn't watch her cry in the middle of her living room, surrounded by chaos.

She felt good in his arms. Warm and soft. That much was for sure and for certain, as Katie would say.

Slowly her tears subsided. *"Danki,"* she whispered as she tilted her head upward to look at him.

Her beautiful face was so close that he could feel the short puffs of her breath on his face. What if he kissed her? Would that be *verboten*?

His memory of that Pennsylvania German word rocked him backward on his feet. How many times had he heard his father use that word as his excuse for running away from his faith? He had thought that the Amish forbade too many things. And yet here was his son with his arms around a pretty young Amish woman, wondering what a plain life with her would be like.

Sirens sounded in the distance, and Adam immediately dropped his hold on Katie. No matter what was on his mind and in his heart, he had a job to do and he was determined to do it well. Surprise lit her face. Was that a tinge of disappointment he saw, as well?

"Maybe you should wait in the Tahoe." He hated that his voice was husky and vulnerable, but he couldn't seem to control it. After what he had confided in the sheriff, that he had been a drunkard himself just a few short years ago, he knew he didn't deserve a loving wife or family. He might be a failure at his job, but at least it gave him a reason to get out of bed in the morning, a way to assuage the grief from his father's wreck of a life, a chance to make the world a better place so that others could have a better life than he did. And he certainly wasn't good enough to hold such a beautiful Amish woman in his arms.

"*Jah*, that might be best."

"You'll feel better if you're not in the midst of the mess."

He assisted her back to the SUV and helped her into the front seat. The sheriff and his deputy arrived just as she rolled down her window for some fresh air.

"I know I said to keep me updated, but I didn't expect to hear from you this soon." The sheriff slid out of his vehicle and introduced a freelance photographer he said did some crime-scene work for his department as needed. "We had just barely finished up at the coffee shop when I got your call. What's happened here?"

After Adam filled him in, the sheriff turned to Katie. "I'm so sorry this has happened. A home is a sort of a sacred space, isn't it?"

Katie nodded. "*Jah*, and so many sentimental things that can't be replaced."

"We're doing our best, but would you mind going inside to determine if anything is missing? It sounds as if Special Agent Troyer believes this was related to your brother, and I agree. But we do need to rule out burglary."

She slid out of her seat, leaning on the cane. "Burglary? But I am Amish. What is there to steal?"

Adam offered her his arm, gratified when she accepted. "It's true, Katie, that the Amish don't generally have the typical valuables that burglars look for, things like a cash hoard, jewelry or expensive electronics. But we just want to make sure."

At the door, she continued to lean on Adam's arm as he led her through the rooms. The crime photographer was already busy, working his way through the house and shooting the chaos from every angle imaginable. The deputy followed behind, beginning to dust.

Carefully Adam picked a path through the mess of the house, letting Katie rest on his arm and absorb the surroundings, evaluating what, if anything, was missing. Only a couple of tears leaked out through the process, her strength and courage in this adversity impressing Adam.

As they stood in the kitchen, making footprints in the flour that had been dumped on the floor, Adam donned a pair of disposable latex gloves and opened a cabinet door, as well as the refrigerator and freezer. "Is anything missing?" He looked around the disarray of Katie's belongings, unable to imagine that it wasn't all there in the chaos.

"I don't think so…"

Adam released a breath. "Well, that's a bit of good—"

"Except for a container of cookies I had made two days ago that were on the countertop and maybe a bottle of water I usually keep in the refrigerator."

"What?" Adam shifted his weight. "Cookies and water? So the thug who broke in and destroyed your house was hungry and didn't take anything except food?"

Katie shrugged. "That is all I see. May I return to the vehicle now?"

Adam watched her fiddle with one of the ties to her prayer *kapp*. It seemed obvious to him that it was a gesture of anxiety. She probably longed for what felt like safety in the Tahoe. "I think so. Just let me check with the sheriff."

Sheriff Moore disengaged from a conversation with his deputy when Adam approached. "I don't need anything more from her. She's free to go. But be careful with her. This is a lot to take in, especially for an Amish widow. Home is of utmost importance to the Amish, and this probably feels like a violation of a sacred space."

"I understand that, Sheriff." Adam promised himself he would be extra gentle with Katie, but then the memory of her in his arms rose up. He shook his head, determined to focus on the task at hand. He should also check in with his supervising agent again and give him an update.

"I'll finish up here, but again I don't expect to find anything helpful. The modus operandi so far seems to indicate a professional—or professionals—who knows enough to wear gloves so as not to leave fingerprints. We have a partial shoe print in a bit of flour, but it's small. Whoever it was was careful."

"That's my impression, as well." Adam held out his arm to Katie to lead her through the debris and to the door. "We'll be in touch."

Back out in the Tahoe, with the key in the ignition and his foot ready to press the accelerator, Adam wasn't sure where else to go but to Sarah and Jed's house. Katie had pleaded with him about her need to see her twins, and her friendship with Sarah would be comforting to her. Truth be told, he wouldn't mind seeing the little girls either, with their twinkling blue eyes and mischievous smiles.

The distance between the two homes had not changed, but with Katie's nearly palpable anxiety over her home being violated and his own constant vigil for further danger, the time it took to reach Sarah and Jed's house seemed to stretch to eternity. Katie's breathing had finally evened out by the time her friend's house came into view, but Adam doubted she would be able to relax or take a deep, cleansing breath until she knew beyond a shadow of a doubt that her girls were safe.

That wasn't going to happen just yet, though. The house was there, but instead of turning into the driveway, Adam drove past at an even speed.

Katie hiccupped as she watched the house, and Adam feared her tears would return. But her voice was steady when she asked, "Are we not going to stop?"

"Not yet." Several yards down the country road, Adam pulled the Tahoe into a dirt road. Truly, at this closer proximity, it looked like more of a path that led to a gate for a cow pasture. "I saw this little drive when we were here earlier, and I thought it might come in handy in the future."

He turned the vehicle around to point out to the road but stayed far enough back that they were protected by thick bushes and trees.

"Are we hiding?"

"Hiding and watching. We don't want to bring trouble on your friends, just in case we're being followed, since we drove straight here from your house."

Adam kept a steady watch up and down the road, even glancing in the rearview mirror from time to time. These few minutes would have the added benefit of allowing Katie to steady her nerves and slow her heart rate back toward something resembling normal.

When he was satisfied that all was quiet, he pulled out of the dirt lane and then into Jed and Sarah's drive.

At the crunch of gravel under their tires in Sarah's driveway, two little faces appeared in the window, noses pressed against the glass. Sarah's face appeared above them, and a moment later Ruth and Rebekah came running from around the back of the house, the ties from their prayer *kapps* flying behind them, and each clutching one of his whittled squirrels. Katie opened her passenger door and slid from the seat to rush to her girls, barely leaning on the cane as she embraced the twins.

Adam stood back, giving the little family room to cherish the time of togetherness. He circled around, surveying the area by instinct. Foreboding gray clouds were beginning to fill the western sky. In a couple more hours, they would be overhead, pressing down their rain and wind.

Katie and the twins disentangled themselves from their embrace and headed toward the house, Katie with an arm around each girl. Adam stood still, letting them get a head start on greeting Sarah and Jed and Lyddie. As much as he had come to enjoy Katie's company—truly he had begun to care for her, although he wasn't sure he was ready to admit that—this would end soon, as all cases did eventually. He would move on in his single life, and she would return to her life filled with her children, as well as hopefully her brother and friends. He straightened some of the gravel, pushing it around with his shoe, as a single large raindrop dropped on his shoulder. With another look at the sky, he hurried inside.

Chamomile tea was poured quickly, but it looked like the plate of cookies had been out for some time. Crumbs were scattered on the table in front of each twin, and there were only two cookies left on the plate. He chewed on a cookie absentmindedly while he stared out the window.

"Adam?" Katie's lilting voice with the Pennsylvania German accent broke through his trance. "Is that okay?"

He rubbed at an eye, bringing himself back to the present. "I'm sorry. What were you saying?"

Sarah cocked her head as she looked at him, a quizzical look on her face. "I was asking if I could organize some of the women to clean up Katie's house."

"Oh, yeah. As soon as the sheriff says it's okay."

Thunder cracked overhead, and the twins startled and then ran to Katie. A few heavy drops plinked on the roof and the window. It looked as if the storm wouldn't wait.

But where could Adam find shelter for Katie? Where could he keep her safe tonight? Her house was a mess. He didn't want to bring trouble on her friends by staying there with Sarah and Jed. They had, in fact, probably been there too much and too long already. And although his Tahoe was big, it didn't exactly have two bedrooms, let alone a bathroom. Where could they possibly go to find safety and rest?

Chapter Ten

Katie picked up the teapot and poured more chamomile.

"It is soothing, *jah*?" Sarah leaned forward and touched Katie's arm, smiling with a warmth that comforted Katie.

"*Jah*, but we cannot linger."

"What? You will stay here. Both of you."

Even as Jed began to shake his head to disagree, Adam spoke up. "There is no doubt that whoever is after Katie knows where she lives. He has demonstrated that he will not give up. She can't stay at her house or even return there until this is resolved."

"Right. So she can stay here." Sarah pushed the plate of cookies toward Adam.

Katie shook her head at her friend. As if Amish cookies could sway the *Englischer*! "*Danki*, Sarah, but—"

Adam leaned forward and pushed the cookie plate back toward Katie. "But she—"

Impulsively Katie waved her hand in Adam's direction, and he stopped talking. She surprised herself with her boldness in interrupting him, but perhaps enough danger on the run had strengthened her. "I cannot accept. I will not bring danger onto your house."

Sarah paused as she examined Katie. Finally she sighed. "If that is what you think is best. But where will you go?"

"I do not know. I would not want to bring trouble onto any of the People."

"*Ach*, why did I not think of it before? You can stay at *mein bruder*'s. He will be moving here from Lancaster County soon and has purchased a house. There are a few furnishings that I had extra and loaned to him until his things are moved. It is just a table and chairs, a few plates, glasses. But he is gone for another couple of weeks because he has business to finish up there before he can move here."

"Are you sure?"

"*Jah*, for sure and for certain. I am cleaning and fixing it up for him in the interim, so right now it is empty."

Adam stood as if signaling that it was time to go. "How far is it?"

"It is only a couple of miles away." Sarah looked at Katie. "It is the old Hochstetler place."

Katie nodded and hugged her twins again as Sarah rose to gather some drinks and snacks for them. She had known the Hoschtetlers and knew the house to be a fine, old structure. It would be plenty adequate for their needs. Adam headed toward the door, and Katie knew it was time to leave. Her heart twisted within the confines of her chest, aching fiercely at her current separation from her daughters. But what could she do? There was not anything at all that she could think of except to continue to run and hide with the *Englischer* until the danger passed, since she would never be willing to stray very far from her Amish community. Keeping her distance was the safest for her and for her daughters.

She pulled her twins close and whispered, "*Mein liebchen.* My darlings." She kissed each cheek in turn. "I will be back as soon as I can."

The stop at Jed and Sarah's had been all too short, but it had been a comfort and a relief to hold her children again, even if just for a moment. Their sweetness and innocence had dispelled some of the depression that seemed to linger about her. An impression struck her that that could have been the last time she would see them. It would certainly be safer for them if she stayed away lest she lead her attacker to her children.

Katie easily directed Adam to the Hochstetler place. She stayed in the Tahoe while he checked out the property, both outside and in. Seemingly satisfied with its distance from nearby Amish houses, he retrieved a flashlight from the glove compartment and ushered her inside. At his direction, she stood just inside the door while he found sleeping bags and a battery-operated lantern in the back of his Tahoe.

The furnishings were definitely sparse, with the table and four chairs that Sarah had mentioned as the only furniture on the expansive first floor. Even if she didn't have a leg wound that would ache from climbing the stairs, there was no point in checking the upper level. Those rooms were sure to be barren, as well. It didn't matter. She hoped not to be in the house long.

Night had fallen as they had driven, so Adam flipped the switch to the lantern and led the way to the kitchen table, motioning Katie to a chair. He took the chair opposite, setting the bishop's copy of the *Ausbund* between them. "You still have the note?" He glanced at her prayer *kapp*. "Or should I pull it up on my phone?"

She reached up to her head covering and retrieved the paper. "I have it." She unfolded it, placed it on the surface between them and then opened the hymnal. After checking the numbers her brother had written in the message, she turned to the appropriate page in the book.

Adam turned sideways in his chair, craning his neck to see both the hymnal and the paper. "This isn't working." He stood and circled the table, sitting in the chair to her left.

She continued searching for the proper page, line and word according to the message her *bruder* had written in the book code. Adam's scent of the woods in springtime tickled her senses, and she doubled her efforts at concentrating on the code.

As she worked on the fifth word of the message, her right hand, holding the pencil, brushed against Adam's hand as it rested on the table between them. A tremor raced up her arm at his touch, but she forced herself to hold the writing utensil steady. She glanced at him to see if he had noticed her reaction and was struck by the handsomeness of his angular face in the lamplight. *Ach, I ought not to be having those thoughts!*

"What does all this mean?" His voice sounded husky to her ears, but he was probably just trying to keep his voice low and not break her concentration.

"It is High German, the language of the *Ausbund*. I will translate it after I get the complete message."

She continued on, intent on the book in the low lamplight, trying not to worry about her own safety or the safety of her girls. She carefully wrote out each German word above its corresponding numbers on her brother's note. "There it all is. Now for the English."

A few minutes later, she read it aloud, pointing to each German word as Adam followed along. "Help me. Harm soon. Deliver identity. In shadow of old saw place near tree. Come mid night. Three day."

Intensity creased the lines on Adam's forehead. "So, he needs help to avoid further harm. And it's urgent."

"*Jah*, seems so." Despite the heat and humidity in the house, a chill crept up Katie's arms.

"He's delivering something, or something is being delivered. Perhaps more identification documents, more like that counterfeit social security card you found in his workshop. What could *old saw place* mean?"

The chill seized Katie's shoulders and threatened to wind itself around her neck. She didn't want to think it, but could it be possible? Did her brother mean the sawmill, the location of her husband's horrible and untimely death?

Dizziness threatened as she remembered that day she had been summoned to the terrible scene. The sawmill was a place she had not been back to and had in fact avoided with a passion since then. She must have begun trembling, for Adam put his arm around her as if to stop her shivering. "What is it? What's the matter?"

She swallowed hard, though it did nothing to dispel the lump that had formed in her esophagus. "I think he means the sawmill."

"Oh. Did something bad happen there?"

But the look on her face must have answered his question.

Adam felt himself being torn in two. Was this why most special agents weren't married? A beautiful woman needed comforting. His comforting. And he wanted to provide it, to hold Katie in his arms again.

But he also needed to act on this message, now that he knew what it meant. Something big was going to go down. He knew where and he knew when. He needed to contact his supervising special agent and get the team mobilized. Katie's brother had taken a huge risk in his desperation to seek help, probably hoping that she could contact law enforcement despite the Amish reluctance to involve *Englishers*.

Which was his priority?

Even with his arm still around Katie, he pulled his phone close to make the call. Of course his priority was to catch the bad guys. Justice must be done. That was why he was a special agent. That was his reason for waking up every morning, for getting out of bed, for putting one foot in front of the other. And as long as the bad guys were on the loose, wreaking their havoc, the woman he wanted to comfort was in danger.

Then again, if he could put an end to this chase, perhaps there could be more time spent with the lovely Amish woman.

What? He shook his head and pulled his arm from around Katie, focusing on his phone. There could not be more time spent with the Amish woman, for one simple reason. She was Amish. He was not. That would be the end of their love story.

He tapped the button to speed-dial his supervisor and relayed the new information. It was all starting to come together, although Adam still wanted to interrogate Katie's brother to get the details. With this heads-up as to when and where the big transaction was taking place, Adam and his supervisor determined that an ICE team should be at the sawmill at midnight the next night. Factoring in the time that had lapsed since Timothy had snuck his note to Katie, it seemed that the night for the meet-up was tomorrow. As he spoke to his supervisor, Katie sat beside him, her eyes closed and her lips moving in what Adam guessed was a silent prayer that they could rescue her brother from whatever he had been forced into.

As he finished the call, Katie opened her eyes and focused on him. "How do you think Timothy became mixed up in this?"

"I'm not sure, but I plan to ask him when I get a chance." Adam's blood pounded through his arteries as he thought of all the trouble Timothy had put on his sister. "He must be seeking help to stop these criminals and protect both himself and you. Without his note, we wouldn't have any idea where to find him or these thugs."

"I have wondered what you must think of my brother, Adam. But I believe he must be in agony over what he has been forced to do. I do not think he chose that life of secrecy and, perhaps, crime." She pleaded with him for a moment with her wide, dark blue eyes, then looked down at the table, her delicate lashes hiding the flashing of her eyes.

"Probably. And perhaps when that man came after you, Timothy knew his usefulness to them was done and it would only be a matter of time before he and you would be eliminated." At that horrible thought, his arm moved without his permission to rest on the back of Katie's chair.

"Eliminated? *Ach*, that is what this is all about." A tear escaped, but she waved a hand at Adam to ward him off. "Of course I knew that already. I am Amish, but I am not ignorant of the ways of evil. It just can be hard to admit."

"To the best of my ability, I will make sure that all is all right. You're safe now, and I'll do whatever is necessary to protect you." He fought hard not to gather her in his arms. This was business, and he was determined to remain professional.

"Even at the sawmill?"

Adam cut his eyes at Katie even as his mind spun, trying to figure out why she would ask about that particular location. "Why would you think you're going to the sawmill?" With the probable danger there, in the midst of that transaction, whatever it was, there was no way he would allow her to go to the sawmill. He would tuck her away someplace safe to wait out the meeting.

"Because I am. My brother will most likely be there. I need to encourage and support him, no matter how difficult it is to return there."

Apparently there was more here he needed to know. "Why difficult? And when have you been there before?"

"That is where my husband was killed."

Adam gasped, experiencing a feeling in his chest as if he'd been hit by a truck. Her bravery, her willingness to return to a place that must hold untold trauma, all in service to her brother, astounded him. "What happened?"

She swallowed and then began. "My husband used to work part-time there while we were trying to get our farm going. I was selling baked goods to help pay the bills, but I had twin toddlers underfoot and could not do much. I was also pregnant with our third child and having a rough time of it."

"Third child?" Adam shook his head. Katie only had the two girls. He hated to think what had happened to that baby.

"*Jah.* And then my neighbor came running into the kitchen one day. She said there had been an accident, and I needed to get to the sawmill right away. She had summoned the Amish Taxi, and it was waiting to take me there." She ran her hand across the smooth wood of the table. "They did not know I had arrived, and I saw everything. I saw…him. His mangled body."

A look of horror swept over her face, and she dissolved into tears. Adam put his hand over hers, the softness of her skin contrasting with the rough wood of the tabletop, and whispered a prayer for comfort.

"The trauma was too much, and I miscarried." She sniffed and swiped away some tears. "It was a boy."

"Are you sure you want to go back?"

"*Jah*, I must go back. For Timothy. He is my only family. I am afraid of the memories at the sawmill, and I am afraid of the bad men. But I am more afraid of losing Timothy forever. If there is something I can do, then I will do it."

Adam was not convinced that Katie should be at the sawmill at the appointed time, especially not since the place was surrounded by such great emotional difficulty. If it came right down to it, his duties did not include her emotional well-being. At least according to ICE regulations. Would her presence be a distraction to him? But there was no point in concerning himself with it now. He would know more as the time approached.

"I admire and applaud your tenacity. But we're in this together, remember? I'm doing everything I can to resolve your and your brother's difficulties." He didn't want to see her hurt. But did his increasing emotional attachment to her impair his judgment? Absentmindedly he rubbed his thumb over the back of her silky hand.

She shivered and looked up at him, fear in her eyes, her lower lip trembling. The lantern cast a soft glow over the room, throwing shadows into the corners and around the edges. How easy it would be to kiss her.

But it would be wrong. Very wrong. His mind shouted at him to leave her alone. Nothing could come of an Amish-*Englisch* romance. Absolutely nothing.

How could he change the way his heart was feeling about her? He couldn't stop it. It was involuntary. Perhaps it was simply a reaction to the close quarters and being on the run. But what if it wasn't? He had never been in love before, never allowed himself to be that vulnerable and never been willing to admit that he was a person who wanted to be loved. Is that what this was—the beginning of love? What if he did want a love and a family to call his own? Was that wrong?

He leaned down, his lips an inch from hers. Her breath came in short puffs. Was that anticipation?

For the briefest of moments, he gently touched his lips to hers. Electricity seemed to crackle around them.

A huge crack of thunder pounded on the roof and

sent shudders through the walls of the house. Lightning turned night into day. In that moment, Adam saw, in an instant, a flash of regret across her beautiful face as brilliant and clear as the lightning.

Yes, it was wrong to want a family of his own. He had a commitment to justice. But not only that—he would never be deserving of Katie. Not even close.

She shoved the chair back and stood in a rush, crossing quickly to the window, hugging her arms around her middle. Another flash of lightning made a jagged streak across the sky, lighting up the yard. But her gasp and exclamation drove all agonizingly romantic thoughts from his head.

"I think someone is out there!"

Chapter Eleven

The thunder was delayed by only a second, and it clapped overhead. The windows rattled in their casements, seeming to shake some sense into her head. What had she been thinking? She had been *ferhoodled* by the handsome face and strong shoulders and protective attitude of this *Englischer*, for sure and for certain. Admiration was one thing. But a kiss? That seemed too much like commitment.

But it wasn't only the *Englischer* watching out for her. *Gott* was watching out for her, protecting her from the *Englischer*. The summer thunderstorm had arrived in just the right timing to bring her back to her Amish reality. She shook her head as if to clear the cobwebs formed by her attraction to Adam, and if he took it as a *nein*, then all the better.

She turned back toward the window. The severe storm had rolled in fast. Lightning had lit up the outside like daytime, but for that split second, it was enough. She stared out into the dark. Had she really seen someone, or had it just been her imagination, fueled by fear?

Then lightning struck again, this time cracking a

tree wide-open, half of it toppling to the side. As it fell, a person ran to the left, seeming to hide behind another tree or the nearby shed.

She spun away from the window and pressed herself against the wall, her heart beating a wild tempo. "Adam," she cried out. "There is someone there."

He slid the button on the battery-powered lantern and plunged the house into darkness. Quickly and quietly, he crossed to the window, hiding himself against the wall on the opposite side from Katie. He held a finger to his lips to signal that she should remain silent, and Katie closed her eyes in an attempt to calm her rapid breathing.

But when lightning struck again, she opened them quickly, unwilling to miss anything. She wanted to see everything that she could in case it would be helpful to Adam. And in that flash of light, she saw a figure run from behind the shed to a tree closer to the house. He held something in his hand, but it didn't look like a gun.

Adam stayed steady but narrowed his eyes at the man. "Is that his tactic?" His voice was so low that Katie thought he must be talking to himself. "That's pretty extreme."

And then, in the space of a heartbeat, as Adam moved away from the window in reaction to the man outside, pulling Katie with him, a light sparked and flared up in the darkness outside.

"Let's move!" He grabbed Katie's shoulders and spun her to face away from the door that was right next to the window. Adam pushed her down and away from the door but stayed right behind her. He was too slow, though.

The door exploded in a flash of light and flame.

Adam served as a human shield, protecting her from the blast. The door flung into him, pushing him against her and hurling both of them against the far wall. She cried out in pain as her foot caught on a chair, pulling on her leg and ripping her gunshot wound open.

Katie clutched at the injury as Adam pushed the door off them and then drew his weapon from the holster. She curled onto her side to see him crawl to the door and fire his weapon into the night. Large, hot flames licked at the doorjamb and the base of the kitchen cabinets. In the glow of the fire, she saw the man run away through the pasture and toward the woods. Lightning sizzled again as if to help her see his escape.

Adam watched through the door a minute more and then turned back to help her sit up. "He's gone, but that's no guarantee he won't be back."

"What was that? A bomb?"

"Kind of. It was a homemade incendiary device." He grabbed a couple of dish towels from the countertop and handed them to her. She immediately applied direct pressure to her oozing wound. "Most likely a Molotov cocktail."

"Something that explodes."

"Yeah."

The door was completely on fire, as well as the edge of the floor and the kitchen cabinet closest to the door. The odor of gasoline and the acrid smell of fire filled her nostrils. Flames licked up the walls, higher and higher, as she pressed the towels to her leg. The heat threatened to burn her skin and singe her hair.

Adam's jaw was set with grim determination as he surveyed the increasing flames. "Fire extinguisher?"

Even as he asked, he ran to the kitchen to begin fling-
ing open cabinets. "Under the sink?"

"If there is one—"

But Adam pulled open what looked like it should
have been used as a broom closet and then held up a
fire extinguisher triumphantly. He blew dust off the
top and the handle. "Pray it works."

Katie maneuvered herself to a standing position, despite the deep throbbing in her leg. She pulled the towels away and began beating at the flames with them,
but Adam motioned for her to sit. "You stay put. Don't
injure yourself further. This extinguisher will do it."

With a little extra tugging, the pin came loose. Adam
swept the nozzle of the extinguisher's hose across the
base of the flames, slowly dousing them. As the foam
squirted onto the fire, he stayed low and as much away
from the door as he could manage.

After several minutes with the extinguisher, the fire
was finally out. Katie drew a deep, ragged breath, ignoring as best she could the overpowering odor of
smoke that burned her nostrils, and tried to put on a
brave face for the pain. But the truth was that it hurt
something fierce and it still trickled blood. It must
have shown in her face, for Adam retrieved his phone
from the table and slid to her side on the wood floor.
He tapped three numbers and then spoke for a few seconds, giving their location.

"I called nine-one-one, but I don't think we should
wait for an ambulance or backup law enforcement.
They could take too long to get here. You need the
emergency room now. I can call the sheriff personally
on the way. Plus it'll be safe there."

She simply nodded, relief flooding her when Adam

lifted her into his arms and carried her to the Tahoe. He settled her into the front seat and then jogged around to the driver's side. Soon they were speeding down the country road, toward the closest hospital.

"I'm afraid our presence there caused great damage to the house." His voice was apologetic.

"*Jah*, and I am sorry, as well. We Amish take care of each other, though."

"Perhaps if we had found somewhere else. Somewhere far away?"

"*Nein.* We are a community. They would not have wanted me to leave, even for safety." The thought of leaving sent a tremor of fear through her. Then, with her eyes closed, she let the darkness flow over her.

The glow of the GPS monitor set in the dashboard drew Adam to check that he was headed in the right direction. So far he was fine, but it looked like it might get a little tricky when they got to the city. He pulled his cell phone out and quickly called the sheriff, who said he would get to the Hochstetler place immediately.

Katie's labored breathing also drew his attention, but so far she seemed to be handling it with strength, as she kept a firm hand on the wound. The dish towels were soaked with her blood, but the bleeding did seem to be slowing now that she was sitting still. The inside of the Tahoe smelled like a fireplace, but at least they were alive.

"How long until we are at the hospital?"

He glanced at the GPS screen again. "Should be about twenty minutes. Are you all right until we get there?"

"*Jah*. It does not hurt that much." But as she shifted in her seat, a grimace told Adam otherwise.

"Can you tell me more about this...this bomb? What did you call it?"

"A Molotov cocktail. It's a...yeah, a homemade bomb." Giving it a fancy name didn't take away the damage it had caused.

"How does it work?"

"It's simply a flammable substance like gasoline, perhaps with some motor oil mixed in, in a breakable glass bottle. Then it just needs a wick to ignite it, like a bit of cloth or a rag, often soaked in alcohol. Could be kerosene, as well."

"I have all those things at home."

"I'm sure you do. Lots of folks do. That's probably why he used that method. He may even have found all of that in the storage shed out back."

"It is worrisome that there are the makings of a bomb around most houses."

"Well, but you aren't going to be making any bombs." Following the blue dot on the GPS screen, Adam turned onto another country road.

"That is true. So, this man would just light the wick, like lighting a candle or a kerosene lamp?"

"Yeah. Light it up and throw it at the target. The bottle smashes when it hits. So then the flame from the wick ignites the fuel that was inside the glass bottle. Boom! There's a fireball that spreads flames. The attacker thinks his mission is accomplished."

"*Ach*, what a terrible thing to do to someone. Why would someone want to do such evil?"

"That's what we're trying to find out." But as they fell silent, Adam couldn't help but wonder at her innocence. She clearly had lived a protected life. Some might even say it was sheltered. Was that best, or did she need to know more of the real world?

He stopped at a light and turned to admire her in the red glow. What was wrong with sheltering, anyway? He thought of the guys he knew in ICE. Many of those agents ate antacids like candy or took blood-pressure medication even though they were still young. They might say they were fulfilled in their jobs, but were they truly satisfied? Pleased with their situations and relaxed about the future? Perhaps he would be happier or more content if he lived a sheltered life like it seemed Katie did. Sometimes the things he knew about the evil in the world and what he had experienced on the job felt downright oppressive and overwhelming.

The light turned green, and he pressed on the accelerator. He could hear her whispering again. With a sideways glance, he saw that her lips were moving in what must be silent prayer. He could probably stand to do a little more praying himself. She had certainly been a good influence on him in such a short time, coming along at just the right moment. Just as he was beginning to feel like a crusty curmudgeon, too far from God.

How much did this relationship mean to him? It had only been a short time that they had known each other, and yet she had influenced him in ways he never would have imagined. Even if nothing came of it and they never spoke again, he would always be changed because of their time together.

Adam scoured a hand through his hair. Was he going soft? *Stop thinking about the girl and think about the job.*

A couple of turns later, the lights of the hospital loomed ahead.

The emergency room was quiet, and a nurse wheeled a chair out for Katie. Inside, Katie gave her basic information, explained the nature of her wound and then was wheeled back to an examination room. Adam followed, but as soon as the nurse was ready to examine the wound, she turned to him and said, "Perhaps you'd like to wait outside. Unless you're the patient's husband?"

Katie giggled as Adam choked a cough into his arm. "*Nein.* He is not my husband."

Despite Adam's discomfort with the question, he was glad for a lighthearted moment for her. Perhaps it would provide some relief from the intensity of the chase. "I'll… I'll just wait out there. Could you let me know when you're done?"

"Of course."

He stepped toward the exit and then turned back. "It's not life-threatening, is it?" He must sound like a moron. She hadn't been brought in on a stretcher or unconscious or any other number of ways a person could be brought into the ER when life was ebbing away.

The nurse smiled at him, a teasing look in her eye. "I haven't seen much of the wound yet, but from what you and the young lady said, I'm guessing she just needs the stitching repaired and maybe some antibiotics to prevent infection."

"Okay. Sure. I'll let you get to work." An overwhelming urge to comfort Katie with a kiss on the forehead swept over him. But he denied it, pressing it back deep down inside, where it belonged. It wouldn't be professional, and it wouldn't be appropriate in front of the nurse.

Adam left the bay, with his hat in his hands, and the nurse jerked the curtain shut behind him. The curtain rings screeched on the rod above, and the breeze from the curtain ruffled his shirtsleeves. He meandered to the empty waiting room, uncertain what to do with himself now that it seemed there was nothing to do except be on guard for Katie. His ICE team was getting into formation and on the road, and there was nothing he could do from this distance. The sheriff was heading to the old Hochstetler place to comb it for evidence. So now he would wait.

He poured coffee into a cup and chose a seat away from the window but facing the entrance to the area. He sipped the brew, grimacing when it tasted old and bitter on his tongue, and placed the cup on a side table. Determined not to worry about Katie, he retrieved his cell phone and called the sheriff.

Sheriff Moore didn't even answer with *hello*. "You running into more trouble, son?" A smile sounded in his tone.

"No, sir. Just wanted an update."

"We're about two minutes away now. If I find something, I'll be sure to let you know. You sure the fire was out when you drove away?"

"Definitely. You'll see the foam all over the kitchen and doorway."

"No call has come in about a fire, so it must have stayed settled down." There was a pause before the sheriff spoke again. "Hadn't Sarah Miller's brother purchased the place?"

Adam dragged his foot over a spot in the carpet. "Yeah. I told Jed and Sarah that we wouldn't stay with them because we didn't want to bring trouble to their family. Now I'm glad we left there. But what about the damage to the house? It'll need a lot of repair."

"When we're done at the old Hochstetler place, I'll drive by and tell Jed and Sarah what happened."

"It'll be expensive."

"You're probably right. And the Amish don't typically carry homeowner's insurance. They believe they should trust in God rather than an insurance policy. But they'll take care of it. You know how they all come together to raise a barn in a day? Same idea here, except they'll repair and clean up a house."

With thanks to the sheriff, Adam hung up and gulped another bitter swallow of the coffee. It was certainly admirable the way the Amish took care of each other without judgment or bitterness. The repairs to the house would probably be what his grandmother had called a work frolic, and the community would clean it up and set it to rights in no time.

Adam picked up a magazine and absentmindedly flipped through it. Advertisements assaulted him for white teeth, glossy hair and healthy cereal. An article boasted of a decorating makeover of a house on the beach. What was the point of those superficialities, though? He glanced at an orderly walking by and remembered Katie's full lips moving in silent prayer nearly all the way to the hospital. Health and safety were the most important needs in his life right now.

And where was God in all of this trauma and turmoil? Apparently Katie's faith didn't suffer when trou-

ble arose. Why did his? Why did he doubt, especially
when bad things happened? Did he really expect that
believing in God would just make every moment perfect and serene and wonderful?

Perhaps he should give God another chance. People
always wanted a second chance in relationships. His
own father had wanted a third and fourth and fifth
chance, as well. So why was he so reluctant to give
God, Maker of everything, a second chance? His father had made his own choices to leave his faith, and
then everything had spiraled down from there, until
the drinking was out of control and Adam's brother
had also been pulled into that lifestyle. Yet where had
that gotten him? In a body bag on the side of the road.

Even Adam had descended into the life of a drunkard for a few years. But all that time on the sofa in a
semiconscious state? Opportunities had been lost, until
he had managed to pull himself up out of the abyss. He
had overcome, mastered the temptation and become a
special agent with ICE.

He took one more swallow of the bitter brew and
then tossed the cup in the trash. Even with his im-
proved station in life, he still wasn't good enough for
the wholesome Amish woman who was now receiv-
ing treatment. And he definitely wasn't good enough
to join the church. What would God want with someone like him?

But what if he had had the faith of his grandparents?
He walked to the window and then returned to his seat,
uncomfortable with being still. If he had adopted that
level of faith, Amish or not, where would he be right
now? His decisions about life and faith had so much
depended on someone else through the years. He had

let his father and his father's weaknesses determine the trajectory of his own life of faith, or until this point, his life of no faith. Why? Sure, Adam had kicked the drinking habit and made his own choice there. So why couldn't he make his own choice here?

His grandparents, and even an aunt and uncle, had sent him letters through the years, gently urging him to come home. It had been several years since he had seen them, but he still received letters every now and then, inviting him to visit. His grandmother in particular liked to include a description of the meal she would make for him, usually topped off with his favorite pie and homemade whipped cream. If she couldn't get his head to decide to visit, then she appealed to his stomach.

But he couldn't quite make the decision of faith. These last couple of days with Katie had shown him that he wasn't making the difference as an agent that he had thought he would when he'd entered the academy a few years back. And what was he missing of a regular life as he continually ran after the bad guys? But even if he could be accepted among the Amish, wouldn't an Amish life be boring? It didn't seem to count for much contribution to the improvement of life. What can one man working a field do to make the world better? The Amish just hid from the world. His stomach roiled with the agony of a decision. How could he know which sort of life was right and good?

The nurse stepped into the waiting room, and Adam jumped to his feet, closing the distance between them in just a few steps. "How is she?"

"The bleeding has stopped, and she's all stitched up. We also put her on intravenous antibiotics as a precaution, so she'll stay overnight tonight to make sure she rests and that the wound isn't reopened or exacerbated in any way."

"May I see her?" Adam caught himself trying to twist his straw hat and forced himself to stop.

"We're moving her to a room, so you can find her there. Would you like to stay, as well?"

"That's allowed?"

"Sure. I can have them set up the cot in her room."

"Thanks." Adam headed toward the elevator, relief trickling over his shoulders. Katie would be fine, and they had someplace safe to sleep tonight. Perhaps by tomorrow night, all would be well again.

Two floors up, he found Katie sitting up in a white-sheeted bed, wearing a green hospital gown and an IV tube. Her prayer *kapp* was askew, and a few tendrils had escaped and curled on her neck. A weary smile lit her face as he came into the room. "I will be stuck here overnight, but the nurse said I will heal just fine in the end."

"Yeah, that's what she told me, too." He glanced around the room. The recliner had been pulled out into a cot, a white sheet tucked in around its edges.

"*Danki* for saving me. I appreciate your devotion to my safety." An adorable shade of pink crept into her cheeks.

"No problem. Just part of the job."

She looked down, her eyes hidden from him, as the color drained from her face.

When she didn't say anything, he sat on the recliner and laid back. Weariness consumed him. As he drifted off to sleep, he wondered what had made him say that it was just his job to protect her. He raised a hand to rub his eye. Wasn't it true, though? He should forget the whole thing, really. He wasn't good enough for the Amish church or an Amish girl. The past couldn't be erased.

Chapter Twelve

An antiseptic odor tickled Katie's nose, and she lifted a hand to rub away the irritation. But when a pricking sensation caused her forearm to jerk, she immediately stopped that movement. She slid her eyes open to find a white room and Adam dozing nearby.

She inhaled deeply, forcing the memories to return. A nurse had stuck an IV into her arm, telling her it would give her antibiotics to fight infection. It sure hurt, though, and she longed to rub it, although she doubted that would help. Limb by limb, she took inventory of what was wrong and what pained her.

Her left arm was sore from the tetanus shot they had stuck her with yesterday, saying something about it being standard procedure after a wound of that sort. Her leg wasn't too bad, perhaps because the IV had contained both fluids and some sort of painkiller in addition to the antibiotic. A slight headache was coming on, but that could be because of the uncomfortableness of the bed and pillow, as well as her stress over her current condition.

Sunlight streamed in the window, and she stared out

at the cloudless sky. Had they kept her overnight partly because of the IV but also because it would be safer in the hospital? Whether that was true or not, she hated to put this financial burden on the community. She had no health insurance to pay the bill. The cost would be distributed among the members of her church district, and all would contribute. But that was the way of the Amish. Insurance of any kind was forbidden because it was deemed to be a reliance on man and not on *Gott* to provide. Neither did she have a husband with a steady income to help pay a bill that was sure to be large. She glanced around the room at the equipment and monitors. None of this was cheap, for sure and for certain.

Being careful of her tether to the pole that held the IV bag, she stretched, working out the kinks in her back and neck. She did feel somewhat rested. Perhaps she had slept better than the past couple of nights because her protector was right here in the same room.

Adam. She looked over at him on the cot, twisted in the sheet while he still wore his homespun trousers and blue shirt. He wouldn't be much help like that, sound asleep, but perhaps he would wake easily if needed. After his years of training and experience, he was probably a light sleeper.

His hair was mussed from his night of sleep. It was cut so short and so differently from the Amish men she knew. He was certainly different from her husband, who had had blond hair and fair coloring. Adam had a darker tone, with light chestnut hair and brown eyes that seemed to see to the depths of her soul. She continued to stare at him, picturing him with the traditional bowl-style Amish haircut. *Ach*, it didn't take long to determine that he would still be handsome. Maybe even more so.

The door swung open, and a nurse pushed through a rolling cart with a blood-pressure cuff dangling over a hook. Adam woke instantly, sitting up and pulling the sheet away from him. His gaze found her right away, a satisfied smile reaching his eyes when he caught her looking at him. Heat rose up her neck and to her cheeks, and she focused on the nurse, who positioned a cover of some sort on a thermometer and placed it in her ear.

A gentle clamp went on her fingertip, preventing her from straightening her *kapp*. She should have just removed it last night to sleep, but she had been so tired that she had been asleep before she could even think about normal bedtime preparations.

The nurse checked the thermometer and tapped on a computer keyboard on the cart. "Everything checks out, so I think you'll be going home today, but it's up to the doctor."

"Home would be *gut*." Home *would* be *gut*, but she couldn't go there. Where would she go?

"It's nice that your husband could stay overnight with you. Do you have children?"

She had felt flushed already, but now the temperature in the room seemed to rise several degrees. Adam sat behind the nurse, and she looked at him to see him shake his head just enough to seem to signal to her that it wasn't worth the time and trouble to correct the nurse. She would be discharged soon anyway.

"*Jah*, I have twin girls. They are with friends."

"Oh, twins. How fun." She spun to Adam, and Katie smiled to see how quickly he put on a straight face.

"Breakfast will be here soon. Would you like a meal so you can eat with your wife?"

Adam maintained his serious expression as he replied, "Yes, thank you."

"Good. I'll order that, and the doctor will be in when he arrives, but it should be this afternoon, if not sooner." She returned to Katie. "Let me know if your pain meds wear off."

She left quickly, and Katie's abdomen twisted with anxiety at the prospect of leaving the safety of the hospital. Her attackers were out there, looking for her, and that knowledge made her pulse race. She closed her eyes and breathed deeply. Maybe for this brief moment, she could heal.

The breakfast wasn't bad for hospital food, according to Adam. After the trays were removed, Adam spoke to the sheriff again. It seemed that the forensics team couldn't lift a single fingerprint or locate even a few fibers from the Hochstetler place. Whoever the attacker was, he hadn't left a single clue.

As Katie dozed, still waiting for the doctor to arrive with the discharge orders, the door opened. She groggily opened her eyes, expecting the doctor.

"Timothy!"

The tall, light-blond man held a straw hat in his hands and quickly stepped forward to grab one of Katie's hands and kiss her on the cheek. A frown creased his high forehead. "Sister, are you all right?"

"*Jah*, I will be fine. Everything is better now that you are here, safe and in one piece." Katie's heart leapt within her chest at seeing her *bruder* again after more than a month of separation. She nodded to Adam, who had stood and stepped forward. "This is Adam Troyer. He is a special agent and is the reason I am alive."

Adam shook Timothy's hand. "I wouldn't say that, but I'm glad you're here. How'd you manage it?"

"The Amish Taxi is how I got to the hospital. But how I knew that my sister was here is not important." Timothy turned back to Katie, anguish carved across his countenance. "This is all my fault, and I am afraid that my presence here may make things worse. But I could not be a part of that group of criminals any longer. I saw a chance, and I took it."

"*Nein, mein bruder.* All is within *Gott*'s will. I do not understand it, but I accept it."

"It was not *mein* will." Timothy turned his straw hat in his hands, nearly crushing it as he spun it round and round, anxiety radiating from him. "It was forced upon me. I had no choice. They threatened you and the twins if I did not do as they said. Are my nieces all right? Where are Ruth and Rebekah?"

"They are fine and in good care. They are hidden away with some friends."

"Who is in this group of criminals?"

"There are too many people involved, and I have only met those I am forced to deal with. I do not know everybody's names."

Adam leaned in, intense concentration creasing his forehead. "Who is your handler? The man who tells you what to do?"

"I know him as Vic Barthold, but I do not think he is the one in charge. He is what you *Englischers* call a middleman. I am afraid that if he is caught, Katie may still be in danger because there are men above

Vic. I do not think that anyone knows Vic's real name or true identity."

Adam looked at the ceiling, deep in thought for a moment as if he were running the name of Vic Barthold through his mental grid. "I can't place the name, but I'll check with my supervisor."

Katie shifted on the bed. "What about the man you hired a couple of months ago? The one who dressed in Amish clothing but did not look or act Amish? Who is he?"

"I do not know his real name. Vic, the man who seemed to be in charge of me, the one who forced me into this smuggling in the first place, sent him to me and said he would be there to watch over me and make sure I did as they wanted. He would even ride with me to deliver the furniture. Vic called him Little Joe. The story Vic told me is that his father is Big Joe, in one of the Amish districts in Holmes County, Ohio, but clearly no one in Indiana knows him. He tried to disguise himself as Amish so that he would be less noticeable."

Adam crossed his arms over his chest and sat on the edge of the bed. "What exactly did they tell you to do?"

Katie struggled hard to maintain the sense of peace she had had earlier that morning. This was the question she had longed to ask her *bruder* for many weeks. And now he was here, about to tell all he knew. Was she ready and prepared to know the truth?

Whether Katie was ready or not, Timothy plunged forward, apparently eager to get it all off his chest and into the hands of a law enforcement officer, who might be able to do something about it. "I make furniture that then is sold to *Englischers* in stores all around the Midwest. Vic—my handler—stopped me on a routine trip to deliver some finished product to the buyer. He said he had a business proposition for me, and when I refused, he held a gun to me. He already knew about you, Katie, and the girls. He said he would harm you if I did not do as he said. There was nothing else I could do but go along. Now I know too much, and that got you involved."

Katie felt as if her heart would slam out of her chest. The love her *bruder* had for her was overwhelming. He hadn't been doing any of this for himself or because of a pull away from the Amish community. It had all been for her and her daughters.

Timothy drew a deep breath and continued. "I was supposed to begin using a new supplier. There, along with my order of materials, I picked up packages of social security cards and birth certificates. Identity documents I assume were falsified. Then I would hide the papers in panels of the furniture I made. *Ach*, I knew what I was doing was criminal, but I did not know how to make it stop."

"What happened to the furniture after you were done?"

"It was delivered to the different furniture stores across the area. The orders that contained the false documents had fabricated customer names, and then, I assume, men involved in this criminal ring picked up the furniture at that end point, with the documents stashed inside."

Adam stood and walked to the window to look out and then returned to perch on the bed. "That answers a lot of questions that ICE couldn't figure out. We had suspicions of a criminal counterfeiting ring in Northern Indiana, but we couldn't figure out where those documents went. Bringing in the Amish on their part was a smart strategy. Who's going to suspect an Amish man in a buggy to be involved in criminal activities?"

"*Jah*, exactly." Timothy sat heavily in the chair, his forearms resting on his knees and his head hanging. "And now they have found out that Katie knows something, since she went to my workshop and found that social security card. That means that my cooperation with them will not protect her any longer."

Katie sat forward, her hands flying to her throat. "But I do not know anything. I did not know what that card was for or why it was there. I only wanted to talk to you."

"I know that, but they do not, especially now that you have a law enforcement officer protecting you." He nodded toward Adam. "It looks suspicious to them." He paused. "And you do know something. Did you figure out my note?"

Adam groaned, probably remembering the visit with the bishop.

"*Jah*, but it was not easy to find the right copy of the *Ausbund*."

"So now I am in need of protection, as well." Timothy looked at Adam. "Can we work together to make this all stop?"

Katie bit her lip to try to keep the tears from flowing. Tears of joy that her *bruder* was back, but also tears of sorrow that more danger seemed to lie ahead.

Adam sat up straighter, his mind tingling as he connected the dots. Months of legwork had not yielded the results he was getting with a single conversation with

Timothy. Hope surged that this case could finally be closed.

An odd sense of eagerness settled over him as he rubbed the back of his neck. This case felt different. More final. He glanced back at Katie as she straightened the sheet. Did it have anything to do with her? He just wasn't as eager as he usually was to move on to the next case.

He forced himself to focus on Timothy, the man with almost all of the answers. "What does your handler know about the law enforcement that's after him? Has he mentioned any names or agencies or departments?" It was always wise to know what one's opponent knew.

"I do not know how much he knows. He has always been quite careful around me to say only what I need to know to do what he wants me to do. There has been no mention of law enforcement." Timothy crumpled the hat that he still held in both hands. "*Ach*, I am sorry that I cannot be more helpful."

"You're right. That's not very helpful. And we still don't know exactly who is after Katie." Adam scrubbed a hand over his chin. "But it's not your fault. Not at all. These guys are good, and they're careful. I'm sure this Vic Barthold has a dozen different identities at his disposal."

"What more can I do?"

"As soon as Katie's discharged, let's get back to the sheriff's office. I'd like you to tell him what you've told me. He knows the area and the people better than I do, and he's been quite helpful to me. Also, a team of ICE agents are going to rendezvous there, so we can formulate a strategy for tonight. Sound good?"

"I will do whatever I can to be helpful." Timothy grinned at Katie, and she nodded in agreement.

A couple of hours later, after a late lunch, the doctor finally arrived to tell Katie that she could go home. She said *danki* and then just shrugged at Adam. She had no home to return to, but Adam determined not to worry about that until after his meeting with his ICE team. She stepped into the restroom with her clothes and a comb the nurse had loaned her and emerged several minutes later, looking refreshed and put-together. Her sage-green dress accentuated the flashing blue of her eyes, and it looked as if she had combed her hair, straightening the part in the middle and smoothing it back into a bun underneath her prayer *kapp*.

Despite what he had heard about the difficulty of sleeping in a hospital, Adam felt well-rested and even energetic after a full night of sleep and both breakfast and lunch. A renewed hope that the conclusion of the case was near filled him as he led Katie and her brother to the elevator and pushed the down button.

The ride down was quiet, but at the door, Timothy pulled Adam back. "He's here!" His voice was a hoarse and panicked whisper.

His adrenaline spiking instantly, Adam thrust his arms out to hold Katie back from going through the automatic sliding door. All three stepped back in unison, and Adam tilted his head toward a nearby hallway to indicate they should congregate there, away from the windows. "Who's here?"

"Vic. My handler. He is in the driver's seat of that white cargo van." Timothy and Adam peeked around the corner of the hallway. "The unmarked van just pulling away."

"This isn't good." Adam scraped a hand across his jaw. "They know we're here. The trick will be getting out of the hospital and to the sheriff's office without being seen." He looked at Katie and her brother. "Either of you know a back way out?"

Katie shook her head. "*Nein.* I try to spend as little time as possible at the hospital."

"Okay, we'll figure something out." He grabbed Katie's hand and, with Timothy following, led her down the hallway and around a corner. He peered carefully out every single window they passed, careful not to get so close as to be seen from the outside, but the van was nowhere to be found. The hallway continued to wind around, and with a couple of turns, Adam found an exit door near the back of the building.

A thorough check through the window of the door revealed no threats outside, so Adam pushed the door open and cautiously stepped halfway out to survey further. A narrow street wound past, and he scanned both ways to see if the white cargo van had found them. The alley was vacant, but through a passageway between two other hospital buildings, he could see what looked like a farmer's market.

He quickly turned back to Katie. "What's going on over there?"

Her eyes widened with realization. "*Jah*, of course. It is the Saturday farmer's market held every weekend in the summer."

"As large as a craft festival, since many come to sell more than just produce. It is in the parking lot of the outdoor shopping mall." Timothy nodded. "A *gut* hiding place."

Still holding Katie's hand, Adam led them across

the alley and through the passage to the farmer's market. Tents and awnings and canopies stood sentinel over tables of produce and craft goods, arranged in a way to provide walkways for customers. A few of the vendors had pulled pickup trucks into the fray, to sell sweet corn or melons out of the truck bed, but there was no way to drive a vehicle, let alone a large cargo van, through the market. Adam felt fairly safe that Vic wouldn't come gunning for them with his vehicle as long as they were within the confines of the farmer's market.

"Let's stay close to the vendors and away from the open middle." Adam reluctantly dropped Katie's hand. A glance back confirmed that Katie and Timothy had fallen in behind him in single-file formation, with Timothy protecting Katie from the rear. "And let's wind our way back to my SUV so we can get to the sheriff's office."

As he tried to match the walking speed of the other customers, Adam kept his eye on the perimeter of the market, the closest place Vic could drive. Just when they passed a wagon full of early corn, Adam spied between the booths the white cargo van cruising slowly, the driver hanging his arm out of the window and craning his neck to peer between the booths and vehicles.

"He's here." Adam kept his voice low.

Timothy immediately stepped backward, and Katie and Adam followed, ducking behind the wagon and the tractor that had pulled it. The sweet-and-sticky smell of the ripe corn tickled his nose, and he stifled a sneeze. In between the slats of wood that formed the sides of the wagon, Adam spied the cargo van moving forward. Figuring there was no better way to stay hidden than to keep his opponent in his own crosshairs, he motioned to Katie and Timothy to follow.

Fresh flowers, including some early sunflowers, were set out in five-gallon buckets on rough wooden boards separated by cement blocks to form display shelves. In between the large round flower clusters of some pink hydrangeas, Adam watched the van drive slowly on until it was out of sight. He needed to hurry everyone on to the next vendor so he could keep the van in sight.

The sweet cinnamon aroma of the roasted nuts at the next booth met Adam as he led Katie and Timothy forward. An older man stood behind the high counter made of a couple of two-by-fours, and he nodded at Adam as he walked past, holding out a sample of the nuts. As delicious as they smelled, Adam couldn't afford distraction. Not when lives were on the line. He murmured a *no thanks* and continued on.

At a table of tomatoes and cucumbers, he turned to seek Katie's advice as to which way to go to begin to head back to the hospital parking lot and his Tahoe. "How do we—"

He cut himself off when he saw Katie but not Timothy. His training kicked in to mask his concern, although his heart began a wild thumping beneath his Amish-made blue shirt. Without showing any reaction, he began to scan the many customers walking behind and around them.

"What is the problem?" Katie's voice was low but controlled.

Without ceasing his visual survey of the crowd, he asked, "Where is Timothy?"

"Timothy?" She spun in a complete circle and then

grabbed his arm. "Where is he? Did they get him?" Her breath hitched and when breathing resumed, it was shallow and staccato.

"I don't know. Would he have left us voluntarily?"

"No. They got him." Her breath came in short spurts now, and her grip on his arm tightened. "Timothy!" Her voice carried across the crowd, a tinge of panic in it. Several customers turned to look at the loud Amish woman.

"Shh. We can't draw attention to ourselves, or they will find us and not just Timothy." He pried her hand off and grasped her upper arm to steer her past the garden produce and into a walkway created by the divide between two booths.

With no idea how to find Timothy in the crush of customers, Adam was determined to get back to his Tahoe and drive to the sheriff's office. But at the end of the walkway, as they neared the parking lot, a tall, burly, bearded man stepped into their path, blocking their exit.

It was Vic, Timothy's handler, with a malicious sneer snaking across his face.

Chapter Thirteen

"Gotcha." Vic stepped forward, a menacing grin on his red face.

He was not what Adam was expecting at the end of the walkway, and Adam reeled backward, his hand grasping Katie's arm even more tightly. Katie whimpered, although whether it was from fear of Vic or Adam's pressure on her arm, he could not tell. There wasn't time to figure it out either.

Adam quickly double-stepped them both backward, but there were only a few feet before they would run into the crowd of customers.

"He was at the cabin." Katie's voice was low as she turned her head toward Adam but didn't take her eyes off the man.

"That's right, sister." Vic grabbed her free arm with his meaty hand and pulled. Katie finally broke her staring contest with Vic to toss a frightened glance at Adam.

"Let her go, Vic." Adam refused to let loose of Katie.

"Vic? I don't know anyone by that name." Maliciousness spread across his face like a rash. "Come on, Super Agent, aren't you going to fight for her?"

Vic pulled on her arm, nearly tugging her out of Adam's grasp.

"I have been fighting for her." Adam nearly growled through his clenched teeth. "You haven't gotten her yet."

"Got her now." Vic pulled again as he gruffed out his commands. "Come with me." He pulled back his open button-down shirt to reveal a Glock in a holster.

Whoever this guy really was, he wasn't fooling around with his firepower. Even though Adam still had his piece, he couldn't reach it without calling attention to it. And then Vic would surely take it away.

Katie relaxed her arm in his grip, staring at him until he looked at her. "Adam." She appeared as if she had a mighty struggle to remain calm, which would only be human. But her voice was composed and somehow, with just her tone, she had taken command of the situation, or at least of Adam. "I will go. *Danki* for your protection."

"Not just you, sister." Vic nodded in Adam's direction. "Him, too."

There was nothing more to argue. Vic had the upper hand, and the best Adam could do was to go along and search for an escape.

With his hand still clamped firmly around Katie's upper arm, Vic forced them to cross the parking lot with strict orders to look normal. The white cargo van was idling along the curb, with a second thug sitting behind the wheel. The nondescript vehicle truly was unnoticeable in the parking lot full of other cargo vans and trucks, the vehicles of the vendors at the farmer's market.

With all of the busyness of the market behind them, the parking lot was surprisingly empty of people. Adam's mind reeled with possible scenarios of escape, but every one of them ended with Katie getting hurt.

Could they make a run for it, hiding behind other vehicles until they got to his Tahoe? But as he scanned the parking lot, it seemed that all of the other vehicles were too far away. They would surely be shot before they could make it ten feet. Besides, Vic still had a hold on Katie's arm.

Could Adam get his weapon out before Vic could react? But Adam's weapon was tucked in a holster at the small of his back. With Vic right next to him, the man would surely be able to retrieve his Glock even before Adam could reach his arm around enough to grab his gun.

Could Adam lunge for Vic and acquire his Glock? But the driver was watching their approach from the van, and professional thugs, as Vic seemed to be, didn't usually travel with only two. There were most likely more standing guard nearby and ready to come to Vic's aid in an instant.

No, escape was impossible.

As Adam mentally ticked off the scenarios, they arrived at the van.

Vic held out his hand to Adam. "I know the Amish don't have phones or weapons, but I'm sure you're packing, Super Agent. Hand over the phone first."

Vic grabbed it when Adam held it out, threw it on the asphalt and ground the heel of his military-style boot into the screen. Even if Adam could still retrieve the phone, it certainly wouldn't work now.

"Now the weapon. Slow and careful."

Adam saw in his peripheral vision that the man behind the wheel held his own Glock low, just below the edge of the open window. He retrieved his weapon from the holster and handed it to Vic. With a sneer, Vic took it and stuffed it into a cargo pocket in his pants.

"All right. In you go." Vic pushed around to the back of the cargo van, where he pulled open the doors to reveal Katie's brother. Timothy was handcuffed and guarded by a third thug.

Adam heard Katie suck in her breath at the sight of her brother, but she wisely kept quiet. Talking would come later, and antagonizing Vic would only make things worse for them all.

Katie stepped up into the cargo van, and Adam followed. His chest clenched at the discouraging thought that they were now hostages. Vic pulled out a second pair of handcuffs and fastened Adam and Katie together. Even as the van doors closed, Adam scanned the parking lot, but there was no one nearby they could holler to for help.

Adam helped Katie get comfortable on the floor of the van and then sat next to her, across from Timothy and their guard. Katie stared at Timothy, her façade of strength cracking a little as she gazed at her brother, who was being held captive in his own set of handcuffs. A tear fell slowly down her cheek, and she lifted her free hand to swipe it away.

"Timothy, what happened?" As Adam asked his question, he watched their guard to see if he would stop them from talking. But the man only glared at him.

"A family with little children stepped right in front of me, and I got separated from you two. Then I was grabbed from behind. I guess I was not careful enough, and the noise of the market covered my words." He shrugged, a gesture of resignation and acceptance of what he probably thought was inevitable. "*Ach*, I am an Amish man. I do not know, like you do, the intricacies of watching out for danger."

The driver nodded to someone Adam couldn't see and then pressed his foot down on the accelerator. The van jerked forward, and Adam ended up leaning into Katie. But when he straightened, Katie continued to lean into him, as if seeking solace and comfort.

"You did nothing wrong." Adam did his best to reassure Timothy. "We're here also, so I didn't do so well watching out for danger either."

Adam was glad they had been able to have a private conversation earlier in the hospital. Would Timothy have been willing, or even allowed, to share all of those necessary details as they rode in the back of the cargo van? It was certainly all information that would be helpful in bringing down this ring of smugglers.

Timothy leaned forward and nodded toward the driver, who was wearing a T-shirt, cargo pants and military-style boots. "That's Little Joe, my Amish employee." Timothy's voice carried a hint of disdain. "When I was forced to switch woodworking suppliers, he came along to make sure I did what I was supposed to with the social security cards and passports that were hidden in the boxes and packages of supplies. He was also the one who supplied the customer names."

Little Joe glanced in the rearview mirror, with a

scowl stretched across his face. "That's enough talking." His voice sounded like tires on gravel.

Timothy shrugged again and focused on a spot above Adam's head. Apparently that was all the information he would get.

The van turned to the right and then sped up along what seemed to be a winding road. Since Adam was in Northern Indiana on assignment and didn't know the area well, he couldn't identify many of the roads they might be traveling. Speed and curves and the sound of the tires meant nothing to him. Even if he were allowed to talk to Timothy or Katie, they probably wouldn't be able to name the streets either. Surely each lane, drive and road felt and sounded different in a buggy than in an automobile. He stared out the front windshield, desperate for some idea of their location. But from his position on the floor of the van, all he could see was blue sky with a few clouds and, every now and then, the top of a tree. That wasn't any help at all.

He tried to lift his hand to run it through his hair, a habit he had when he was anxious. But a few inches up, the handcuffs bit into his wrist. Katie whimpered, and Adam whispered an apology as he lowered his hand. If he could whittle, that might help him think. But he hadn't had his pocketknife since he changed into the Amish clothing.

Was an escape possible? He hadn't been able to come up with a plan before they were forced into the van. Discouragement settled heavily on his shoulders as he looked around the inside of the vehicle, their prison.

Could they buy some time to figure out an escape plan by offering to work for Vic and his minions?

Maybe a federal special agent and an Amish woman and man would be helpful in their ring? A bump in the road jostled them about, just enough to shake sense into Adam. Their usefulness would not last long, even if they were accepted into the scheme. Eventually they would be eliminated. And why was he trying to kid himself anyway? He would be completely unwilling to join in any criminal activities, and he knew without a doubt that Katie and Timothy would also be unwilling, no matter what the benefits of the deception might be.

God would protect and provide, and Adam knew that Katie would trust in His sovereignty.

"Are you okay?" He bowed his head to whisper to Katie, praying that he wouldn't be noticed by the thug at the wheel.

Katie turned to look at him, her eyes wide, her eyebrows raised. It was a look of forlornness, of weariness, and Adam's heart twisted within his chest at how he had failed her. She simply nodded, but Adam also saw a hope, or at least a peacefulness, that shone through her.

He longed to put his arms about her and absorb that peacefulness. For as long as she would let him.

It made his palms sweat to think of how he had come to care for her in such a short time. Could he imagine a lifetime with her? With every minute that ticked by, the answer became a more resounding *yes*.

He broke the eye contact and looked out the windshield again. His throat felt thick and he swallowed hard with the thought of his desire of a family to call his own, a wife and children. He had no standing, no authority, to want that. A man in his position, with his training and experience, couldn't afford a family. A wife and children would only pull him off course.

Loving and raising a family wouldn't make a difference in this evil world anyway.

He may be a failure at his job, as evidenced by his and Katie's current predicament, but his job was what defined him. It gave him a reason to get out of bed in the morning. It assuaged his grief over his father and brother and the way they had wasted their lives, at least for the moments that he was working.

Changing the world for the better was a good goal, but was his job truly accomplishing that? And if it wasn't, then what else was he supposed to do?

Thirst pulled at him. He swallowed hard but it didn't help much. He didn't have much experience trying to gauge speed while riding in a moving vehicle, especially when he couldn't see the road and surroundings. But if he had to guess, he would figure they were moving at about forty miles per hour. The stops and starts had ceased, so they didn't seem to be in town any longer. And the road sounded smooth, like asphalt. But overall, none of that information helped him much.

He glanced back at Katie to see that her eyes were closed and her full lips were moving slightly. Praying again, no doubt. But suddenly that made a lot of sense to Adam. His own resources hadn't helped in this particular case. The way he was choosing to live his own life hadn't brought the fulfillment and satisfaction that he had hoped. But Katie's steady faith in the face of adversity was something he wanted.

It was a faith he needed and a faith that had been ebbing back into his life through the past few days.

Katie, too, was something he needed. He savored the feeling of her arm against him as she leaned into him for comfort and strength. It seemed that every nerve ending on the outside of his arm was acutely aware of her touch. And then a thought struck that forced him upright with the realization of it.

He was falling in love with her.

Katie shifted against him, and he glanced quickly at Timothy across the van, as if the man could read his thoughts about his sister. But Timothy also had his eyes closed as if praying silently. The thug sitting with Timothy made eye contact with Adam, a smirk splayed across his face. Adam quickly looked away, checking the windshield again to see if he could see anything more, but there was nothing new.

What more was there to do but pray? His resources, his strength and his control of the situation were spent. This case had beaten him, and all he had left was God.

He closed his eyes to shut out distraction and began to whisper a prayer. But would the Lord hear him after all his years of trying to live life on his own?

Lord, I need You. With those simple words, a peace Adam had never known seeped through his soul.

Tears dampened Katie's cheeks, but she didn't try to swipe them away this time. The tears, just like her grief, would have to run their course. She glanced at her brother, feeling grateful that he had not left the Amish faith and was now returned to her, but also grieved at all that he had gone through in the past couple of months. Being forced into criminal activity, yet powerless to fight back, must have felt crippling. *Jah,* the Amish were pacifists. But being forced to disobey the law of God seemed to be an entirely different situation, and one where he had no choice but to comply.

How could *Gott* have allowed this situation? Her

brother was a fine, upstanding Amish man, who loved God and obeyed His will.

Another tear fell from her cheek and onto the bodice of her white starched apron. *Ach*, but how could she question the sovereignty of *Gott*?

Gott, help my unbelief!

A lull had fallen over their little group, and she used the silence to try to listen to the sound of the road. Could she hear anything that might help her to know where they were going? *Jah*, she had traveled by bicycle or by horse and buggy over most of the roads in the surrounding countryside, but those modes of transportation only made her feel the bumps and dips even more. Perhaps if she could speed up those bumps and dips, she would have a better chance of determining what road they were on. From her angle, as she sat on the floor of the van, she could tell that evening sunlight was slanting in through the windshield, but she couldn't get much of a view of the outside.

The driver had not stopped for a while and the speed seemed fairly consistent now, so they were probably on a country road. She had been on the interstate a couple of times, a road where the speed had become absolutely dizzying. So she probably wasn't a good judge of how fast they were traveling. But it didn't seem fast enough for the highway. Did that mean they weren't going too far?

But wasn't this line of thinking truly a lesson in futility? If she could figure out their destination, what could she possibly do about it? They were guarded by two men who were armed and in control. Surely this was her darkest moment.

She sighed more heavily than she intended, and

Adam leaned farther into her, lending her his strength and comfort. At least she wasn't facing this alone.

If she had decoded Timothy's message correctly—and that seemed to be a big *if*—they could possibly be going to the sawmill. But could a criminal mind even be understood, let alone predicted? They could be going anywhere, like someplace where they would be held for a while or where they would be killed. But there was no way she could ask her *bruder* if she had interpreted his message right. That communication would reveal their knowledge to the thug currently guarding them. And if that thug knew that Katie and Adam and Timothy knew about the meeting, then the criminal gang could be on the lookout for Adam's team coming. That would ruin all possible chances for survival.

Deep in thought, Katie lifted her hand to try to tuck a stray strand of hair back into her prayer *kapp*. But the handcuffs clinking together brought her back to her present surroundings, and she quickly lowered her hand.

"Sorry," she whispered to Adam. The man sitting next to Timothy glared at her but didn't say anything.

She licked her dry lips and wished for a drink. How far from home was she? Her thoughts meandered to her little twins, Ruth and Rebekah, and what they were doing right then. Perhaps eating supper, or depending on what time it was, *redding* up the kitchen after the meal. Jed might be bringing out his big Bible for the after-supper reading of *Gott*'s Word. *Ach*, how she longed to be there.

One thing was for sure and for certain. Sarah and Jed were the truest of friends, and Sarah was the closest thing she had to a sister. Friendship like that was a gift from *Gott*. Her twins may be without her for the moment, but she trusted Sarah and Jed implicitly with her girls. Would she see them again? Ever? Only the Lord knew the answer to that question. Her heart raced at the notion that the end of her life was approaching. It seemed to be a distinct possibility that her twins could be left as orphans.

A thought struck her, shaking clear through to her very soul. The only One who could save anybody was *Gott*. Sure, she had known this for most of her life, but it was only head knowledge. Now that her life was at risk, and it seemed that *Gott* was the only One who could save her physically, the notion that *Gott* was the only One who could save someone spiritually became much more real.

With so much of her efforts and energies directed toward figuring out what had been wrong with her *bruder*, had she actually accomplished anything? Had she made any progress at all? Maybe it was only Jesus who could save him now. Perhaps it was honestly and truly out of her hands.

A shiver coursed through her at the realization. It had been Jesus all along...the only One who could save Timothy. The only One who could save her or Adam or anybody. *Gott* was the One who had saved her and guided her and blessed her, but she hadn't been turning to Him, seeking Him, laying her soul bare as she asked Him for help with her biggest problem. She had prayed plenty, but it had been prayer as a habit, as something that everyone else in the Amish church did. It was a rote practice. It had not been a real conversation with

Gott, sprinkled with plenty of quiet in order to listen to His response.

Did Adam have faith? A real faith? She glanced at him, but he seemed lost in thought and didn't return the look. She thought back over the past couple of days. Sometimes it had seemed that he did, but other times she had thought that he didn't. *Gott,* she prayed, *help him to know Your love.*

Did Adam realize that she loved him, as well? Katie gasped and jerked her head up at the revelation. From the corner of her eye, she saw Adam look at her, but she refused to meet his gaze. *Jah*, it was true, although she had not realized it until the quiet moments available for reflection. Yes, he was an *Englischer*. But she was falling in love with him, whether it was wise or not.

The van lurched to a stop, and Little Joe turned from the wheel, a malicious grin on his face. "Everybody out."

Katie's heart beat wildly in her chest at the announcement. What fate waited for them outside the van doors?

Chapter Fourteen

The sun had just dipped below the trees as the doors at the back of the cargo van opened. Katie peered over Timothy's shoulder for a glimpse of their destination. An eerie glow cast itself over the landscape, and trees loomed large and menacing around the dirt parking lot.

The thug pushed Timothy out first. Katie followed, but she stumbled over the edge of the van and fell toward the ground. Timothy stuck out his bound hands to stop her fall, and she gripped the cold metal of the cuffs, grateful for the help. Adam, still handcuffed to Katie, followed closely behind.

"Move it." With a gun to her back, the man pushed her and Adam around the van and toward a large, dark building.

The sawmill! Katie gasped to see the ominous structure rise up before her. *Jah*, she had interpreted her *bruder*'s message correctly, but that was little comfort she most likely marched to her death. Of even less comfort was the thought that she would die in the same place as her husband had. She bit her lip to fight back the tears at the irony of it all.

The dark descended rapidly, which meant it was after work hours and no employees would be around to summon help. But it was also Saturday. That meant the mill was closed for the whole next day as well, giving the bad guys a day and a half to carry out their evil deeds at the empty sawmill. There was no hope for employees to return to work to find and rescue them.

Despair gripped her heart like the vise that her *bruder* had in his woodworking shop. Not only had she not succeeded in saving her *bruder*, but her death would orphan her twins. *Jah*, the Amish community would surround her girls with love and provide for their care, but it would not be the same as having a mother and an uncle.

As she stepped slowly across the dirt parking lot, a verse from the Psalms sprang to her mind. *I will bless the Lord at all times: His praise shall continually be in my mouth. Ach, mein Gott, help me to praise You, even here and in these circumstances.*

Her foot landed on the edge of a dip in the packed dirt, and she wobbled, her ankle twisting down into the hole. With his free hand, Adam grabbed her arm to keep her from tumbling to the ground. In her efforts to right herself, a straight pin from her prayer *kapp* pricked her in the scalp. Inspiration struck, and she quickly reached up to straighten her *kapp*.

"I have an idea," she whispered to Adam, tamping down the feel of a smile flitting around her lips.

He continued to stare at the sawmill, his expression serious, but he nodded so slightly that she could barely see it. It was an agreement that in this, their most desperate hour, she should proceed with whatever her idea was.

She suppressed the smile, eager not to draw attention to herself. Staring straight ahead and with what she wanted to be a somber expression, she removed one of the straight pins used to fasten her *kapp* into place. Hopefully it would look to an observer like she was simply adjusting her head covering.

Lowering her hand, she tucked the straight pin into one of the creases in her palm, the cold metal of the pin pressing against her flesh. Perhaps at some point in time, she could pick the lock of the handcuffs. Her mind reeled with what she was planning. Normally on a Saturday evening, she would be at home, finishing her pies and *redding* up her house for visiting on an off Sunday. And yet here, today, she was trying to figure out how to get out of handcuffs and save her life, as well as the life of her *bruder* and a special agent.

She glanced at Adam, his jaw fixed in grim determination. If she had learned anything about him over the past couple of days, she knew from the set of his eyebrows and the wrinkles in his forehead that he was working hard to formulate a plan. She had no idea what all his training and experience encompassed, but surely he would have some idea how to pick the lock of the handcuffs if she couldn't make it work.

The pace was slow and steady, but the sawmill loomed large in front of them anyway. Adam walked close by, but not just because they were still handcuffed together. He cleared his throat softly, and as she looked his way, he cast a reassuring look at her, a smile hidden in the crinkles around his eyes.

"It'll be fine." He kept his voice so low, she could barely hear him.

She nodded in return. "*Jah, Gott* is with us."

Little Joe stepped up from behind them and stuck the barrel of his weapon into Adam's side. "No talking."

Adam grunted his defiance and picked up the pace, edging away from the gun, but the thug matched him. The other thug had his weapon on Timothy, and the five of them hurried on toward the sawmill.

The pace was too much for smooth walking though, especially with the unevenness of the ground. Red welts were beginning to mar her skin as the handcuff pulled on her wrist. Subconsciously she began to list the ingredients for a homemade salve that would soothe her skin, if she survived the night. She couldn't rub her wrist either, or hold it to keep the cold metal of the handcuff away from the skin because she was still tightly holding the straight pin in her free hand. Was there a way to transfer the pin to her other hand?

But then they were at the door, the thug right behind her so that his hot breath blew on the back of her neck, and there was no opportunity.

Little Joe stepped around her to grab the door, and the second thug pressed them into the building. Darkness enveloped the structure, and the gloominess of the interior tried to penetrate to her soul. Katie stumbled over the threshold of the door, the pin jabbing into the flesh of her palm. A cry of pain rose to her lips, but she suppressed it so she wouldn't draw attention to herself.

Little Joe grabbed her arm, pulled her up and shoved her farther inside. The second man closed the door behind them with a resounding thud of finality. She shuffled along behind Timothy, trying to see through the gloom and yet afraid to look around. The sweet scent of sawdust overwhelmed her and resurrected vivid memories of the day two years ago when she had been summoned to that same sawmill because her husband had been in an accident.

"Keep moving." The round end of the gun barrel pressed into her shoulder blade as Little Joe growled near her ear.

She forced herself to keep plodding, one foot in front of the other, as she passed the large bay door, where the ambulance had pulled up in an effort to get as close to her husband's body as possible. A muscle jumped under her neck as she thought, as she had a million times since the accident, that her husband never should have taken that part-time job at the mill. Their farm-and-produce income had been enough, but he had wanted to build up some savings as their family grew.

That pregnancy had been an easy one, up until that point. She had had a little morning sickness and had been plenty tired, but after managing twins through infancy and the toddler stage, those symptoms hadn't bothered her that much. Her crochet hook had flown fast through the green-and-white baby blanket, as well as a pair of booties, and even though it was too early for such preparations, her excitement had driven her to retrieve the twins' old baby clothes that had been tucked away in the attic.

On the morning of that fateful day, she had just brought the laundry in from the line and had planned to bake some oatmeal cookies for the twins before she started crocheting a little cap. Miriam from next door, whose husband had a telephone in the barn for his harness business, had come running as Katie stood at the sink, washing the morning's dishes. The message had been grim, and her heart had begun a wild thump even before she had heard the word *accident*. Miriam had volunteered to stay with the twins, who thankfully, at age two, were completely unaware of what was transpiring.

Five long minutes later, the Amish Taxi had pulled up in the lane, though she had not called for it. With hugs from the twins, she had been whisked away by the van, riding in the same vehicle, along the same road, that her husband traveled every day to his job at the mill, since it was too far for horse and buggy. The ride had been silently frantic, and all too soon for her emotions to adjust and her heart to rest, they had arrived at the sawmill, where ambulance lights flashed through the morning sunshine, and huddled groups of workers had cast forlorn looks at her as she approached the entrance.

Inside, the scene had been gruesome. She had learned later that she wasn't supposed to have seen her husband like that. Her husband's boss and the paramedics didn't know she would arrive so soon, and they had not finished their repositioning of him or their cleanup of the area. As soon as they realized she was watching and listening, they rushed her away to an employee lounge and made her sit on a red leather couch.

The miscarriage had struck later that day. While she had lain on a hospital bed on the second floor, being attended by an obstetrician, her husband had lain on a metal slab in the basement morgue, being attended by a coroner.

Now, despite her husband's efforts and good intentions, she had neither savings nor family beyond the twins.

Lost in her memories and dazed by being back at

the sawmill, a place she had avoided since her husband had died, Katie stumbled into Adam. The thug had stopped them near several large stacks of boards. Adam grasped her hand, his hand warm and strong over her cold flesh. Her pulse beat through her, threatening to pull her back into a state of being overwhelmed, and she glanced at Timothy. With both of his wrists handcuffed, he was even more limited than she was.

She swallowed hard, forcing the memories and emotions to the back of her mind. Her *bruder* needed her, and she would do her best for him. For Timothy, and for Ruth and Rebekah.

Adam stroked his thumb over the back of her hand, a gesture that was both comforting and thrilling at the same time. And *jah*, she would do her best for Adam as well, and for whatever the future may hold for them.

A tear trickled down Katie's cheek, and Adam's heart twisted within his chest at her obvious anguish. She had told him that her husband had died in an accident at the sawmill, and now here they were. She had been forced to enter the very place where her happy life had ended, and there was nothing Adam could do to protect her from it. It took all his restraint not to slam his fist into the stack of boards or lunge for the closest criminal or make a wild dash for the door with Katie. But none of those actions would help, and would in fact only bring further harm to all three of them.

Self-control, a level head and a compassionate heart were what Katie needed now. God would help him, especially now that Adam had asked Him.

As they had been marched through the sawmill and into the middle of the enormous building, Adam had scoured the structure for exits. There were not many options that he could see, except for the one they had just entered. A few skylights dotted the ceiling, but unless he had a grappling gun, a weapon that could shoot a rope with grappling hooks on one end around the transom and allow them to ascend through the roof, the skylights weren't helpful.

Several windows lined the very top of the walls, near the ceiling. But at a height of at least fifteen feet, those windows couldn't provide an escape. The tiniest bit of setting sun filtered through the opaque glass. It would be completely dark in a matter of minutes. One small light was on, a lamp on a table a few yards away. But considering the time spent driving, they were probably so far out in the country that no one would see it. And who would care anyway? Lots of business owners left lights on in their places of business overnight and through the weekend for security. It was ironic, really. The little light in the dark sawmill should indicate to someone on the outside that someone was inside, yet lights were left on inside a business for security. Adam would have chuckled to himself if he had been capable of finding anything funny at that moment.

He continued his survey of the building.

One entire end of the building looked like a giant garage door, but it was closed and most likely locked. Adam had no doubt that it was secure and would not provide a viable exit. The walls reflected a bit of shine from the low lamplight. They looked to be made of sheet metal, which would mean that he couldn't grab an ax and break through drywall. It also meant that, even if he did have his weapon, which he didn't, it wouldn't be wise to shoot. A bullet could ricochet off many surfaces in that sawmill, and then there would be no telling where it might end up.

Adam didn't know much about milling, but none of the machines in that part of the building looked safe. He was sure that much safety equipment was required to be worn while operating them. One looked like it was designed to skin the bark off logs, and another probably cut them up into boards. Conveyor belts, perhaps for moving the logs and the resulting lumber, stretched back and forth. And almost every bit of equipment contained vicious-looking teeth. They were all machines that would be plenty capable of hurting people. Adam sent up a quick prayer that that was not what this criminal gang had in mind for the three of them.

Timothy cast a forlorn look at Adam as the thug called Little Joe stationed them in front of a stack of what looked like freshly cut boards. Sawdust clung to the top in clumps, and Katie sneezed.

"Stay there," Little Joe ordered them as if they were dogs and then sauntered toward the folding table where Vic huddled with a couple of other men.

After Joe had moved far enough away, Adam looked to Katie and Timothy. "It'll be fine." He wasn't sure exactly what he meant by that, but it seemed he should say something reassuring. Even if their end was death, they would be with the Lord, and that was fine.

"Do you have a plan?" Katie whispered and then sniffled, the sawdust in the air obviously affecting her breathing.

"Not yet, but I'm working on it." He nodded toward the table. "So, Vic is there, as well as the driver of our van and the guy who was in the back with us. Who's the fourth man? Do you know, Timothy?"

Timothy cut his eyes at the foursome, seeming to study the men. "*Nein*, I do not recognize him."

"Maybe he was the advance man and broke into the sawmill before we arrived. There's no way to know for sure." Adam studied the men some more and the stacks of papers spread out over their table. "Any idea what all the paper is? Did Little Joe ever say anything that might indicate what's going on?"

"*Nein*. He was quiet all the time, except for when he was giving me orders."

The papers were most likely counterfeit birth certificates and social security cards that would be handed over tonight to the other part of the counterfeit ring. Why it couldn't pass through the usual channels, such as Timothy, Adam couldn't figure, except perhaps because Timothy wasn't cooperating any longer. Perhaps they had so much material that it was easiest to hand it all over at once. Or maybe they were sure that they could avoid detection by law enforcement.

No matter what the reason, the counterfeiting gang's chances for success increased greatly when they kidnapped Adam. Adam and Katie thought they had determined the location based upon Timothy's secret encoded message. But Adam couldn't lead his team to the location if he was a hostage.

Katie sniffed again. "What should we do?"

Adam's heart broke for her obvious emotional anguish, being held captive in the very place where her husband had been killed. But he prayed that he could save her from that fate and that God would allow him to bring love and security back into her life. He searched the nooks and crannies of his mind for any idea of how to escape, as well as something reassuring to say to the beautiful Amish woman. "Katie—"

"No talking." The thug whom Timothy had called Little Joe had walked up while Adam had been lost in concentration.

Vic stood behind his thug, a sneer stretched across his lips. "Okay, Super Agent, time for a few questions. I need to know what you know."

Adam didn't respond.

"Do you know why we're here? How many ICE agents have you summoned? Do they know where we are? How and when will they be arriving?" Vic held his weapon to Adam's side. "What about that incompetent local sheriff? Will he be joining our party tonight?"

Adam shifted sideways, away from the gun barrel that was jammed into his ribs, but still did not answer. He ground his teeth together as he was forced to admit to himself that he didn't know the answers to those questions. It was better for Katie and Timothy if he didn't assume that help would be coming. It would force him to make a way for their escape.

"That's what I figured." Vic shoved his face up into Adam's personal space. "Either you don't know anything or you're playing tough. Both ways work for me. I'm expecting quite a party here tonight, so even if you are hoping for some reinforcements, I guarantee you they'll be outmanned and outgunned. I'll also get to show you off to my superior. It's quite a badge of honor to capture a federal agent."

Smugness radiated from the man so strongly, it was nearly overwhelming. He obviously believed he had the upper hand. And from all appearances, Adam had to admit that he did. The handcuffs cut into his wrist, and if they were hurting him, he could just imagine how they were hurting Katie and her delicate skin.

Adam clenched his jaw and refused to speak. In his peripheral vision, he could see Katie and her brother watching him, but Adam would not be the first to break the staring contest with Vic. Adam may be in handcuffs, but that didn't mean he was giving up without a fight.

"Got nothing to say?" The man's foul breath punched Adam in the face.

Vic was obviously a man of malicious intent, stopping at nothing to achieve his goals. Instead of stopping this counterfeiting ring, what if Adam was forced to join them? What if Adam's goal of making some good come from the senseless deaths of his father and brother was turned against him, and he was put in a position where he had no choice but to join the very thugs he had been working to bring down?

What could be better than an ICE agent hiding their activities, so that they're never found? Would Adam's team get there in time? Or would the team be ambushed before they could even breach the door?

Adam couldn't stand idly by any longer. As he continued to return Vic's stare, he made a fist and tensed the muscles in his free arm. Vic blinked, and in that split second, Adam shoved his elbow up and smashed it into Vic's gun hand.

Shock registered on the man's face. Katie screamed. As Vic's arm jerked upward from the impact, a gunshot rang out across the sawmill.

Chapter Fifteen

Clammy perspiration popped out on Katie's forehead as she dropped to the floor. The handcuff jerked on her wrist, but that pain was minimal compared to what a gunshot felt like. The wound on her leg throbbed as her full skirt made sawdust billow up from the floor.

"Vic! You all right?" One of the thugs stood up at the table, peering at them.

His gun still in his hand, Vic took a quick step back, out of the reach of Adam. "Think you can fight your way out of here, Super Agent?" A hateful laugh erupted from the men at the table.

Timothy bent down to lend Katie a hand and help her up, sympathy and strength in his eyes. An artery pulsated on Adam's temple, but he still stared at Vic. Apparently no one had been shot, and she quickly found the bullet lodged in a board above their heads and to the side. It seemed that one of the men at the table had fired a warning shot.

"You understand what we're capable of now? This is not a training exercise, Super Agent."

"Vic, need you to look at something." The guys at

the table sorted through a stack of papers, completely nonchalant, as if gunplay were an everyday occurrence for them. Katie's heart grieved within her at the thought of what a desolate and violent life they each must lead.

With one last glare, Vic growled to Adam, "Next time it won't just be a warning." Then he turned on his heel and marched back to his cohorts.

Katie exhaled a long breath that felt like it had been trapped in her lungs all day. She wanted to sag down on the floor and just let it all be over, but the thought of her twins invigorated her to trust *Gott* and trust Adam with her immediate future.

They were alone again and without a guard, at least as alone as they could get with the gang at the table several yards away but still in the same area.

"Katie." Adam kept his voice low and didn't look at her as he continued his watch of the men at the table. "Got the straight pin?"

Ach, the pin! She had forgotten about it completely in the melee. "*Jah*, it is here." As she maneuvered it in her palm in order to hand it to Adam, it jabbed her in the flesh. She winced with the pain.

"Hopefully a team will be here soon. I called them with the location, and when we didn't arrive at the sheriff's office, they should have assumed something went wrong."

Timothy leaned forward. "What about guards posted outside?"

"And are there not more of their gang to arrive?"

"The team's been trained to deal with various scenarios. They'll be careful." Adam took the straight pin from her and began to work on the lock of the handcuffs. "Keep an eye on those guys, and let me know if anyone looks this way."

Katie focused on the men at the table, fighting hard to keep her lip from trembling. Adam lifted the handcuffs that bound them just slightly, and after a few moments of prying the pin into the lock, his cuff came loose. She wanted to sag with relief at their small victory, but she forced herself to stay upright and keep watch.

As Adam began to work on her cuff, Vic looked up from his papers and stared directly at her.

"Adam," Katie whispered out of the corner of her mouth. "He is looking."

Katie felt Adam stand upright, his arms dangling at his side, probably trying to look as if nothing had happened.

Vic looked back at the documents, seemingly satisfied, and Adam resumed his lock picking. The cuff bit into her wrist as Adam worked at it, and a few moments later her cuff also came loose.

But then Vic looked up again, and although Adam jolted back to position, Vic left the table and sauntered in their direction.

"Look normal. Be cool." Adam whispered encouragement to her.

Katie grasped the handcuff and, with her wrist nearly twisted backward, struggled to hold it in place to make it look as if it were still locked around her wrist. Adam seemed to be doing the same with his cuff, since it did not dangle. Would he try to overtake Vic now that they were free from the handcuffs? Was that his escape plan?

But Vic didn't notice the handcuffs. He just walked

up to Adam and sneered at him, as if he were quite satisfied with the presence of his hostages. Katie felt all her muscles tense as she waited to see what Adam would do. But he only returned the stare, and a few moments later, Vic turned back to the table.

Katie forced her shoulders to relax as she snuck a glance at Adam. His jaw seemed softer now, not quite so grim. Did she dare to hope that he was trusting *Gott* a little bit more with their situation? Was he softening to a renewal of his faith? Gratitude flooded her that he hadn't tried to overtake Vic. Of course Adam was a smart man, and he surely had factored into his thinking the fact that the men at the table had all the weapons. If it had been revealed that they were free, the others at the table would certainly have opened fire. All would have been lost.

When the men seemed engrossed in their stacks of paper again, Adam angled slightly toward Timothy to work on his handcuffs. Katie watched her brother's face as he maintained a vigil for anyone approaching. His expression was somber and unrevealing, like she had seen many times before. But as his sister, she knew the heart for *Gott* that beat inside him, as well as the trust of *Gott* that gave him peace. Memories from the calm they had shared before the current storm, before the counterfeiters had sunk their criminal claws into their family, washed over her. Life had been normal, predictable. Even comfortable, or at least as comfortable as it could be after the loss of a husband. And despite the loneliness she had endured, and in fact continued to endure as a widow, she would return to that time in an instant, that time where none of this had happened.

As he maneuvered to reach the lock better, Adam's shoulder bumped hers. She looked at his face, his growth of stubble because he hadn't even taken the time to shave in his vigilant protection of her, the intelligence that shone from his light brown eyes, the handsomeness in the strength of his jaw.

Ach, would she return to the life she had had before this danger? Suddenly she did not know for sure and for certain that she would. That was before Adam had come into her life. Was he not worth knowing—and loving—even if this peril was the price she had to pay? She had already admitted to herself that she was falling in love with him. Was there any hope, any prayer, that they might survive and that he might decide that the Amish life was for him?

Before a petition to *Gott* could spring to her lips, Adam's husky voice reached her. "Let's go."

Had Timothy been freed from his handcuffs while she had been lost in thought? She spun to her brother, and he simply nodded toward the door they had come in through.

Adam grabbed her hand and tugged her along. At first they sidestepped slowly, trying not to be noticed. But when Little Joe looked up, his eyes widened as he realized their escape plan. His weapon was out of the holster in a split second, and his movement caused the other thugs to stand in a rush. In an instant, all guns were pointed at them.

"Run!" Adam pulled on Katie, and Timothy followed closely behind. Her leg pained her, but she gritted her teeth and forced herself to put her full weight on it in order to keep up with Adam. She didn't want to be the one to keep them from getting away.

As they passed the stacks of boards, the exit door

came into sight. But a series of loud pops suddenly filled the mill. Immediately it felt as if her leg were on fire, and her flesh seared. She stumbled on the cement floor, a cry escaping as pain engulfed her. Had her leg been hit again? The entire limb burned as the floor rushed up to meet her.

"Adam!" His name was the only thought in her mind.

She landed on the cold cement, her shoulder hitting first. The mill swirled around her consciousness. Adam's face appeared above hers, and she battled to focus on it. But the spinning only increased, a dizzying swirling and whirling, until darkness overtook her.

"Katie!" Her name sprung to Adam's lips. As if he were caught in quicksand, unable to move, he watched her go down, her hand involuntarily clutching her leg, where the bullet had hit.

Adrenaline pulsed through him. He lunged for her, to catch her, to keep her conscious, to do something or anything to save her life, when a searing agony ripped through his biceps. In that nanosecond, a thousand thoughts flitted through his mind. He would have to turn away from Katie, ignoring her and her need of him, and face Vic. Otherwise he would be shot dead. If he were killed, he could no longer be a help to Katie or her brother. At least by obeying the thug with the gun, there was still a chance, however slight, to survive and to get Katie help before it was too late.

He turned to find the source of his pain and saw Vic pointing his weapon directly at him. Behind him, the other three had their guns drawn and pointed at the would-be escapees.

Out of the corner of his eye, Adam saw that Timothy's face was contorted with anguish as he stole glances at his sister, his only family left, lying unconscious on the floor. Unable to stand still and do nothing any longer, Timothy moved toward Katie.

Vic took a step forward. "Don't move, boy." His voice growled like a threatened dog. "You stay put, and I'll deal with you in a minute."

Adam shook his head slightly at Timothy, cutting his eyes in the direction of where Timothy was standing before he moved. Would he get the message that he should return to his position? When he didn't move, Adam ventured to speak, despite the risk of further angering Vic. "Best to obey the man's orders, Timothy."

A sneer snaked across Vic's lips. "Yes, Timothy." His tone was laced with malice. "It's best to obey me."

As Timothy inched back, forcing his gaze from Katie, Adam tried to assess Katie's injury from what he could see in his peripheral vision. He couldn't see much blood coming from her leg wound, and there was no puddle under her. So he dismissed, tentatively, the possibility that she could bleed out. But if she was in shock, if that was the reason for her unconsciousness, then she would need treatment fast. Her face looked pale, but was her skin clammy? Did she have a rapid pulse? If he could just examine her, lift an eyelid to see if her pupils were dilated, he could tell more about her condition. She needed an ambulance, direct pressure on her wound to stop any bleeding, elevation of her legs.

And did she hit her head on the floor? He had no way to tell from that distance. At least Vic seemed to have forgotten about her. That increased her chance of survival.

But for now he was stuck where he was until Vic looked away. Or shot him again.

"What's your plan here, Vic?" Adam shrugged. Why not just ask a direct question? "Are you going to let her die?" He gestured toward Katie, sneaking another glance at her.

"I might. She's not necessary anyway." Vic leveled the weapon at Adam. "You know what? You're expendable, as well."

Adam refused to close his eyes in anticipation of the gunshot. He wanted to be conscious and alert to his very last moment.

One of the guys still at the table hollered, interrupting their staring contest. "Vic, got a call."

Vic lowered his weapon slightly and half turned back, rolling his eyes at the interruption. "Can't you deal with it?"

With Vic distracted, Adam grabbed the opportunity to shuffle backward toward the stack of boards nearby. He had noticed on the way in that there seemed to be boards stacked everywhere with different levels of sawdust coating them. That fact hadn't seemed important at the time, but now inspiration struck him. One inch back led to another inch back as Vic and his minions argued about the phone call and who would do what. Timothy just looked at him wide-eyed and held his ground as if he knew that he should stay still to reduce the chance of Vic noticing them.

With just a few inches left between him and the stack of boards, Adam reached back, moving as slowly as an inchworm. He grabbed a handful of sawdust from the top of the stack and clenched it in his fist. The more he could manage, the better his chances of success.

Immobilizing Vic could buy them the time needed for an escape.

The bickering ceased, and Vic turned his attention back to Adam, not seeming to notice Adam's fist clenched at his side or that he had edged backward. Vic stepped forward, his weapon pointed again at Adam's heart, and sneered in Adam's face, a malicious smile that showed a couple of yellowed teeth and emitted his foul breath. "This is it. Say goodbye."

Adam brought his hand up to his hip. "That's right. Goodbye."

Confusion darted across Vic's face. Adam seized that moment to bring his hand up, unclench his fist and blow the sawdust into Vic's face.

The cloud hovered around Vic, clinging to his hair, his eyelashes, his cheeks. He stumbled backward, immediately dropping his weapon and grabbing at his eyes as if he could claw out the minuscule bits of wood. Vic howled with pain.

A vicious-looking tool lay on top of a nearby stack. Adam grasped the solid-wood handle, leaving the large metal hook swinging on the underside. Despite his wound, adrenaline surged, and his arms tingled with the anticipation of swinging the weapon and defending himself. Old habits usually died hard, and it was in his training to fight to defend those who needed his protection, including the woman he loved.

Yet his fingers loosened their grip on the hook as a new and unusual sensation of calm soaked through him. He honestly didn't want to harm the man. He didn't want to do it. But was his faith rebuilt? Was he ready to adopt the Amish idea of peacefulness with his fellow man and pacifism? *Jah*, definitely so.

Vic clawed at his eyes, groaning more loudly and attracting the attention of his cohorts in crime. As the other brutes approached, weapons at the ready, loud shouts sounded from the door as more men entered.

Suddenly they were surrounded.

Chapter Sixteen

"Drop your weapons!"

As men in tactical gear streamed in around him from every corner of the building, Adam recognized many faces as those of his own team, as well as several more men sent as reinforcements.

Vic's weapon had already been dropped, but Little Joe and the other thugs behind him quickly lowered their guns, letting them clatter to the cement floor. Their smirks turned to grimaces as they raised their hands in defeat.

Adam slowly unclenched his fists as his heart rate began to slow to a more normal pace.

"Troyer, we got them on the outside, too. Good work, son." Sheriff Moore followed the others in as another ICE agent took up a position to protect the door.

It was over. There wasn't success with every case, but this one was ending well. Adam closed his eyes as tension flowed from his body.

"Can we get some help over here, please?" Timothy rushed to Katie's side and dropped to his knees.

His call drew Adam's attention. It had barely been

a couple of seconds since the team had arrived, but his heart raced anew with the sight of Katie on the ground. Her chest still rose and fell with breath as two paramedics arrived with a stretcher. He breathed easier to see that sign of life. But as he stepped toward her, eager to see to her care and well-being, the sheriff caught his arm.

"Your team needs you." He nodded toward the folding table, where a couple of special agents were looking through Vic's documents.

Adam looked at his fellow agents and then back at Katie as she was lifted onto the gurney. Timothy held her hand as the paramedics began their assessment. Adam's abdomen twisted within him. Shouldn't *he* be the one holding her hand?

"Need to do your job first, son. Leave the woman to her brother." The sheriff's voice was low but firm with his admonishment.

His brow pulled down in concentration, Adam watched a paramedic elevate Katie's feet with a pillow and cover her with an emergency blanket. The sheriff was right. Adam needed to do his duty and complete his mission. Katie was being cared for, and Adam's first obligation was to ICE and his team.

But all he wanted in that moment was to be by her side. He wanted to forget about the job and just be with her, secure her health and safety, comfort her as she returned to consciousness.

He forced himself to turn away from her and trudge toward his team as they began to process evidence. But one thought remained in the back of his mind.

What job could he do in which he wouldn't have to leave her again?

* * *

Katie's eyelashes fluttered against her cheeks like butterfly wings on her skin. A dull throb began to pulse in her head with the effort it seemed to take to open her eyelids. She forced them open a fraction of an inch, but bright light made her drop them closed again. With a wiggle of her hands, she tested the strength of her wrists. She tried to lift a hand to brush some hair off her forehead, but she quickly dropped it to the bed again for lack of strength. As she began a physical inventory of aches and pains, the wiggle of her feet brought a sudden jolt of pain to her leg.

Her gunshot wound. It all came back in a rush. She wiggled her wrists again to find that the handcuffs were gone. The mattress was soft beneath her, so she wasn't on the hard floor of the sawmill any longer. A soft blanket comforted her. Her heart leapt within her as she remembered everything that had happened and realized she was safe.

Katie steeled her nerves for the harsh white light. Slowly she forced her eyes open once more. A white ceiling overhead came into view, although it was fuzzy. She cut her eyes to the side, and a face appeared in her vision.

"Timothy." Her throat scratched as she wobbled out the name.

Her brother grasped her hand. "Do not move. I think you will hurt less if you stay still."

"Ambulance?" She looked around to see small cabinets of supplies and a kind-looking woman on her other side.

"*Jah*, you are in the ambulance. And you will be fine…eventually."

"Mrs. Schwartz? Or may I call you Katie?" The paramedic smiled at her with a comforting warmth and held a cup with a bendable straw toward her.

Katie sipped the cool water and let it soothe her throat before she answered. "*Jah*, call me Katie."

The paramedic set the cup on a small counter. "How do you feel?"

"Like I have been through the wringer."

The woman removed her protective glasses. "A bullet grazed your leg and reopened your wound, so you probably feel some aching. I've given you something for your pain." She gestured toward an intravenous bag hanging from the ceiling of the vehicle. "You had passed out from shock before we arrived, but I believe you'll have a full recovery."

"*Danki* for taking care of me." Katie also appreciated that the paramedic spoke in language she could understand, not her medical jargon.

"Thank your brother. He's stayed by your side the entire time."

She rolled her head to look back at Timothy. "Is it all over, then?"

He smiled at her. "*Jah*, the bad men are all in custody. There are so many law enforcement officers in there, it makes my head spin. *Ach*, it is an evil world we live in."

"There has always been evil, *mein bruder*, even back to the Garden of Eden. Please. We are together again. Let us dwell on that right now." She squeezed his hand, savoring his presence.

"But this is all my fault. I am why you became involved in this mess. I am why you are in this ambulance right now." He cast his gaze down at the floor.

"*Nein*, it is not your fault. It was out of your control. Besides, it is done now, for sure and for certain." Tears trickled from the corners of her eyes and dropped to the sheet that covered the cot.

It thrilled her that Timothy was safe and out of danger now, and there with her. But what about Adam? Her heart thumped and bumped as she looked about for him from her limited view on the gurney. Did he survive? Where was he? Was he alive and well or in a body bag?

Tightening her abdominal muscles, she strained to sit up, the line from the IV bag pulling on her arm.

The paramedic quickly and gently pushed her back down. "You need to lie still a bit longer. And soon we'll transport you to the hospital. You're going this time. No arguments."

The hospital? She couldn't, not without finding out about Adam. "But what about…? I mean, where is…" She slumped back into the cot and picked at the blanket that covered her. Was she betraying her *bruder*, and even her Amish faith, with her concern for Adam? Adam was an *Englischer*. *Jah*, over the past few days he had seemed to soften toward the Amish. Had even kissed her, a *wunderbar* kiss that had *ferhoodled* her, for sure and for certain. But now that the danger was done, would he change his mind? Were his words of care and concern only uttered because of the danger of the moment?

The paramedic tapped her arm, and Katie looked up into her warm and understanding gaze. The woman inclined her head toward the open back door. Adam stood there, gazing at her, his look intense and concentrated.

And suddenly, with his presence, all was right with her world.

Timothy cleared his throat next to Katie and rose from his stool. "I will go see what more I can do for the sheriff."

After he squeezed through the door, Timothy shook Adam's hand. "*Danki.* We would never have survived this without your help and protection. *Danki* especially for taking care of Katie." Her brother's voice broke as he said her name.

As Timothy walked back toward the sawmill, Adam hopped into the ambulance with her.

Tears pooled in her eyes, but she did not care. This man had seen her at her worst and had still taken care of her. "You are hurt?"

"Not really. Just a scratch. I was treated in a second ambulance, and it'll be fine." His gaze relaxed, and little lines crinkled at the edges of his soft brown eyes. "I wanted to check on you."

Katie glanced back at the paramedic to see if she would answer, but the woman had turned her back on them and seemed to be busy organizing a small cabinet. "I am told that I will be fine, but I have to go to the hospital this time."

"Yes, and I'll go with you." With no apparent thought for the presence of the paramedic, Adam drew her into his arms, being mindful of the IV. "I know we've only spent a few days together, and the circumstances have been extreme."

"*Jah.*" The interior of the ambulance swirled around her, but it was not a medical condition this time. Any lingering sense of cold she had had disappeared with his arms around her.

"But I think you should know that I'm falling in love with you."

* * *

Even with a small bandage on her forehead, her dark blond hair mussed and her prayer *kapp* askew, she was beautiful. Adam could look at her face for the rest of his life.

Whoa, really?

He scrubbed a hand through his hair, not caring that that nervous gesture would dishevel him even more. This lovely creature had been with him in the most dire of circumstances in the past few days, and she had seen him through thick and thin.

Yes, really.

It only took a moment of remembrance of the strength that she had exhibited, her loving interactions with her twins and her care for him even when she had been in danger. He knew.

How could he voice those emotions? He wasn't sure he had the strength or the presence of mind just then. A lot had happened over the past days that he would need to analyze and process. But there was something he could say.

Should he ask the paramedic to leave? But did it matter if she had heard? It was no secret, certainly not now, that he cared for this lovely Amish woman. And after that night's pulse-racing danger and the scare of losing Katie, he was certain. "Katie, this might seem sudden to you. But God has been at work in me, and I want to join the Amish church. To slow down. To worship and praise God within the community of believers." He wanted to wake up every morning with her. To raise a family of a dozen children. To get his hands dirty growing crops or raising chickens or whatever it was he would do to support a family. He could whittle. Maybe he could develop those woodworking skills into an occupation.

Katie looked down at the blanket, sending his heart into a tailspin. What if she didn't return his affection, his love? What if he had to leave that ambulance alone and without hope? Would he be able to return to the life he had considered normal just a few short days ago?

"I'm sorry it isn't romantic." His voice was husky, but he couldn't help the emotion swelling within him. A thousand times it had been on his lips to tell her that he was falling in love with her. Why hadn't he? And now, would it be too late?

She looked up at him, her dark blue eyes luminous and—could he dare to hope?—expectant.

In her silence, the clink and clatter of bins and supplies sounded around them. He didn't care. He wasn't a man of many words, but those particular words said everything he was trying to communicate, so he repeated them. "I love God, and I love you."

Slowly, like the sun sending out its first rays in the morning to warm the earth, a smile radiated across her face. "Wherever we are together, that is where I want to be. I love you, too, Adam. But please, no more ambulances."

Epilogue

Crisp, colorful leaves had crunched under Katie's feet that morning as she and the twins left the house for the service on Preaching Sunday. The autumn was becoming so chilly that she would soon have to pull their black winter capes out of the attic.

Now warmth and wonderful fall aromas surrounded her as she stood in the serving line at Jed and Sarah's house, dishing out pieces of pie as the men passed by. Adam stepped through, accepting a piece of raspberry pie and looking handsome in his blue shirt and home-spun pants. He smiled at her with a mischievous look twinkling in his eyes.

His baptism into the Amish church had been a beautiful event, and Katie had had to dab at her eyes several times. It was a *wunderbar* thing when a person turned from a focus on the world and sought a focus on the Lord, accepting a life of simplicity in communion with other like-minded believers.

After the men were seated at long tables outside, an arrangement that wouldn't last too much longer as the days turned chillier, the women filled their plates.

Katie was halfway through her piece of pineapple up-side-down cake and almost ready to jump up to refill coffee cups when Adam snuck up behind her.

"May I steal you away for a few minutes?" His voice was low in her ear and tickled the back of her neck.

She nodded and stood. The other women at the table smiled at Adam and then at her and then back at Adam. These past few months, Adam had taken baptismal classes, become better acquainted with the men in the community, met with the bishop and spent plenty of time with her. He had also been putting his whittling skills to good use by working closely with Timothy to learn woodworking. Soon he would make and sell Amish furniture. The district had accepted him with-out hesitation and had not failed to notice the growing romance between them.

Adam led her past the tables of church members eating. Girls were jumping rope in the lane, and some bare-footed boys were throwing a ball back and forth. Timothy waved in greeting from where he stood, talk-ing to the bishop in what looked to be an easy and ca-sual conversation. Vibrant mums of orange and yellow and purple graced the flower beds, the color so vivid that it seemed like the mums were competing with the oranges and reds and golds of the surrounding trees. Leaves crunched under their boots as they meandered toward the barn.

They left the crowd behind, and Adam held the branches of a weeping willow to the side to allow Katie to pass ahead of him into the enclosed space inside the drooping leaves. As the sun shone through the leaves, a golden glow surrounded them.

She leaned against the tree's trunk. "It was a beautiful service, *jah*?"

"Jah." He smiled at his own use of the Pennsylvania German. "It is *wunderbar* to sing from the *Ausbund* and use it as it is intended. Not for decoding a secret message."

"Definitely." She returned the smile. "And you are pleased with your decision to join the Amish church?"

"I always thought the only way I could change the world was to catch the bad guys and put evil behind bars. But you helped me to see that I can have an impact on the world from inside the Amish church, by raising a good family and keeping the simple ways."

"Jah, family is important." Through the branches, she glimpsed the green shirt of her brother. "That is why I had to get *mein bruder* back."

"He seems quite content to be back in the fold, and his business is going well. I also saw him making eyes at the young lady serving the casseroles this afternoon."

Katie had noticed that, as well. Her brother would probably be courting soon, now that life was getting back to normal. "What about the trial coming up?"

"Well, Vic and Little Joe and the others are still behind bars, and they'll stay there until they are tried. So all is safe and well. Considering the amount of evidence against them, I don't doubt they will be convicted. The only real question is how long they'll serve."

"Will you attend the trial? What did the bishop say?" Katie hugged her arms around her middle at the idea of Adam in the courtroom. The Amish did not, as a rule, become involved in legal proceedings, but perhaps there wasn't any other option in this situation.

"I'll have to testify since I'm an eyewitness. The bishop has given me permission to don my ICE uniform one more time for the trial. If I'm there testifying in my capacity as an ICE agent during those events, then the lawyer and jury will expect me to dress the part. I don't want to cast doubt on my testimony or endanger the chances of a proper sentence by appearing in my Amish clothes."

"*Jah*, I understand that."

"That's over. Let's not talk about those events anymore." The twinkle reappeared in his light brown eyes, the gold specks nearly shining. He smiled wide and ran his hands down her arms, grasping both hands in his.

Katie's heart beat harder as she let him hold her hands. It seemed there was only one other thing he might want to talk about, considering the nervousness mixed with anticipation that spread across his smile, but she did not want to assume what he was feeling and thinking.

He leaned forward and kissed her on the forehead. "I don't have a lot to offer. I'm still learning the business of making furniture. But I'm a hard worker, and I trust in *Gott* to provide and answer prayer. What I can give you is my love, my affection, my devotion, for as long as we both shall live."

Her throat tightened at those words, and tears of joy stung her eyes. *As long as we both shall live?*

Adam squeezed her hands. "Katie, will you marry me?"

A tear trickled down her cheek unbidden. "*Jah*, I will. For sure and for certain."

He leaned in again, but this time he touched his lips to hers, a sealing of their commitment to each other.

His lips were soft and warm, and she wanted him to linger there forever.

With a shout, the twins parted the branches and ran in to grab Katie's legs. Adam pulled back but not before he whispered in her ear, "We'll continue this later."

Her heart thrilled at the promise. The twins each reached their arms around her waist, and Adam pulled them all into his embrace. Another tear of joy escaped, and her heart felt as if it would burst. *Gott* was blessing her with family again.

* * * * *

SPECIAL EXCERPT FROM

LOVE INSPIRED
INSPIRATIONAL ROMANCE

*When a television reporter must go into hiding,
she finds a haven deep in Amish country.
Could she fall in love with the simple life—
and a certain Amish man?*

Read on for a sneak preview of
The Amish Newcomer *by Patrice Lewis.*

"Isaac, we have a visitor. This is Leah Porte. She's an *Englischer* friend of ours, staying with us a few months. Leah, this is Isaac Sommer."

For a moment Isaac was struck dumb by the newcomer. With her dark hair tamed back under a *kapp*, and her chocolate eyes, he barely noticed the ugly red scar bisecting her right cheek.

Leah stepped forward. "How do you do?"

"Fine, *danke*. Where do you come from?"

"California."

"Please, sit. Both of you." Edith Byler gestured toward the table.

Isaac found himself opposite Leah and gazed at her as the family gathered around the table. When all heads bowed in silence, he found himself praying he could get to know the visitor better.

At once, chatter broke out as the family reached for food.

"We hope you'll have a pleasant stay with us." Ivan Byler scooped corn onto his plate .

"I…I'm not familiar with your day-to-day life." The woman toyed with her fork. "I don't want to be seen as a freeloader."

"What is it you did before you came here?" Ivan asked.

"I was a television journalist," she replied. Isaac saw her touch her wounded cheek and glance toward him. "But after my…my car accident, I couldn't do my job anymore."

Journalist! What kind of God-sent coincidence was that? He smiled. "Maybe I should have you write some articles for my magazine."

"Magazine?"

Edith explained, "Isaac started a magazine for Plain people. He uses a computer to create it. The bishop gave him permission."

"An Amish man using a computer?"

"Many *Englischers* have misconceptions of how much technology the *Leit* allows," Ivan intervened. "You won't find computers in our homes, or cell phones. But while we try to live not *of* the world, we still live *in* the world, and sometimes technology is needed to keep our businesses running. So, some bishops have decided a little technology is allowed."

"What's the magazine about?" Leah asked.

"Whatever appeals to Plain people. Farming. Businesses. Land management."

"And you want *me* to write for it?" she asked. "I don't know anything about those topics."

"But that's what a journalist does, ain't so? Learn about new topics," Isaac replied. Her opposition made him more determined. "Besides, you're about to get a crash course while you stay here. Maybe you'll learn something."

"I already said I had no intention of being a freeloader."

He nodded. "*Gut.* Then prove it. You can write me an article about what you learn."

"Sure," she snapped. "How hard could it be?"

He grinned. "You'll find out soon enough."

**IF YOU ENJOYED THIS BOOK
WE THINK YOU WILL ALSO LOVE**

LOVE INSPIRED

INSPIRATIONAL ROMANCE

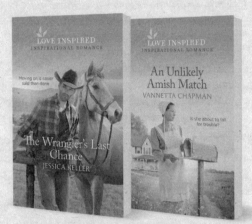

Uplifting stories of faith, forgiveness and hope.

Fall in love with stories where faith helps
guide you through life's challenges, and discover
the promise of a new beginning.

6 NEW BOOKS AVAILABLE EVERY MONTH!

LIXSERIES2020

SPECIAL EXCERPT FROM

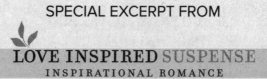

LOVE INSPIRED SUSPENSE
INSPIRATIONAL ROMANCE

A K-9 officer and a forensics specialist must work together to solve a murder and stay alive.

Read on for a sneak preview of
Scene of the Crime *by Sharon Dunn,*
the next book in the True Blue K-9 Unit: Brooklyn series available September 2020 from Love Inspired Suspense.

Brooklyn K-9 Unit Officer Jackson Davison caught movement out of the corner of his eye: a face in the trees fading out of view. His heart beat a little faster. Was someone watching him? The hairs on the back of Jackson's neck stood at attention as a light breeze brushed his face. Even as he studied the foliage, he felt the weight of a gaze on him. The sound of Smokey's barking brought his mission back into focus.

When he caught up with his partner, the dog was sitting. The signal that he'd found something. "Good boy." Jackson tossed out the toy he carried on his belt for Smokey to play with, his reward for doing his job. The dog whipped the toy back and forth in his mouth.

"Drop," Jackson said. He picked up the toy and patted Smokey on the head. "Sit. Stay."

The body, partially covered by branches, was clothed in neutral colors and would not be easy to spot unless you were looking for it.

He keyed his radio. "Officer Davison here. I've got a body in Prospect Park. Male Caucasian under the age of forty, about two hundred yards in, just southwest of the Brooklyn Botanic Garden."

Dispatch responded, "Ten-four. Help is on the way."

He studied the trees just in time to catch the face again, barely visible, like a fading mist. He was being watched. "Did you see something?" Jackson shouted. "Did you call this in?"

The person turned and ran, disappearing into the thick brush.

Jackson took off in the direction the runner had gone. As his feet pounded the hard earth, another thought occurred to him. Was this the person who had shot the man in the chest? Sometimes criminals hung around to witness the police response to their handiwork.

His attention was drawn to a garbage can just as an object hit the back of his head with intense force. Pain radiated from the base of his skull. He crumpled to the ground and his world went black.

Don't miss
Scene of the Crime *by Sharon Dunn,*
available wherever Love Inspired Suspense books
and ebooks are sold.

LoveInspired.com

HARLEQUIN

Heartfelt or suspenseful, inspiring or passionate, Harlequin has your happily-ever-after.

With new books published
every month, you are sure to find the
satisfying escape you know you deserve.